PAX SAMSON

THE COOKOUT

ONI PRESS

AN ONI PRESS PUBLICATION

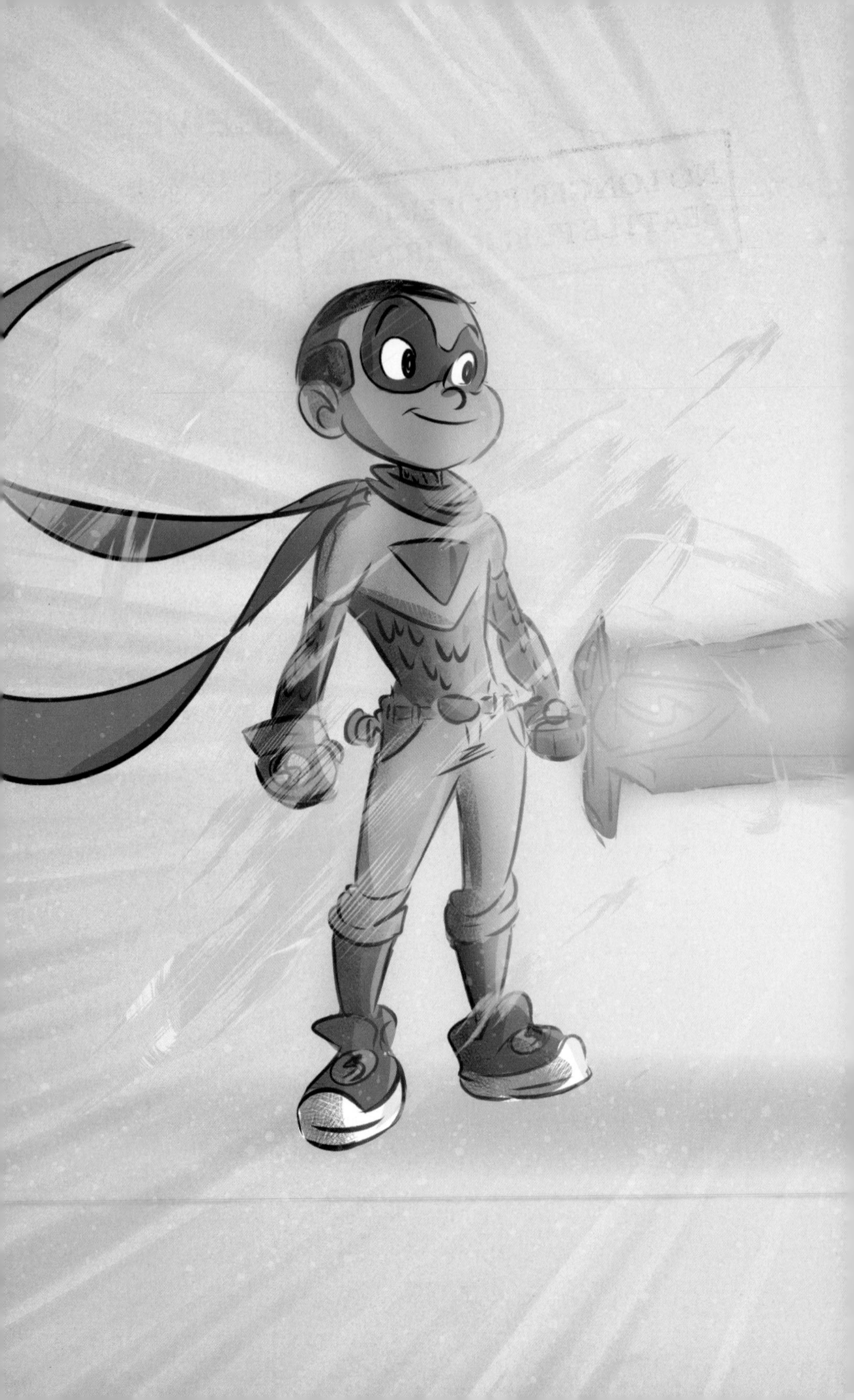

PAX SAMSON

THE COOKOUT

RASHAD DOUCET * JASON REEVES

Written by RASHAD DOUCET & JASON REEVES
Illustrated by RASHAD DOUCET
Color assistance by JUAN MURILLO
Letters by LORIS RAVINA
Title Logo by SHAWN LEE
Consulting Reader JASMINE WALLS
Designed by SONJA SYNAK
Edited by ANDREA COLVIN & GRACE SCHEIPETER

PUBLISHED BY ONI-LION FORGE PUBLISHING GROUP, LLC

James Lucas Jones, president & publisher • **Sarah Gaydos**, editor in chief • **Charlie Chu**, e.v.p. of creative & business development • **Brad Rooks**, director of operations • **Amber O'Neill**, special projects manager • **Margot Wood**, director of marketing & sales • **Devin Funches**, sales & marketing manager • **Katie Sainz**, marketing manager • **Tara Lehmann**, publicist • **Holly Aitchison**, consumer marketing manager • **Troy Look**, director of design & production • **Kate Z. Stone**, senior graphic designer • **Sonja Synak**, graphic designer • **Hilary Thompson**, graphic designer • **Sarah Rockwell**, graphic designer • **Angie Knowles**, digital prepress lead • **Vincent Kukua**, digital prepress technician • **Jasmine Amiri**, senior editor • **Shawna Gore**, senior editor • **Amanda Meadows**, senior editor • **Robert Meyers**, senior editor, licensing • **Desiree Rodriguez**, editor • **Grace Scheipeter**, editor • **Zack Soto**, editor • **Chris Cerasi**, editorial coordinator • **Steve Ellis**, vice president of games • **Ben Eisner**, game developer • **Michelle Nguyen**, executive assistant • **Jung Lee**, logistics coordinator

Joe Nozemack, publisher emeritus

1319 SE Martin Luther King, Jr. Blvd.
Suite 240
Portland, OR 97214

ONIPRESS.COM   ▪ · ◆ · ⊚   LIONFORGE.COM

rashaddoucet.artstation.com | @RashadDoucet
Jason Reeves: 133art.com | @133art

First Edition: August 2021
ISBN: 978-1-62010-851-2
eISBN: 978-1-62010-852-9

1 2 3 4 5 6 7 8 9 10
Library of Congress Control Number: 2020939648

Printed in Canada.

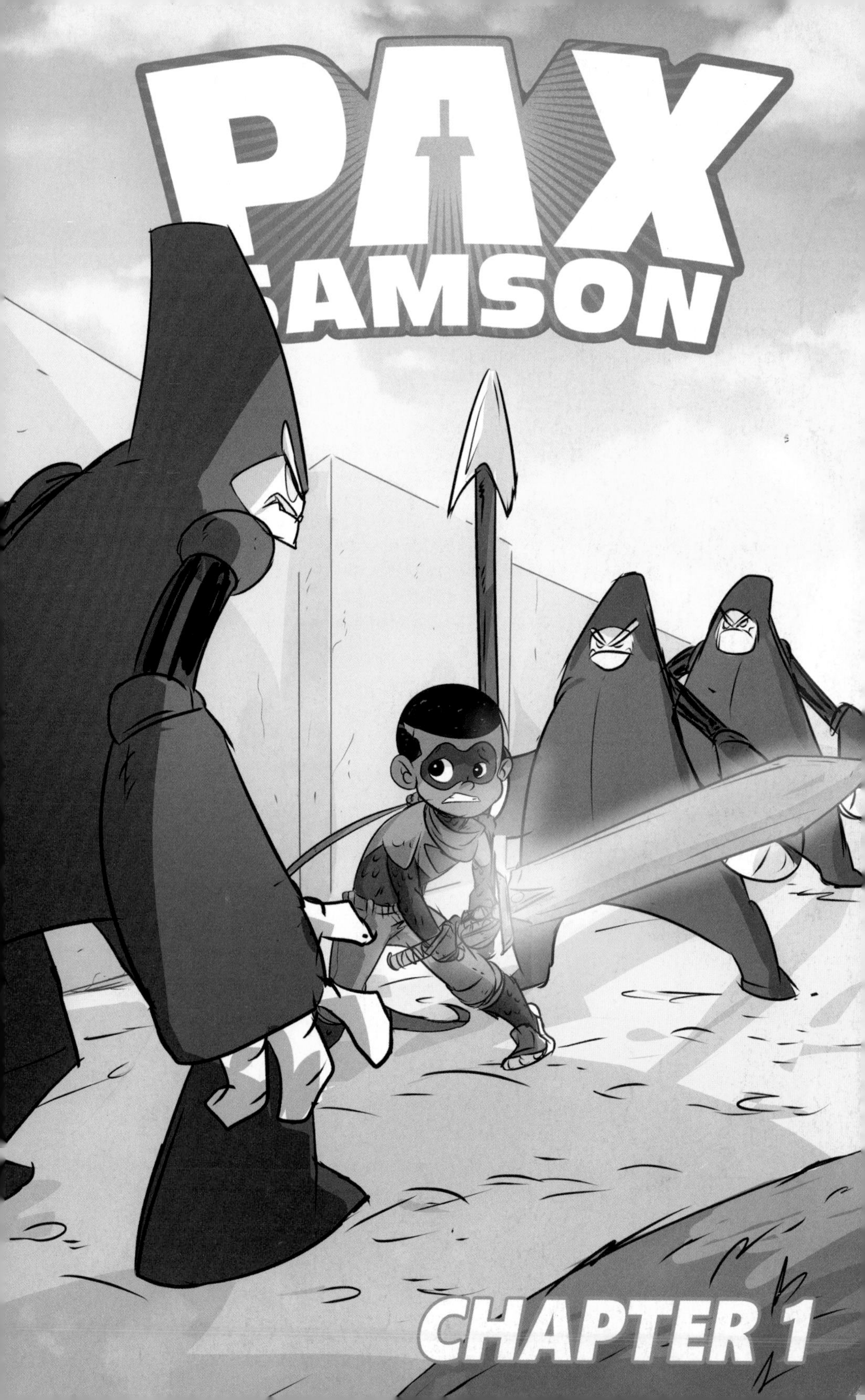
PAX
SAMSON
CHAPTER 1

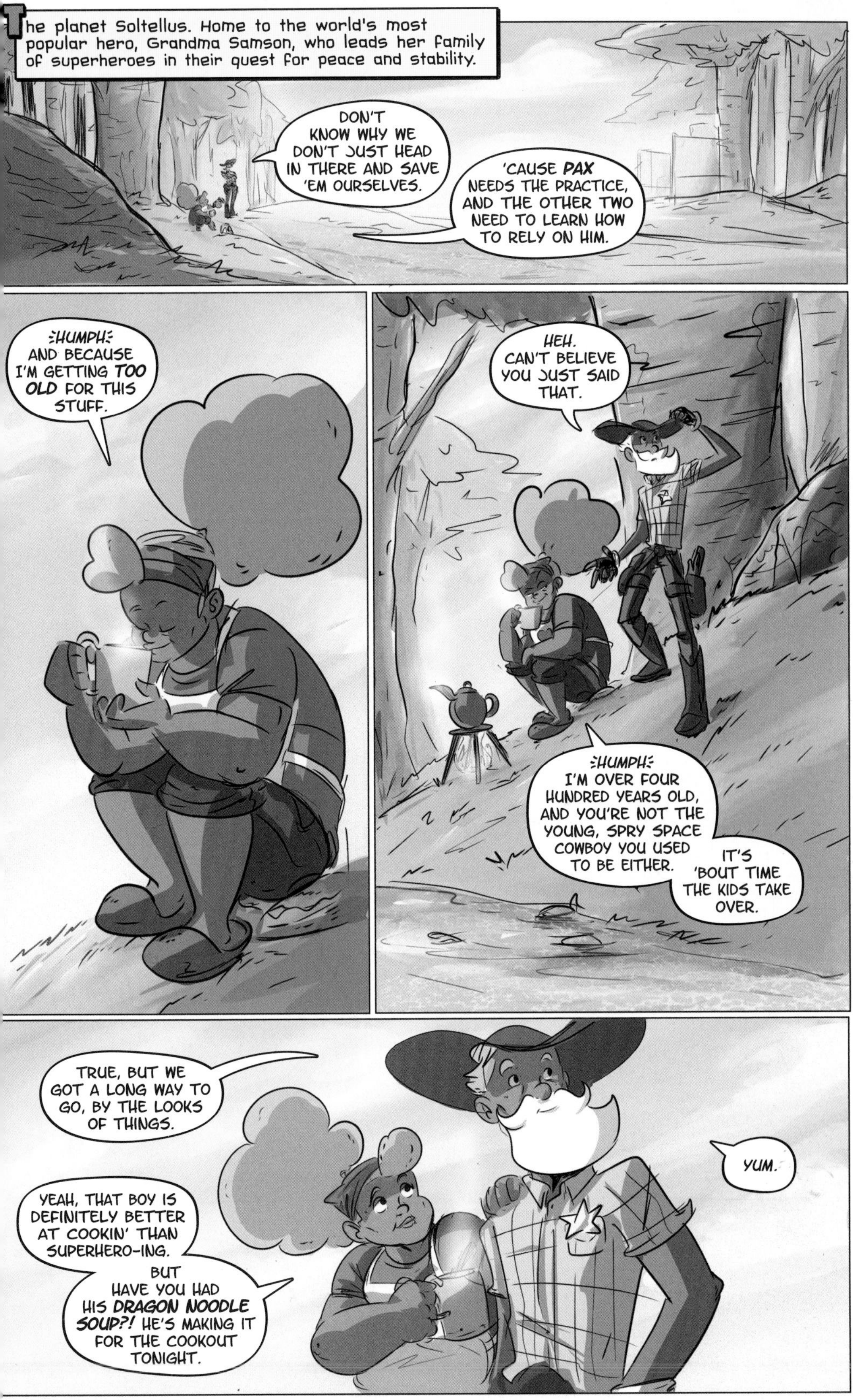
The planet Soltellus. Home to the world's most popular hero, Grandma Samson, who leads her family of superheroes in their quest for peace and stability.
DON'T KNOW WHY WE DON'T JUST HEAD IN THERE AND SAVE 'EM OURSELVES.
'CAUSE PAX NEEDS THE PRACTICE, AND THE OTHER TWO NEED TO LEARN HOW TO RELY ON HIM.
HUMPH AND BECAUSE I'M GETTING TOO OLD FOR THIS STUFF.
HEH. CAN'T BELIEVE YOU JUST SAID THAT.
HUMPH I'M OVER FOUR HUNDRED YEARS OLD, AND YOU'RE NOT THE YOUNG, SPRY SPACE COWBOY YOU USED TO BE EITHER.
IT'S 'BOUT TIME THE KIDS TAKE OVER.
TRUE, BUT WE GOT A LONG WAY TO GO, BY THE LOOKS OF THINGS.
YEAH, THAT BOY IS DEFINITELY BETTER AT COOKIN' THAN SUPERHERO-ING.
BUT HAVE YOU HAD HIS DRAGON NOODLE SOUP?! HE'S MAKING IT FOR THE COOKOUT TONIGHT.
YUM.

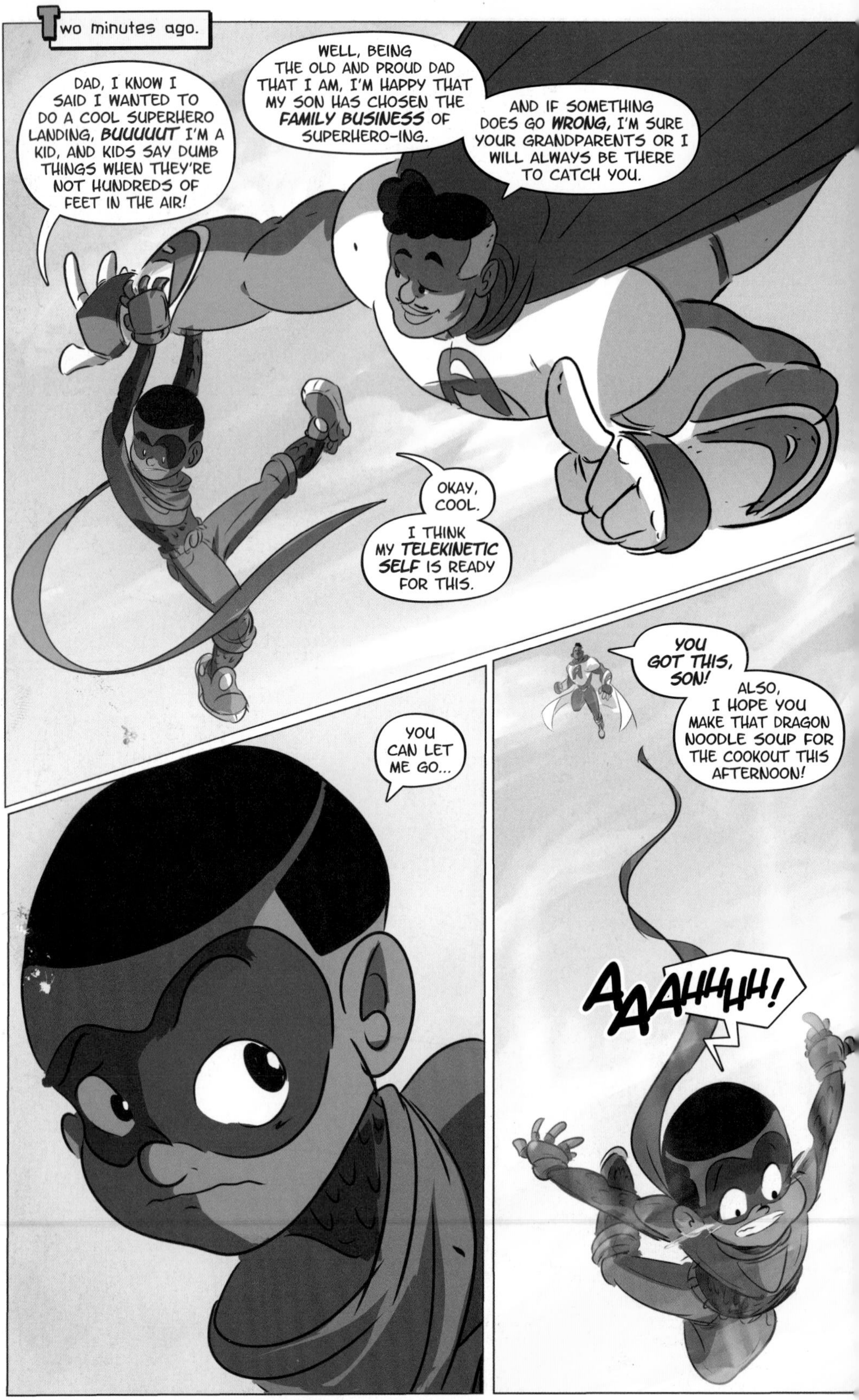
Two minutes ago.
DAD, I KNOW I SAID I WANTED TO DO A COOL SUPERHERO LANDING, BUUUUUT I'M A KID, AND KIDS SAY DUMB THINGS WHEN THEY'RE NOT HUNDREDS OF FEET IN THE AIR!
WELL, BEING THE OLD AND PROUD DAD THAT I AM, I'M HAPPY THAT MY SON HAS CHOSEN THE FAMILY BUSINESS OF SUPERHERO-ING.
AND IF SOMETHING DOES GO WRONG, I'M SURE YOUR GRANDPARENTS OR I WILL ALWAYS BE THERE TO CATCH YOU.
OKAY, COOL.
I THINK MY TELEKINETIC SELF IS READY FOR THIS.
YOU CAN LET ME GO...
YOU GOT THIS, SON!
ALSO, I HOPE YOU MAKE THAT DRAGON NOODLE SOUP FOR THE COOKOUT THIS AFTERNOON!
AAAHHHH!

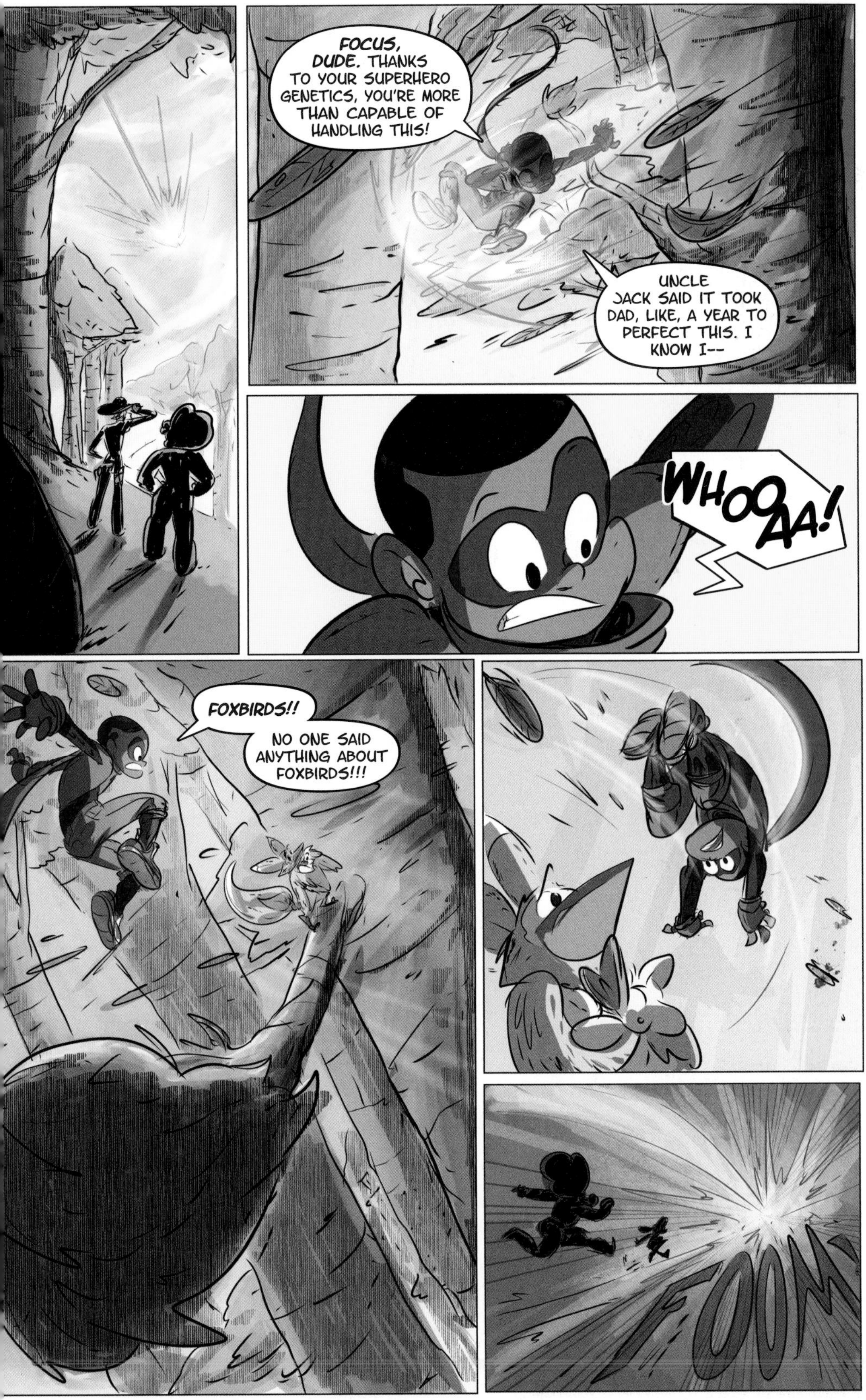
FOCUS, DUDE. THANKS TO YOUR SUPERHERO GENETICS, YOU'RE MORE THAN CAPABLE OF HANDLING THIS!
UNCLE JACK SAID IT TOOK DAD, LIKE, A YEAR TO PERFECT THIS. I KNOW I--
WHOOAA!
FOXBIRDS!!
NO ONE SAID ANYTHING ABOUT FOXBIRDS!!!
FOOM!

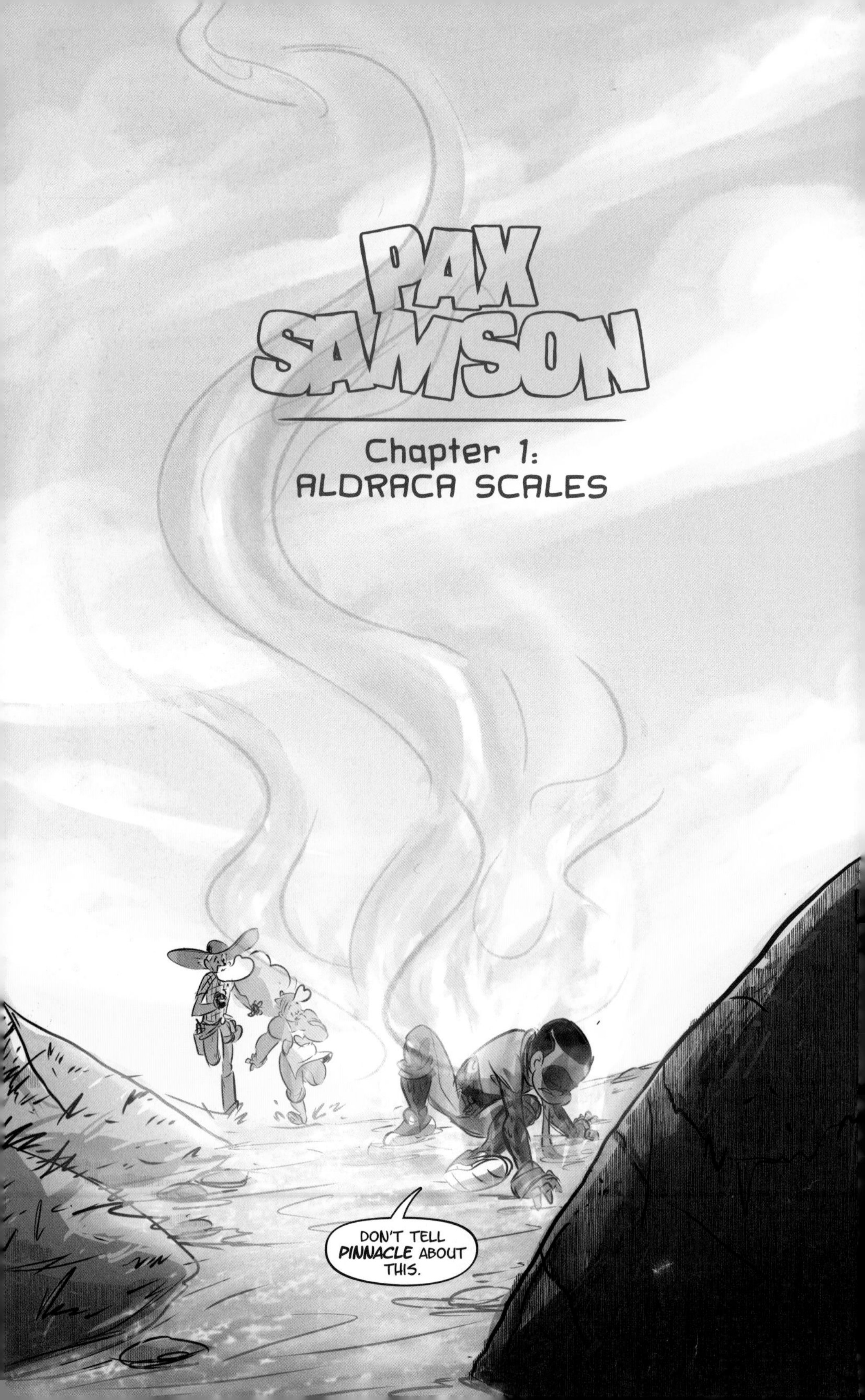
PAX SAMSON
Chapter 1:
ALDRACA SCALES
DON'T TELL PINNACLE ABOUT THIS.

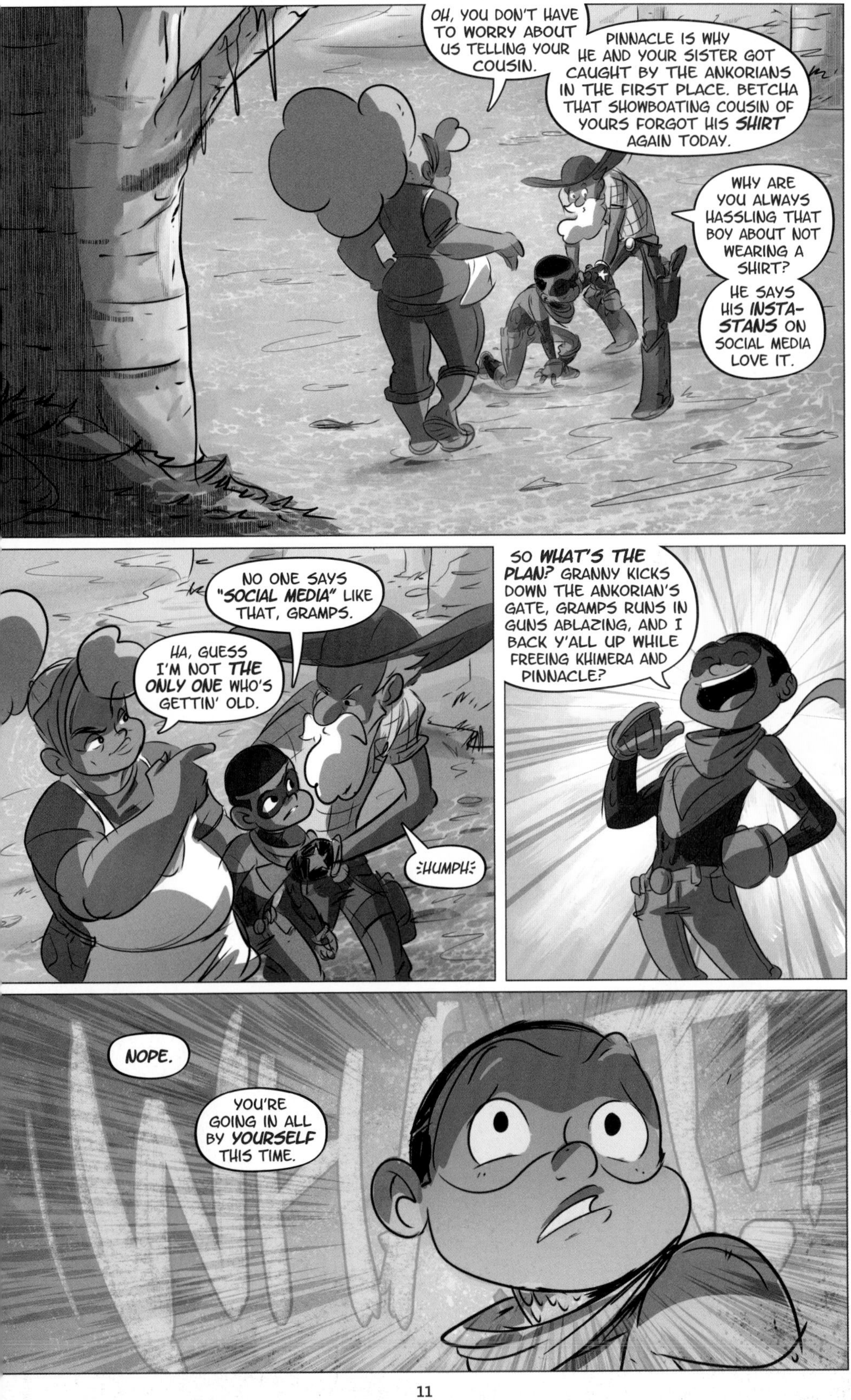
OH, YOU DON'T HAVE TO WORRY ABOUT US TELLING YOUR COUSIN.
PINNACLE IS WHY HE AND YOUR SISTER GOT CAUGHT BY THE ANKORIANS IN THE FIRST PLACE. BETCHA THAT SHOWBOATING COUSIN OF YOURS FORGOT HIS SHIRT AGAIN TODAY.
WHY ARE YOU ALWAYS HASSLING THAT BOY ABOUT NOT WEARING A SHIRT?
HE SAYS HIS INSTA-STANS ON SOCIAL MEDIA LOVE IT.
NO ONE SAYS "SOCIAL MEDIA" LIKE THAT, GRAMPS.
HA, GUESS I'M NOT THE ONLY ONE WHO'S GETTIN' OLD.
HUMPH
SO WHAT'S THE PLAN? GRANNY KICKS DOWN THE ANKORIAN'S GATE, GRAMPS RUNS IN GUNS ABLAZING, AND I BACK Y'ALL UP WHILE FREEING KHIMERA AND PINNACLE?
NOPE.
YOU'RE GOING IN ALL BY YOURSELF THIS TIME.

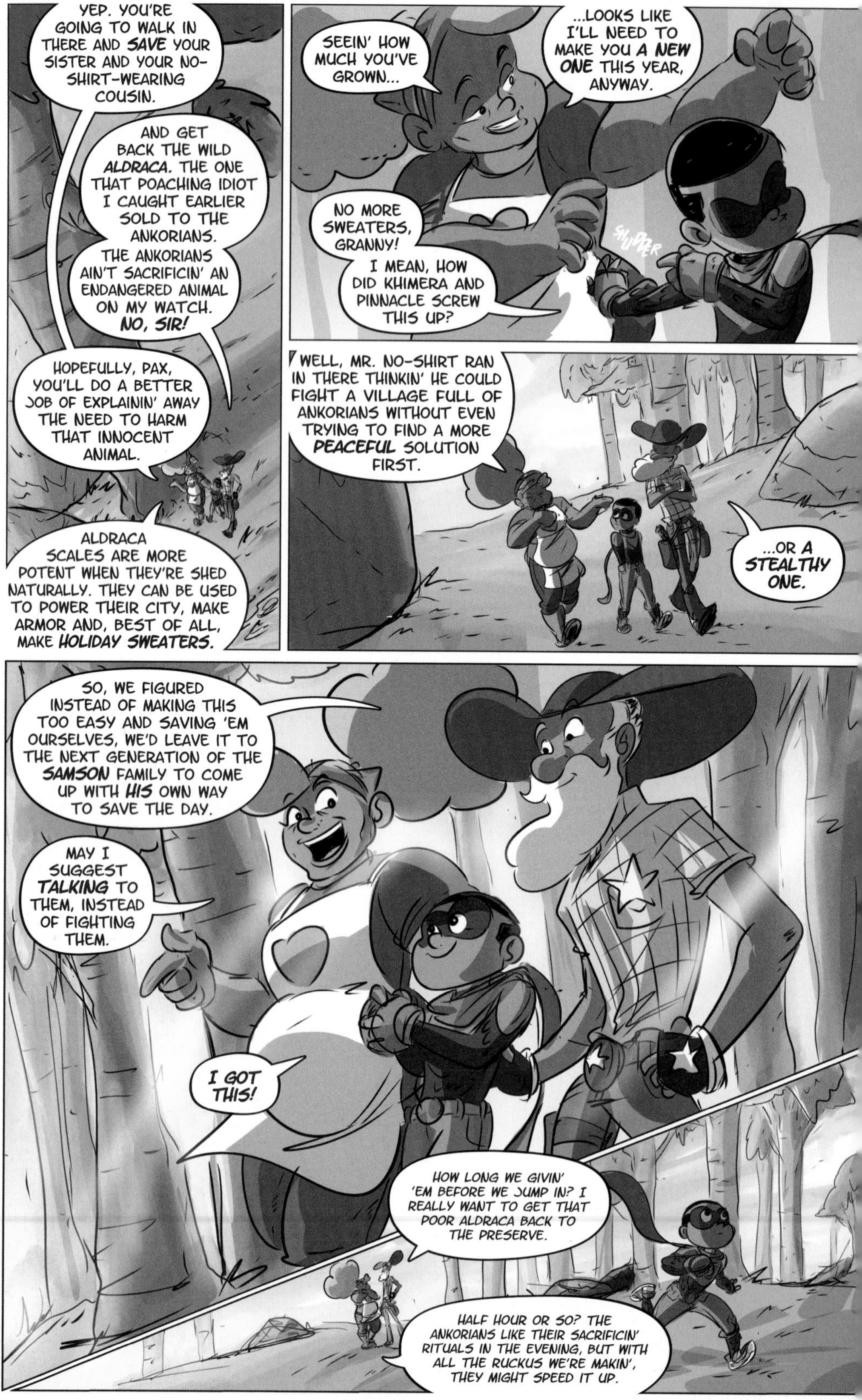
YEP. YOU'RE GOING TO WALK IN THERE AND SAVE YOUR SISTER AND YOUR NO-SHIRT-WEARING COUSIN.
AND GET BACK THE WILD ALDRACA. THE ONE THAT POACHING IDIOT I CAUGHT EARLIER SOLD TO THE ANKORIANS.
THE ANKORIANS AIN'T SACRIFICIN' AN ENDANGERED ANIMAL ON MY WATCH. NO, SIR!
HOPEFULLY, PAX, YOU'LL DO A BETTER JOB OF EXPLAININ' AWAY THE NEED TO HARM THAT INNOCENT ANIMAL.
ALDRACA SCALES ARE MORE POTENT WHEN THEY'RE SHED NATURALLY. THEY CAN BE USED TO POWER THEIR CITY, MAKE ARMOR AND, BEST OF ALL, MAKE HOLIDAY SWEATERS.
SEEIN' HOW MUCH YOU'VE GROWN...
...LOOKS LIKE I'LL NEED TO MAKE YOU A NEW ONE THIS YEAR, ANYWAY.
NO MORE SWEATERS, GRANNY!
SHUDDER
I MEAN, HOW DID KHIMERA AND PINNACLE SCREW THIS UP?
WELL, MR. NO-SHIRT RAN IN THERE THINKIN' HE COULD FIGHT A VILLAGE FULL OF ANKORIANS WITHOUT EVEN TRYING TO FIND A MORE PEACEFUL SOLUTION FIRST.
...OR A STEALTHY ONE.
SO, WE FIGURED INSTEAD OF MAKING THIS TOO EASY AND SAVING 'EM OURSELVES, WE'D LEAVE IT TO THE NEXT GENERATION OF THE SAMSON FAMILY TO COME UP WITH HIS OWN WAY TO SAVE THE DAY.
MAY I SUGGEST TALKING TO THEM, INSTEAD OF FIGHTING THEM.
I GOT THIS!
HOW LONG WE GIVIN' 'EM BEFORE WE JUMP IN? I REALLY WANT TO GET THAT POOR ALDRACA BACK TO THE PRESERVE.
HALF HOUR OR SO? THE ANKORIANS LIKE THEIR SACRIFICIN' RITUALS IN THE EVENING, BUT WITH ALL THE RUCKUS WE'RE MAKIN', THEY MIGHT SPEED IT UP.

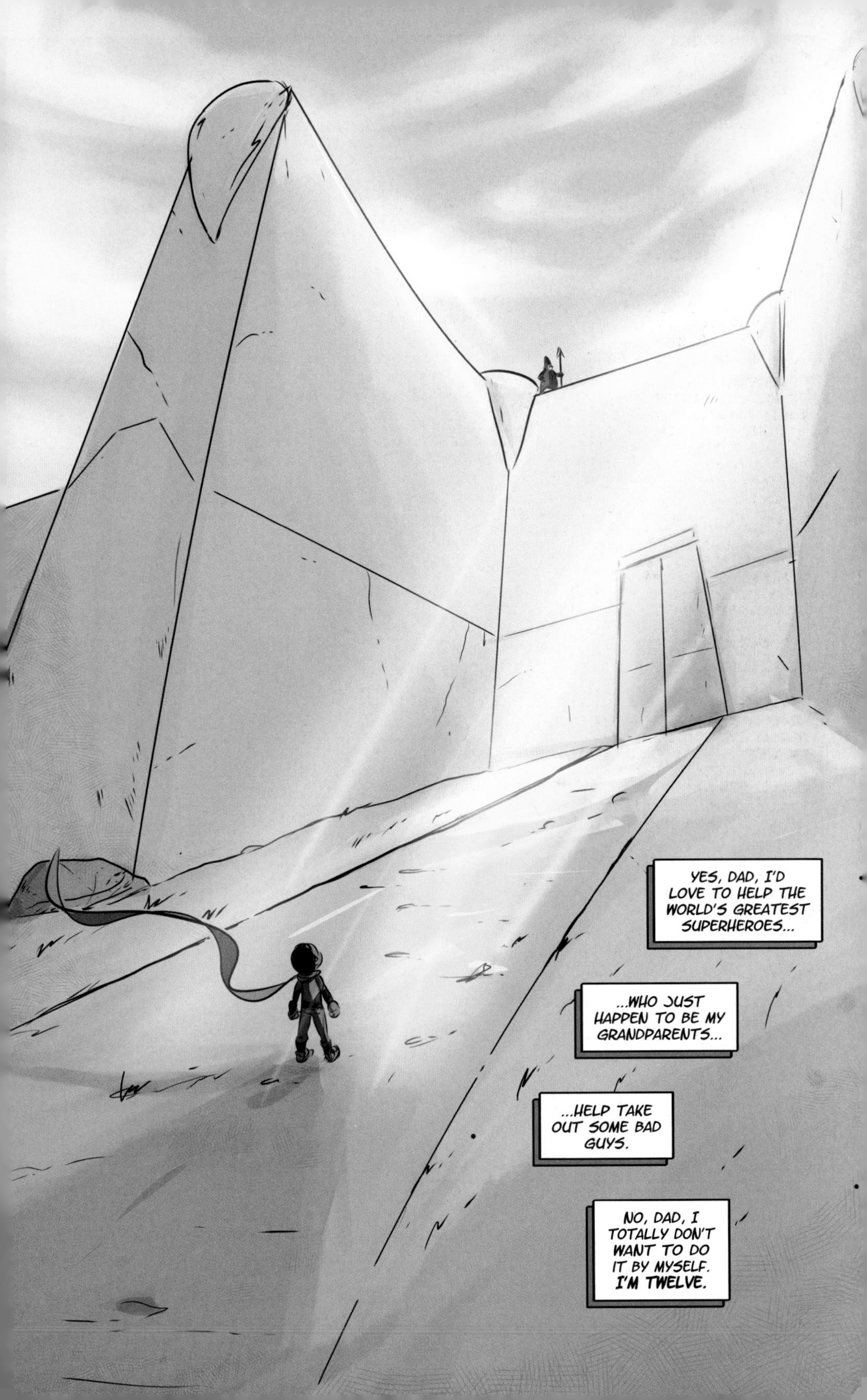
YES, DAD, I'D LOVE TO HELP THE WORLD'S GREATEST SUPERHEROES...
...WHO JUST HAPPEN TO BE MY GRANDPARENTS...
...HELP TAKE OUT SOME BAD GUYS.
NO, DAD, I TOTALLY DON'T WANT TO DO IT BY MYSELF. I'M TWELVE.

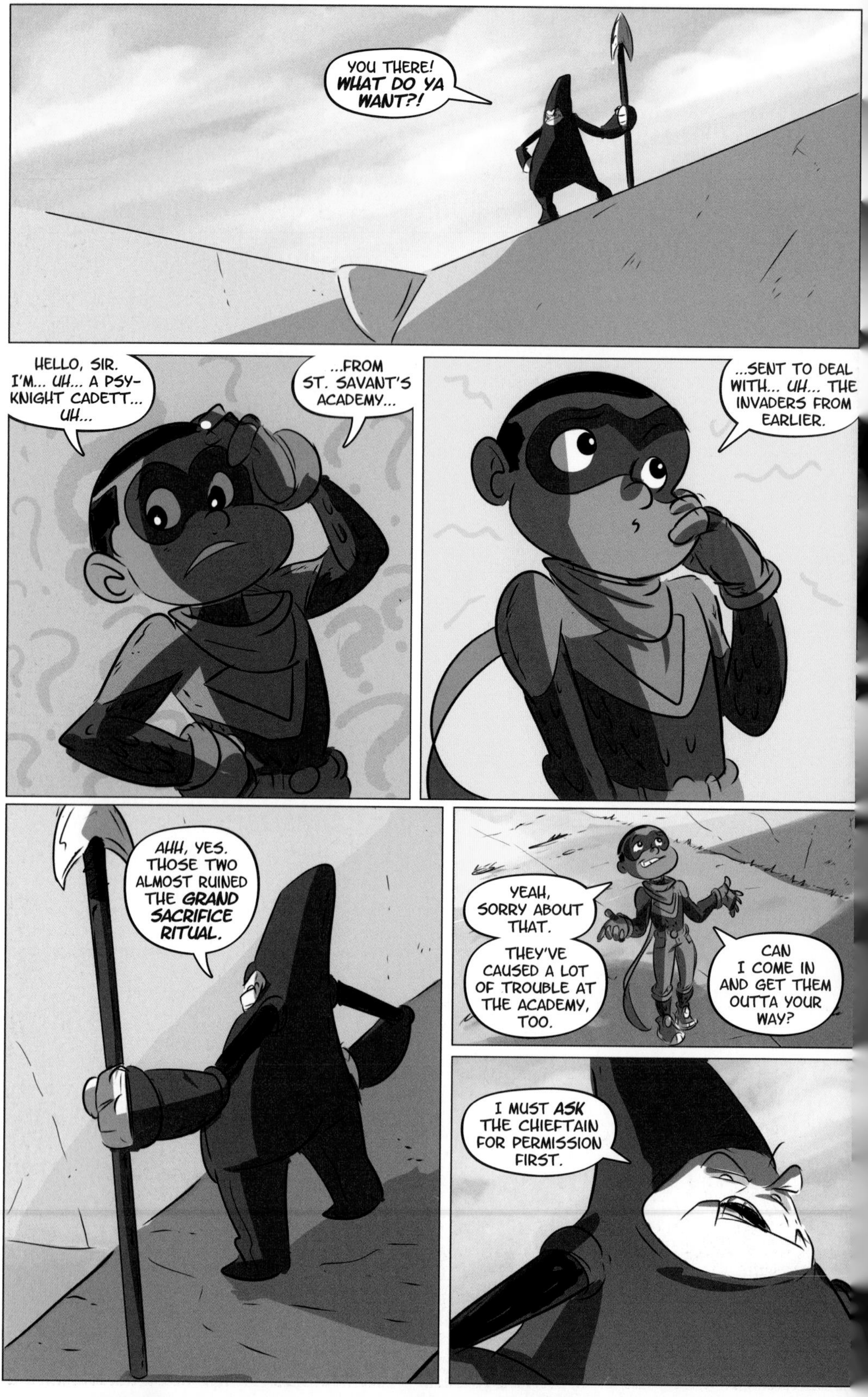
YOU THERE! WHAT DO YA WANT?!
HELLO, SIR. I'M... UH... A PSY-KNIGHT CADETT... UH...
...FROM ST. SAVANT'S ACADEMY...
...SENT TO DEAL WITH... UH... THE INVADERS FROM EARLIER.
AHH, YES. THOSE TWO ALMOST RUINED THE GRAND SACRIFICE RITUAL.
YEAH, SORRY ABOUT THAT.
THEY'VE CAUSED A LOT OF TROUBLE AT THE ACADEMY, TOO.
CAN I COME IN AND GET THEM OUTTA YOUR WAY?
I MUST ASK THE CHIEFTAIN FOR PERMISSION FIRST.

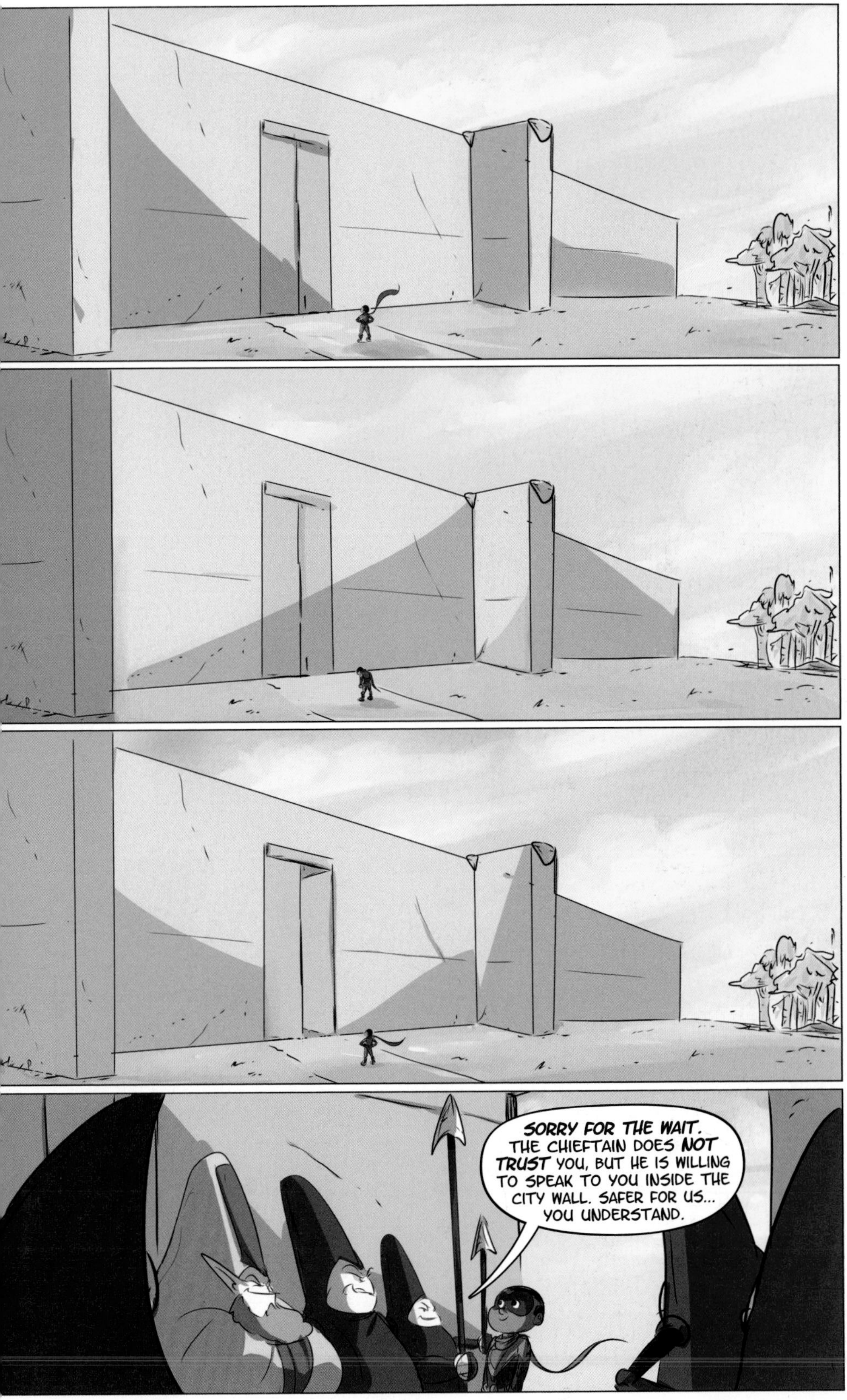
SORRY FOR THE WAIT. THE CHIEFTAIN DOES NOT TRUST YOU, BUT HE IS WILLING TO SPEAK TO YOU INSIDE THE CITY WALL. SAFER FOR US... YOU UNDERSTAND.

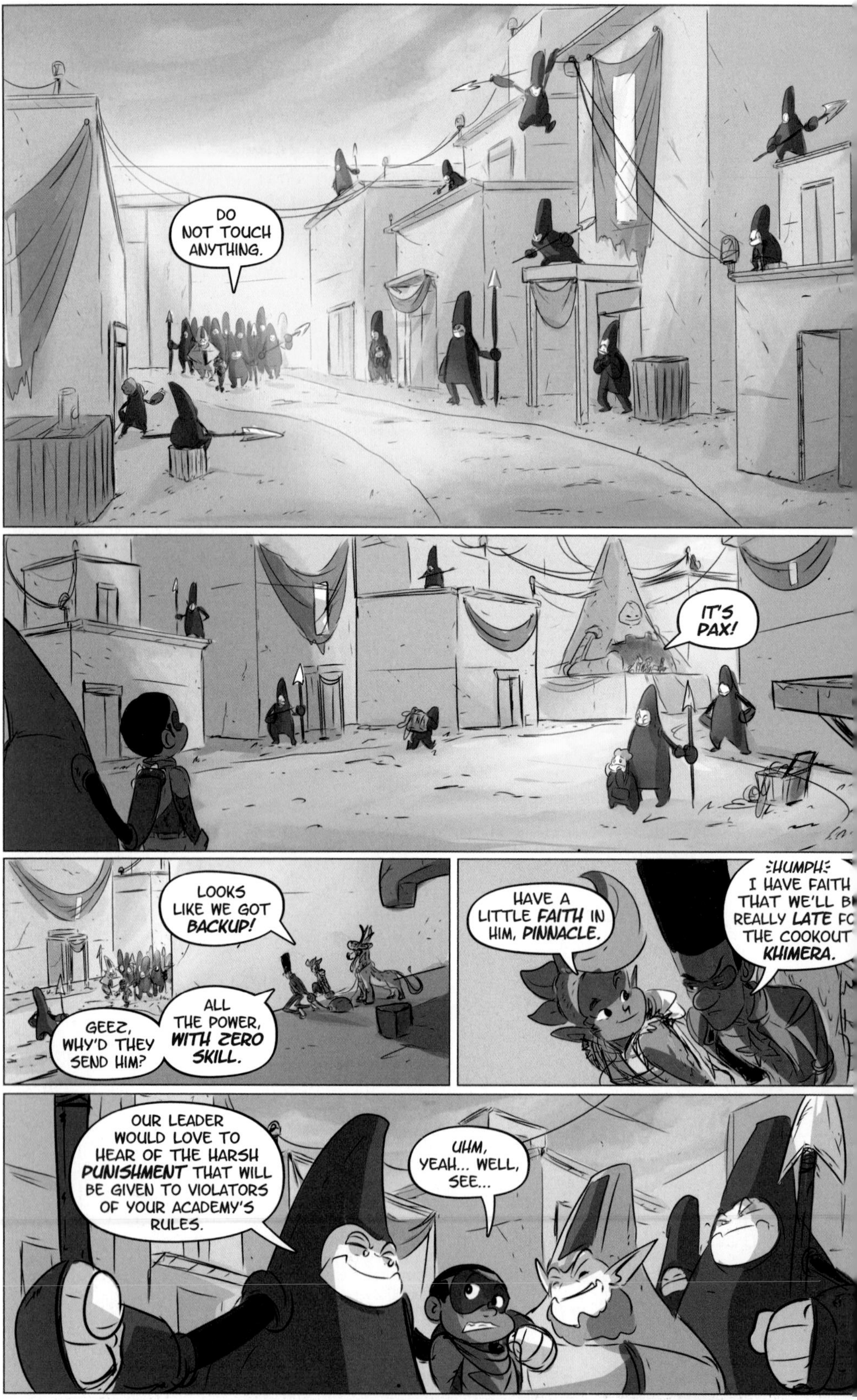
DO NOT TOUCH ANYTHING.
IT'S PAX!
LOOKS LIKE WE GOT BACKUP!
GEEZ, WHY'D THEY SEND HIM?
ALL THE POWER, WITH ZERO SKILL.
HAVE A LITTLE FAITH IN HIM, PINNACLE.
HUMPH
I HAVE FAITH THAT WE'LL B REALLY LATE FO THE COOKOUT KHIMERA.
OUR LEADER WOULD LOVE TO HEAR OF THE HARSH PUNISHMENT THAT WILL BE GIVEN TO VIOLATORS OF YOUR ACADEMY'S RULES.
UHM, YEAH... WELL, SEE...

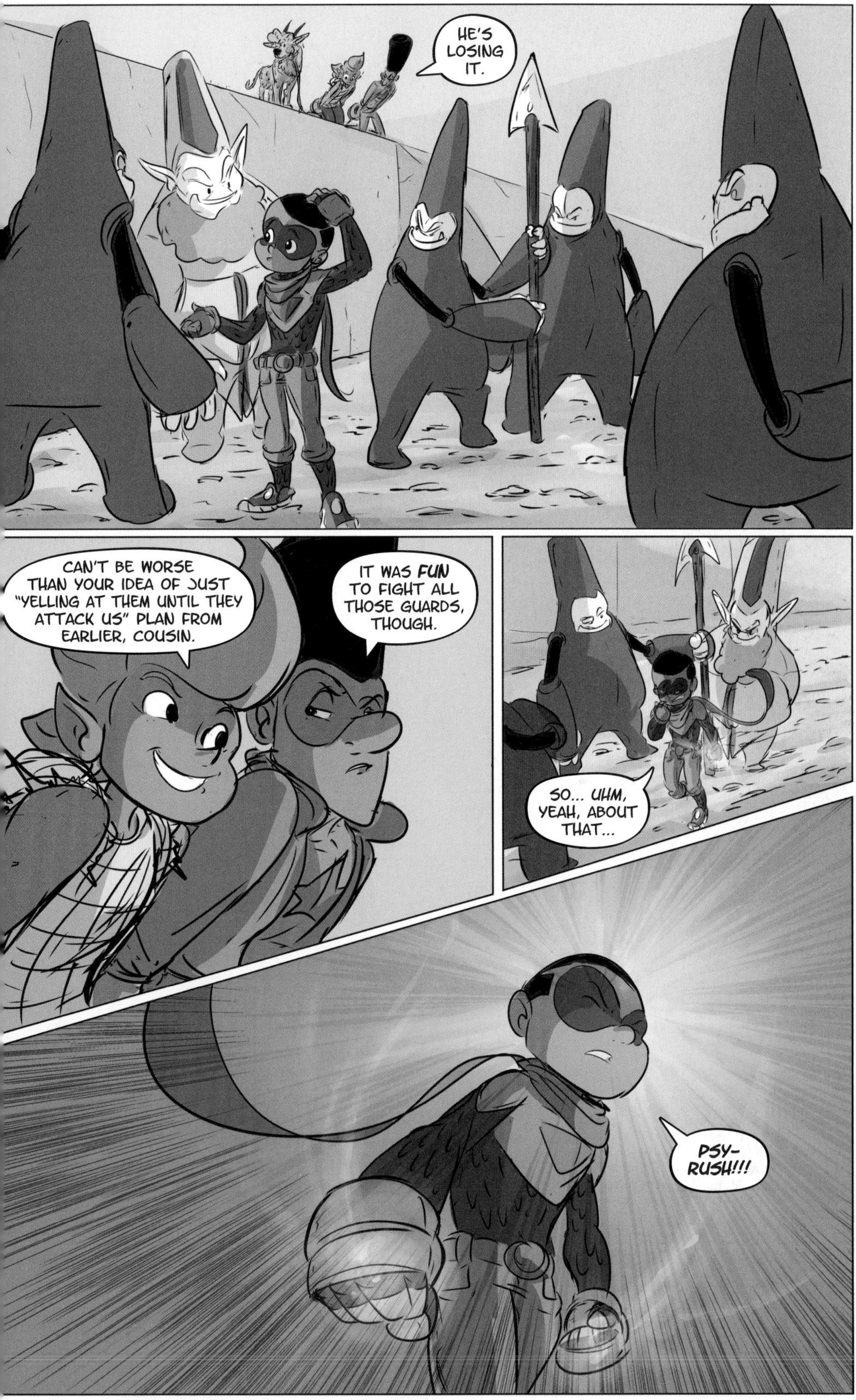
HE'S LOSING IT.
CAN'T BE WORSE THAN YOUR IDEA OF JUST "YELLING AT THEM UNTIL THEY ATTACK US" PLAN FROM EARLIER, COUSIN.
IT WAS FUN TO FIGHT ALL THOSE GUARDS, THOUGH.
SO... UHM, YEAH, ABOUT THAT...
PSY-RUSH!!!

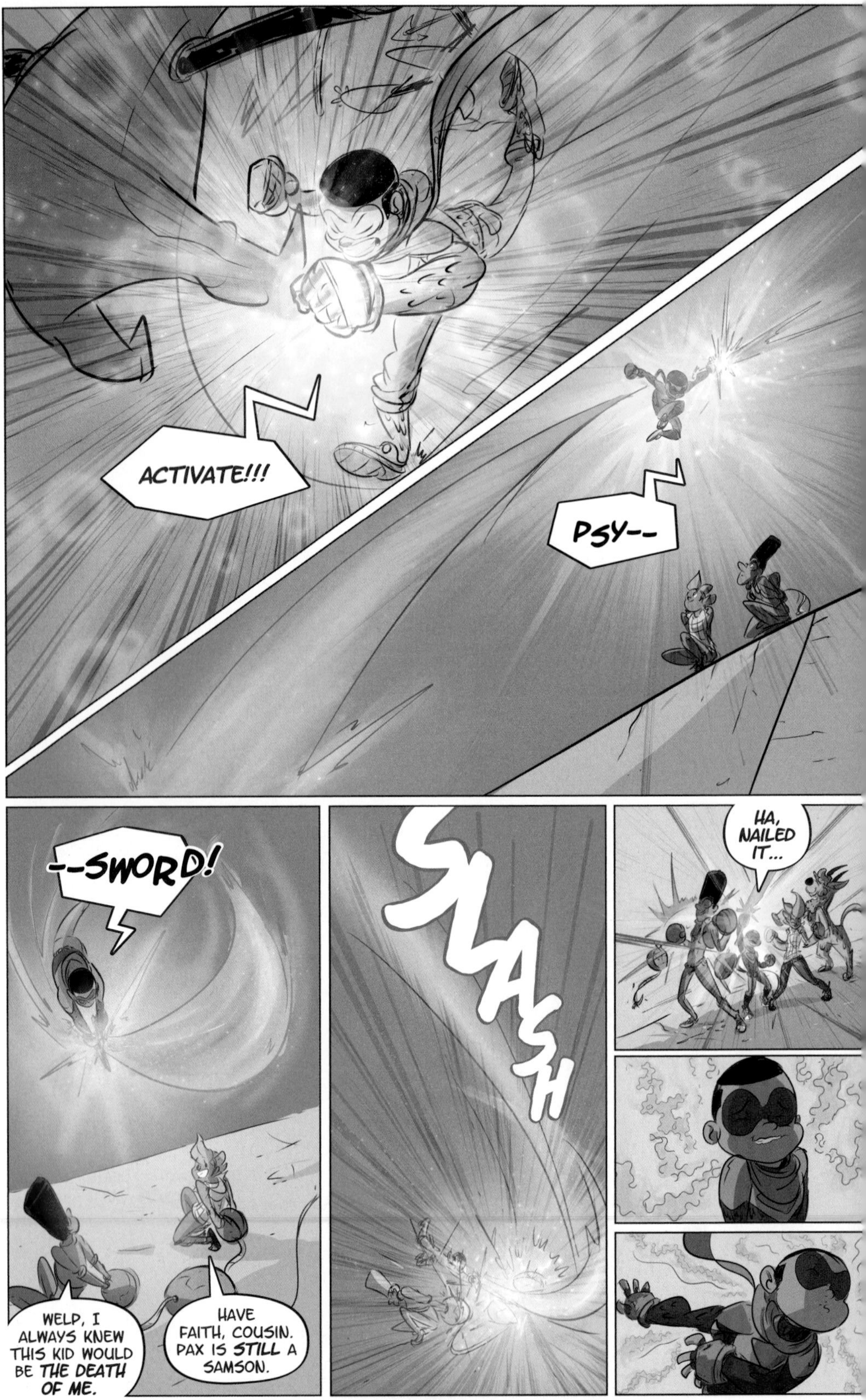
ACTIVATE!!!
PSY--
--SWORD!
WELP, I ALWAYS KNEW THIS KID WOULD BE THE DEATH OF ME.
HAVE FAITH, COUSIN. PAX IS STILL A SAMSON.
SLASH
HA, NAILED IT...

SEE? FAITH.
YEAH, THAT WAS PRETTY COOL.
HOLD ONTO THAT ALDRACA, AND I'LL TAKE OUR SAVIOR HERE. HEAD FOR THE GATES.
SUPER FUN! ALL OF THIS FIGHTING AND A COOKOUT TONIGHT.
SO WE HAVE ABOUT ZERO MINUTES BEFORE WE'RE TOTALLY SWARMED BY GUARDS, AND/OR GRANNY AND GRAMPS COME TO SAVE US.
MAN, THIS THING IS MOLTING...
SIGH LET'S GO.

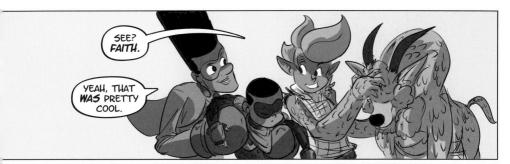

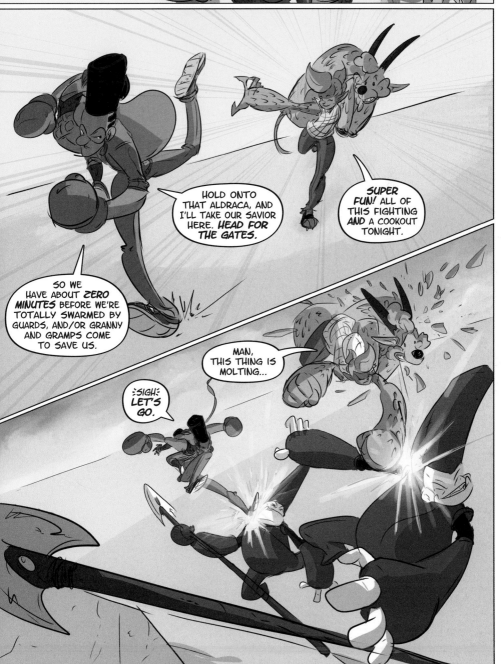

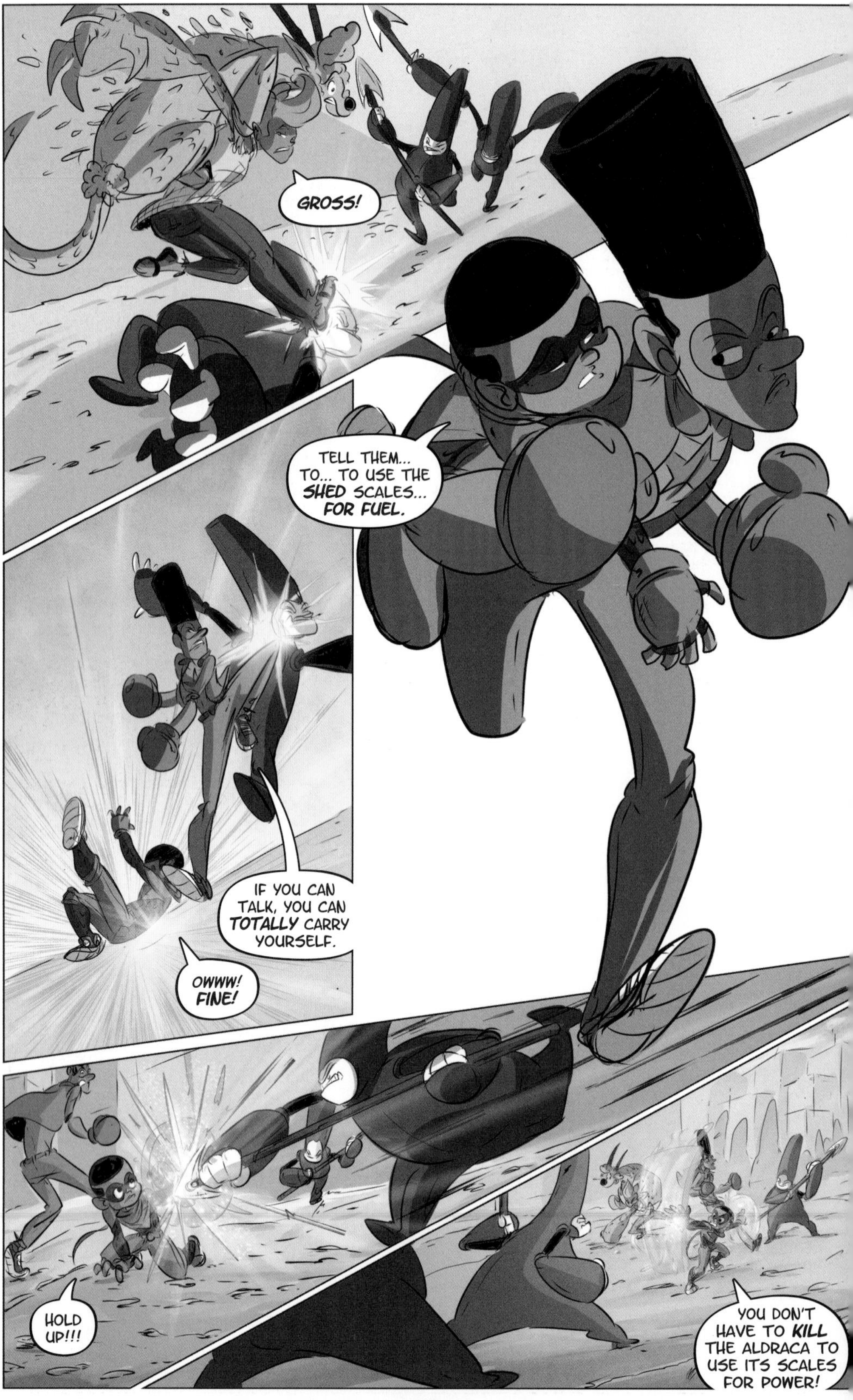
GROSS!
TELL THEM... TO... TO USE THE SHED SCALES... FOR FUEL.
IF YOU CAN TALK, YOU CAN TOTALLY CARRY YOURSELF.
OWWW! FINE!
HOLD UP!!!
YOU DON'T HAVE TO KILL THE ALDRACA TO USE ITS SCALES FOR POWER!

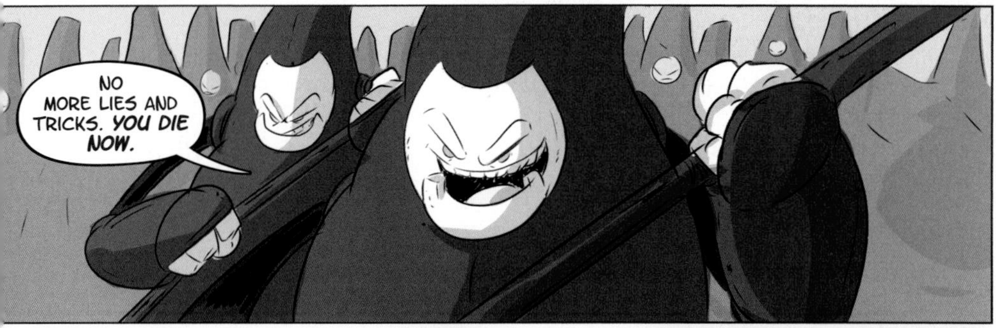
NO MORE LIES AND TRICKS. YOU DIE NOW.

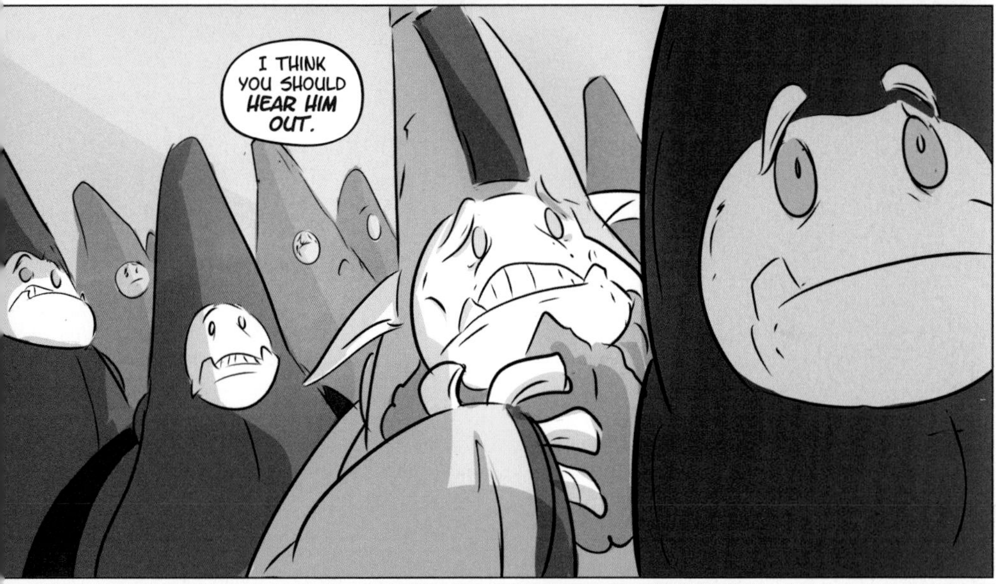
I THINK YOU SHOULD HEAR HIM OUT.

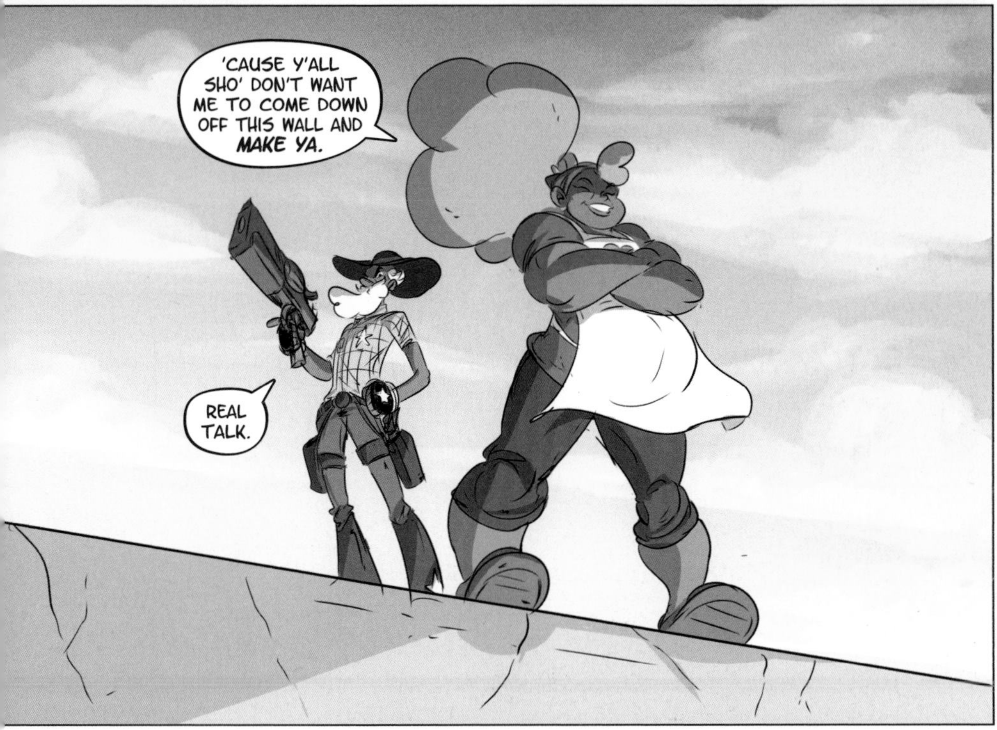
'CAUSE Y'ALL SHO' DON'T WANT ME TO COME DOWN OFF THIS WALL AND MAKE YA.
REAL TALK.

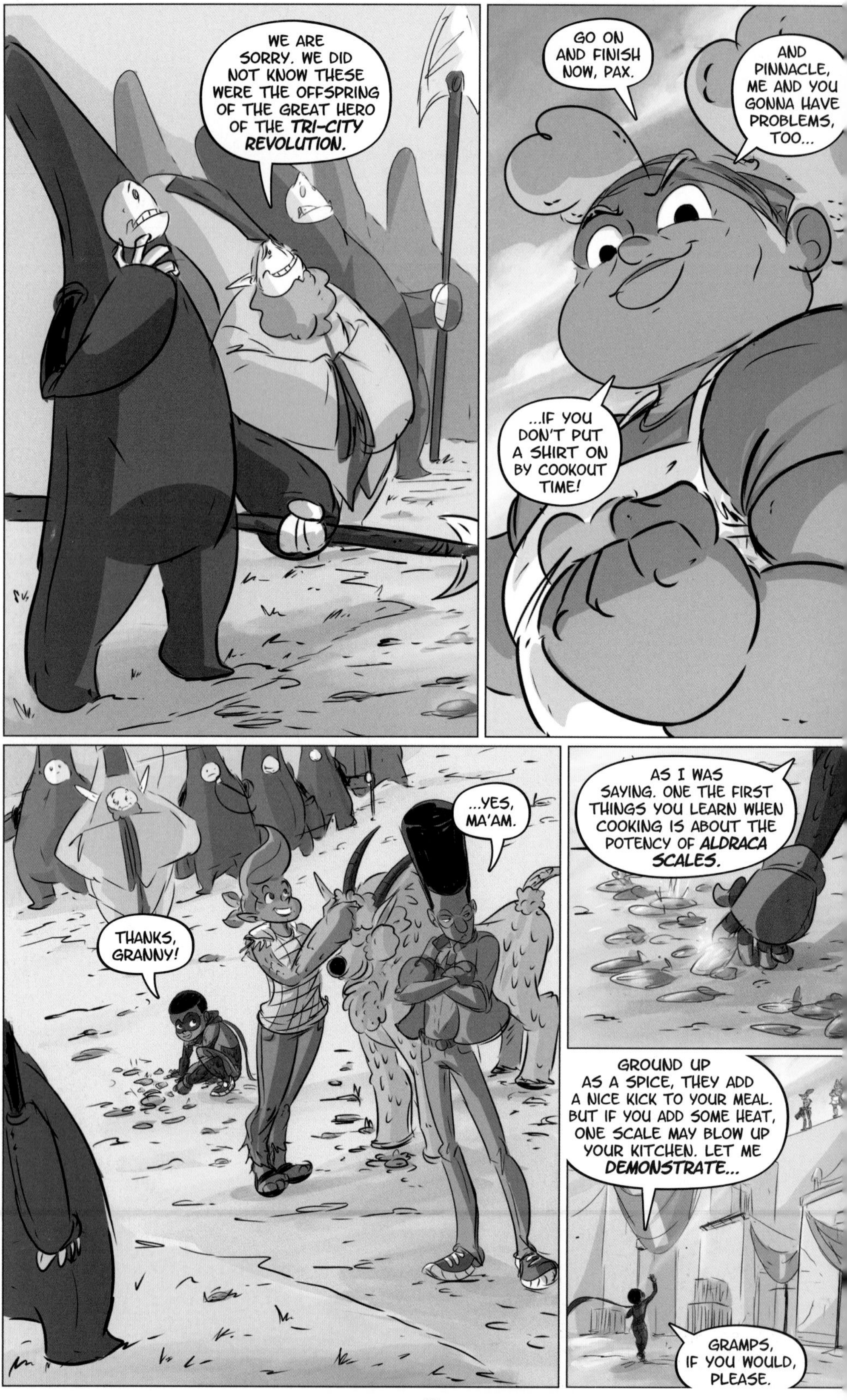
WE ARE SORRY. WE DID NOT KNOW THESE WERE THE OFFSPRING OF THE GREAT HERO OF THE **TRI-CITY REVOLUTION.**
GO ON AND FINISH NOW, PAX.
AND PINNACLE, ME AND YOU GONNA HAVE PROBLEMS, TOO...
...IF YOU DON'T PUT A SHIRT ON BY COOKOUT TIME!
...YES, MA'AM.
THANKS, GRANNY!
AS I WAS SAYING. ONE THE FIRST THINGS YOU LEARN WHEN COOKING IS ABOUT THE POTENCY OF **ALDRACA SCALES.**
GROUND UP AS A SPICE, THEY ADD A NICE KICK TO YOUR MEAL. BUT IF YOU ADD SOME HEAT, ONE SCALE MAY BLOW UP YOUR KITCHEN. LET ME **DEMONSTRATE...**
GRAMPS, IF YOU WOULD, PLEASE.

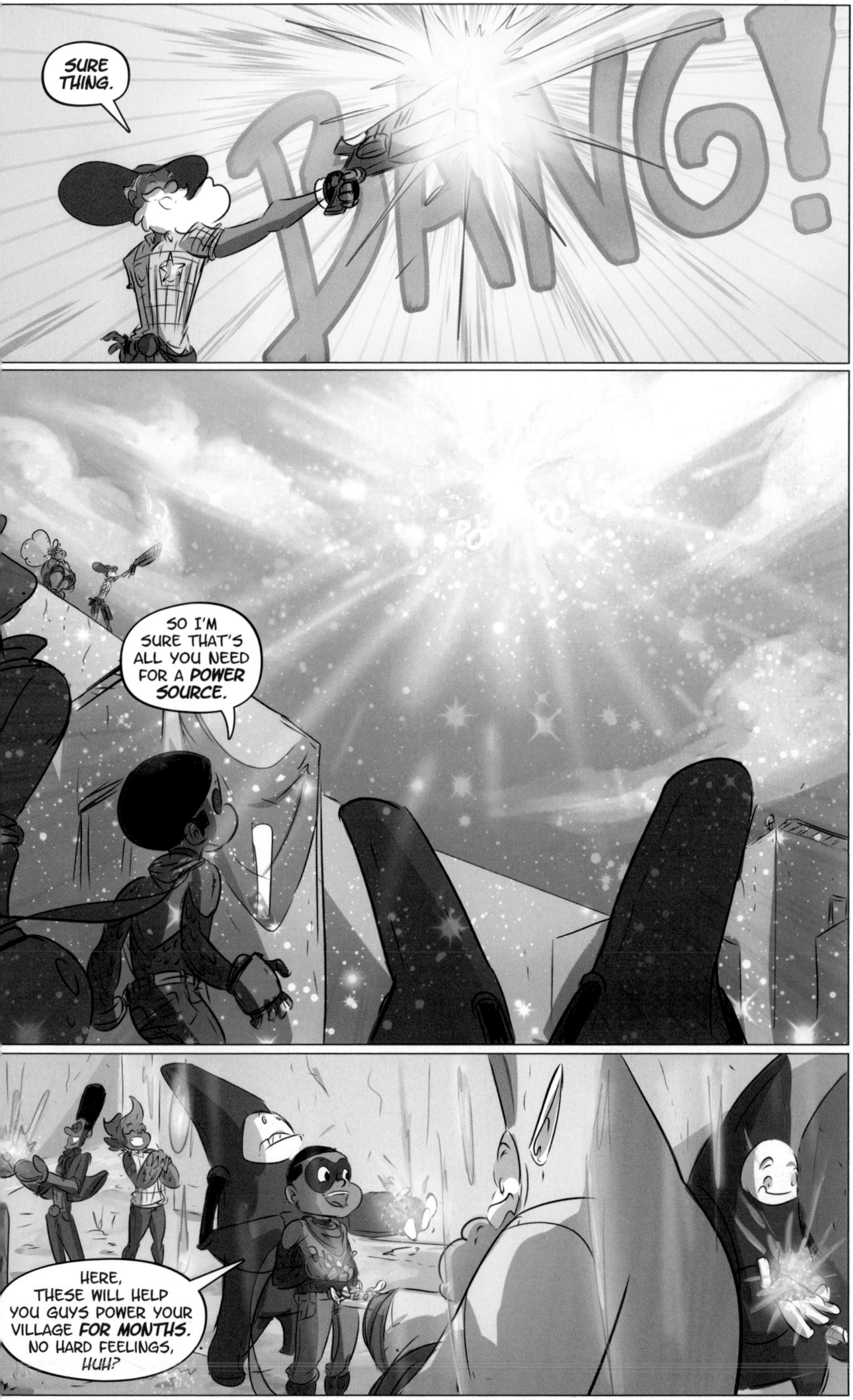
SURE THING.
BANG!
SO I'M SURE THAT'S ALL YOU NEED FOR A **POWER SOURCE.**
HERE, THESE WILL HELP YOU GUYS POWER YOUR VILLAGE **FOR MONTHS.** NO HARD FEELINGS, HUH?

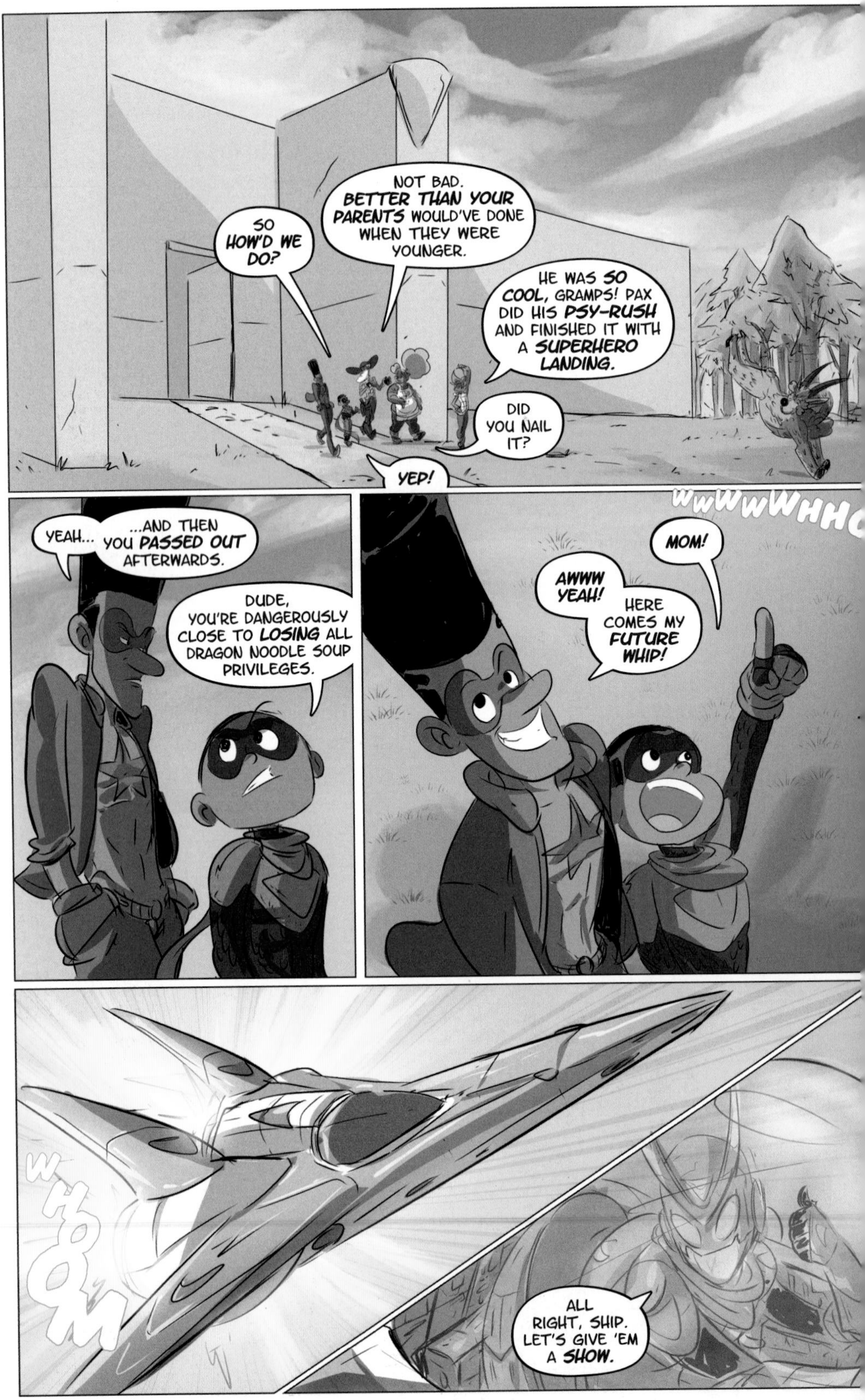
SO HOW'D WE DO?
NOT BAD. BETTER THAN YOUR PARENTS WOULD'VE DONE WHEN THEY WERE YOUNGER.
HE WAS SO COOL, GRAMPS! PAX DID HIS PSY-RUSH AND FINISHED IT WITH A SUPERHERO LANDING.
DID YOU NAIL IT?
YEP!
YEAH...
...AND THEN YOU PASSED OUT AFTERWARDS.
DUDE, YOU'RE DANGEROUSLY CLOSE TO LOSING ALL DRAGON NOODLE SOUP PRIVILEGES.
WWWWWWHHO
MOM!
AWWW YEAH!
HERE COMES MY FUTURE WHIP!
WHOOM
ALL RIGHT, SHIP. LET'S GIVE 'EM A SHOW.

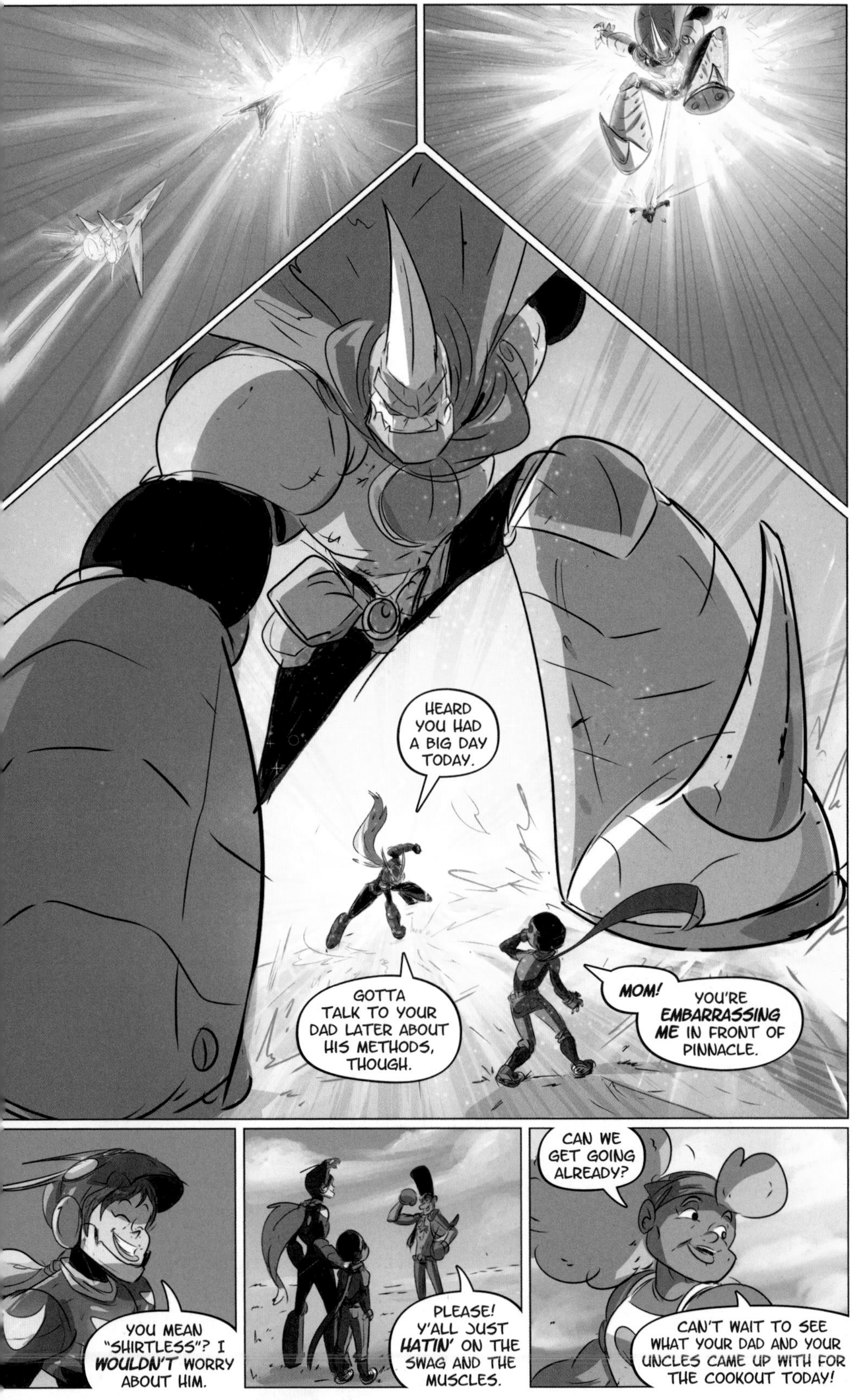
HEARD YOU HAD A BIG DAY TODAY.
GOTTA TALK TO YOUR DAD LATER ABOUT HIS METHODS, THOUGH.
MOM! YOU'RE EMBARRASSING ME IN FRONT OF PINNACLE.
YOU MEAN "SHIRTLESS"? I WOULDN'T WORRY ABOUT HIM.
PLEASE! Y'ALL JUST HATIN' ON THE SWAG AND THE MUSCLES.
CAN WE GET GOING ALREADY?
CAN'T WAIT TO SEE WHAT YOUR DAD AND YOUR UNCLES CAME UP WITH FOR THE COOKOUT TODAY!

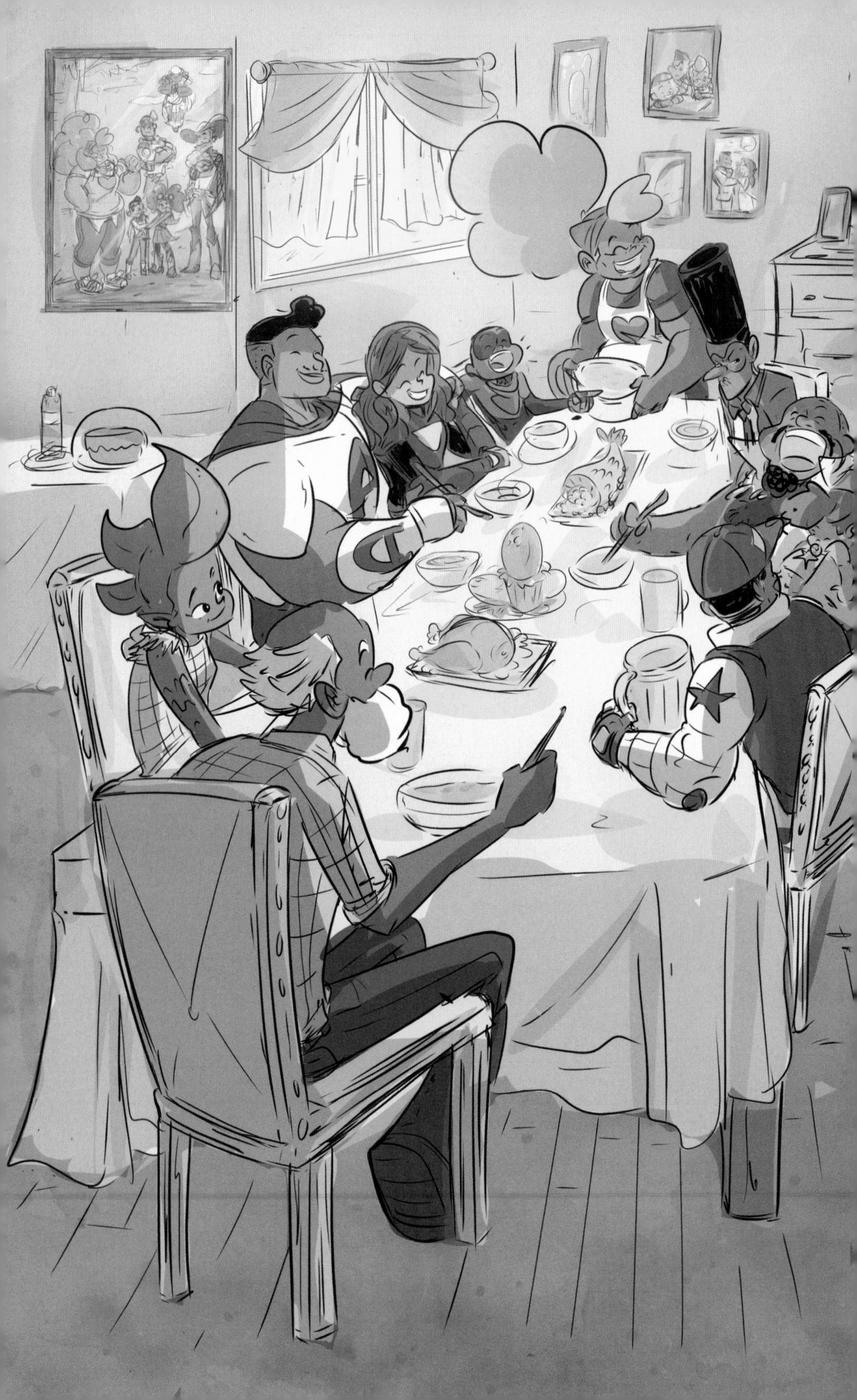

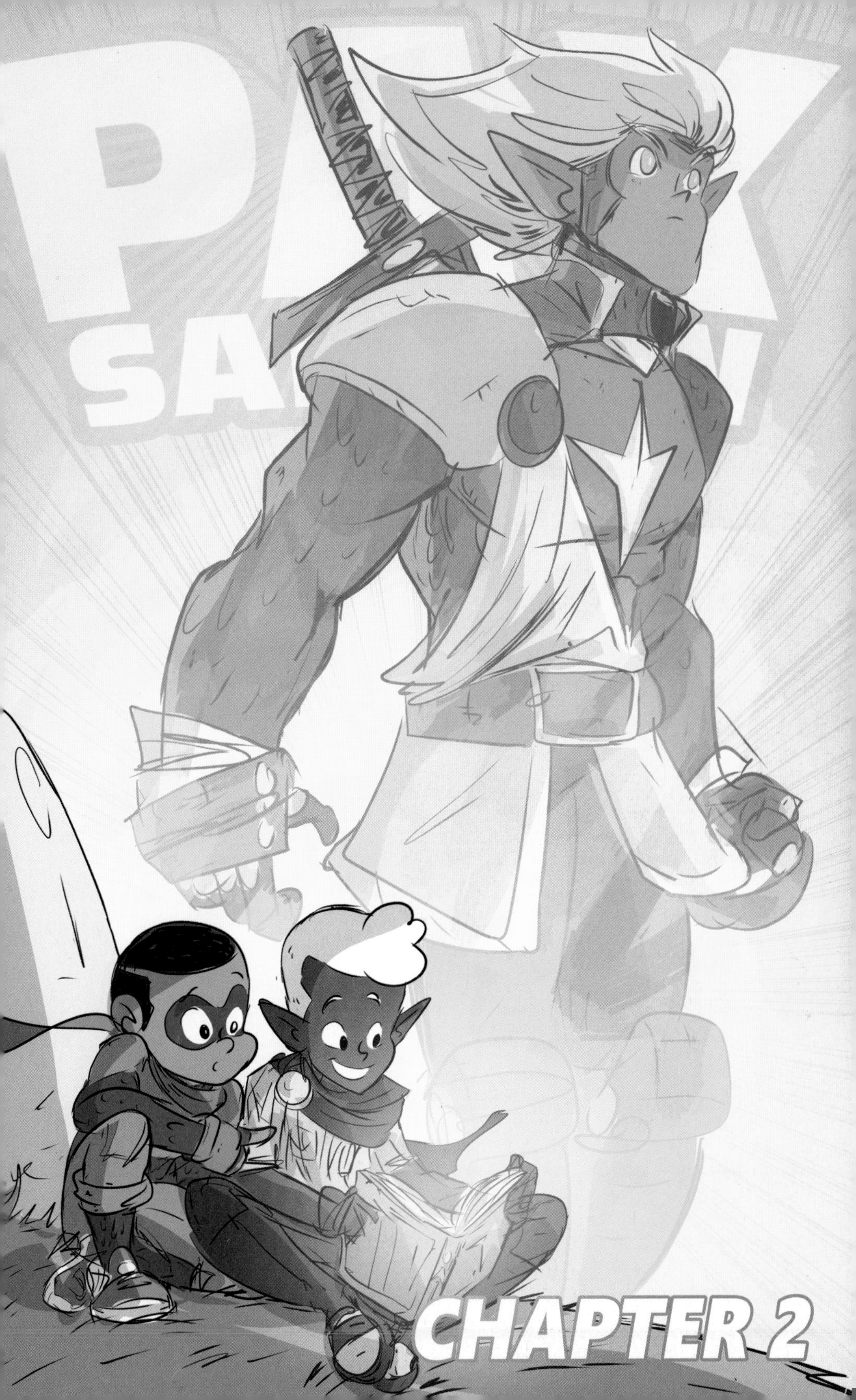
CHAPTER 2

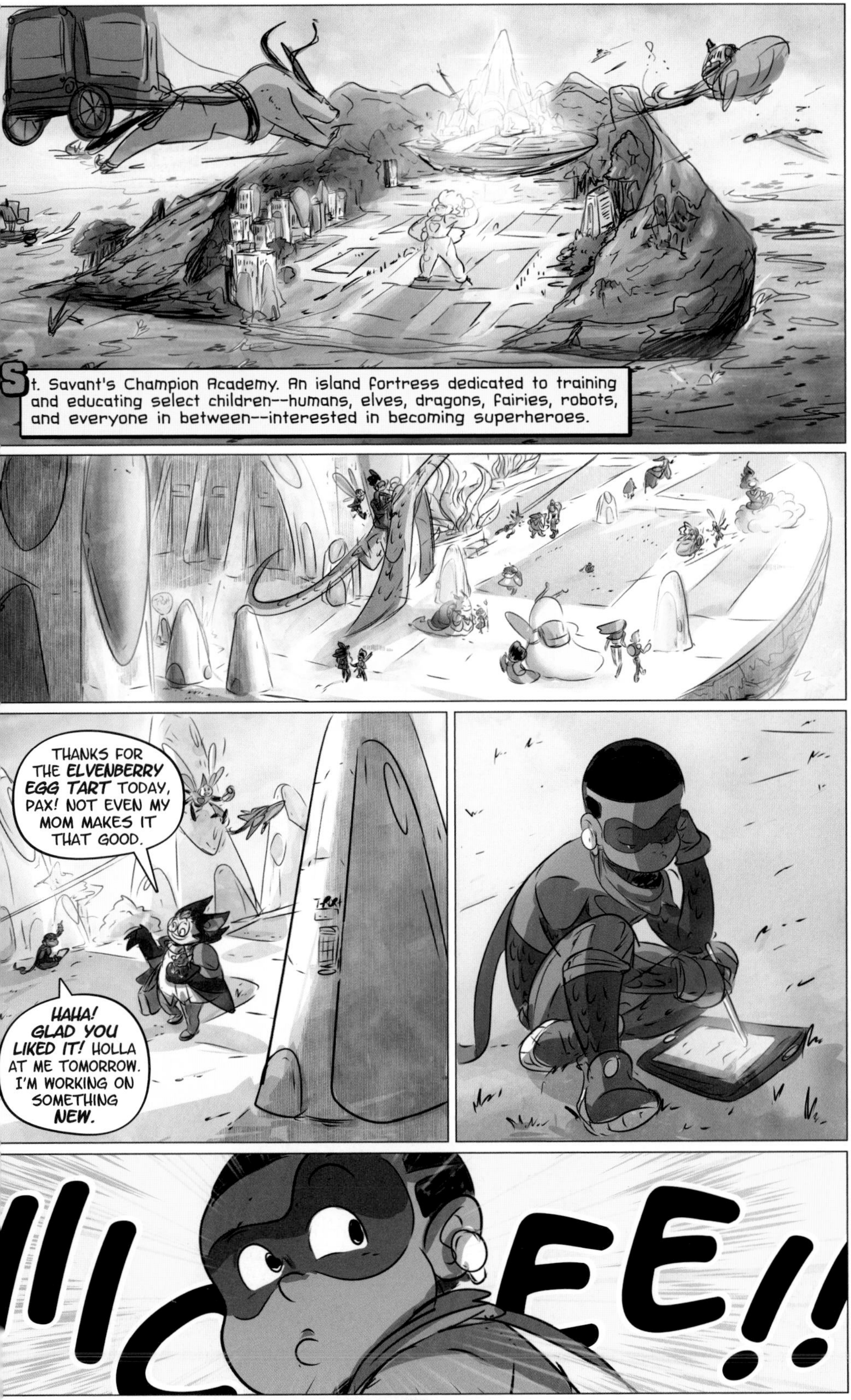
St. Savant's Champion Academy. An island fortress dedicated to training and educating select children--humans, elves, dragons, fairies, robots, and everyone in between--interested in becoming superheroes.
THANKS FOR THE ELVENBERRY EGG TART TODAY, PAX! NOT EVEN MY MOM MAKES IT THAT GOOD.
HAHA! GLAD YOU LIKED IT! HOLLA AT ME TOMORROW. I'M WORKING ON SOMETHING NEW.
IIICEE!!

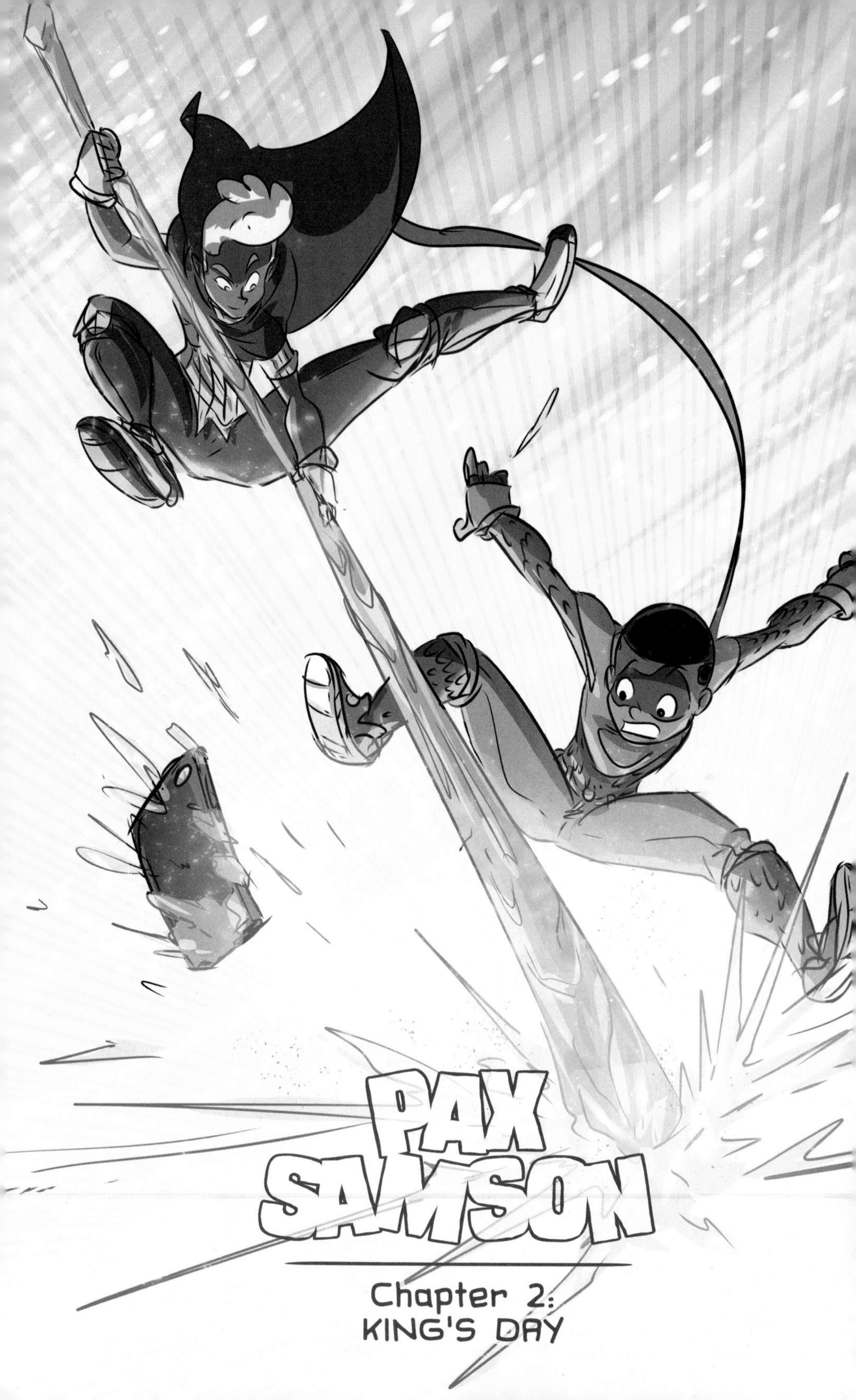

PAX SAMSON

Chapter 2: KING'S DAY

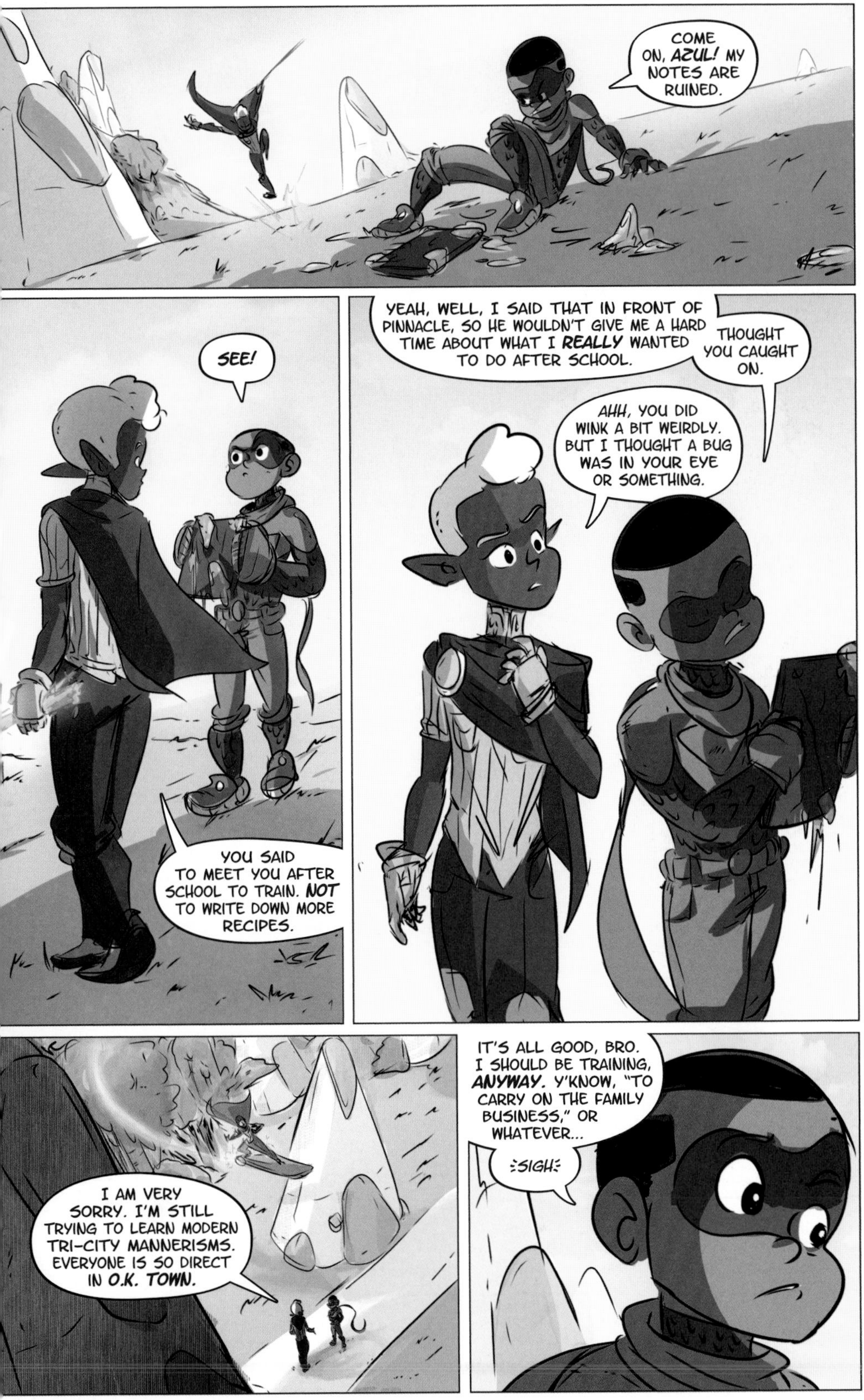
COME ON, AZUL! MY NOTES ARE RUINED.
SEE!
YOU SAID TO MEET YOU AFTER SCHOOL TO TRAIN. NOT TO WRITE DOWN MORE RECIPES.
YEAH, WELL, I SAID THAT IN FRONT OF PINNACLE, SO HE WOULDN'T GIVE ME A HARD TIME ABOUT WHAT I REALLY WANTED TO DO AFTER SCHOOL.
THOUGHT YOU CAUGHT ON.
AHH, YOU DID WINK A BIT WEIRDLY. BUT I THOUGHT A BUG WAS IN YOUR EYE OR SOMETHING.
I AM VERY SORRY. I'M STILL TRYING TO LEARN MODERN TRI-CITY MANNERISMS. EVERYONE IS SO DIRECT IN O.K. TOWN.
IT'S ALL GOOD, BRO. I SHOULD BE TRAINING, ANYWAY. Y'KNOW, "TO CARRY ON THE FAMILY BUSINESS," OR WHATEVER...
SIGH

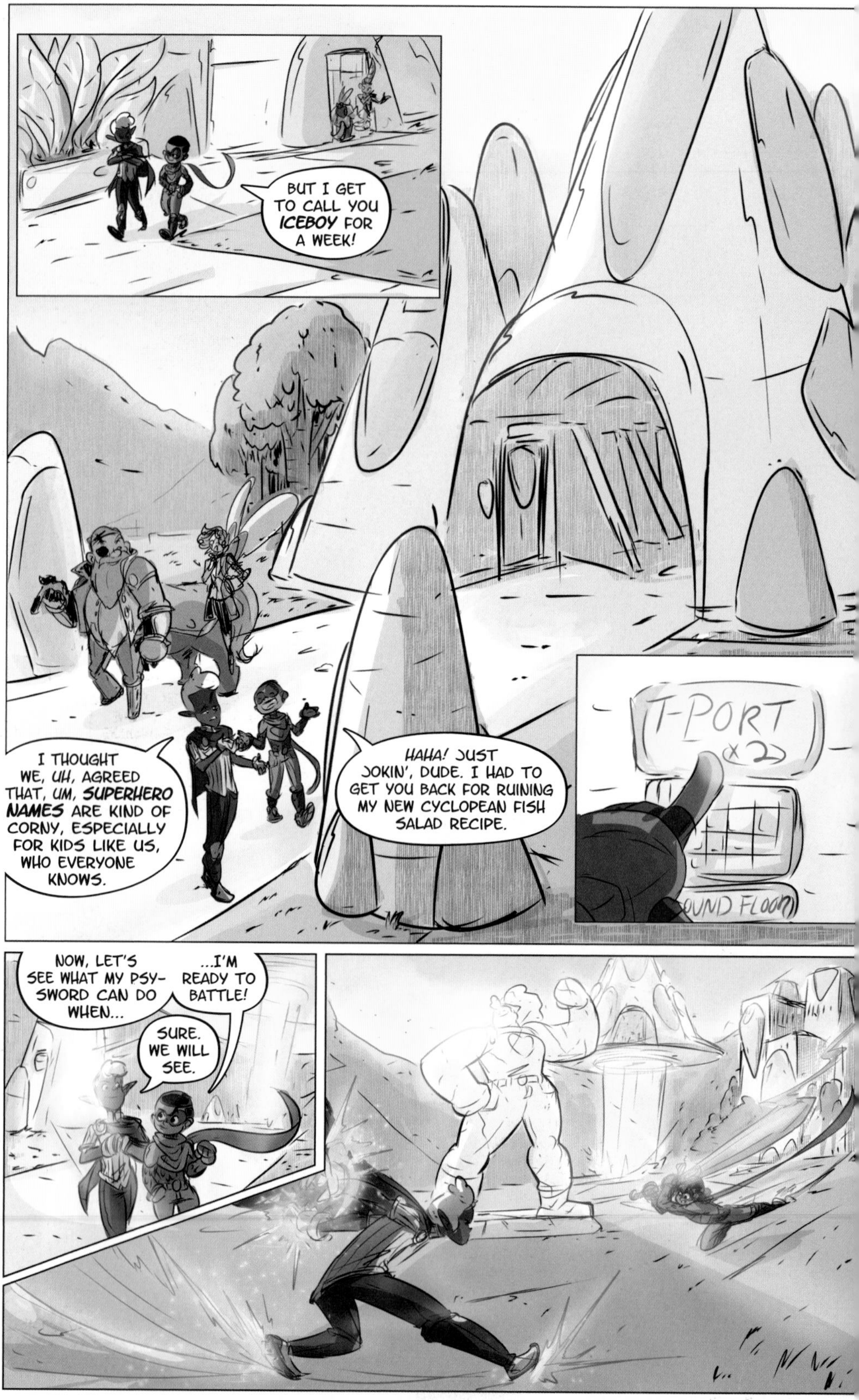
BUT I GET TO CALL YOU ICEBOY FOR A WEEK!
I THOUGHT WE, UH, AGREED THAT, UM, SUPERHERO NAMES ARE KIND OF CORNY, ESPECIALLY FOR KIDS LIKE US, WHO EVERYONE KNOWS.
HAHA! JUST JOKIN', DUDE. I HAD TO GET YOU BACK FOR RUINING MY NEW CYCLOPEAN FISH SALAD RECIPE.
T-PORT (x2)
OUND FLOOR
NOW, LET'S SEE WHAT MY PSY-SWORD CAN DO WHEN...
...I'M READY TO BATTLE!
SURE. WE WILL SEE.

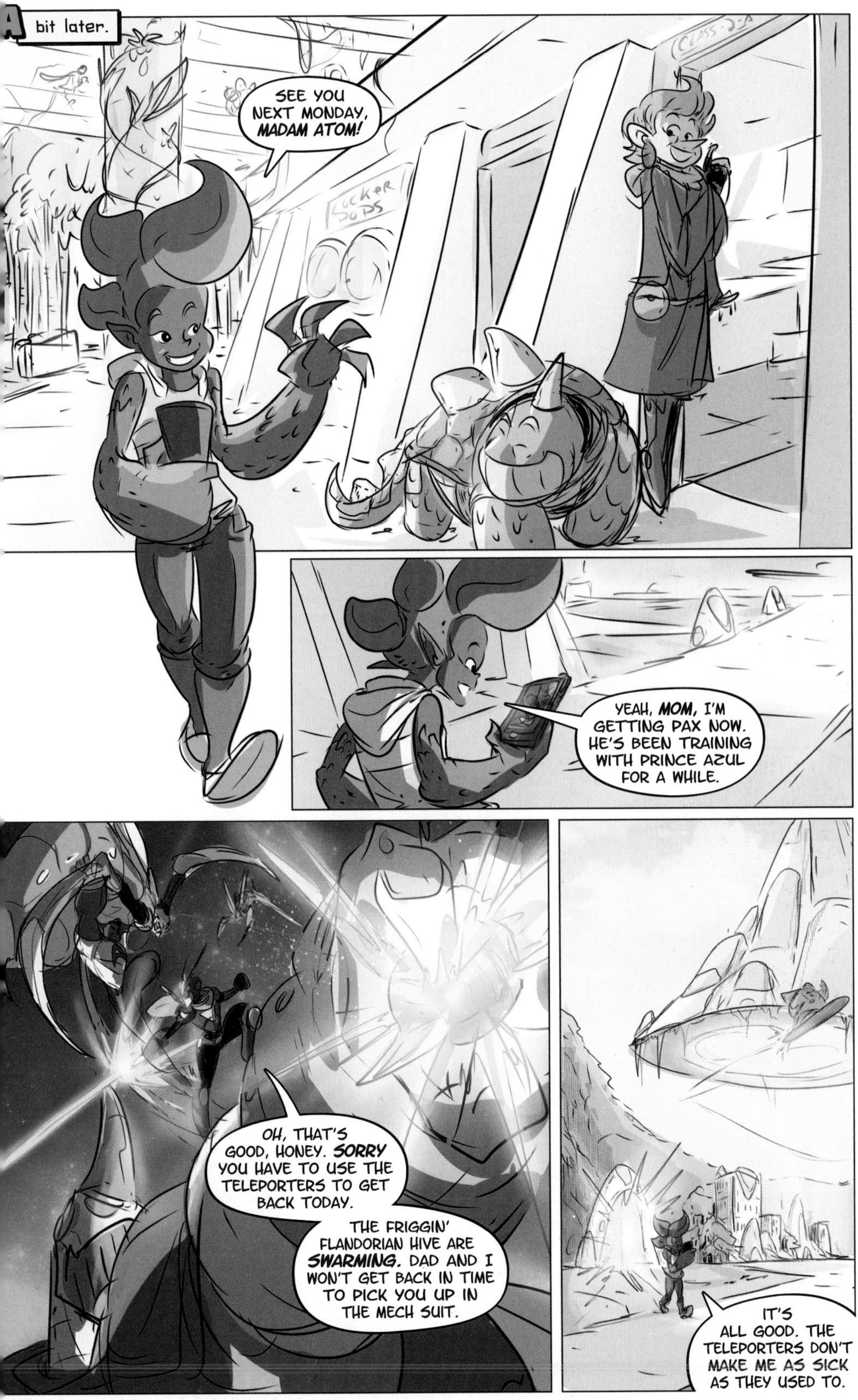
A bit later.
SEE YOU NEXT MONDAY, MADAM ATOM!
CLASS-2-A
LOCKER PODS
YEAH, MOM, I'M GETTING PAX NOW. HE'S BEEN TRAINING WITH PRINCE AZUL FOR A WHILE.
OH, THAT'S GOOD, HONEY. SORRY YOU HAVE TO USE THE TELEPORTERS TO GET BACK TODAY.
THE FRIGGIN' FLANDORIAN HIVE ARE SWARMING. DAD AND I WON'T GET BACK IN TIME TO PICK YOU UP IN THE MECH SUIT.
IT'S ALL GOOD. THE TELEPORTERS DON'T MAKE ME AS SICK AS THEY USED TO.

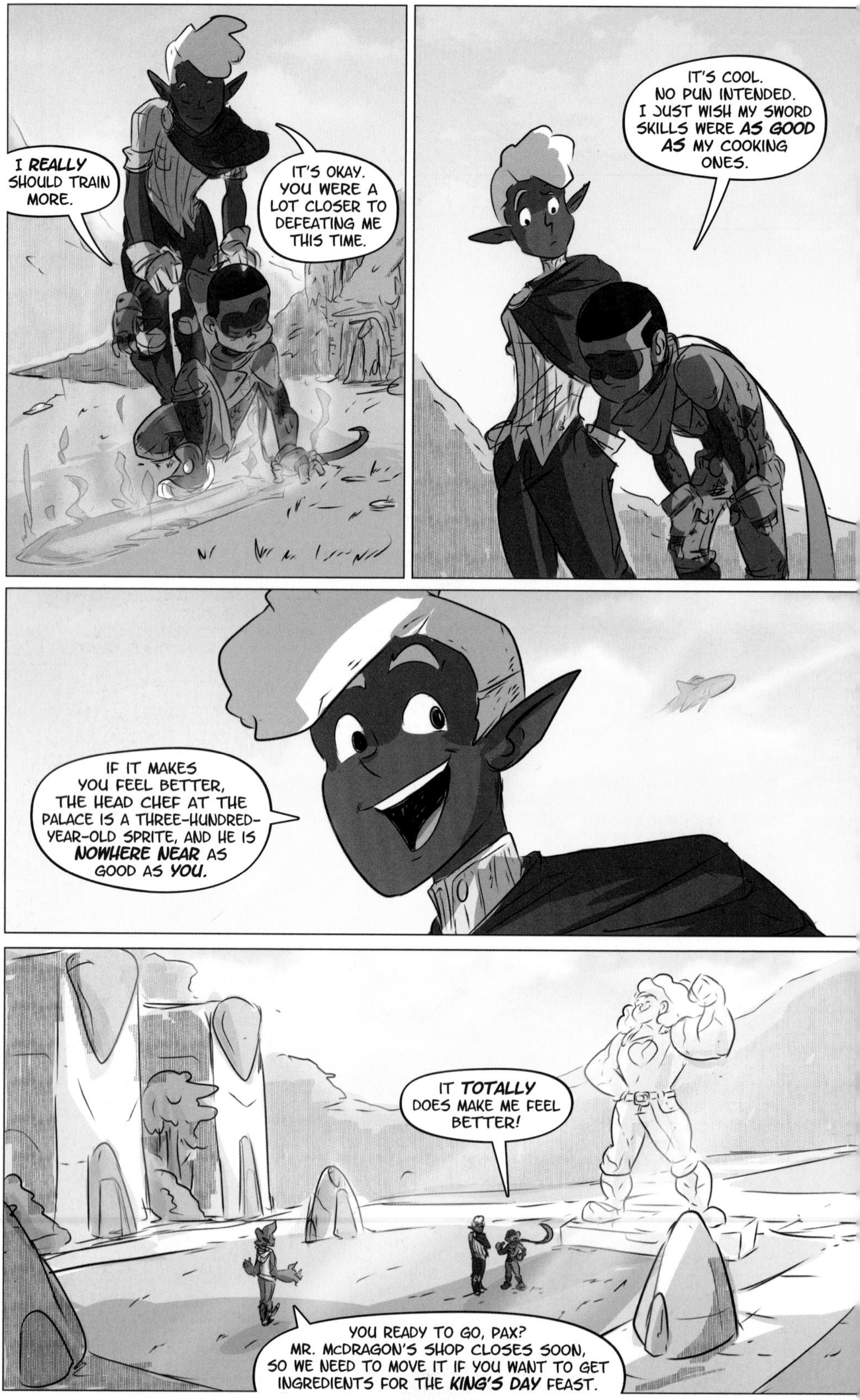
I REALLY SHOULD TRAIN MORE.
IT'S OKAY. YOU WERE A LOT CLOSER TO DEFEATING ME THIS TIME.
IT'S COOL. NO PUN INTENDED. I JUST WISH MY SWORD SKILLS WERE AS GOOD AS MY COOKING ONES.
IF IT MAKES YOU FEEL BETTER, THE HEAD CHEF AT THE PALACE IS A THREE-HUNDRED-YEAR-OLD SPRITE, AND HE IS NOWHERE NEAR AS GOOD AS YOU.
IT TOTALLY DOES MAKE ME FEEL BETTER!
YOU READY TO GO, PAX? MR. McDRAGON'S SHOP CLOSES SOON, SO WE NEED TO MOVE IT IF YOU WANT TO GET INGREDIENTS FOR THE KING'S DAY FEAST.

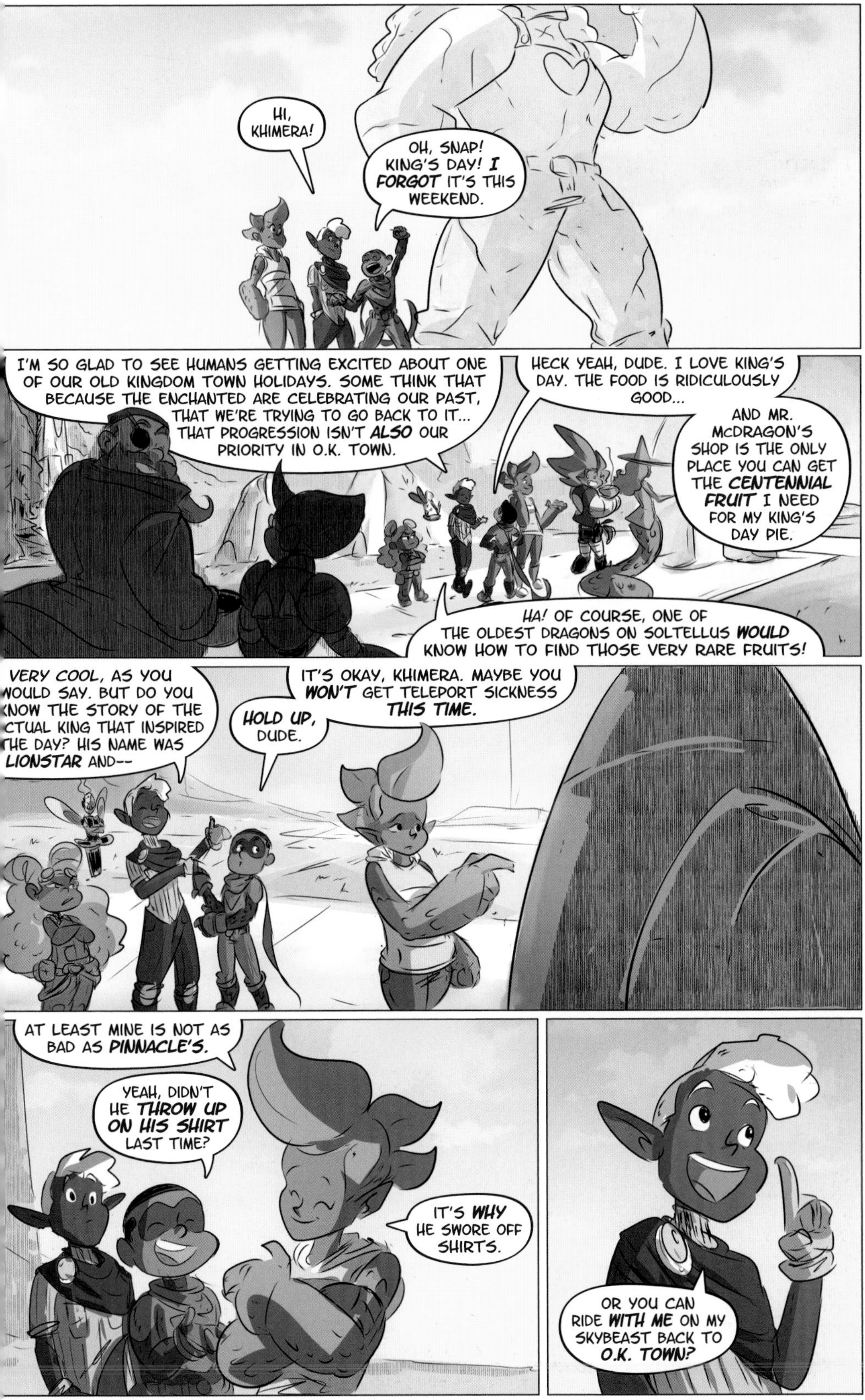
HI, KHIMERA!
OH, SNAP! KING'S DAY! I FORGOT IT'S THIS WEEKEND.
I'M SO GLAD TO SEE HUMANS GETTING EXCITED ABOUT ONE OF OUR OLD KINGDOM TOWN HOLIDAYS. SOME THINK THAT BECAUSE THE ENCHANTED ARE CELEBRATING OUR PAST, THAT WE'RE TRYING TO GO BACK TO IT... THAT PROGRESSION ISN'T ALSO OUR PRIORITY IN O.K. TOWN.
HECK YEAH, DUDE. I LOVE KING'S DAY. THE FOOD IS RIDICULOUSLY GOOD...
AND MR. McDRAGON'S SHOP IS THE ONLY PLACE YOU CAN GET THE CENTENNIAL FRUIT I NEED FOR MY KING'S DAY PIE.
HA! OF COURSE, ONE OF THE OLDEST DRAGONS ON SOLTELLUS WOULD KNOW HOW TO FIND THOSE VERY RARE FRUITS!
VERY COOL, AS YOU WOULD SAY. BUT DO YOU KNOW THE STORY OF THE ACTUAL KING THAT INSPIRED THE DAY? HIS NAME WAS LIONSTAR AND--
HOLD UP, DUDE.
IT'S OKAY, KHIMERA. MAYBE YOU WON'T GET TELEPORT SICKNESS THIS TIME.
AT LEAST MINE IS NOT AS BAD AS PINNACLE'S.
YEAH, DIDN'T HE THROW UP ON HIS SHIRT LAST TIME?
IT'S WHY HE SWORE OFF SHIRTS.
OR YOU CAN RIDE WITH ME ON MY SKYBEAST BACK TO O.K. TOWN?

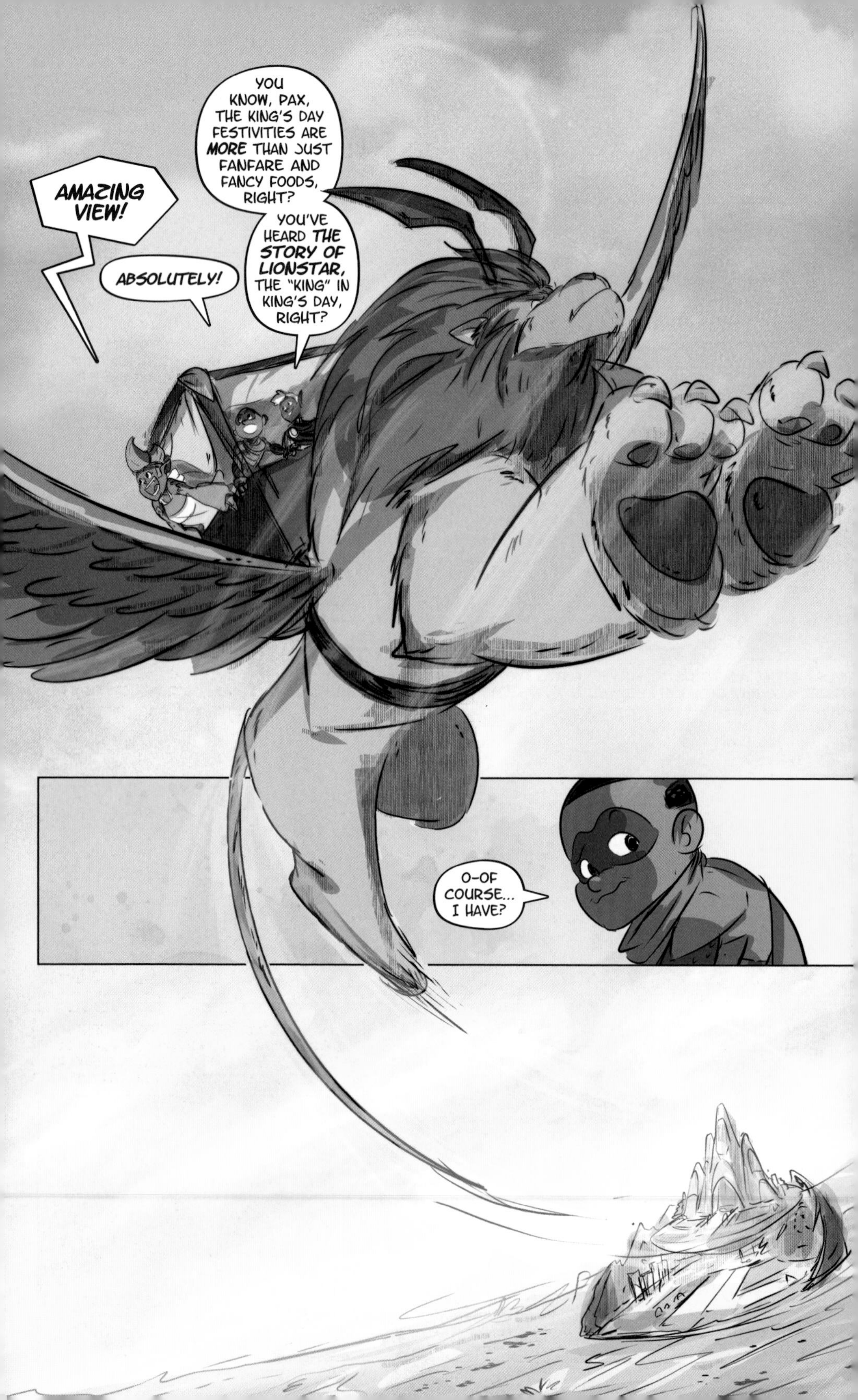
AMAZING VIEW!
ABSOLUTELY!
YOU KNOW, PAX, THE KING'S DAY FESTIVITIES ARE MORE THAN JUST FANFARE AND FANCY FOODS, RIGHT?
YOU'VE HEARD THE STORY OF LIONSTAR, THE "KING" IN KING'S DAY, RIGHT?
O-OF COURSE... I HAVE?

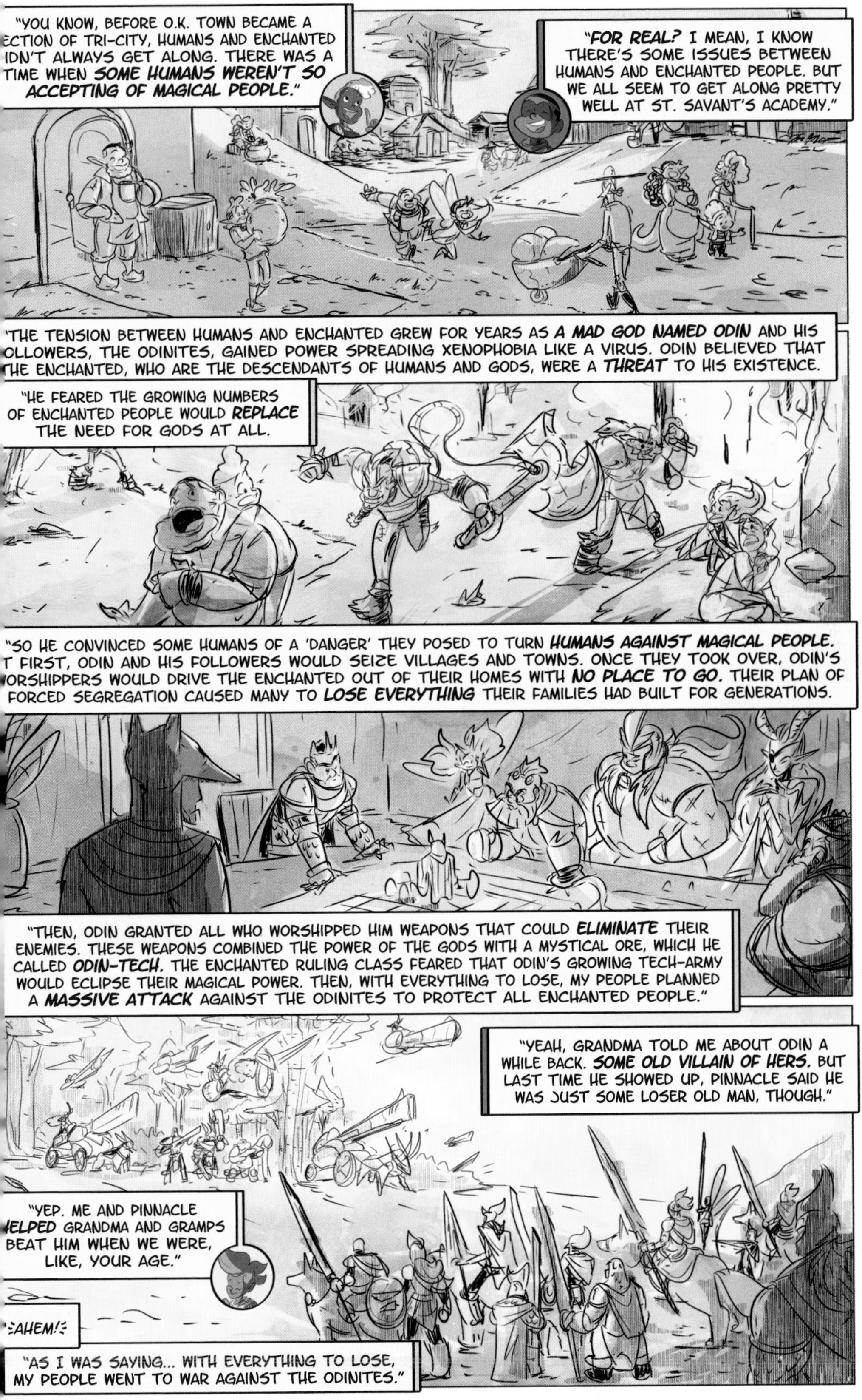

"YOU KNOW, BEFORE O.K. TOWN BECAME A ECTION OF TRI-CITY, HUMANS AND ENCHANTED IDN'T ALWAYS GET ALONG. THERE WAS A TIME WHEN SOME HUMANS WEREN'T SO ACCEPTING OF MAGICAL PEOPLE."
"FOR REAL? I MEAN, I KNOW THERE'S SOME ISSUES BETWEEN HUMANS AND ENCHANTED PEOPLE. BUT WE ALL SEEM TO GET ALONG PRETTY WELL AT ST. SAVANT'S ACADEMY."
'THE TENSION BETWEEN HUMANS AND ENCHANTED GREW FOR YEARS AS A MAD GOD NAMED ODIN AND HIS OLLOWERS, THE ODINITES, GAINED POWER SPREADING XENOPHOBIA LIKE A VIRUS. ODIN BELIEVED THAT THE ENCHANTED, WHO ARE THE DESCENDANTS OF HUMANS AND GODS, WERE A THREAT TO HIS EXISTENCE.
"HE FEARED THE GROWING NUMBERS OF ENCHANTED PEOPLE WOULD REPLACE THE NEED FOR GODS AT ALL.
"SO HE CONVINCED SOME HUMANS OF A 'DANGER' THEY POSED TO TURN HUMANS AGAINST MAGICAL PEOPLE. T FIRST, ODIN AND HIS FOLLOWERS WOULD SEIZE VILLAGES AND TOWNS. ONCE THEY TOOK OVER, ODIN'S ORSHIPPERS WOULD DRIVE THE ENCHANTED OUT OF THEIR HOMES WITH NO PLACE TO GO. THEIR PLAN OF FORCED SEGREGATION CAUSED MANY TO LOSE EVERYTHING THEIR FAMILIES HAD BUILT FOR GENERATIONS.
"THEN, ODIN GRANTED ALL WHO WORSHIPPED HIM WEAPONS THAT COULD ELIMINATE THEIR ENEMIES. THESE WEAPONS COMBINED THE POWER OF THE GODS WITH A MYSTICAL ORE, WHICH HE CALLED ODIN-TECH. THE ENCHANTED RULING CLASS FEARED THAT ODIN'S GROWING TECH-ARMY WOULD ECLIPSE THEIR MAGICAL POWER. THEN, WITH EVERYTHING TO LOSE, MY PEOPLE PLANNED A MASSIVE ATTACK AGAINST THE ODINITES TO PROTECT ALL ENCHANTED PEOPLE."
"YEAH, GRANDMA TOLD ME ABOUT ODIN A WHILE BACK. SOME OLD VILLAIN OF HERS. BUT LAST TIME HE SHOWED UP, PINNACLE SAID HE WAS JUST SOME LOSER OLD MAN, THOUGH."
"YEP. ME AND PINNACLE ELPED GRANDMA AND GRAMPS BEAT HIM WHEN WE WERE, LIKE, YOUR AGE."
AHEM!
"AS I WAS SAYING... WITH EVERYTHING TO LOSE, MY PEOPLE WENT TO WAR AGAINST THE ODINITES."

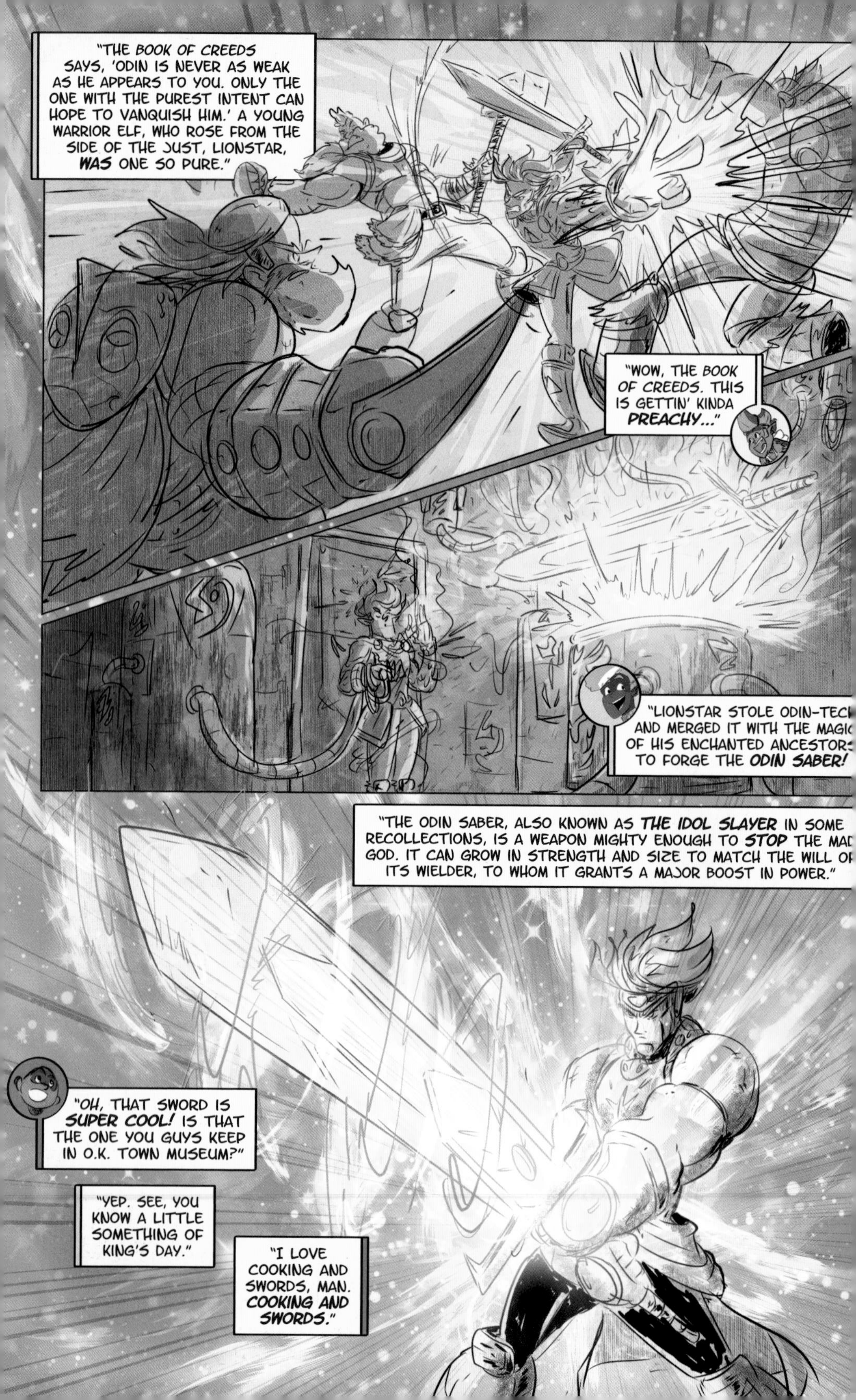

"THE *BOOK OF CREEDS* SAYS, 'ODIN IS NEVER AS WEAK AS HE APPEARS TO YOU. ONLY THE ONE WITH THE PUREST INTENT CAN HOPE TO VANQUISH HIM.' A YOUNG WARRIOR ELF, WHO ROSE FROM THE SIDE OF THE JUST, LIONSTAR, **WAS** ONE SO PURE."
"WOW, THE *BOOK OF CREEDS*. THIS IS GETTIN' KINDA **PREACHY...**"
"LIONSTAR STOLE ODIN-TECH AND MERGED IT WITH THE MAGIC OF HIS ENCHANTED ANCESTORS TO FORGE THE **ODIN SABER!**
"THE ODIN SABER, ALSO KNOWN AS **THE IDOL SLAYER** IN SOME RECOLLECTIONS, IS A WEAPON MIGHTY ENOUGH TO **STOP** THE MAD GOD. IT CAN GROW IN STRENGTH AND SIZE TO MATCH THE WILL OF ITS WIELDER, TO WHOM IT GRANTS A MAJOR BOOST IN POWER."
"OH, THAT SWORD IS **SUPER COOL!** IS THAT THE ONE YOU GUYS KEEP IN O.K. TOWN MUSEUM?"
"YEP. SEE, YOU KNOW A LITTLE SOMETHING OF KING'S DAY."
"I LOVE COOKING AND SWORDS, MAN. **COOKING AND SWORDS.**"

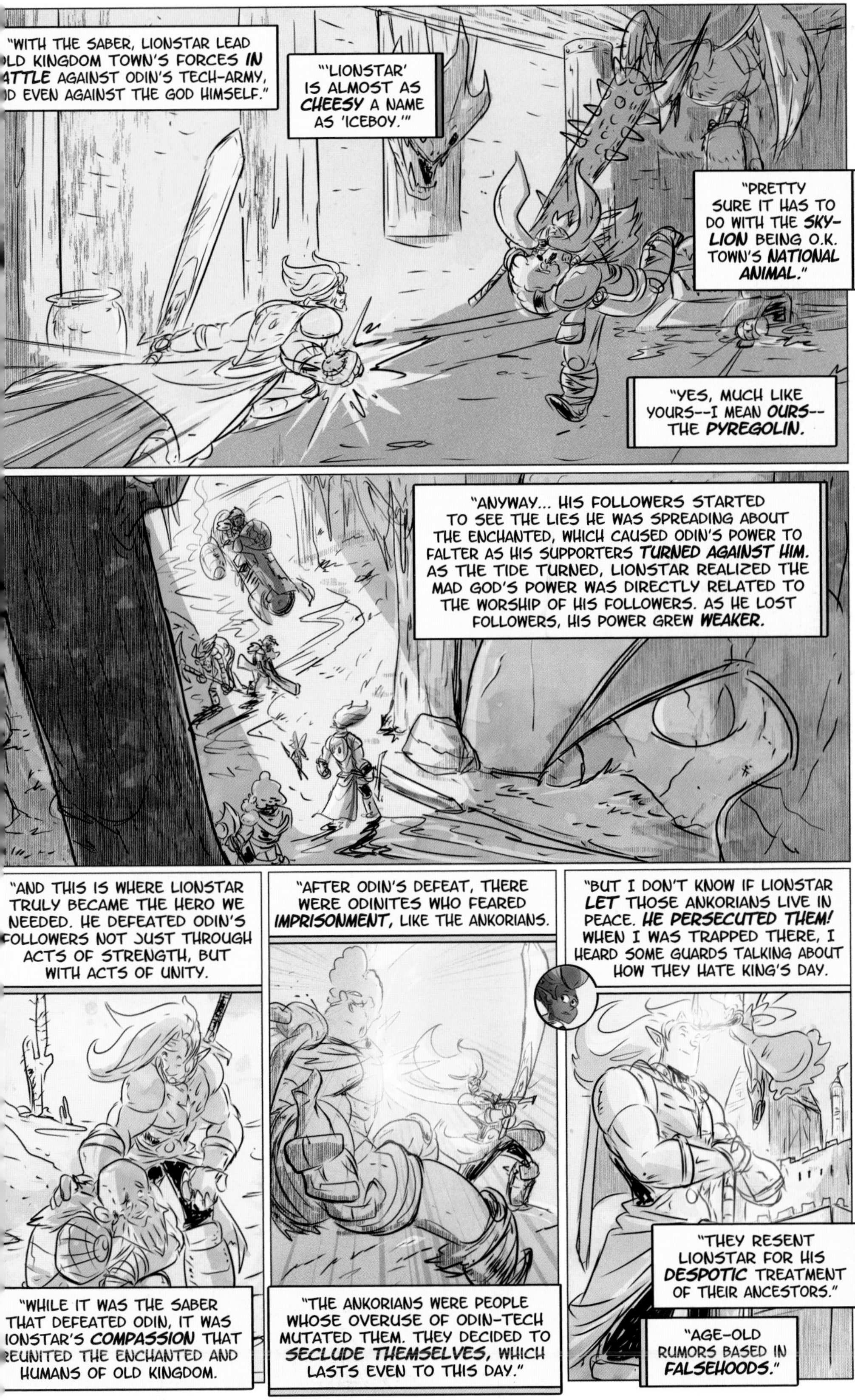
"WITH THE SABER, LIONSTAR LEAD
OLD KINGDOM TOWN'S FORCES IN
BATTLE AGAINST ODIN'S TECH-ARMY,
AND EVEN AGAINST THE GOD HIMSELF."
"'LIONSTAR' IS ALMOST AS CHEESY A NAME AS 'ICEBOY.'"
"PRETTY SURE IT HAS TO DO WITH THE SKY-LION BEING O.K. TOWN'S NATIONAL ANIMAL."
"YES, MUCH LIKE YOURS--I MEAN OURS--THE PYREGOLIN.
"ANYWAY... HIS FOLLOWERS STARTED TO SEE THE LIES HE WAS SPREADING ABOUT THE ENCHANTED, WHICH CAUSED ODIN'S POWER TO FALTER AS HIS SUPPORTERS TURNED AGAINST HIM. AS THE TIDE TURNED, LIONSTAR REALIZED THE MAD GOD'S POWER WAS DIRECTLY RELATED TO THE WORSHIP OF HIS FOLLOWERS. AS HE LOST FOLLOWERS, HIS POWER GREW WEAKER.
"AND THIS IS WHERE LIONSTAR TRULY BECAME THE HERO WE NEEDED. HE DEFEATED ODIN'S FOLLOWERS NOT JUST THROUGH ACTS OF STRENGTH, BUT WITH ACTS OF UNITY.
"WHILE IT WAS THE SABER THAT DEFEATED ODIN, IT WAS LIONSTAR'S COMPASSION THAT REUNITED THE ENCHANTED AND HUMANS OF OLD KINGDOM.
"AFTER ODIN'S DEFEAT, THERE WERE ODINITES WHO FEARED IMPRISONMENT, LIKE THE ANKORIANS.
"THE ANKORIANS WERE PEOPLE WHOSE OVERUSE OF ODIN-TECH MUTATED THEM. THEY DECIDED TO SECLUDE THEMSELVES, WHICH LASTS EVEN TO THIS DAY."
"BUT I DON'T KNOW IF LIONSTAR LET THOSE ANKORIANS LIVE IN PEACE. HE PERSECUTED THEM! WHEN I WAS TRAPPED THERE, I HEARD SOME GUARDS TALKING ABOUT HOW THEY HATE KING'S DAY.
"THEY RESENT LIONSTAR FOR HIS DESPOTIC TREATMENT OF THEIR ANCESTORS."
"AGE-OLD RUMORS BASED IN FALSEHOODS."

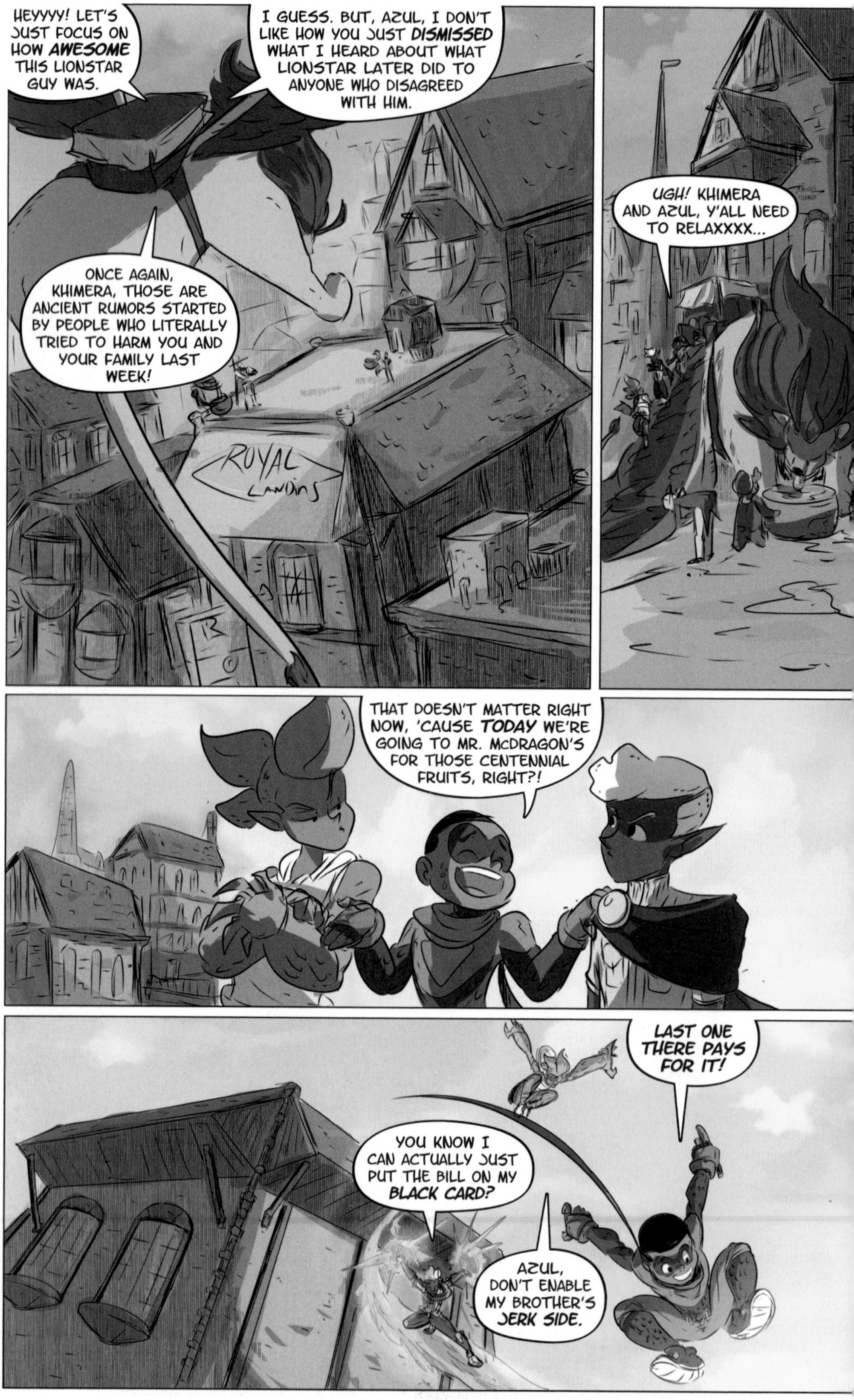
HEYYYY! LET'S JUST FOCUS ON HOW AWESOME THIS LIONSTAR GUY WAS.
I GUESS. BUT, AZUL, I DON'T LIKE HOW YOU JUST DISMISSED WHAT I HEARD ABOUT WHAT LIONSTAR LATER DID TO ANYONE WHO DISAGREED WITH HIM.
ONCE AGAIN, KHIMERA, THOSE ARE ANCIENT RUMORS STARTED BY PEOPLE WHO LITERALLY TRIED TO HARM YOU AND YOUR FAMILY LAST WEEK!
ROYAL LANDING
UGH! KHIMERA AND AZUL, Y'ALL NEED TO RELAXXXX...
THAT DOESN'T MATTER RIGHT NOW, 'CAUSE TODAY WE'RE GOING TO MR. McDRAGON'S FOR THOSE CENTENNIAL FRUITS, RIGHT?!
LAST ONE THERE PAYS FOR IT!
YOU KNOW I CAN ACTUALLY JUST PUT THE BILL ON MY BLACK CARD?
AZUL, DON'T ENABLE MY BROTHER'S JERK SIDE.

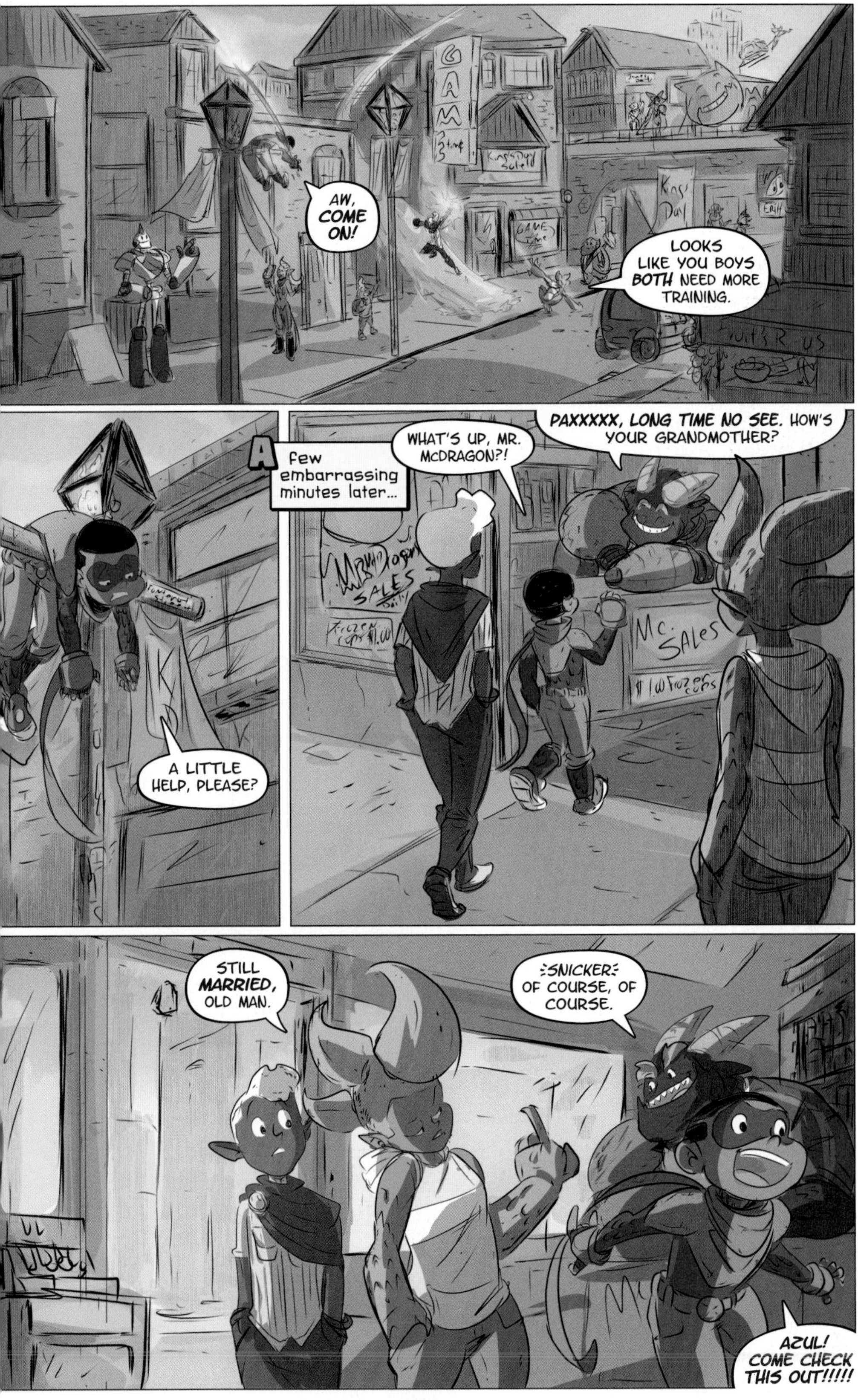
AW, COME ON!
LOOKS LIKE YOU BOYS BOTH NEED MORE TRAINING.
A few embarrassing minutes later...
A LITTLE HELP, PLEASE?
WHAT'S UP, MR. MCDRAGON?!
PAXXXXX, LONG TIME NO SEE. HOW'S YOUR GRANDMOTHER?
Mc. SALES
STILL MARRIED, OLD MAN.
SNICKER
OF COURSE, OF COURSE.
AZUL! COME CHECK THIS OUT!!!!!

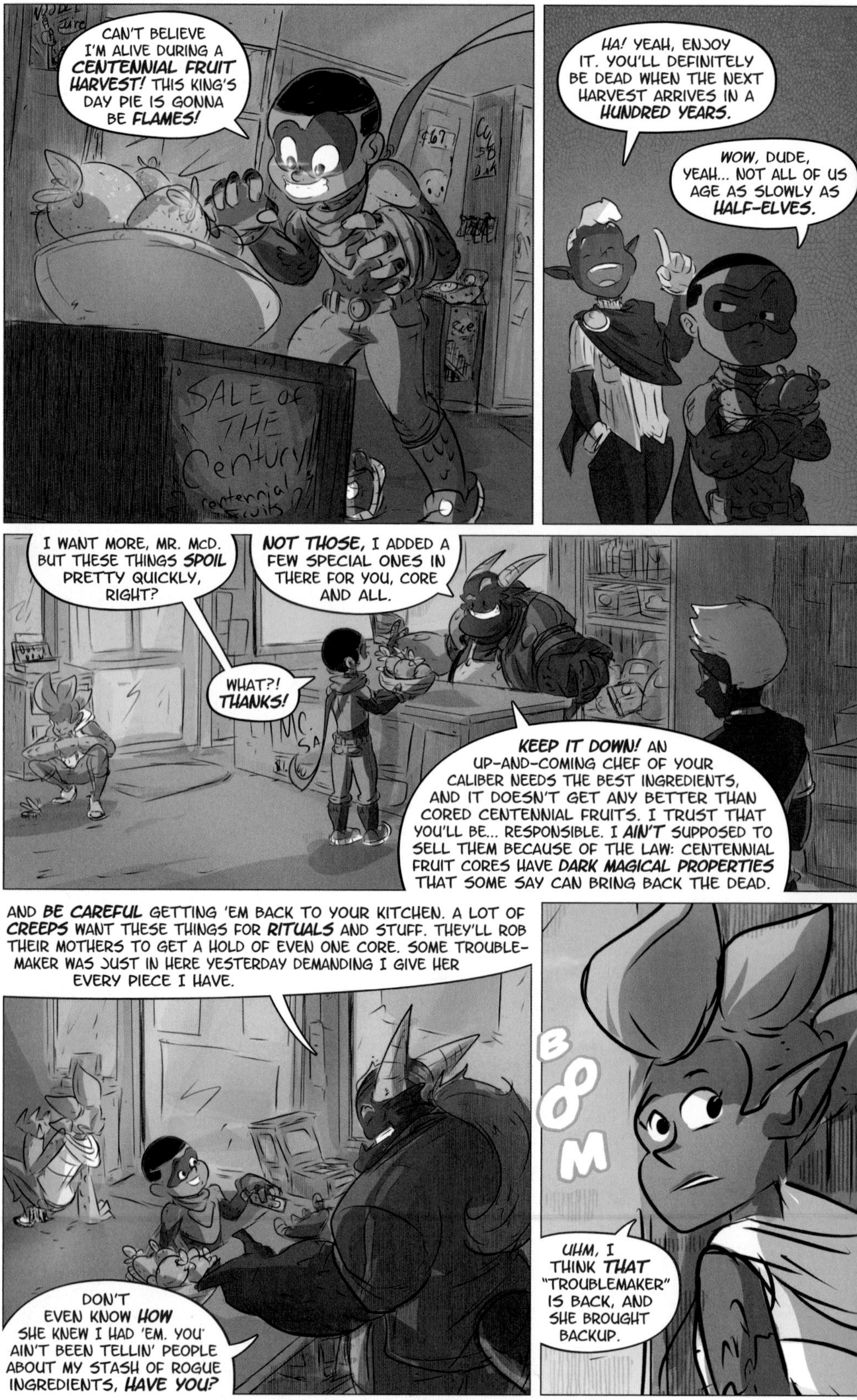
CAN'T BELIEVE I'M ALIVE DURING A CENTENNIAL FRUIT HARVEST! THIS KING'S DAY PIE IS GONNA BE FLAMES!
SALE of THE Century! centennial fruits
HA! YEAH, ENJOY IT. YOU'LL DEFINITELY BE DEAD WHEN THE NEXT HARVEST ARRIVES IN A HUNDRED YEARS.
WOW, DUDE, YEAH... NOT ALL OF US AGE AS SLOWLY AS HALF-ELVES.
I WANT MORE, MR. McD. BUT THESE THINGS SPOIL PRETTY QUICKLY, RIGHT?
NOT THOSE, I ADDED A FEW SPECIAL ONES IN THERE FOR YOU, CORE AND ALL.
WHAT?! THANKS!
KEEP IT DOWN! AN UP-AND-COMING CHEF OF YOUR CALIBER NEEDS THE BEST INGREDIENTS, AND IT DOESN'T GET ANY BETTER THAN CORED CENTENNIAL FRUITS. I TRUST THAT YOU'LL BE... RESPONSIBLE. I AIN'T SUPPOSED TO SELL THEM BECAUSE OF THE LAW: CENTENNIAL FRUIT CORES HAVE DARK MAGICAL PROPERTIES THAT SOME SAY CAN BRING BACK THE DEAD.
AND BE CAREFUL GETTING 'EM BACK TO YOUR KITCHEN. A LOT OF CREEPS WANT THESE THINGS FOR RITUALS AND STUFF. THEY'LL ROB THEIR MOTHERS TO GET A HOLD OF EVEN ONE CORE. SOME TROUBLE-MAKER WAS JUST IN HERE YESTERDAY DEMANDING I GIVE HER EVERY PIECE I HAVE.
DON'T EVEN KNOW HOW SHE KNEW I HAD 'EM. YOU AIN'T BEEN TELLIN' PEOPLE ABOUT MY STASH OF ROGUE INGREDIENTS, HAVE YOU?
BOOM
UHM, I THINK THAT "TROUBLEMAKER" IS BACK, AND SHE BROUGHT BACKUP.

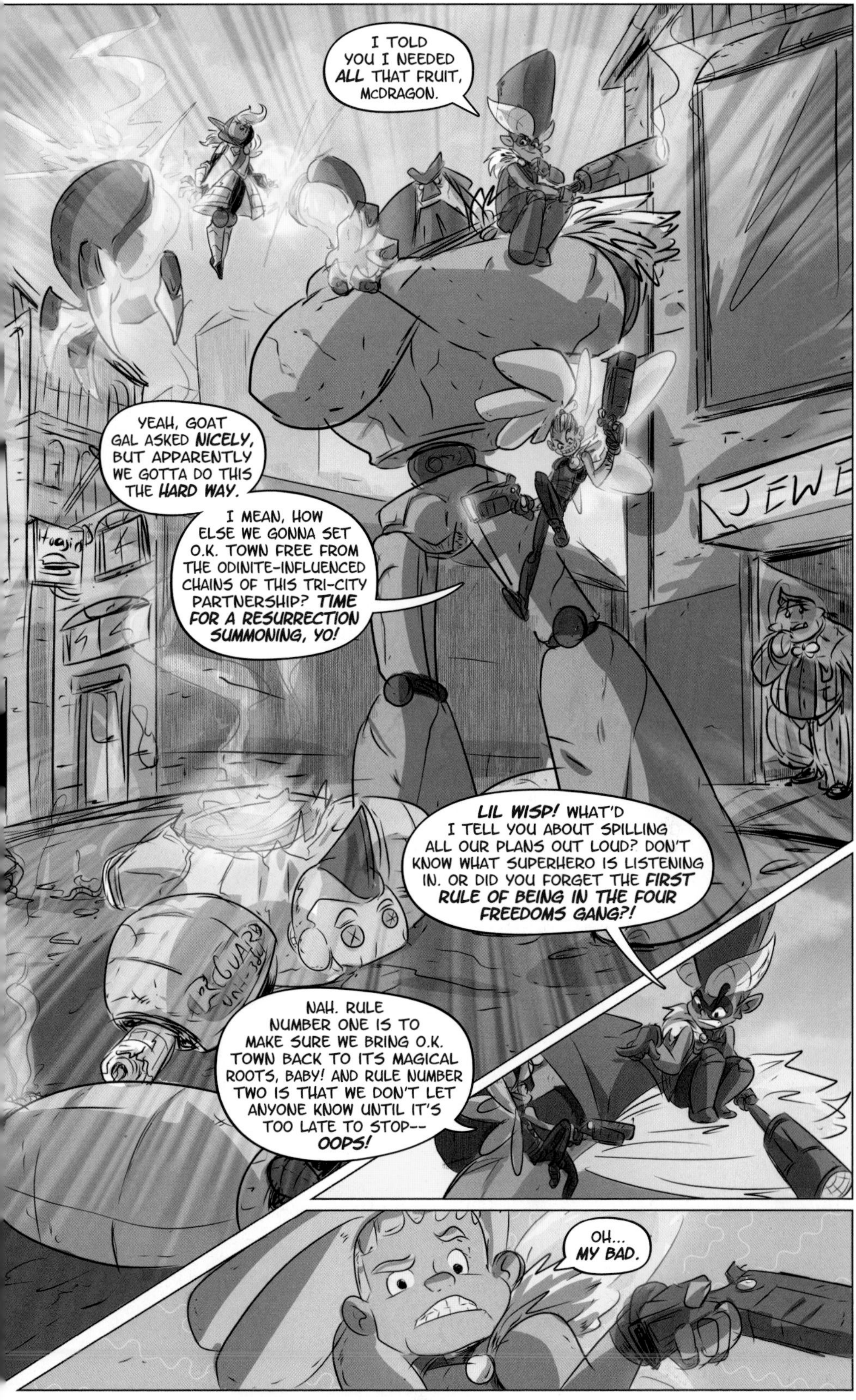
I TOLD YOU I NEEDED **ALL** THAT FRUIT, McDRAGON.
YEAH, GOAT GAL ASKED **NICELY**, BUT APPARENTLY WE GOTTA DO THIS THE **HARD WAY**.
I MEAN, HOW ELSE WE GONNA SET O.K. TOWN FREE FROM THE ODINITE-INFLUENCED CHAINS OF THIS TRI-CITY PARTNERSHIP? **TIME FOR A RESURRECTION SUMMONING, YO!**
LIL WISP! WHAT'D I TELL YOU ABOUT SPILLING ALL OUR PLANS OUT LOUD? DON'T KNOW WHAT SUPERHERO IS LISTENING IN. OR DID YOU FORGET THE **FIRST RULE OF BEING IN THE FOUR FREEDOMS GANG?!**
NAH. RULE NUMBER ONE IS TO MAKE SURE WE BRING O.K. TOWN BACK TO ITS MAGICAL ROOTS, BABY! AND RULE NUMBER TWO IS THAT WE DON'T LET ANYONE KNOW UNTIL IT'S TOO LATE TO STOP-- **OOPS!**
OH... **MY BAD.**

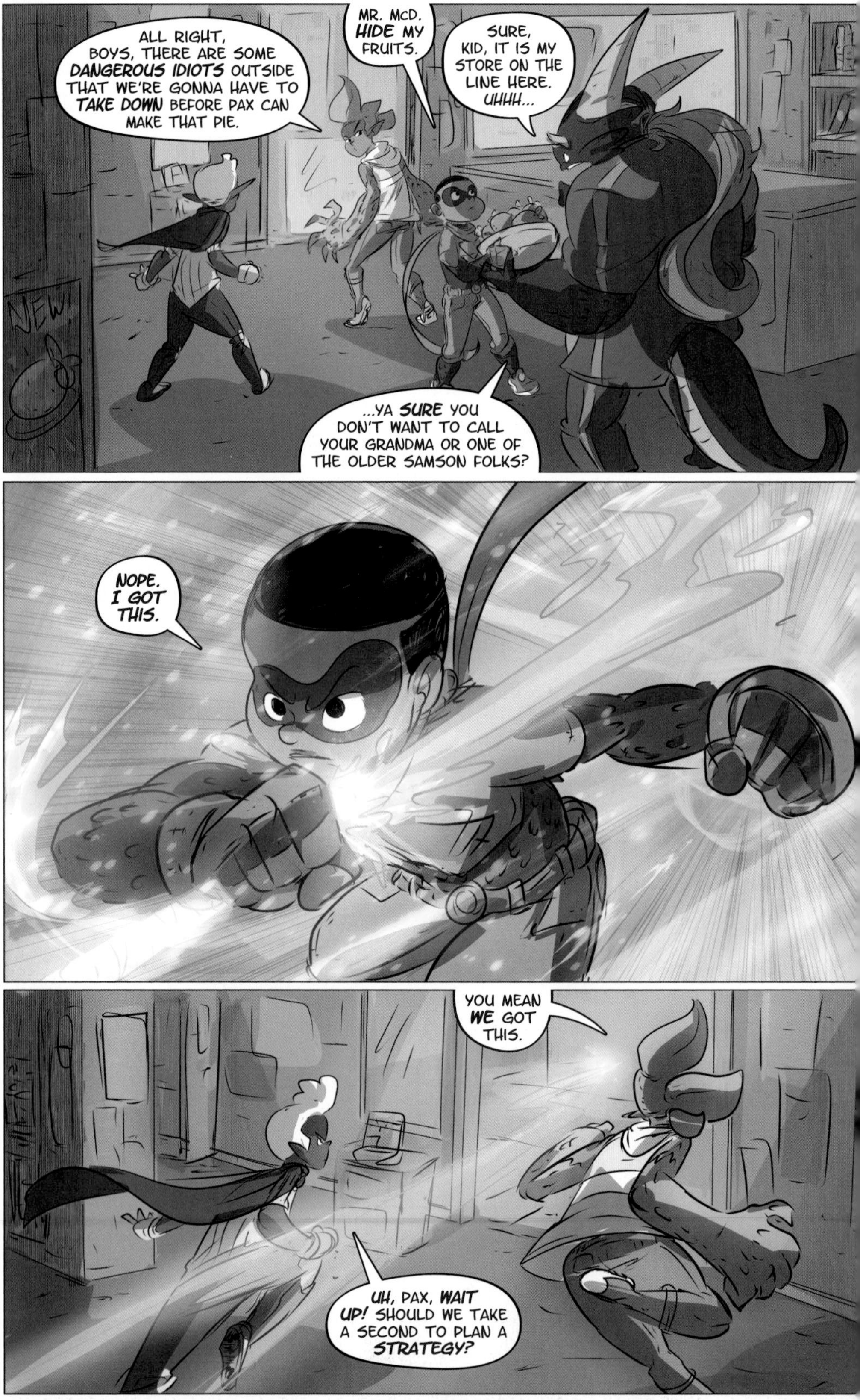
ALL RIGHT, BOYS, THERE ARE SOME DANGEROUS IDIOTS OUTSIDE THAT WE'RE GONNA HAVE TO TAKE DOWN BEFORE PAX CAN MAKE THAT PIE.
MR. McD. HIDE MY FRUITS.
SURE, KID, IT IS MY STORE ON THE LINE HERE. UHHH...
...YA SURE YOU DON'T WANT TO CALL YOUR GRANDMA OR ONE OF THE OLDER SAMSON FOLKS?
NOPE. I GOT THIS.
YOU MEAN WE GOT THIS.
UH, PAX, WAIT UP! SHOULD WE TAKE A SECOND TO PLAN A STRATEGY?

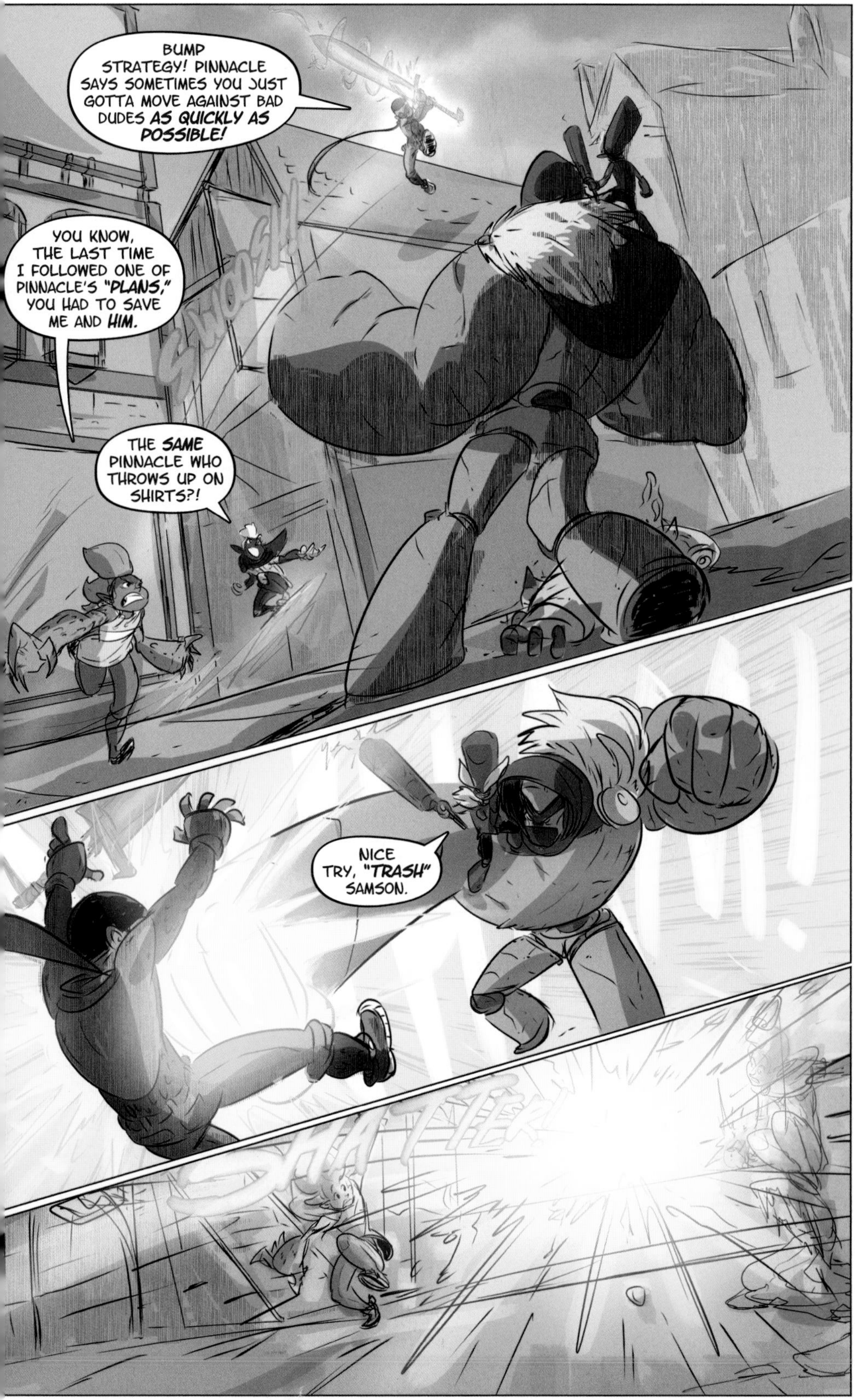
BUMP
STRATEGY! PINNACLE SAYS SOMETIMES YOU JUST GOTTA MOVE AGAINST BAD DUDES **AS QUICKLY AS POSSIBLE!**
YOU KNOW, THE LAST TIME I FOLLOWED ONE OF PINNACLE'S **"PLANS,"** YOU HAD TO SAVE ME AND **HIM.**
THE **SAME** PINNACLE WHO THROWS UP ON SHIRTS?!
SWOOSH!
NICE TRY, **"TRASH"** SAMSON.
SHATTER!

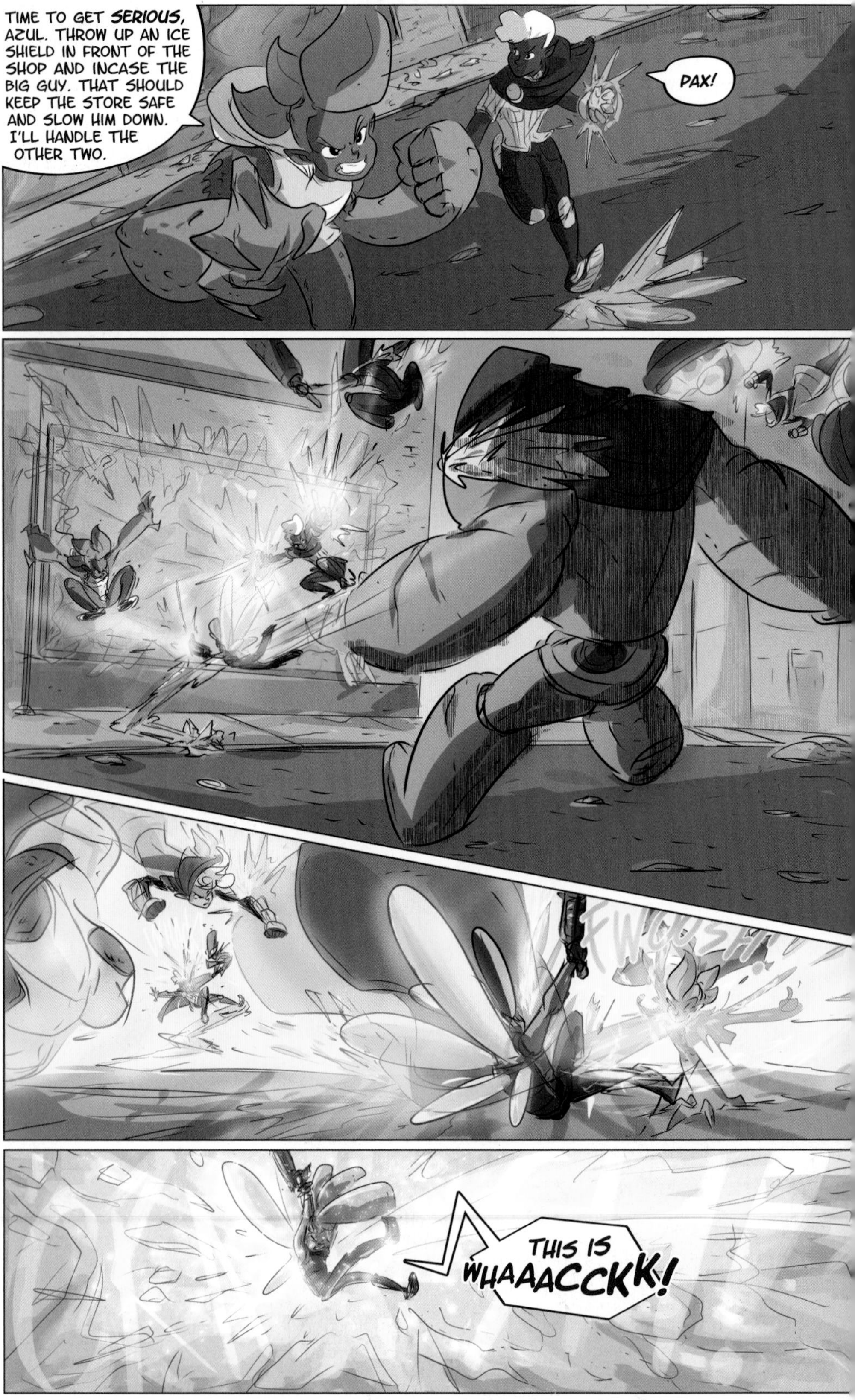
TIME TO GET SERIOUS, AZUL. THROW UP AN ICE SHIELD IN FRONT OF THE SHOP AND INCASE THE BIG GUY. THAT SHOULD KEEP THE STORE SAFE AND SLOW HIM DOWN. I'LL HANDLE THE OTHER TWO.
PAX!
FWOOSH!
THIS IS WHAAACCKK!

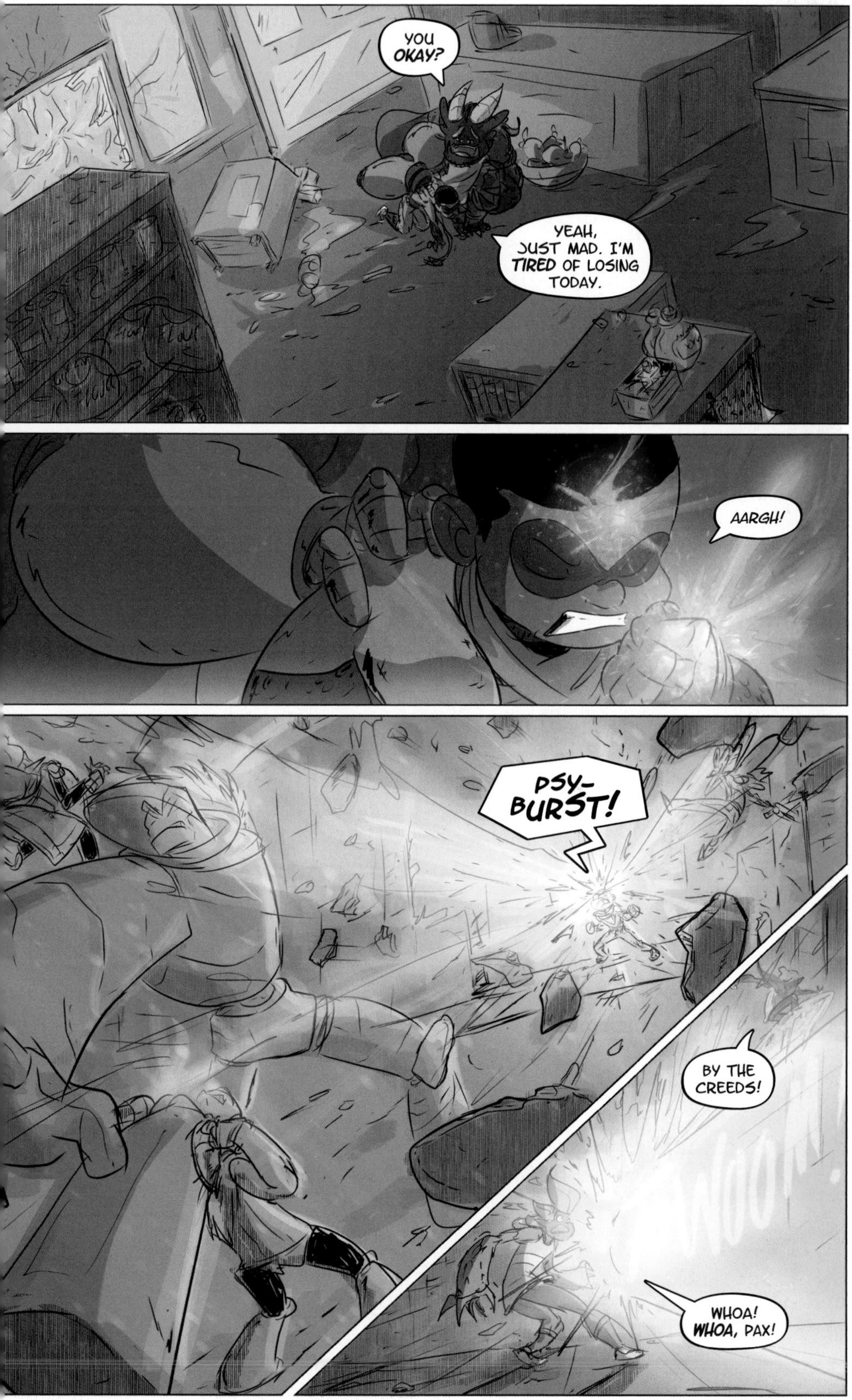
YOU OKAY?
YEAH, JUST MAD. I'M TIRED OF LOSING TODAY.
AARGH!
PSY-BURST!
BY THE CREEDS!
WHOA! WHOA, PAX!

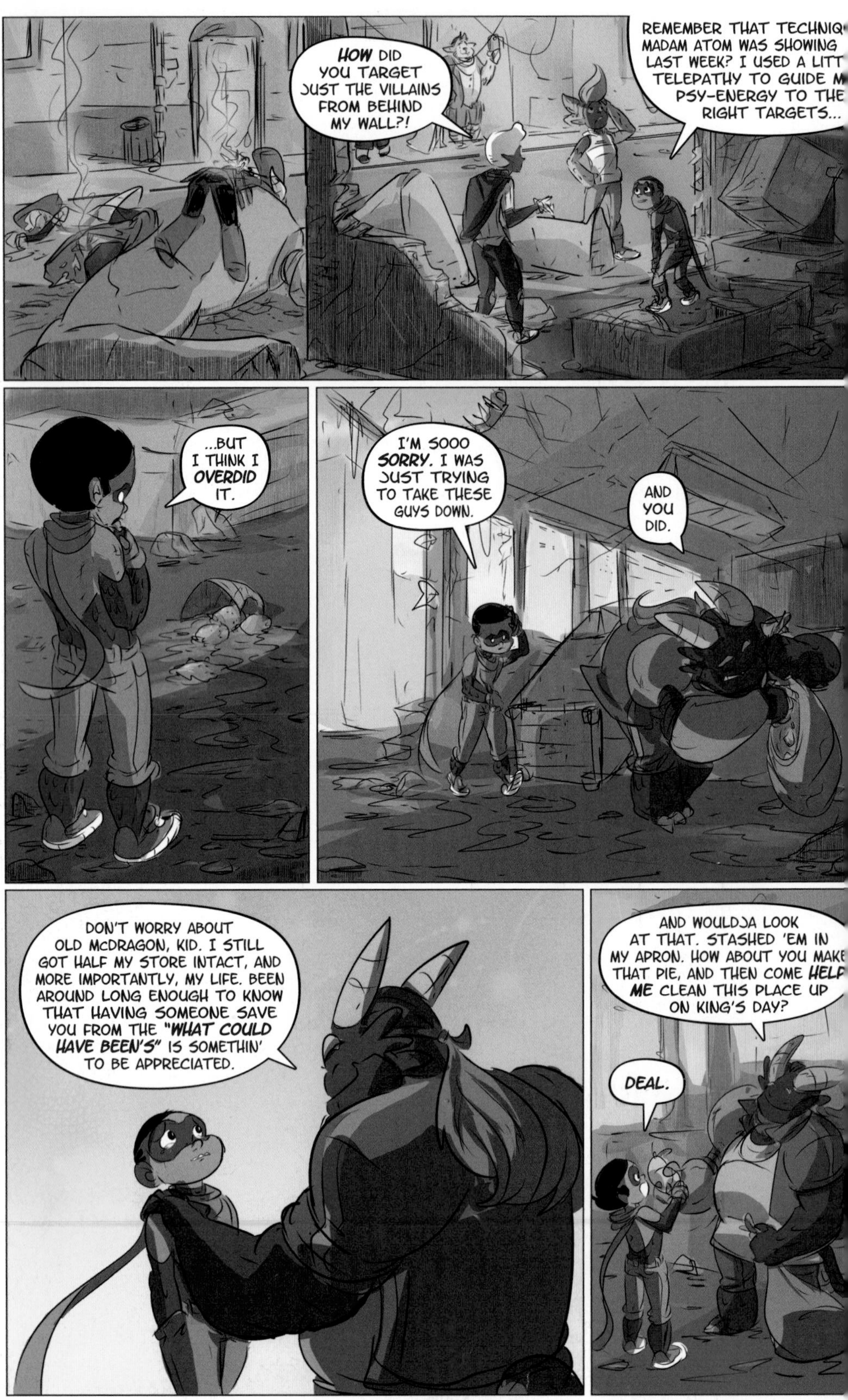
HOW DID YOU TARGET JUST THE VILLAINS FROM BEHIND MY WALL?!
REMEMBER THAT TECHNIQ MADAM ATOM WAS SHOWING LAST WEEK? I USED A LITT TELEPATHY TO GUIDE M PSY-ENERGY TO THE RIGHT TARGETS...
...BUT I THINK I OVERDID IT.
I'M SOOO SORRY. I WAS JUST TRYING TO TAKE THESE GUYS DOWN.
AND YOU DID.
DON'T WORRY ABOUT OLD McDRAGON, KID. I STILL GOT HALF MY STORE INTACT, AND MORE IMPORTANTLY, MY LIFE. BEEN AROUND LONG ENOUGH TO KNOW THAT HAVING SOMEONE SAVE YOU FROM THE "WHAT COULD HAVE BEEN'S" IS SOMETHIN' TO BE APPRECIATED.
AND WOULDJA LOOK AT THAT. STASHED 'EM IN MY APRON. HOW ABOUT YOU MAKE THAT PIE, AND THEN COME HELP ME CLEAN THIS PLACE UP ON KING'S DAY?
DEAL.

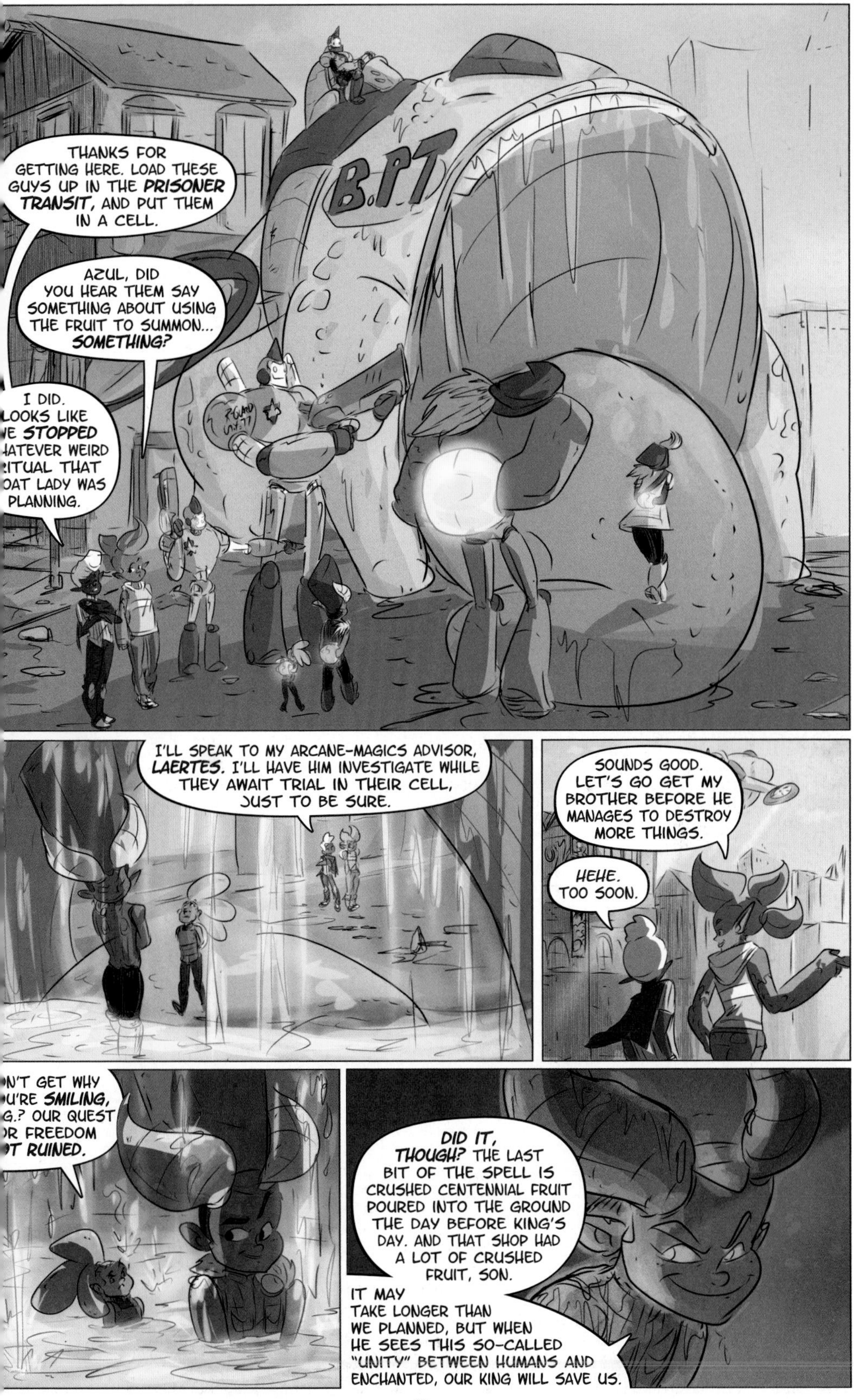
THANKS FOR GETTING HERE. LOAD THESE GUYS UP IN THE PRISONER TRANSIT, AND PUT THEM IN A CELL.
B.P.T
AZUL, DID YOU HEAR THEM SAY SOMETHING ABOUT USING THE FRUIT TO SUMMON... SOMETHING?
I DID. LOOKS LIKE E STOPPED HATEVER WEIRD RITUAL THAT OAT LADY WAS PLANNING.
I'LL SPEAK TO MY ARCANE-MAGICS ADVISOR, LAERTES. I'LL HAVE HIM INVESTIGATE WHILE THEY AWAIT TRIAL IN THEIR CELL, JUST TO BE SURE.
SOUNDS GOOD. LET'S GO GET MY BROTHER BEFORE HE MANAGES TO DESTROY MORE THINGS.
HEHE. TOO SOON.
N'T GET WHY U'RE SMILING, G.? OUR QUEST R FREEDOM T RUINED.
DID IT, THOUGH? THE LAST BIT OF THE SPELL IS CRUSHED CENTENNIAL FRUIT POURED INTO THE GROUND THE DAY BEFORE KING'S DAY. AND THAT SHOP HAD A LOT OF CRUSHED FRUIT, SON.
IT MAY TAKE LONGER THAN WE PLANNED, BUT WHEN HE SEES THIS SO-CALLED "UNITY" BETWEEN HUMANS AND ENCHANTED, OUR KING WILL SAVE US.

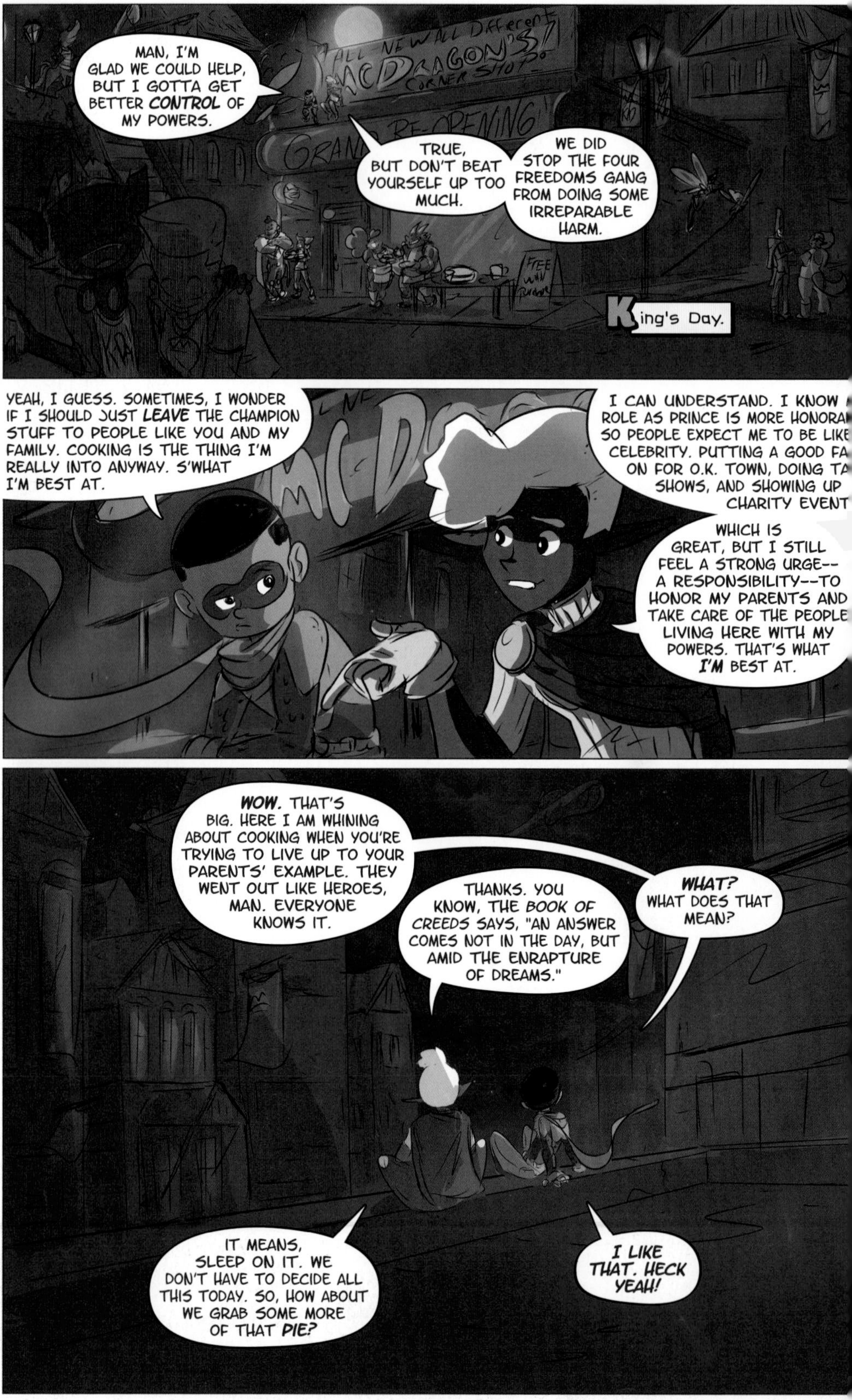
MAN, I'M GLAD WE COULD HELP, BUT I GOTTA GET BETTER **CONTROL** OF MY POWERS.
TRUE, BUT DON'T BEAT YOURSELF UP TOO MUCH.
WE DID STOP THE FOUR FREEDOMS GANG FROM DOING SOME IRREPARABLE HARM.
King's Day.
YEAH, I GUESS. SOMETIMES, I WONDER IF I SHOULD JUST **LEAVE** THE CHAMPION STUFF TO PEOPLE LIKE YOU AND MY FAMILY. COOKING IS THE THING I'M REALLY INTO ANYWAY. S'WHAT I'M BEST AT.
I CAN UNDERSTAND. I KNOW
ROLE AS PRINCE IS MORE HONORA
SO PEOPLE EXPECT ME TO BE LIKE
CELEBRITY. PUTTING A GOOD FA
ON FOR O.K. TOWN, DOING TA
SHOWS, AND SHOWING UP
CHARITY EVENT
WHICH IS GREAT, BUT I STILL FEEL A STRONG URGE-- A RESPONSIBILITY--TO HONOR MY PARENTS AND TAKE CARE OF THE PEOPLE LIVING HERE WITH MY POWERS. THAT'S WHAT ***I'M*** BEST AT.
WOW. THAT'S BIG. HERE I AM WHINING ABOUT COOKING WHEN YOU'RE TRYING TO LIVE UP TO YOUR PARENTS' EXAMPLE. THEY WENT OUT LIKE HEROES, MAN. EVERYONE KNOWS IT.
THANKS. YOU KNOW, THE *BOOK OF CREEDS* SAYS, "AN ANSWER COMES NOT IN THE DAY, BUT AMID THE ENRAPTURE OF DREAMS."
WHAT? WHAT DOES THAT MEAN?
IT MEANS, SLEEP ON IT. WE DON'T HAVE TO DECIDE ALL THIS TODAY. SO, HOW ABOUT WE GRAB SOME MORE OF THAT ***PIE?***
I LIKE THAT. HECK YEAH!

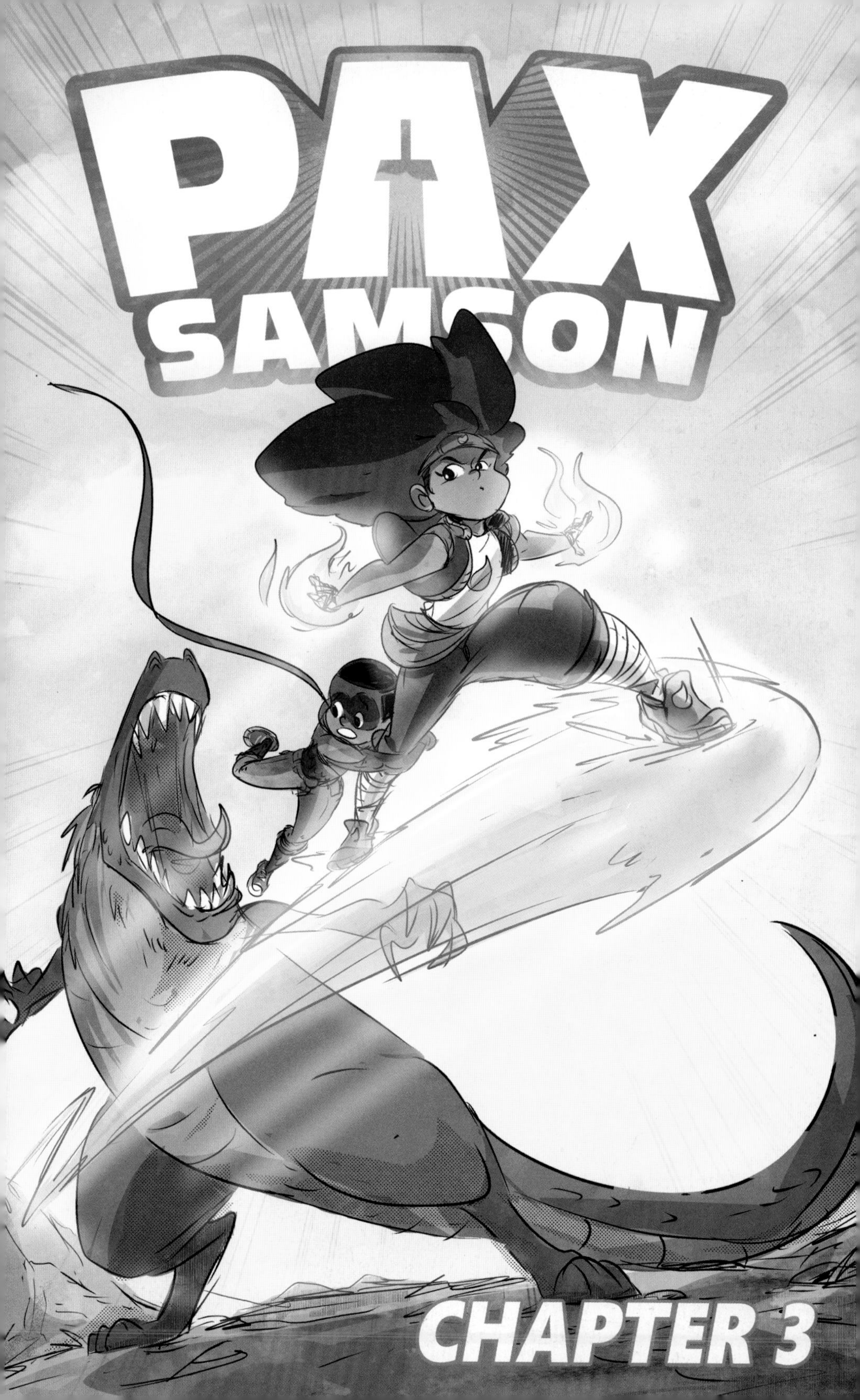
PAX SAMSON
CHAPTER 3

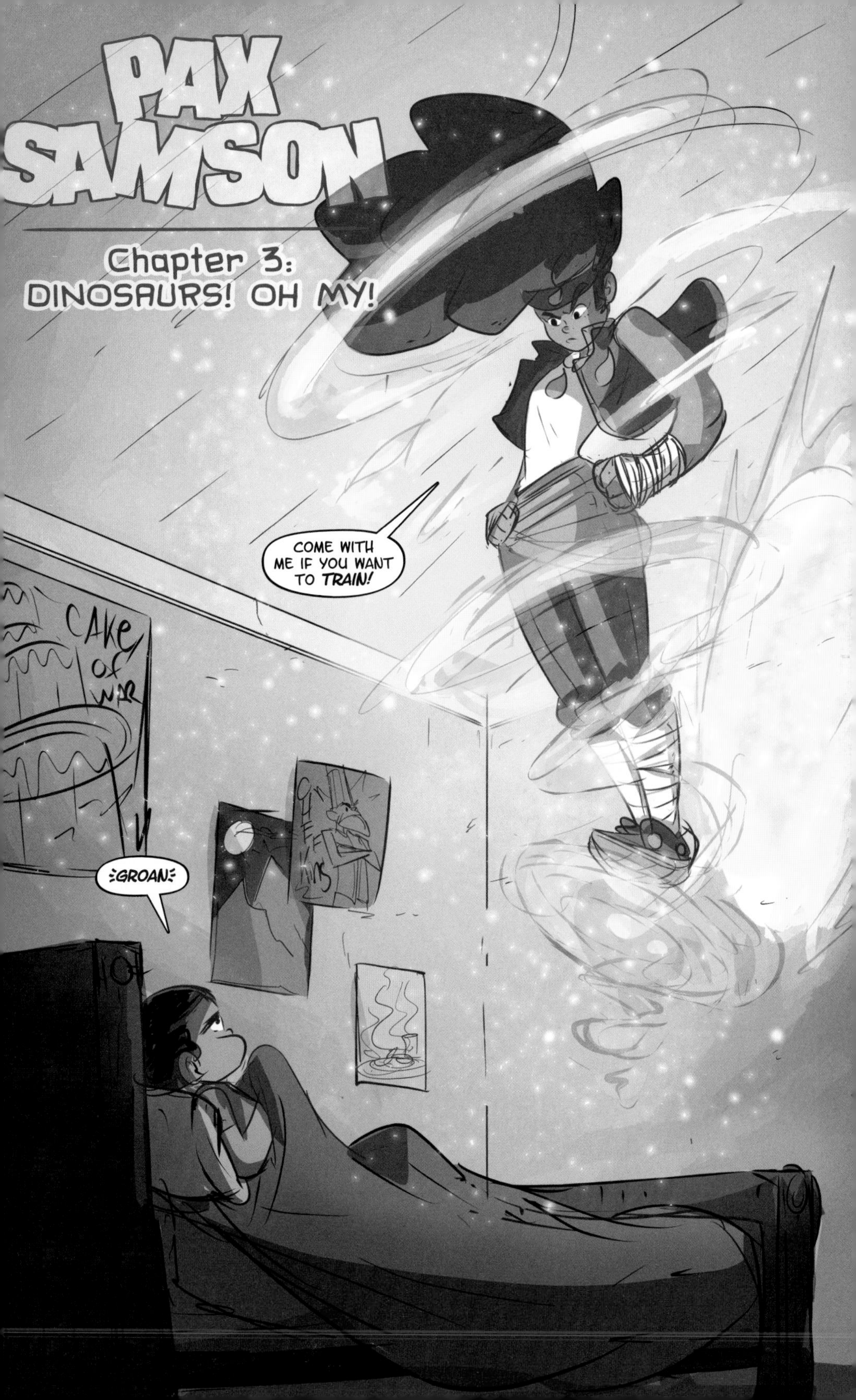
PAX SAMSON
Chapter 3:
DINOSAURS! OH MY!
COME WITH ME IF YOU WANT TO TRAIN!
CAKE of WAR
GROAN

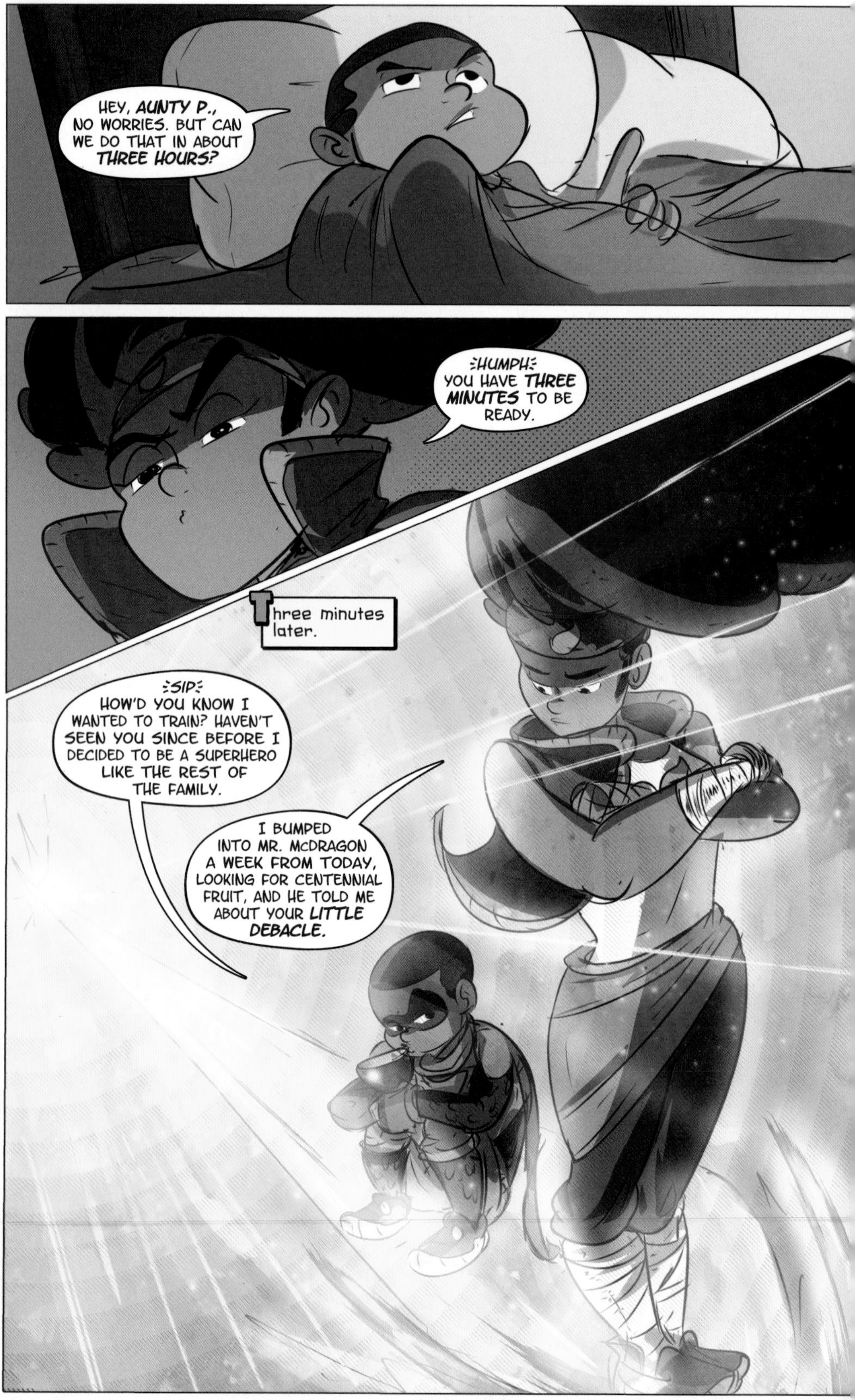
HEY, AUNTY P., NO WORRIES. BUT CAN WE DO THAT IN ABOUT THREE HOURS?
HUMPH
YOU HAVE THREE MINUTES TO BE READY.
Three minutes later.
SIP
HOW'D YOU KNOW I WANTED TO TRAIN? HAVEN'T SEEN YOU SINCE BEFORE I DECIDED TO BE A SUPERHERO LIKE THE REST OF THE FAMILY.
I BUMPED INTO MR. McDRAGON A WEEK FROM TODAY, LOOKING FOR CENTENNIAL FRUIT, AND HE TOLD ME ABOUT YOUR LITTLE DEBACLE.

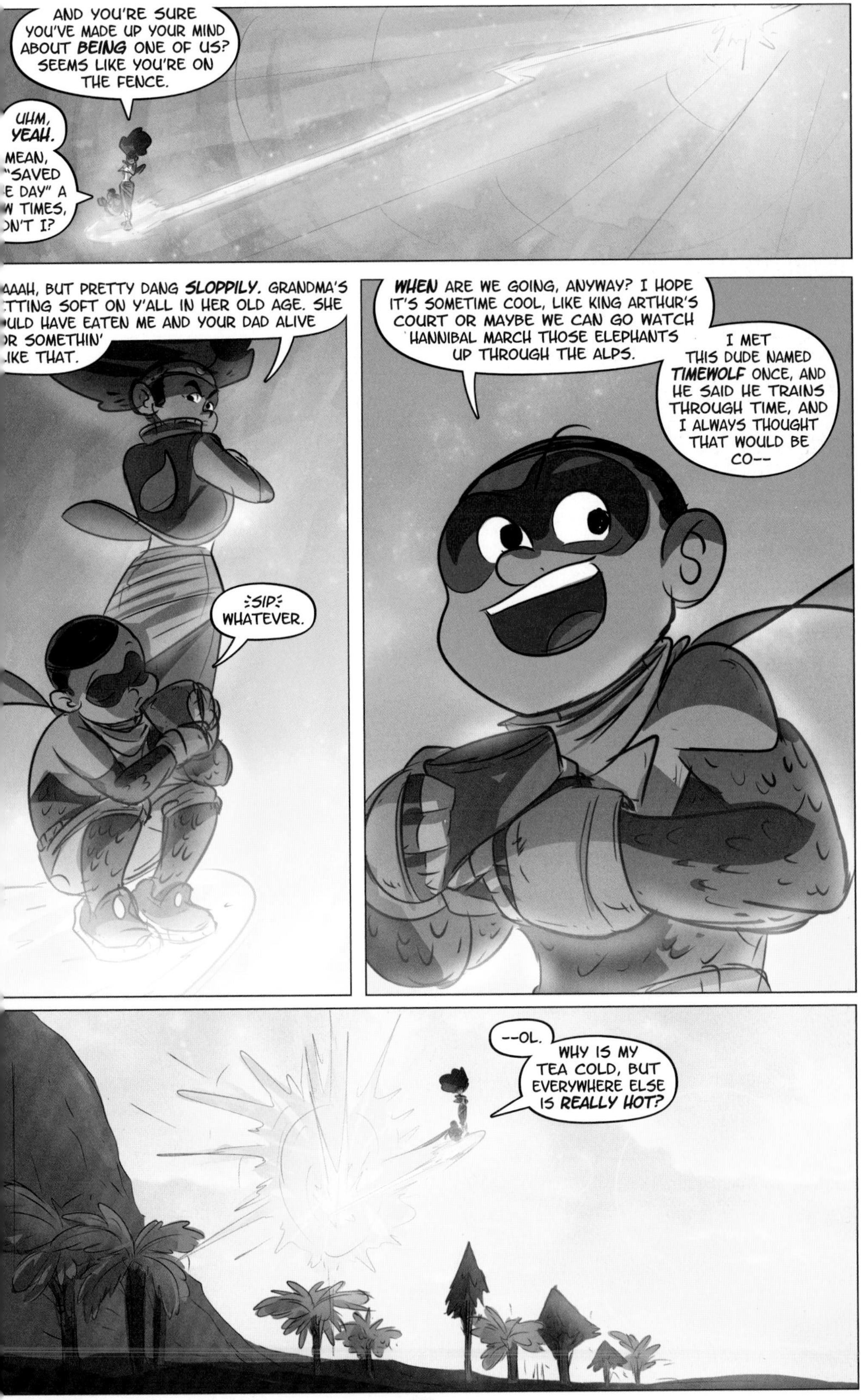
AND YOU'RE SURE YOU'VE MADE UP YOUR MIND ABOUT **BEING** ONE OF US? SEEMS LIKE YOU'RE ON THE FENCE.
UHM, **YEAH.** MEAN, "SAVED E DAY" A W TIMES, ON'T I?
AAAH, BUT PRETTY DANG **SLOPPILY.** GRANDMA'S TTING SOFT ON Y'ALL IN HER OLD AGE. SHE ULD HAVE EATEN ME AND YOUR DAD ALIVE R SOMETHIN' IKE THAT.
SIP
WHATEVER.
WHEN ARE WE GOING, ANYWAY? I HOPE IT'S SOMETIME COOL, LIKE KING ARTHUR'S COURT OR MAYBE WE CAN GO WATCH HANNIBAL MARCH THOSE ELEPHANTS UP THROUGH THE ALPS.
I MET THIS DUDE NAMED **TIMEWOLF** ONCE, AND HE SAID HE TRAINS THROUGH TIME, AND I ALWAYS THOUGHT THAT WOULD BE CO--
--OL.
WHY IS MY TEA COLD, BUT EVERYWHERE ELSE IS **REALLY HOT?**

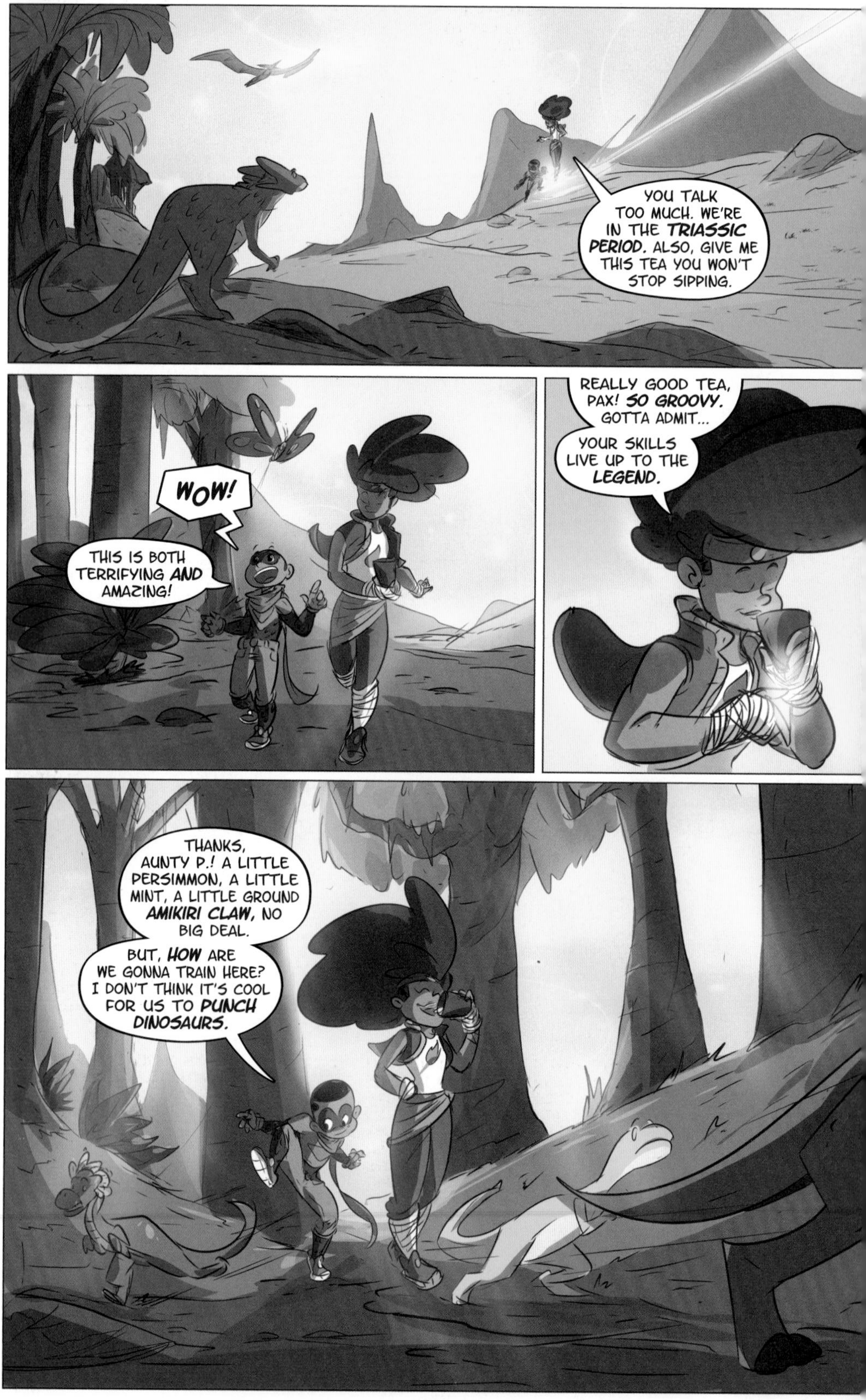
YOU TALK TOO MUCH. WE'RE IN THE TRIASSIC PERIOD. ALSO, GIVE ME THIS TEA YOU WON'T STOP SIPPING.
WOW!
THIS IS BOTH TERRIFYING AND AMAZING!
REALLY GOOD TEA, PAX! SO GROOVY. GOTTA ADMIT...
YOUR SKILLS LIVE UP TO THE LEGEND.
THANKS, AUNTY P.! A LITTLE PERSIMMON, A LITTLE MINT, A LITTLE GROUND AMIKIRI CLAW, NO BIG DEAL.
BUT, HOW ARE WE GONNA TRAIN HERE? I DON'T THINK IT'S COOL FOR US TO PUNCH DINOSAURS.

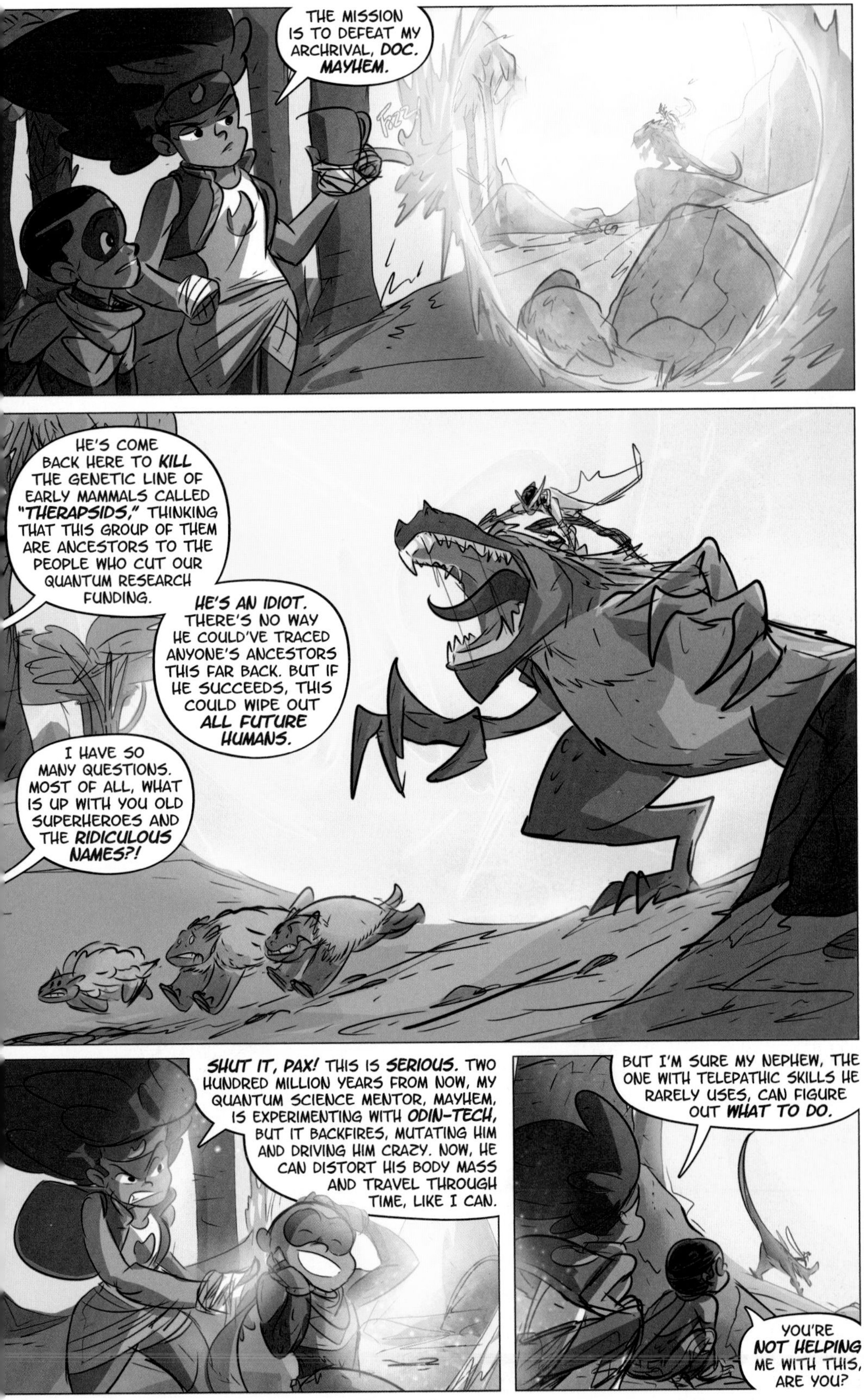
THE MISSION IS TO DEFEAT MY ARCHRIVAL, DOC. MAYHEM.
HE'S COME BACK HERE TO KILL THE GENETIC LINE OF EARLY MAMMALS CALLED "THERAPSIDS," THINKING THAT THIS GROUP OF THEM ARE ANCESTORS TO THE PEOPLE WHO CUT OUR QUANTUM RESEARCH FUNDING.
HE'S AN IDIOT. THERE'S NO WAY HE COULD'VE TRACED ANYONE'S ANCESTORS THIS FAR BACK. BUT IF HE SUCCEEDS, THIS COULD WIPE OUT ALL FUTURE HUMANS.
I HAVE SO MANY QUESTIONS. MOST OF ALL, WHAT IS UP WITH YOU OLD SUPERHEROES AND THE RIDICULOUS NAMES?!
SHUT IT, PAX! THIS IS SERIOUS. TWO HUNDRED MILLION YEARS FROM NOW, MY QUANTUM SCIENCE MENTOR, MAYHEM, IS EXPERIMENTING WITH ODIN-TECH, BUT IT BACKFIRES, MUTATING HIM AND DRIVING HIM CRAZY. NOW, HE CAN DISTORT HIS BODY MASS AND TRAVEL THROUGH TIME, LIKE I CAN.
BUT I'M SURE MY NEPHEW, THE ONE WITH TELEPATHIC SKILLS HE RARELY USES, CAN FIGURE OUT WHAT TO DO.
YOU'RE NOT HELPING ME WITH THIS, ARE YOU?

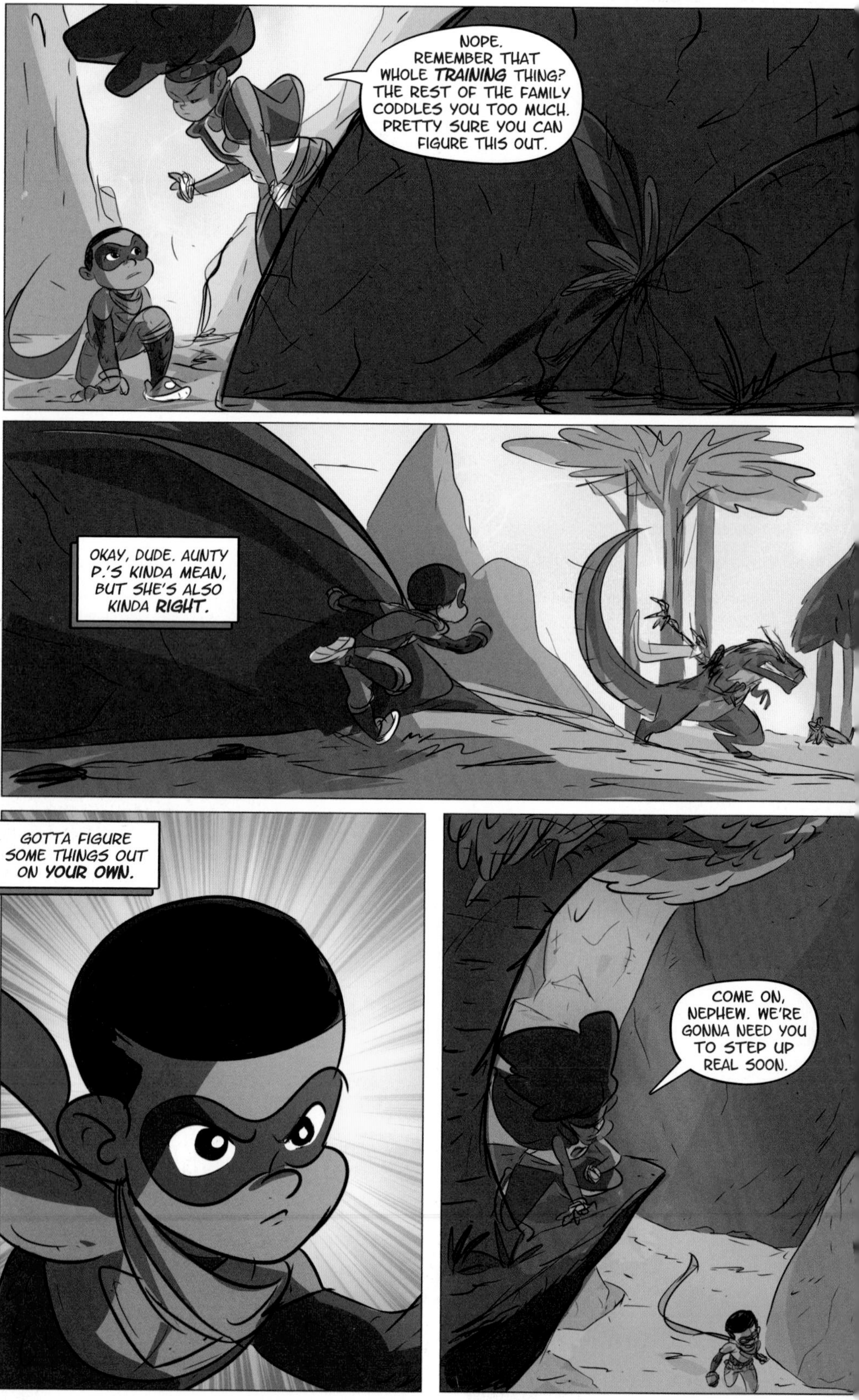
NOPE. REMEMBER THAT WHOLE TRAINING THING? THE REST OF THE FAMILY CODDLES YOU TOO MUCH. PRETTY SURE YOU CAN FIGURE THIS OUT.
OKAY, DUDE. AUNTY P.'S KINDA MEAN, BUT SHE'S ALSO KINDA RIGHT.
GOTTA FIGURE SOME THINGS OUT ON YOUR OWN.
COME ON, NEPHEW. WE'RE GONNA NEED YOU TO STEP UP REAL SOON.

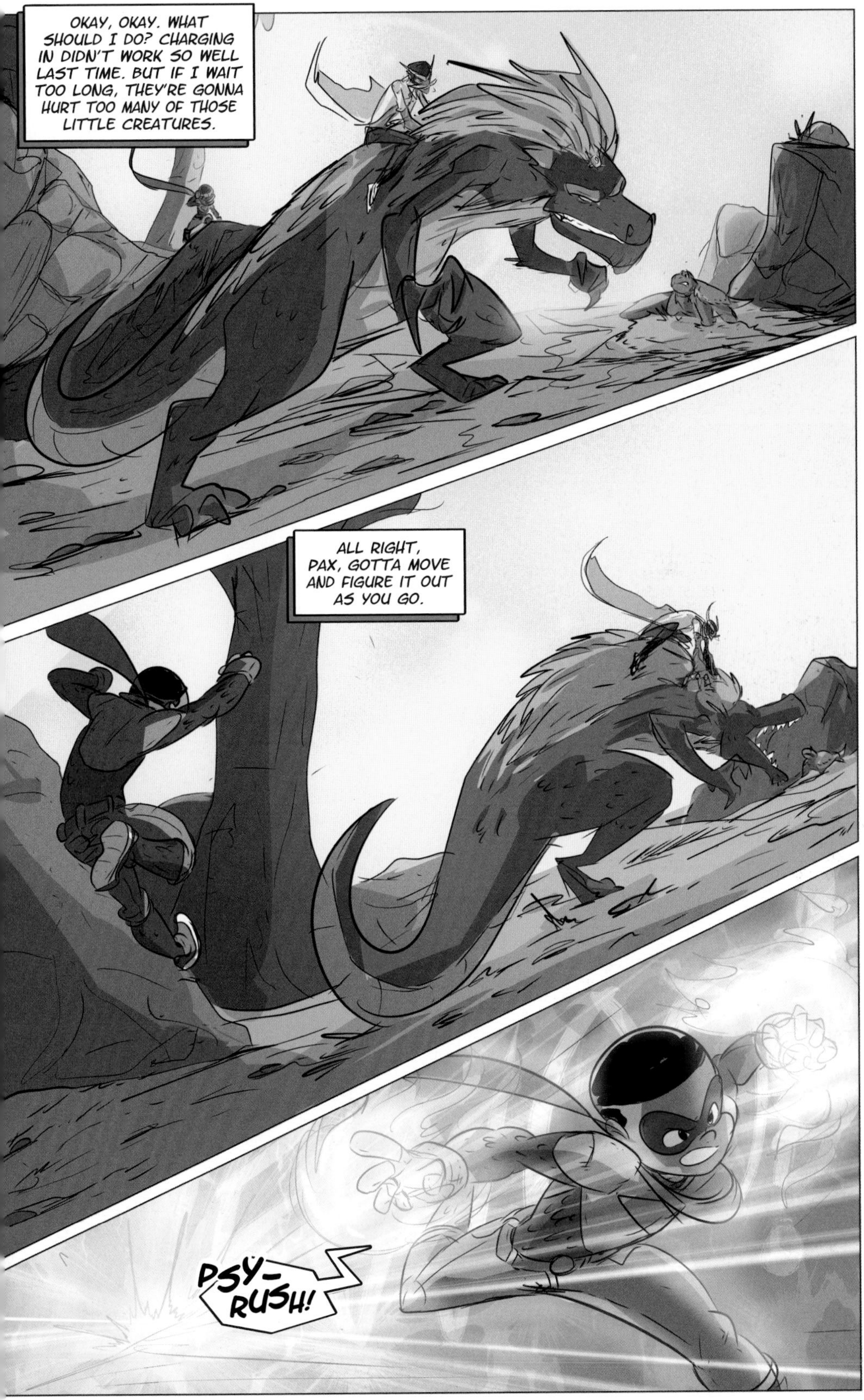
OKAY, OKAY. WHAT SHOULD I DO? CHARGING IN DIDN'T WORK SO WELL LAST TIME. BUT IF I WAIT TOO LONG, THEY'RE GONNA HURT TOO MANY OF THOSE LITTLE CREATURES.
ALL RIGHT, PAX, GOTTA MOVE AND FIGURE IT OUT AS YOU GO.
PSY-RUSH!

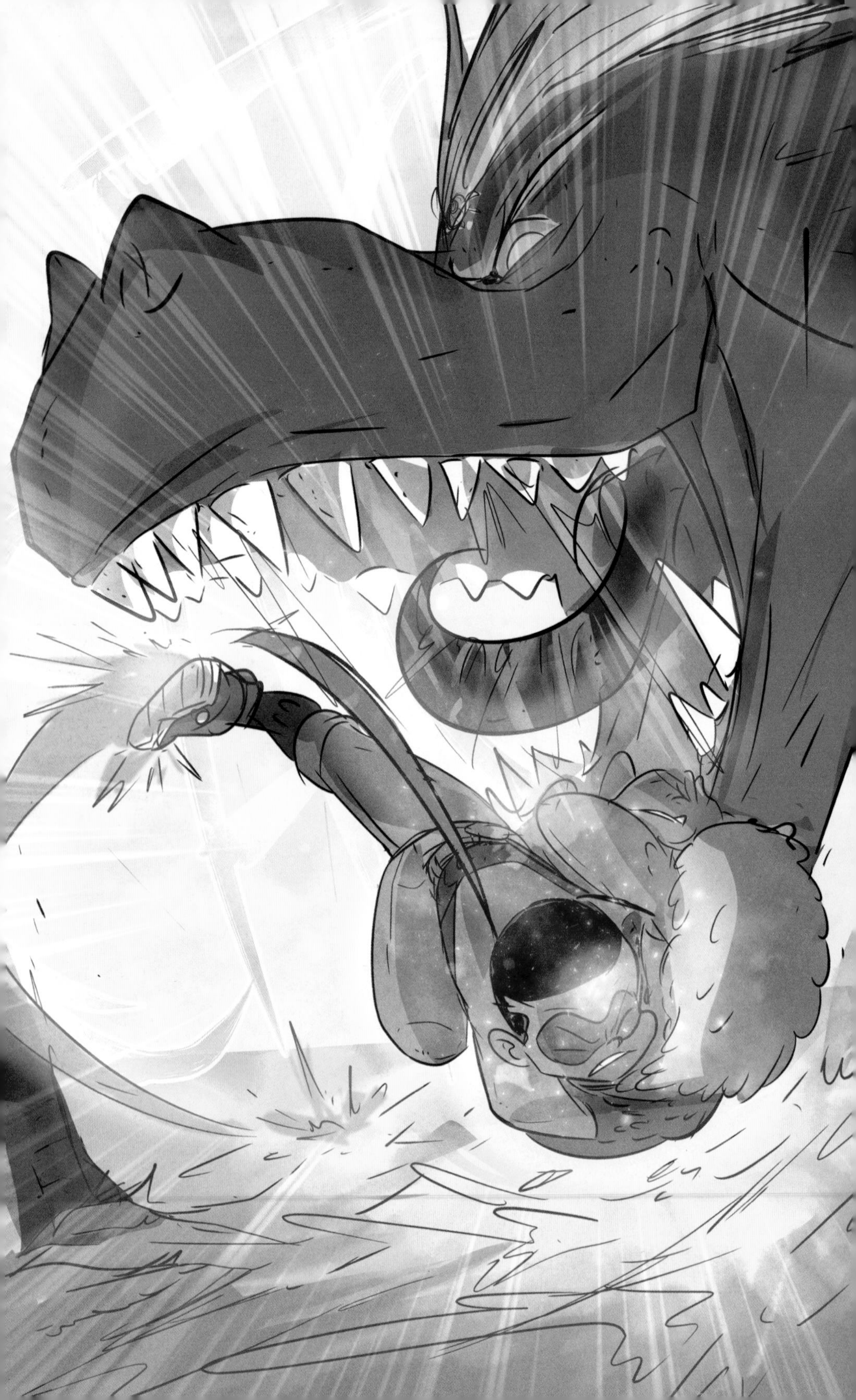

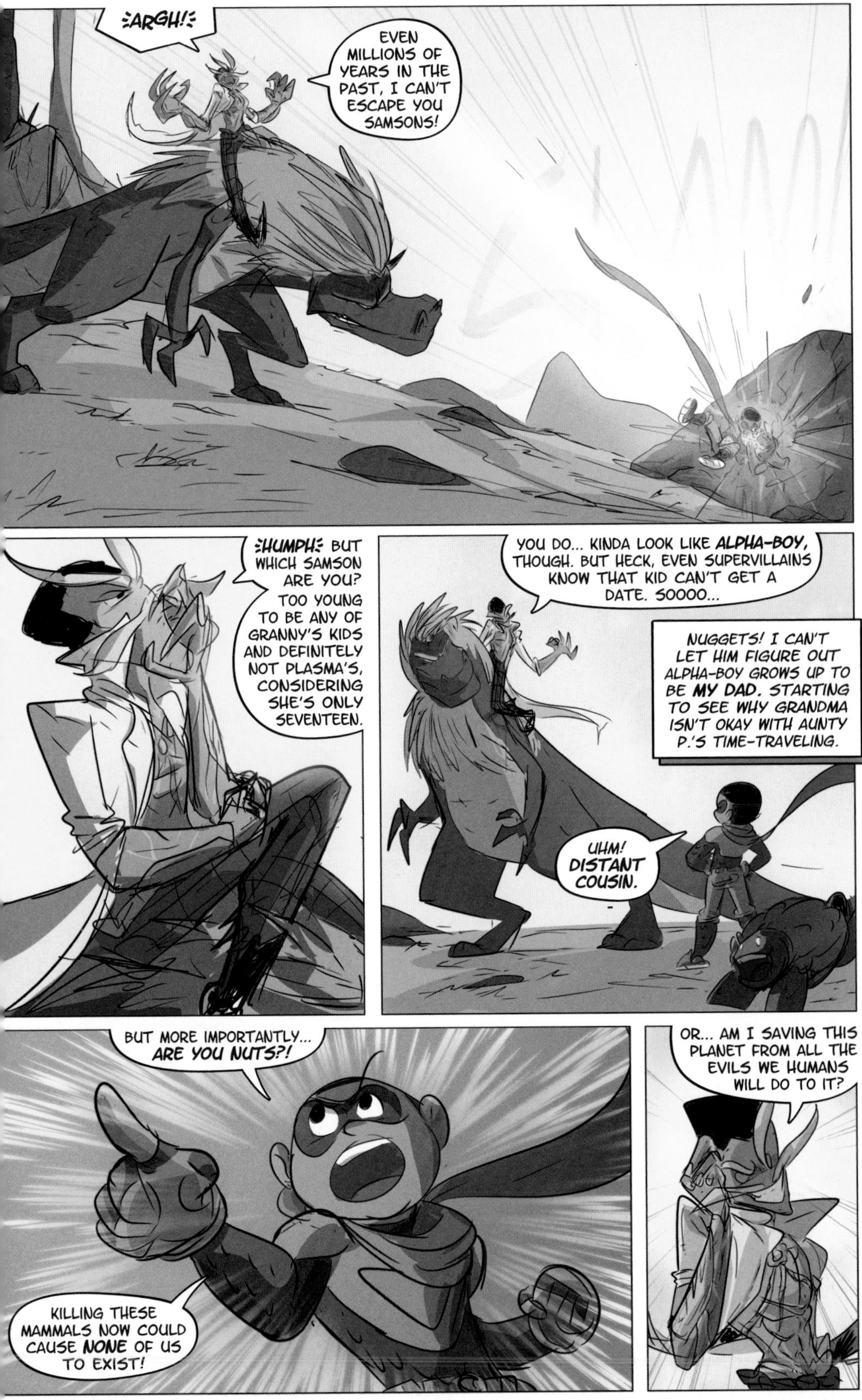
ARGH!
EVEN MILLIONS OF YEARS IN THE PAST, I CAN'T ESCAPE YOU SAMSONS!
HUMPH! BUT WHICH SAMSON ARE YOU?
TOO YOUNG TO BE ANY OF GRANNY'S KIDS AND DEFINITELY NOT PLASMA'S, CONSIDERING SHE'S ONLY SEVENTEEN.
YOU DO... KINDA LOOK LIKE ALPHA-BOY, THOUGH. BUT HECK, EVEN SUPERVILLAINS KNOW THAT KID CAN'T GET A DATE. SOOOO...
NUGGETS! I CAN'T LET HIM FIGURE OUT ALPHA-BOY GROWS UP TO BE MY DAD. STARTING TO SEE WHY GRANDMA ISN'T OKAY WITH AUNTY P.'S TIME-TRAVELING.
UHM! DISTANT COUSIN.
BUT MORE IMPORTANTLY... ARE YOU NUTS?!
KILLING THESE MAMMALS NOW COULD CAUSE NONE OF US TO EXIST!
OR... AM I SAVING THIS PLANET FROM ALL THE EVILS WE HUMANS WILL DO TO IT?

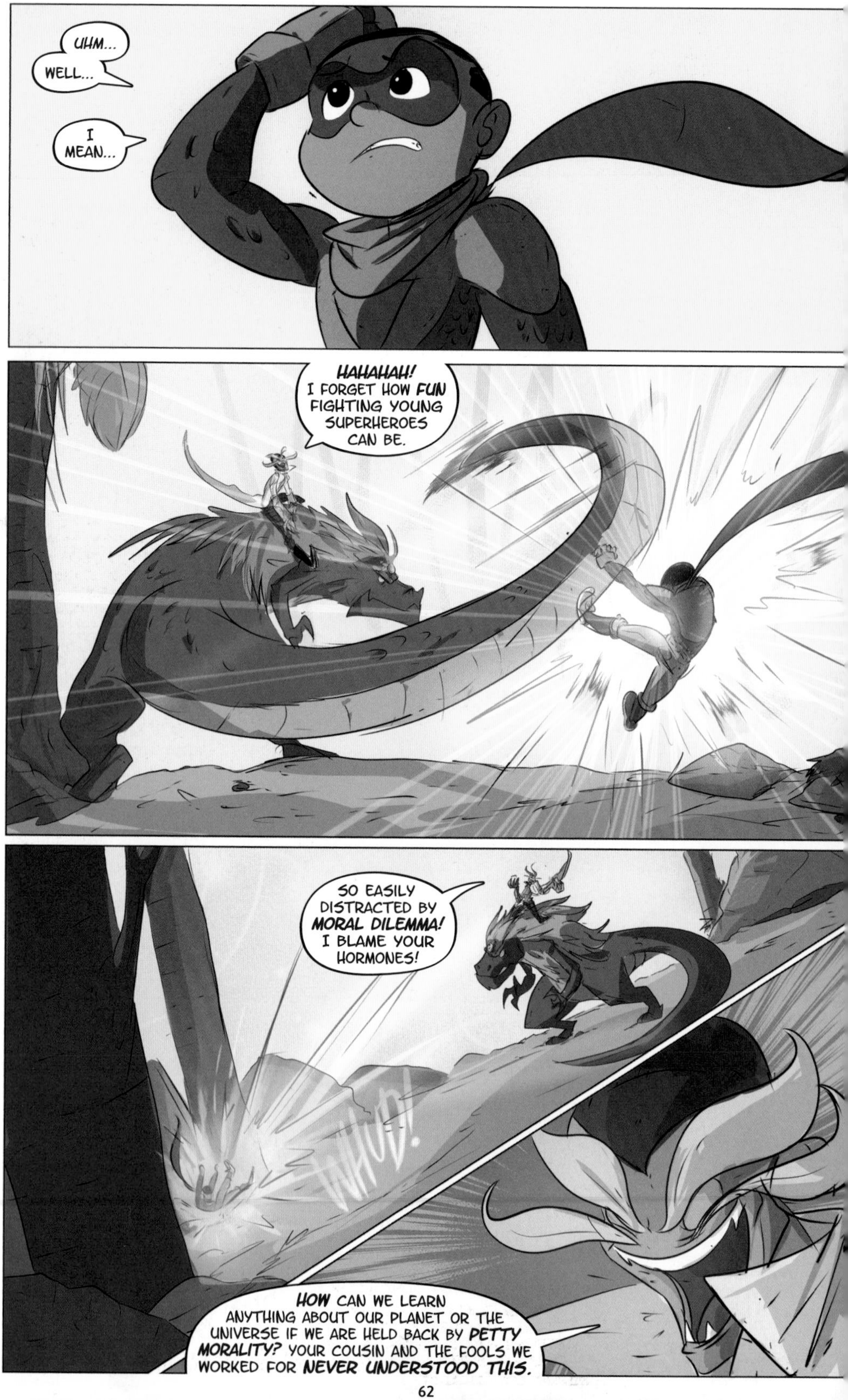
UHM...
WELL...
I MEAN...
HAHAHAH! I FORGET HOW FUN FIGHTING YOUNG SUPERHEROES CAN BE.
SO EASILY DISTRACTED BY MORAL DILEMMA! I BLAME YOUR HORMONES!
WHUD!
HOW CAN WE LEARN ANYTHING ABOUT OUR PLANET OR THE UNIVERSE IF WE ARE HELD BACK BY PETTY MORALITY? YOUR COUSIN AND THE FOOLS WE WORKED FOR NEVER UNDERSTOOD THIS.

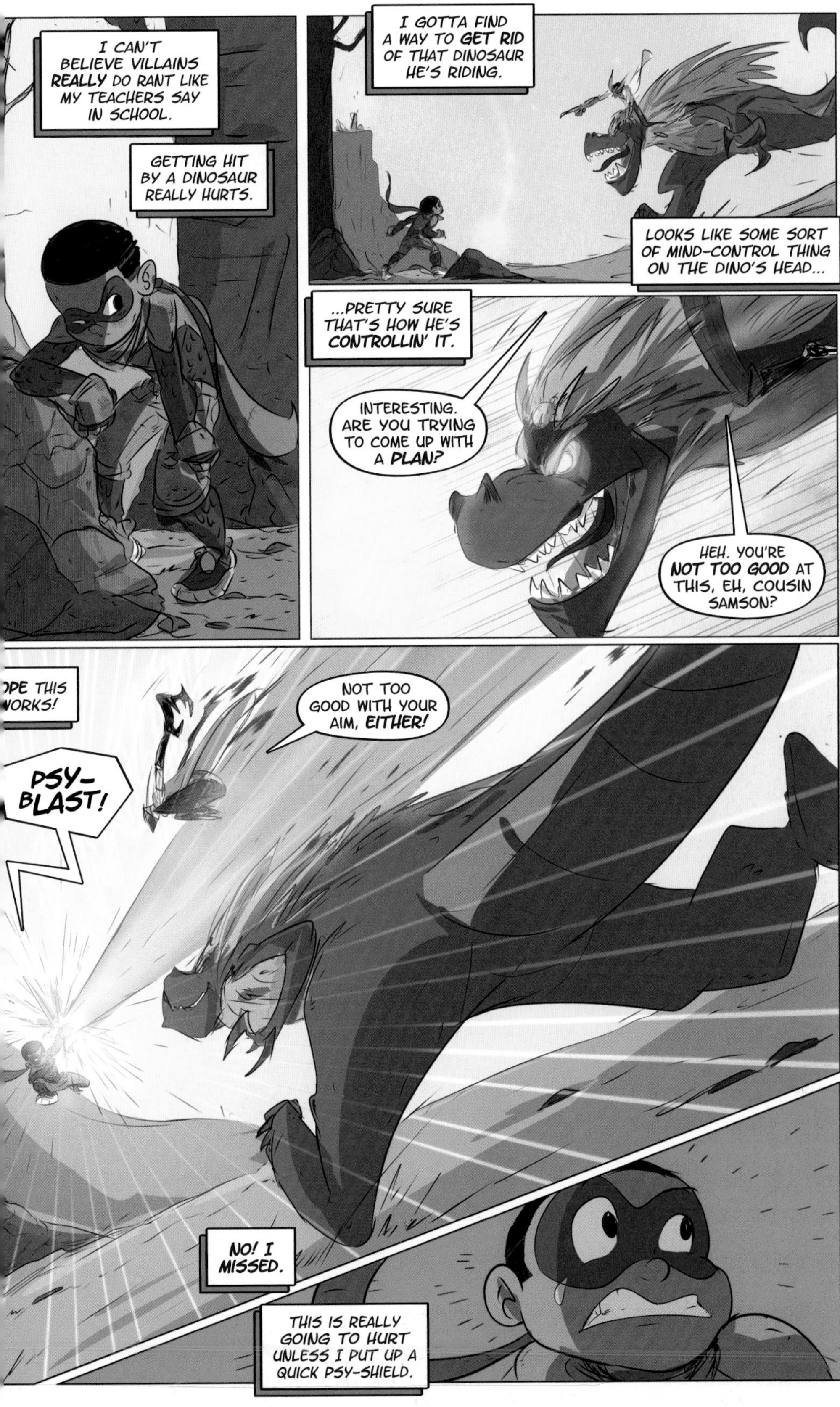
I CAN'T BELIEVE VILLAINS **REALLY** DO RANT LIKE MY TEACHERS SAY IN SCHOOL.
GETTING HIT BY A DINOSAUR REALLY HURTS.
I GOTTA FIND A WAY TO **GET RID** OF THAT DINOSAUR HE'S RIDING.
LOOKS LIKE SOME SORT OF MIND-CONTROL THING ON THE DINO'S HEAD...
...PRETTY SURE THAT'S HOW HE'S **CONTROLLIN'** IT.
INTERESTING. ARE YOU TRYING TO COME UP WITH A **PLAN?**
HEH. YOU'RE **NOT TOO GOOD** AT THIS, EH, COUSIN SAMSON?
OPE THIS WORKS!
PSY-BLAST!
NOT TOO GOOD WITH YOUR AIM, **EITHER!**
NO! I MISSED.
THIS IS REALLY GOING TO HURT UNLESS I PUT UP A QUICK PSY-SHIELD.

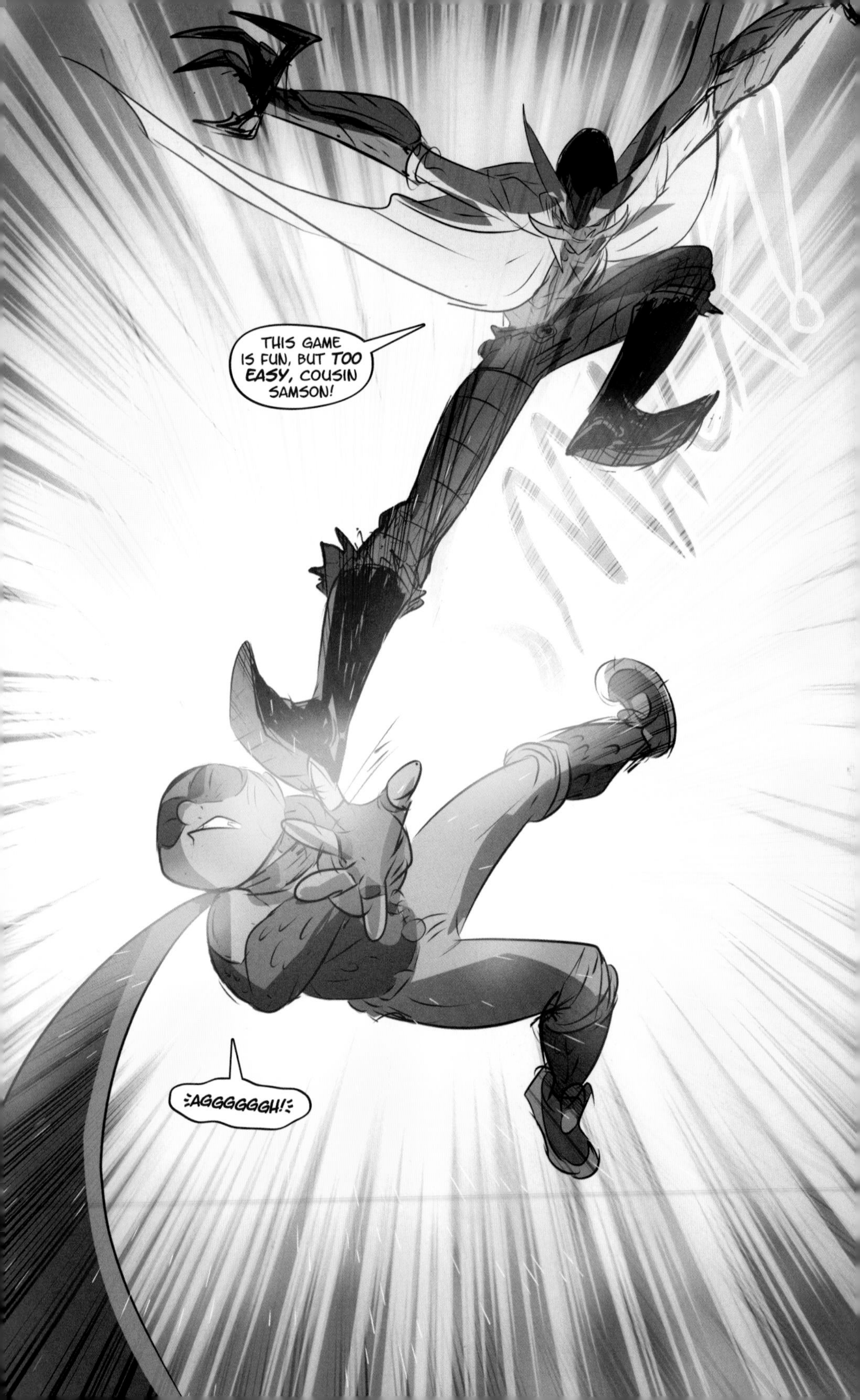
THIS GAME IS FUN, BUT TOO EASY, COUSIN SAMSON!
AGGGGGGH!

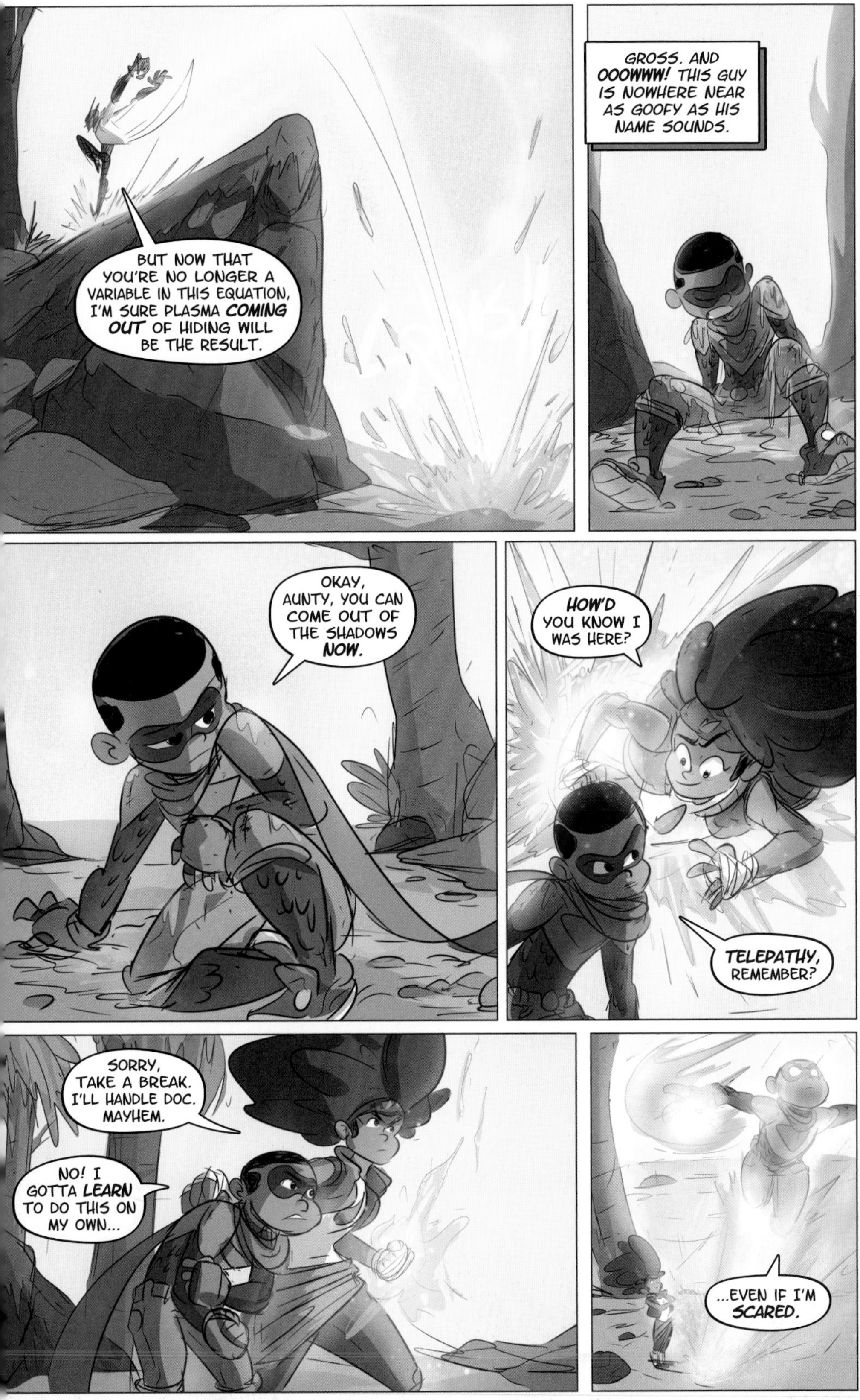
BUT NOW THAT YOU'RE NO LONGER A VARIABLE IN THIS EQUATION, I'M SURE PLASMA COMING OUT OF HIDING WILL BE THE RESULT.
GROSS. AND OOOWWW! THIS GUY IS NOWHERE NEAR AS GOOFY AS HIS NAME SOUNDS.
OKAY, AUNTY, YOU CAN COME OUT OF THE SHADOWS NOW.
HOW'D YOU KNOW I WAS HERE?
TELEPATHY, REMEMBER?
SORRY, TAKE A BREAK. I'LL HANDLE DOC. MAYHEM.
NO! I GOTTA LEARN TO DO THIS ON MY OWN...
...EVEN IF I'M SCARED.

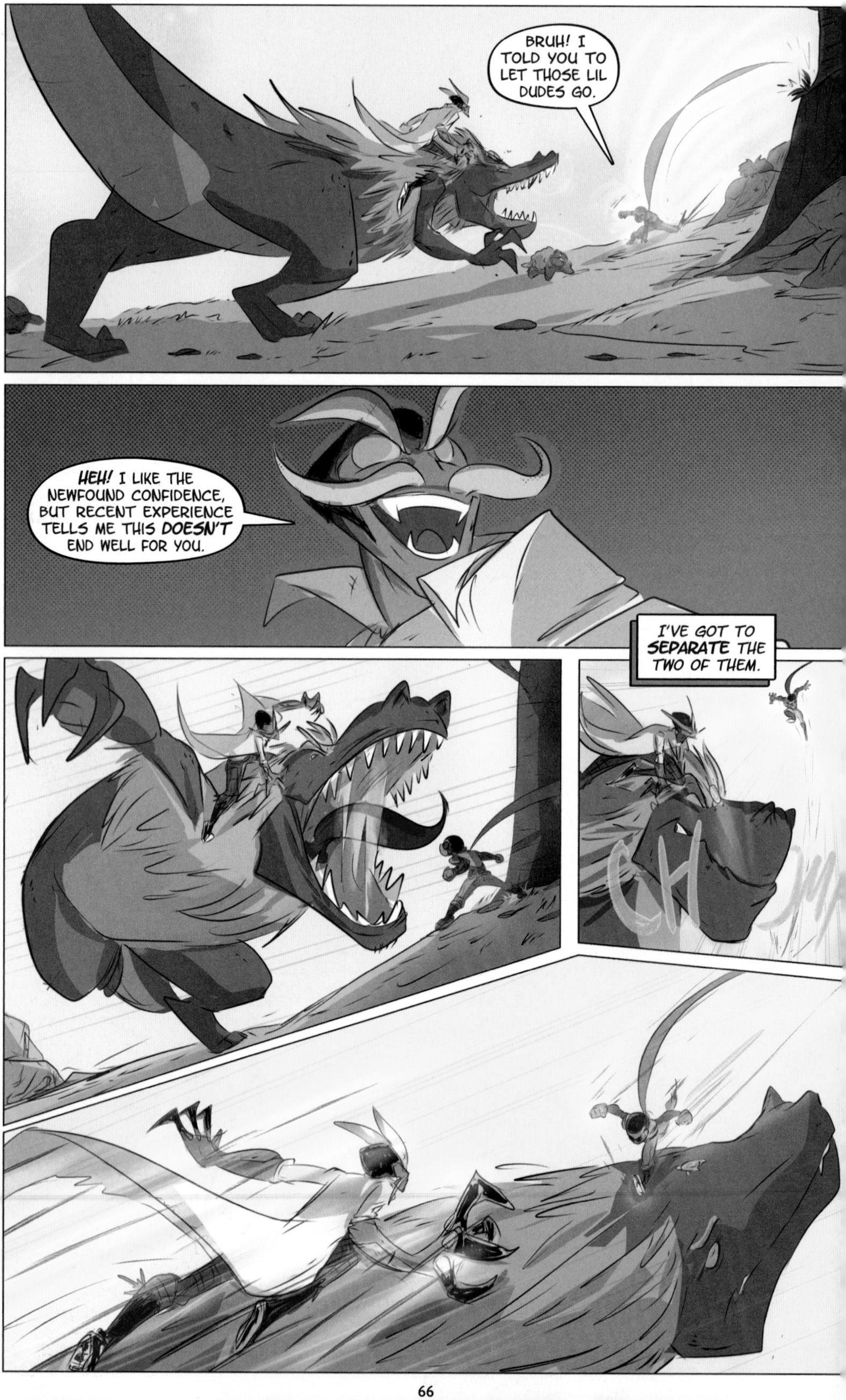
BRUH! I TOLD YOU TO LET THOSE LIL DUDES GO.
HEH! I LIKE THE NEWFOUND CONFIDENCE, BUT RECENT EXPERIENCE TELLS ME THIS DOESN'T END WELL FOR YOU.
I'VE GOT TO SEPARATE THE TWO OF THEM.

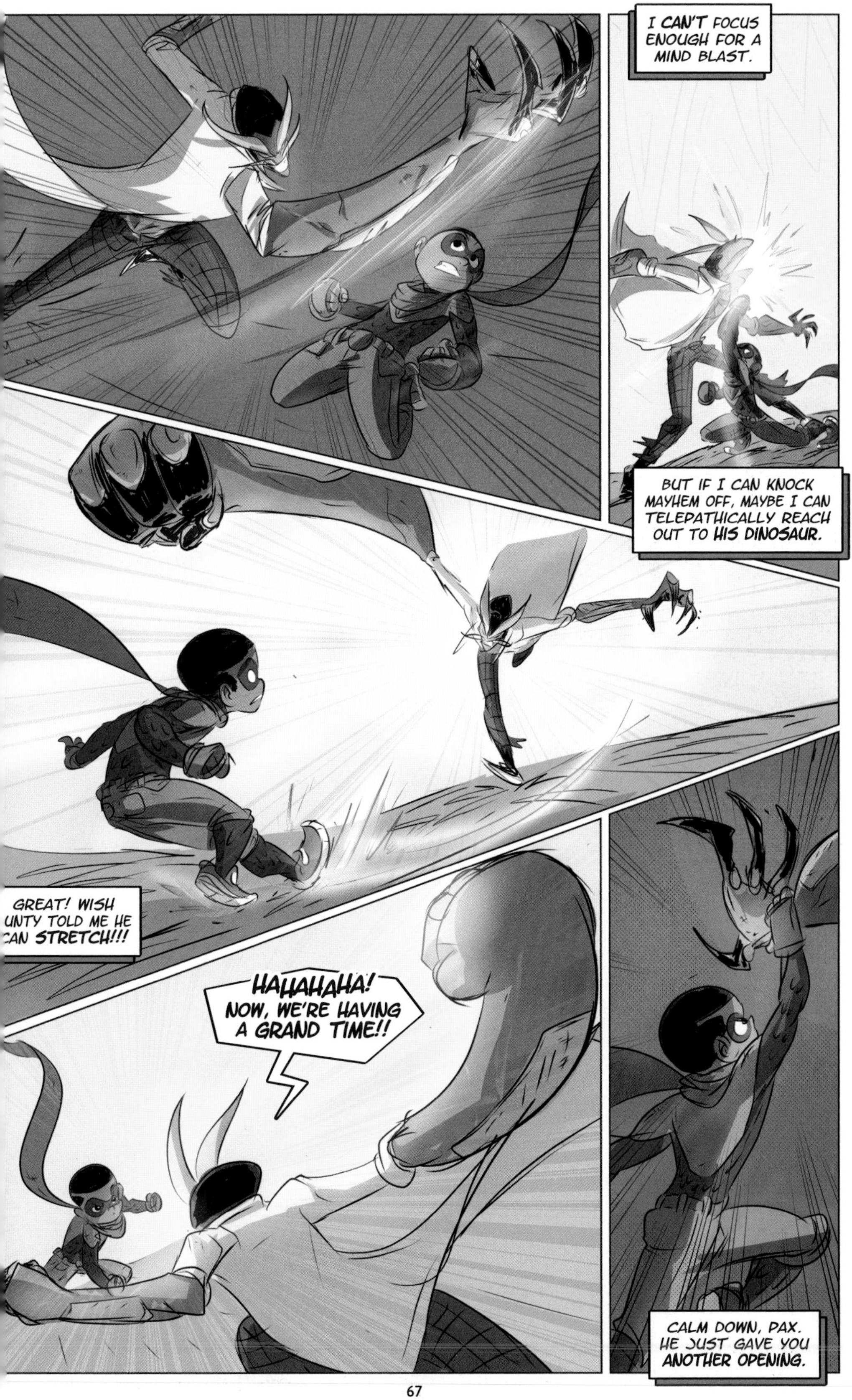
I CAN'T FOCUS ENOUGH FOR A MIND BLAST.
BUT IF I CAN KNOCK MAYHEM OFF, MAYBE I CAN TELEPATHICALLY REACH OUT TO HIS DINOSAUR.
GREAT! WISH
UNTY TOLD ME HE
CAN STRETCH!!!
HAHAHAHA! NOW, WE'RE HAVING A GRAND TIME!!
CALM DOWN, PAX. HE JUST GAVE YOU ANOTHER OPENING.

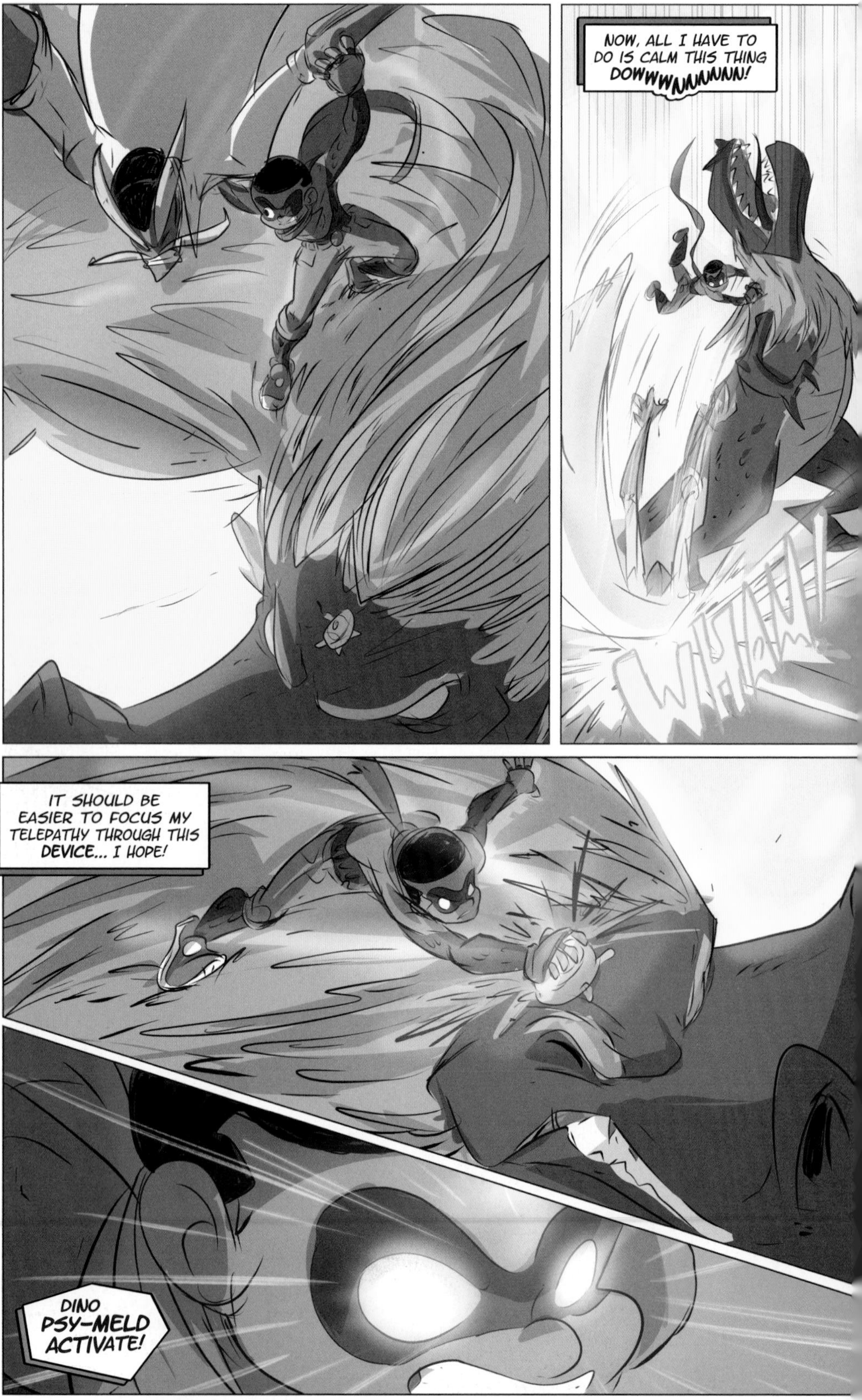
NOW, ALL I HAVE TO DO IS CALM THIS THING DOWWWNNNNNNN!
WHAM!!
IT SHOULD BE EASIER TO FOCUS MY TELEPATHY THROUGH THIS DEVICE... I HOPE!
DINO PSY-MELD ACTIVATE!

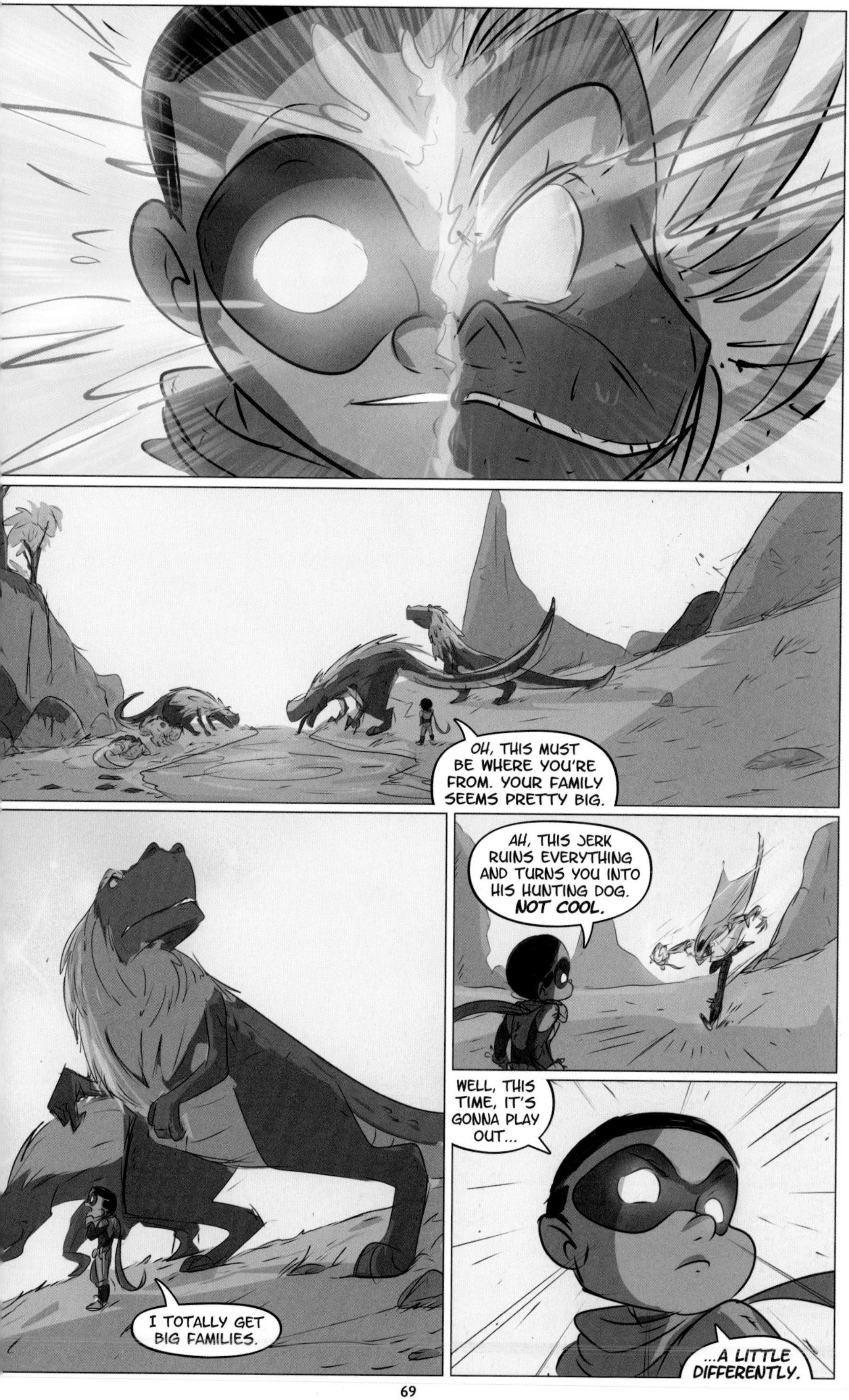
OH, THIS MUST BE WHERE YOU'RE FROM. YOUR FAMILY SEEMS PRETTY BIG.
I TOTALLY GET BIG FAMILIES.
AH, THIS JERK RUINS EVERYTHING AND TURNS YOU INTO HIS HUNTING DOG. NOT COOL.
WELL, THIS TIME, IT'S GONNA PLAY OUT...
...A LITTLE DIFFERENTLY.

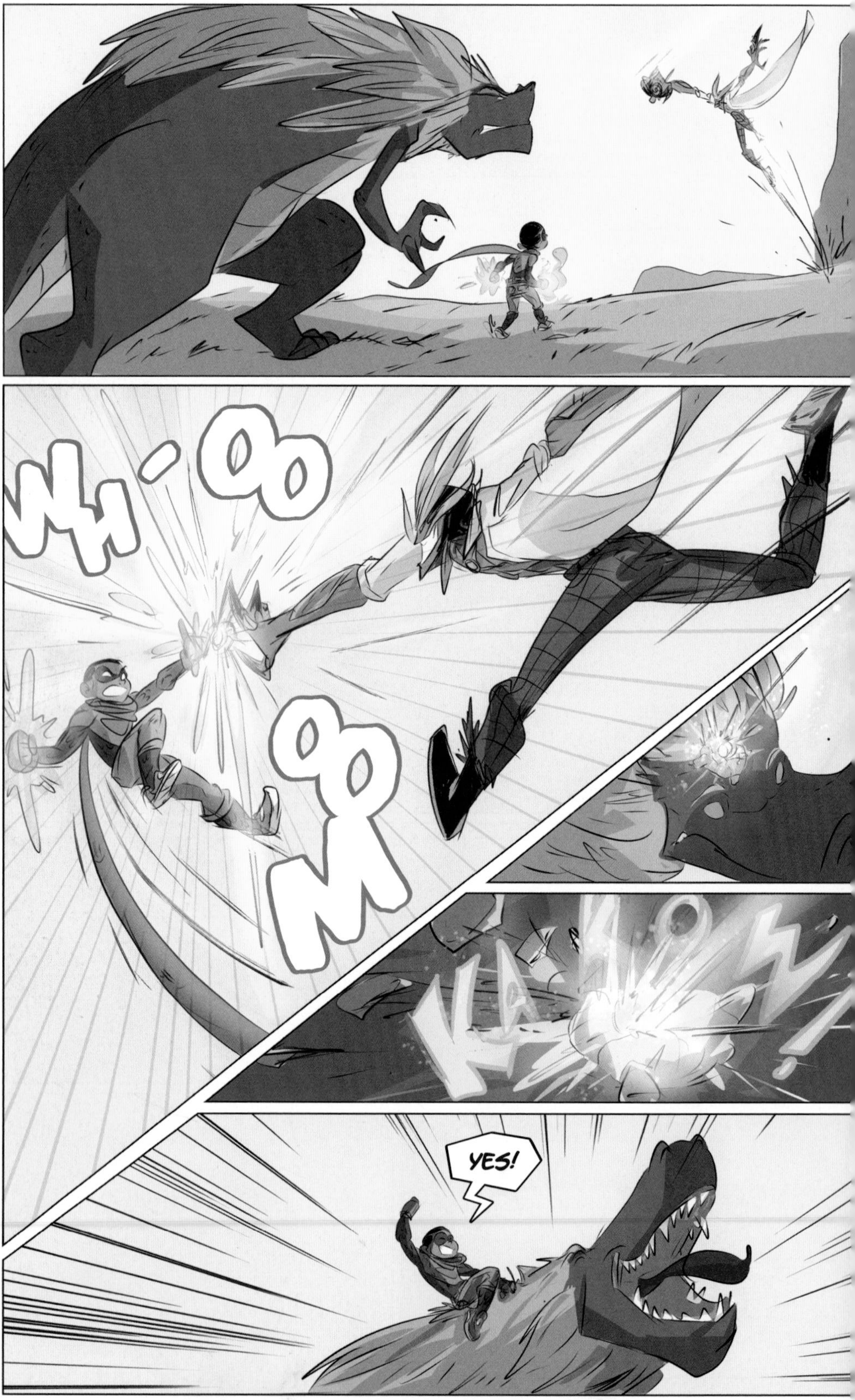
WH-OOOOM
YES!

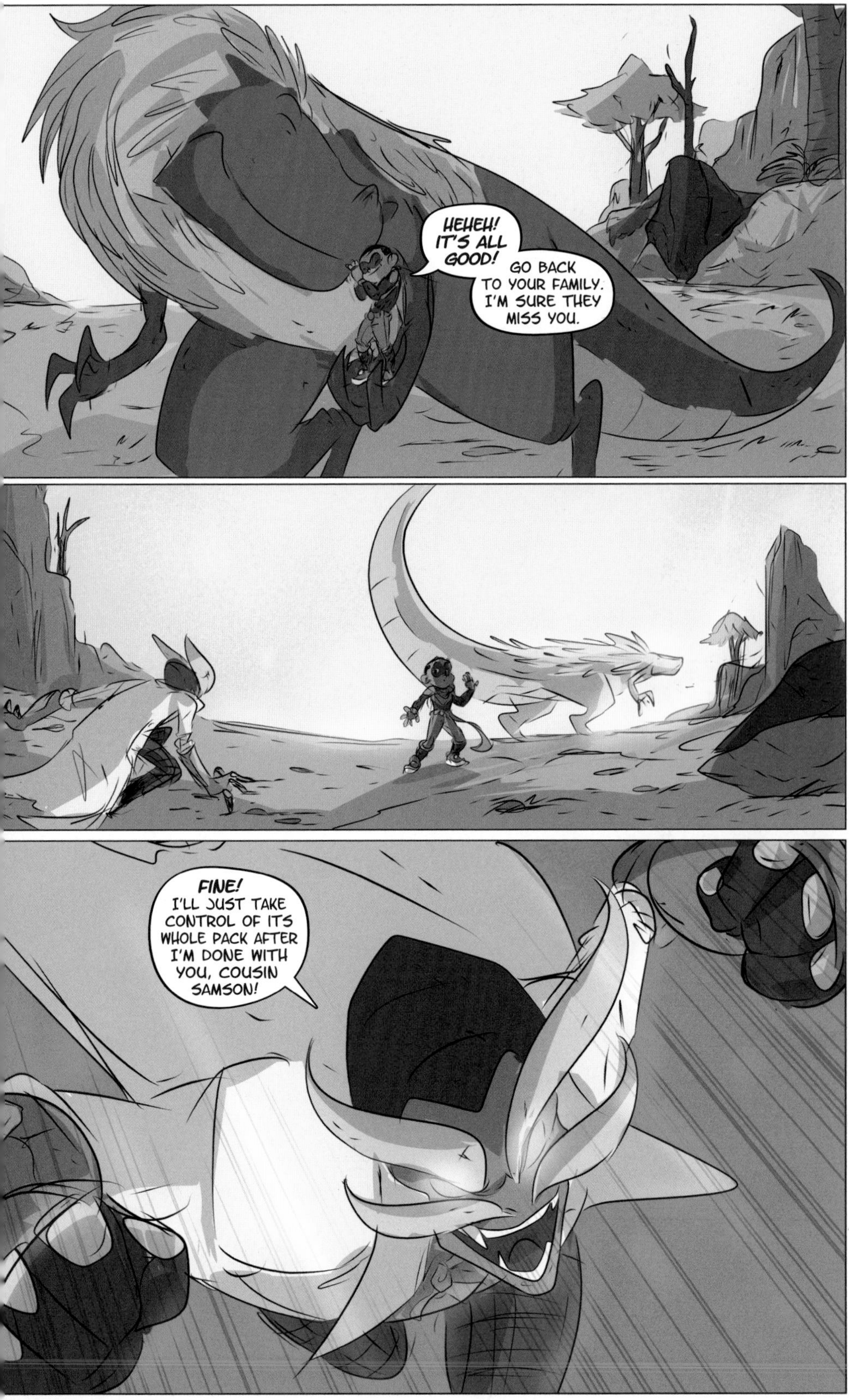
HEHEH! IT'S ALL GOOD!
GO BACK TO YOUR FAMILY. I'M SURE THEY MISS YOU.
FINE! I'LL JUST TAKE CONTROL OF ITS WHOLE PACK AFTER I'M DONE WITH YOU, COUSIN SAMSON!

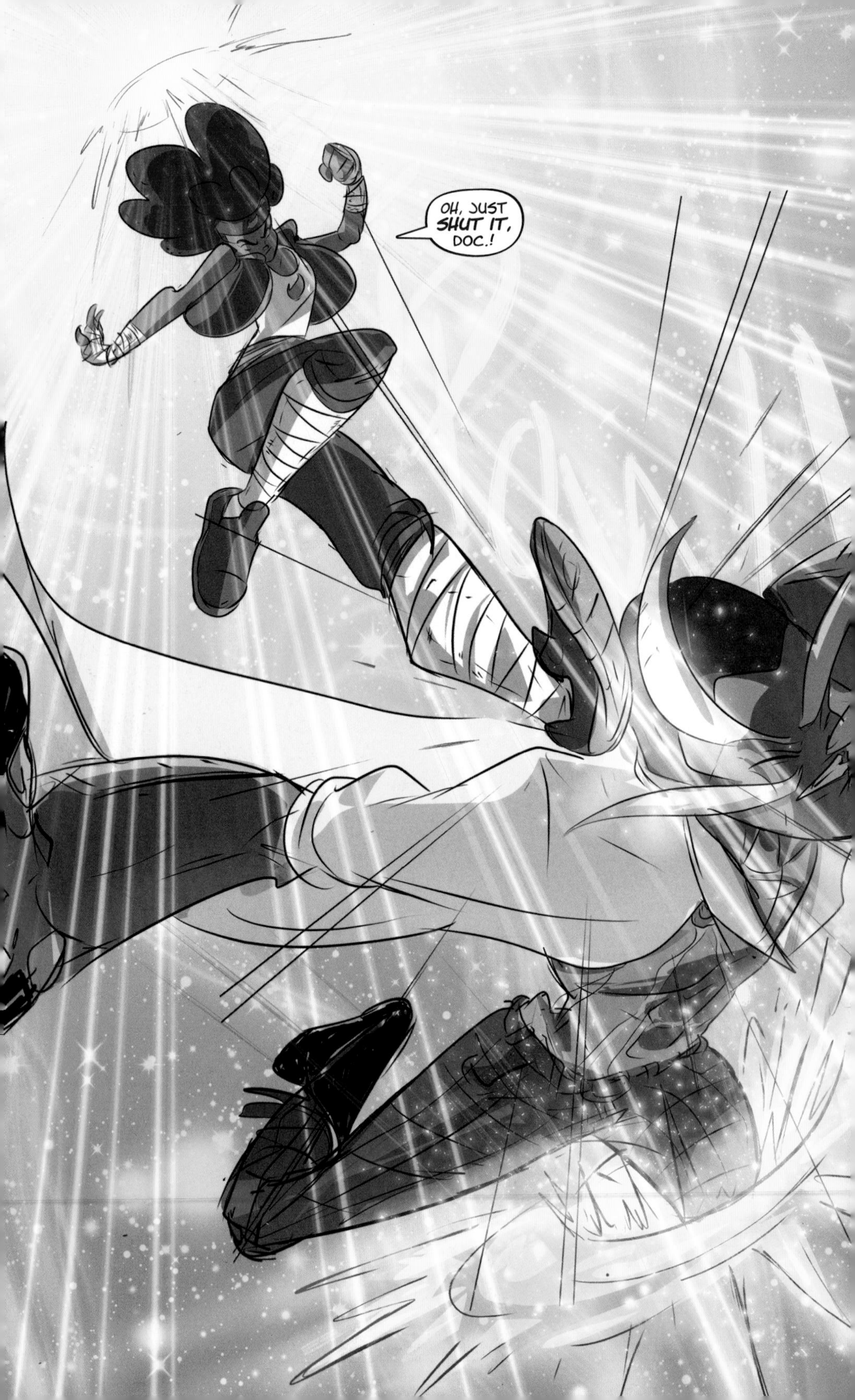
OH, JUST SHUT IT, DOC.!

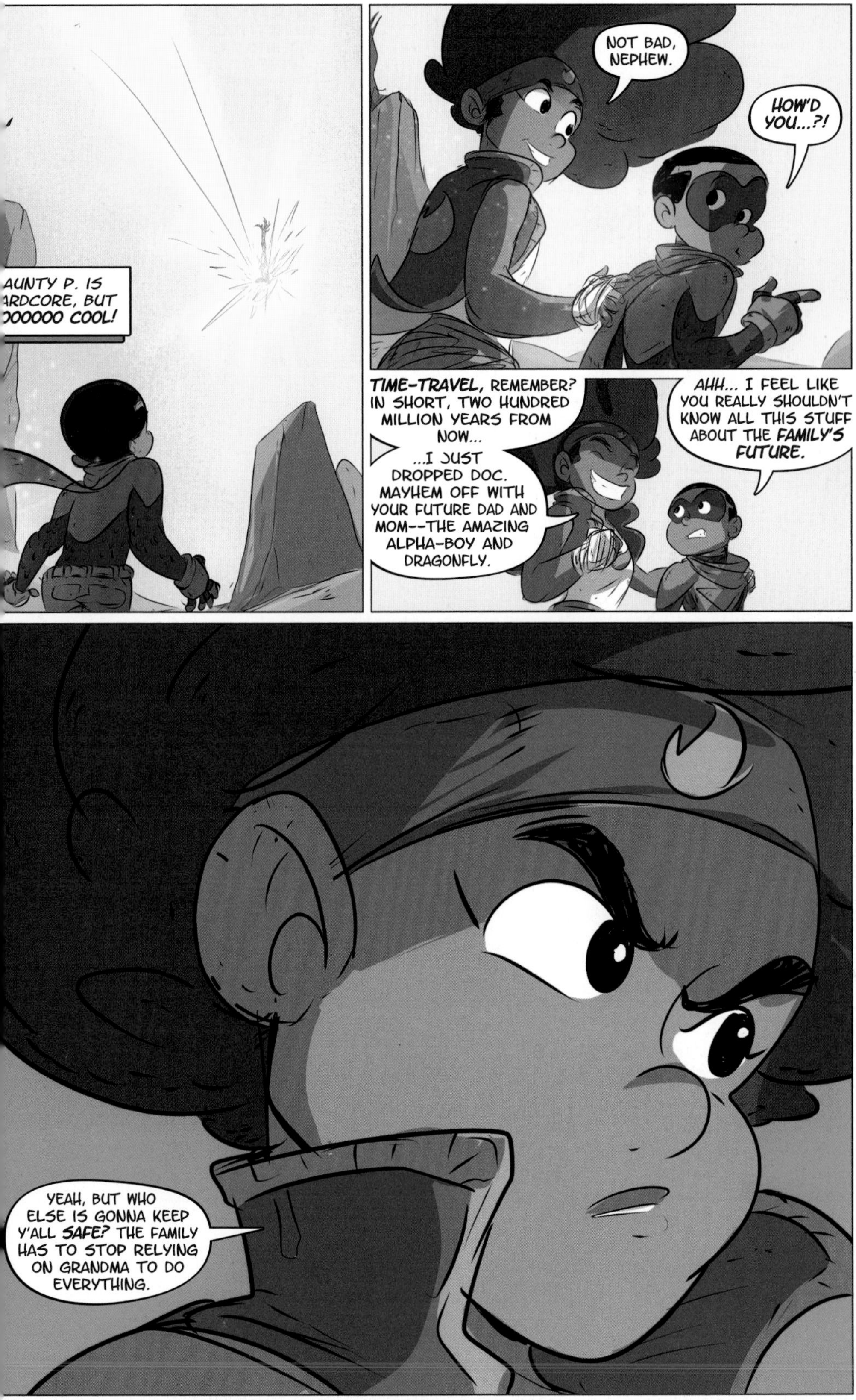
AUNTY P. IS
ARDCORE, BUT
OOOOOO COOL!
NOT BAD, NEPHEW.
HOW'D YOU...?!
TIME-TRAVEL, REMEMBER? IN SHORT, TWO HUNDRED MILLION YEARS FROM NOW...
...I JUST DROPPED DOC. MAYHEM OFF WITH YOUR FUTURE DAD AND MOM--THE AMAZING ALPHA-BOY AND DRAGONFLY.
AHH... I FEEL LIKE YOU REALLY SHOULDN'T KNOW ALL THIS STUFF ABOUT THE FAMILY'S FUTURE.
YEAH, BUT WHO ELSE IS GONNA KEEP Y'ALL SAFE? THE FAMILY HAS TO STOP RELYING ON GRANDMA TO DO EVERYTHING.

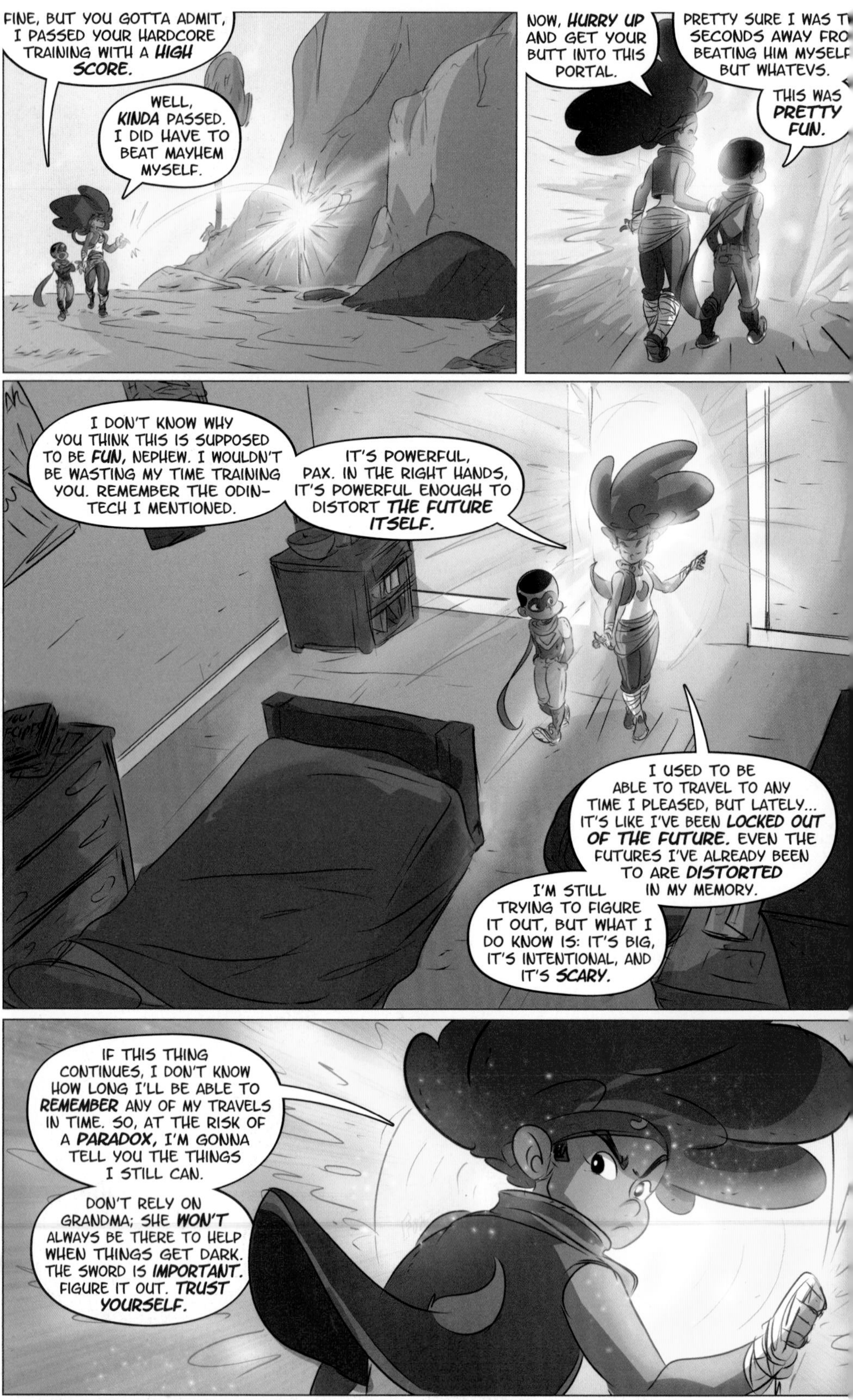
FINE, BUT YOU GOTTA ADMIT, I PASSED YOUR HARDCORE TRAINING WITH A HIGH SCORE.
WELL, KINDA PASSED. I DID HAVE TO BEAT MAYHEM MYSELF.
NOW, HURRY UP AND GET YOUR BUTT INTO THIS PORTAL.
PRETTY SURE I WAS TW SECONDS AWAY FRO BEATING HIM MYSELF BUT WHATEVS.
THIS WAS PRETTY FUN.
I DON'T KNOW WHY YOU THINK THIS IS SUPPOSED TO BE FUN, NEPHEW. I WOULDN'T BE WASTING MY TIME TRAINING YOU. REMEMBER THE ODIN-TECH I MENTIONED.
IT'S POWERFUL, PAX. IN THE RIGHT HANDS, IT'S POWERFUL ENOUGH TO DISTORT THE FUTURE ITSELF.
I USED TO BE ABLE TO TRAVEL TO ANY TIME I PLEASED, BUT LATELY... IT'S LIKE I'VE BEEN LOCKED OUT OF THE FUTURE. EVEN THE FUTURES I'VE ALREADY BEEN TO ARE DISTORTED IN MY MEMORY.
I'M STILL TRYING TO FIGURE IT OUT, BUT WHAT I DO KNOW IS: IT'S BIG, IT'S INTENTIONAL, AND IT'S SCARY.
IF THIS THING CONTINUES, I DON'T KNOW HOW LONG I'LL BE ABLE TO REMEMBER ANY OF MY TRAVELS IN TIME. SO, AT THE RISK OF A PARADOX, I'M GONNA TELL YOU THE THINGS I STILL CAN.
DON'T RELY ON GRANDMA; SHE WON'T ALWAYS BE THERE TO HELP WHEN THINGS GET DARK. THE SWORD IS IMPORTANT. FIGURE IT OUT. TRUST YOURSELF.

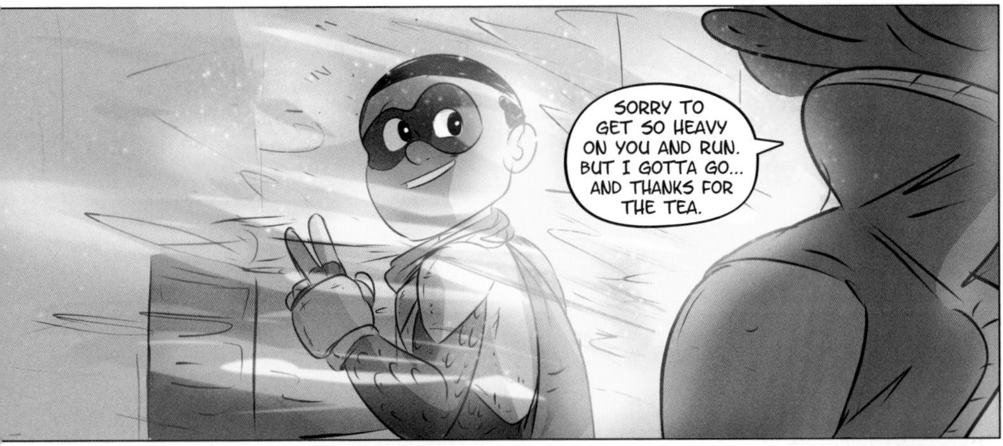
SORRY TO GET SO HEAVY ON YOU AND RUN. BUT I GOTTA GO... AND THANKS FOR THE TEA.

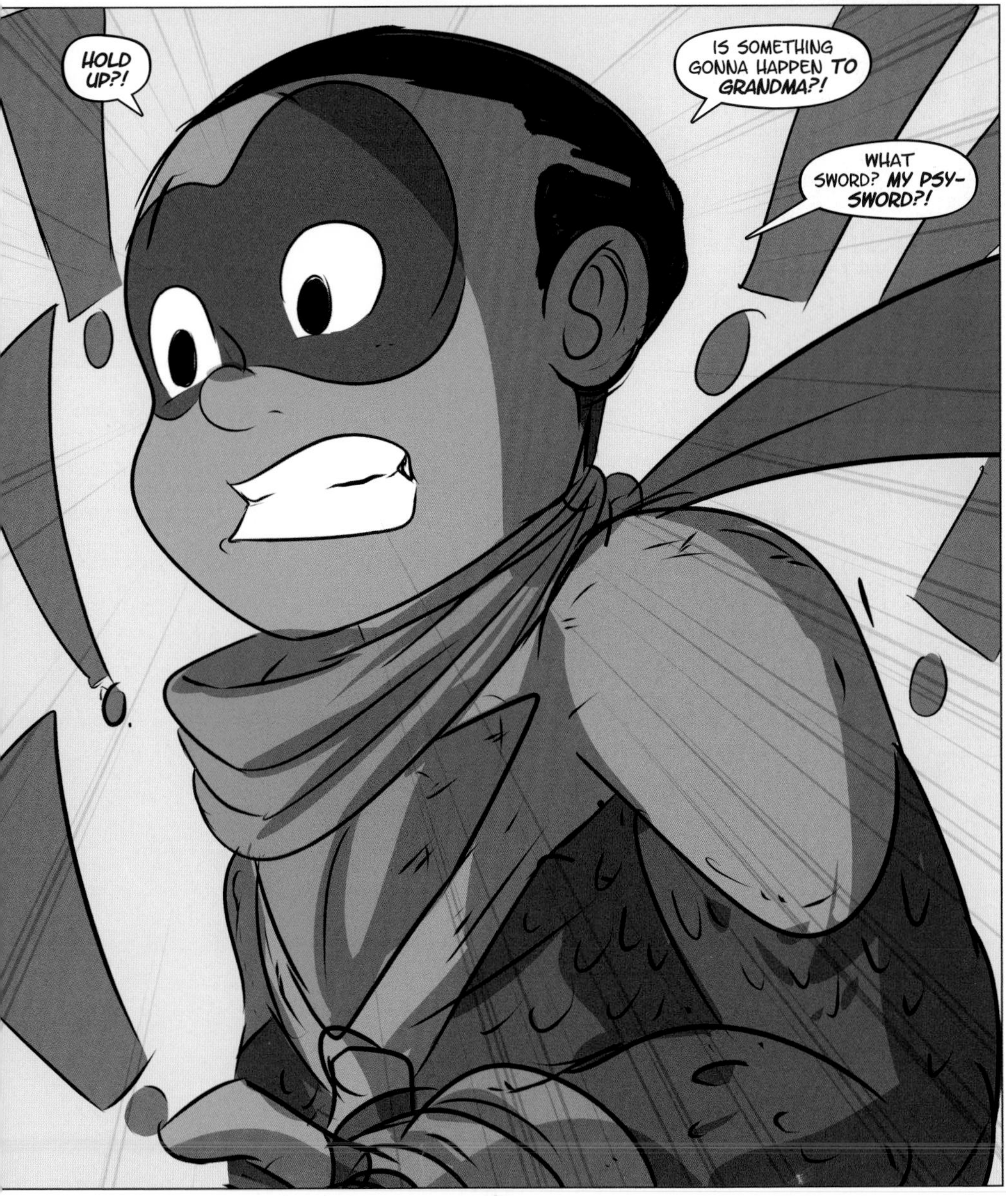
HOLD UP?!
IS SOMETHING GONNA HAPPEN TO GRANDMA?!
WHAT SWORD? MY PSY-SWORD?!

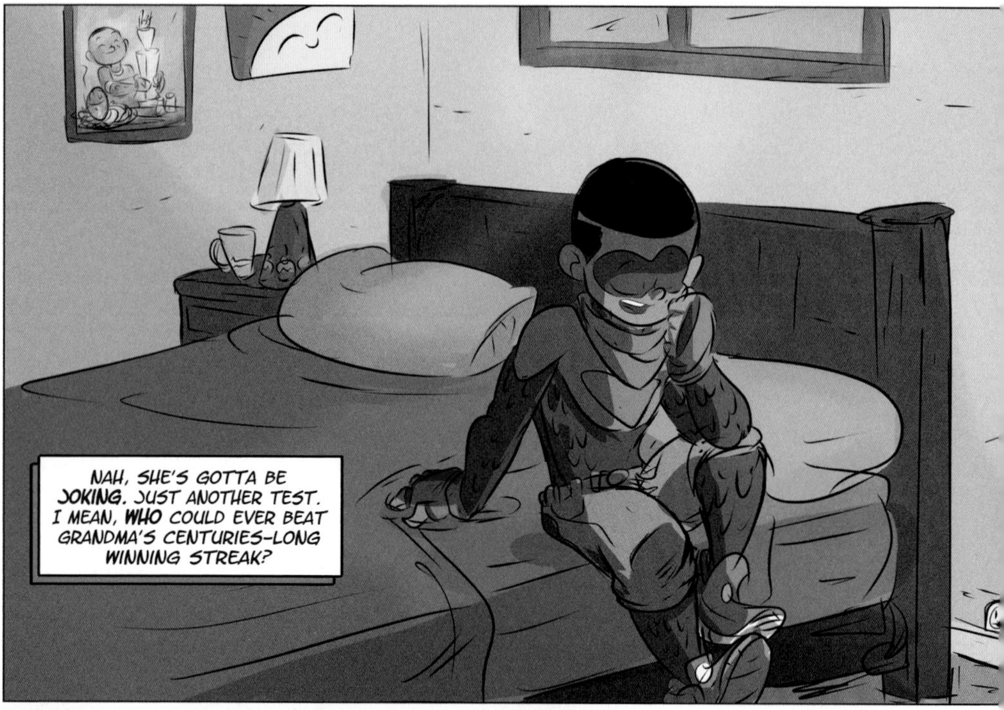
NAH, SHE'S GOTTA BE **JOKING.** JUST ANOTHER TEST. I MEAN, **WHO** COULD EVER BEAT GRANDMA'S CENTURIES-LONG WINNING STREAK?

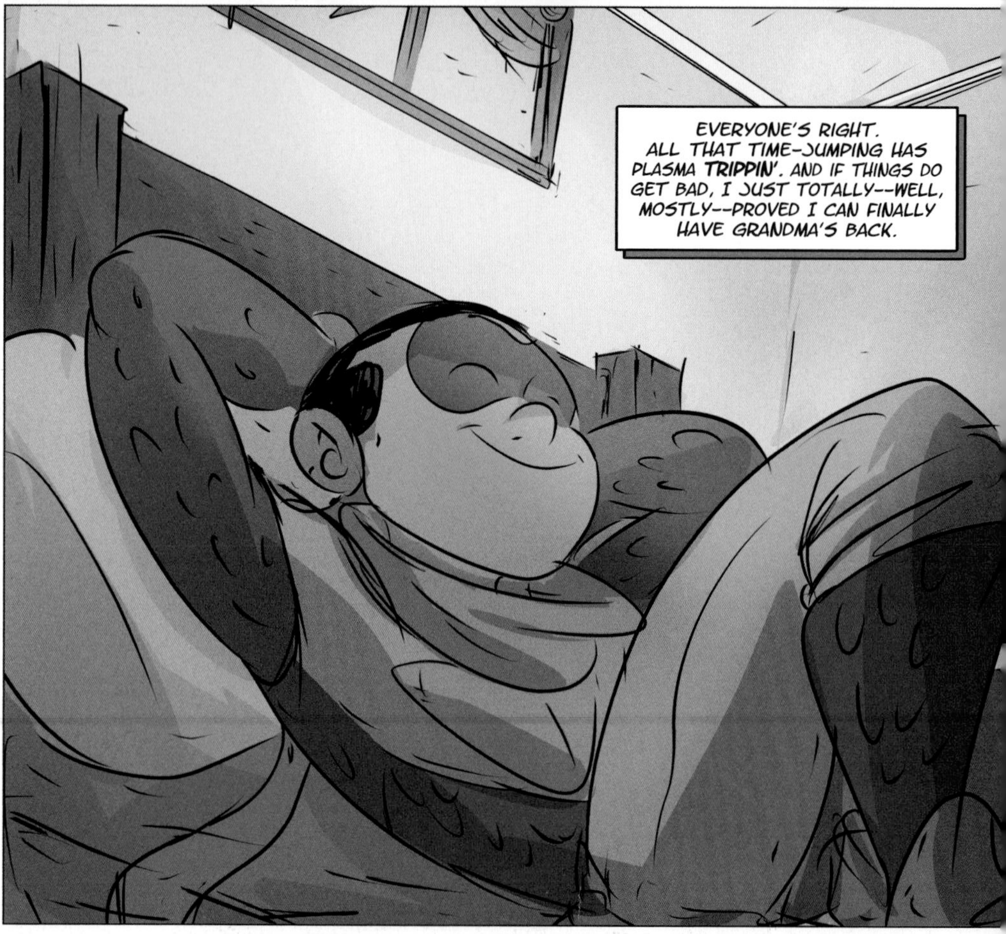
EVERYONE'S RIGHT. ALL THAT TIME-JUMPING HAS PLASMA **TRIPPIN'.** AND IF THINGS DO GET BAD, I JUST TOTALLY--WELL, MOSTLY--PROVED I CAN FINALLY HAVE GRANDMA'S BACK.

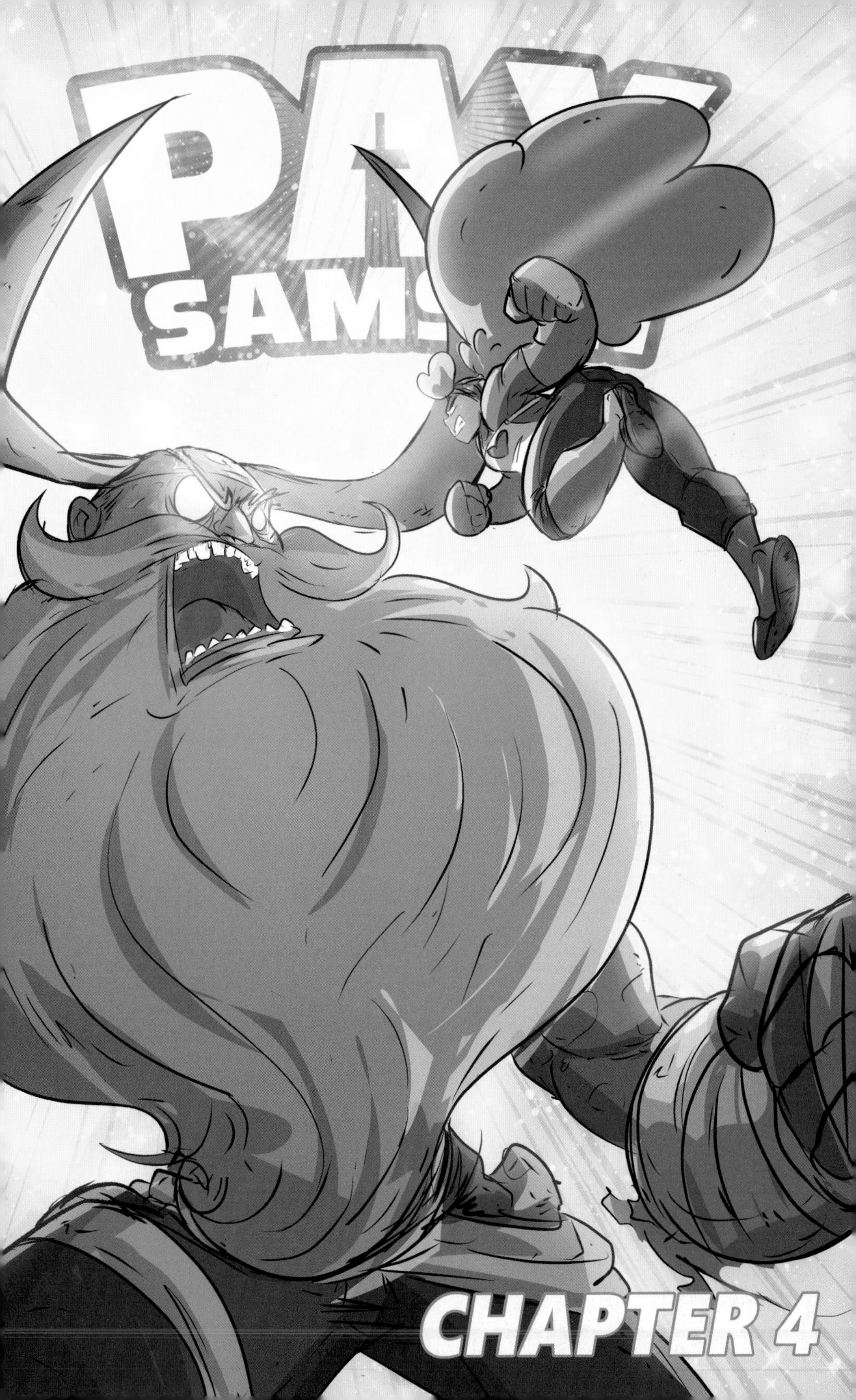
CHAPTER 4

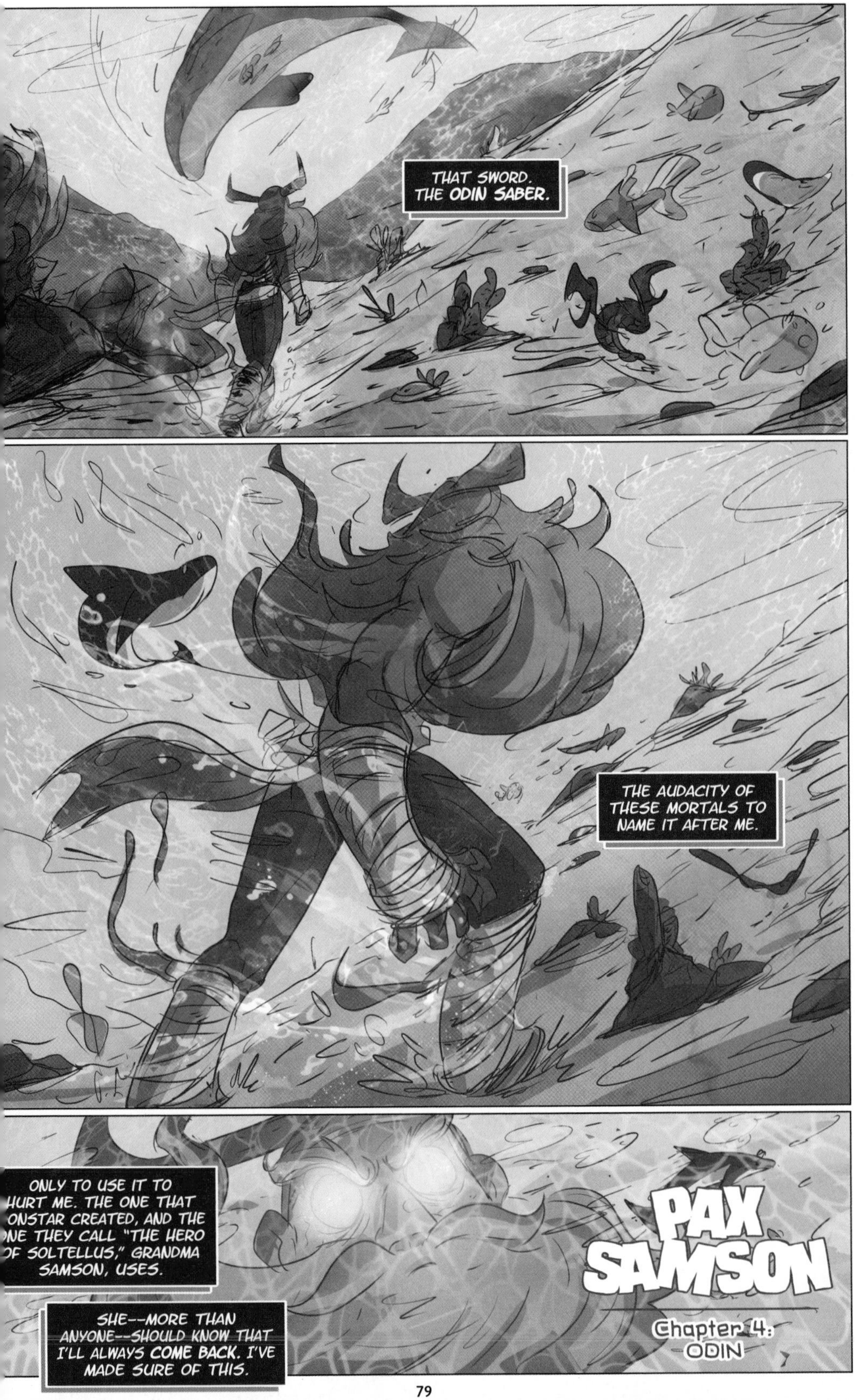
THAT SWORD. THE ODIN SABER.
THE AUDACITY OF THESE MORTALS TO NAME IT AFTER ME.
ONLY TO USE IT TO HURT ME. THE ONE THAT ONSTAR CREATED, AND THE ONE THEY CALL "THE HERO OF SOLTELLUS," GRANDMA SAMSON, USES.
SHE--MORE THAN ANYONE--SHOULD KNOW THAT I'LL ALWAYS COME BACK. I'VE MADE SURE OF THIS.
PAX SAMSON
Chapter 4: ODIN

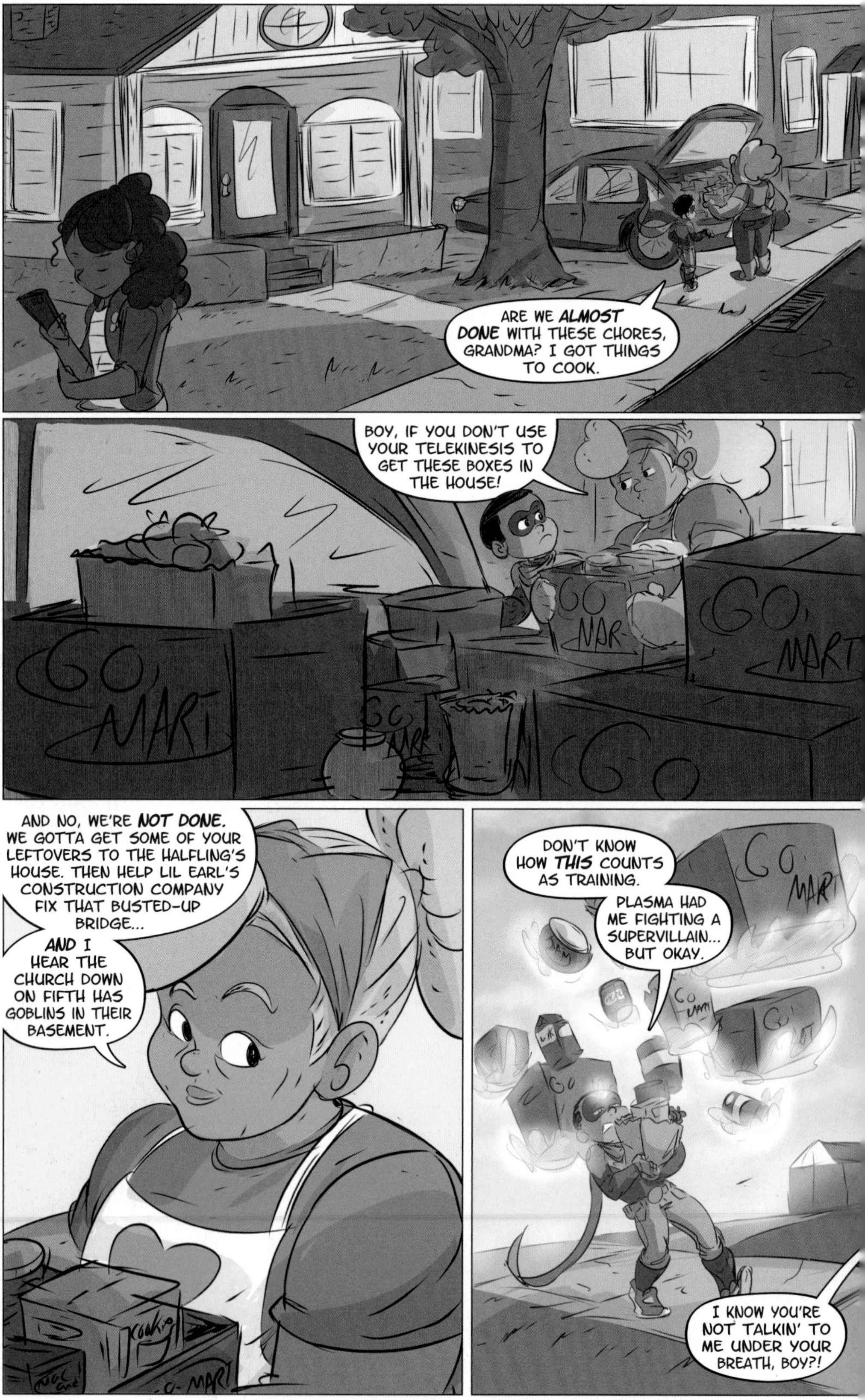

ARE WE **ALMOST DONE** WITH THESE CHORES, GRANDMA? I GOT THINGS TO COOK.
BOY, IF YOU DON'T USE YOUR TELEKINESIS TO GET THESE BOXES IN THE HOUSE!
GO MART
AND NO, WE'RE **NOT DONE.** WE GOTTA GET SOME OF YOUR LEFTOVERS TO THE HALFLING'S HOUSE. THEN HELP LIL EARL'S CONSTRUCTION COMPANY FIX THAT BUSTED-UP BRIDGE...
AND I HEAR THE CHURCH DOWN ON FIFTH HAS GOBLINS IN THEIR BASEMENT.
DON'T KNOW HOW **THIS** COUNTS AS TRAINING.
PLASMA HAD ME FIGHTING A SUPERVILLAIN... BUT OKAY.
I KNOW YOU'RE NOT TALKIN' TO ME UNDER YOUR BREATH, BOY?!

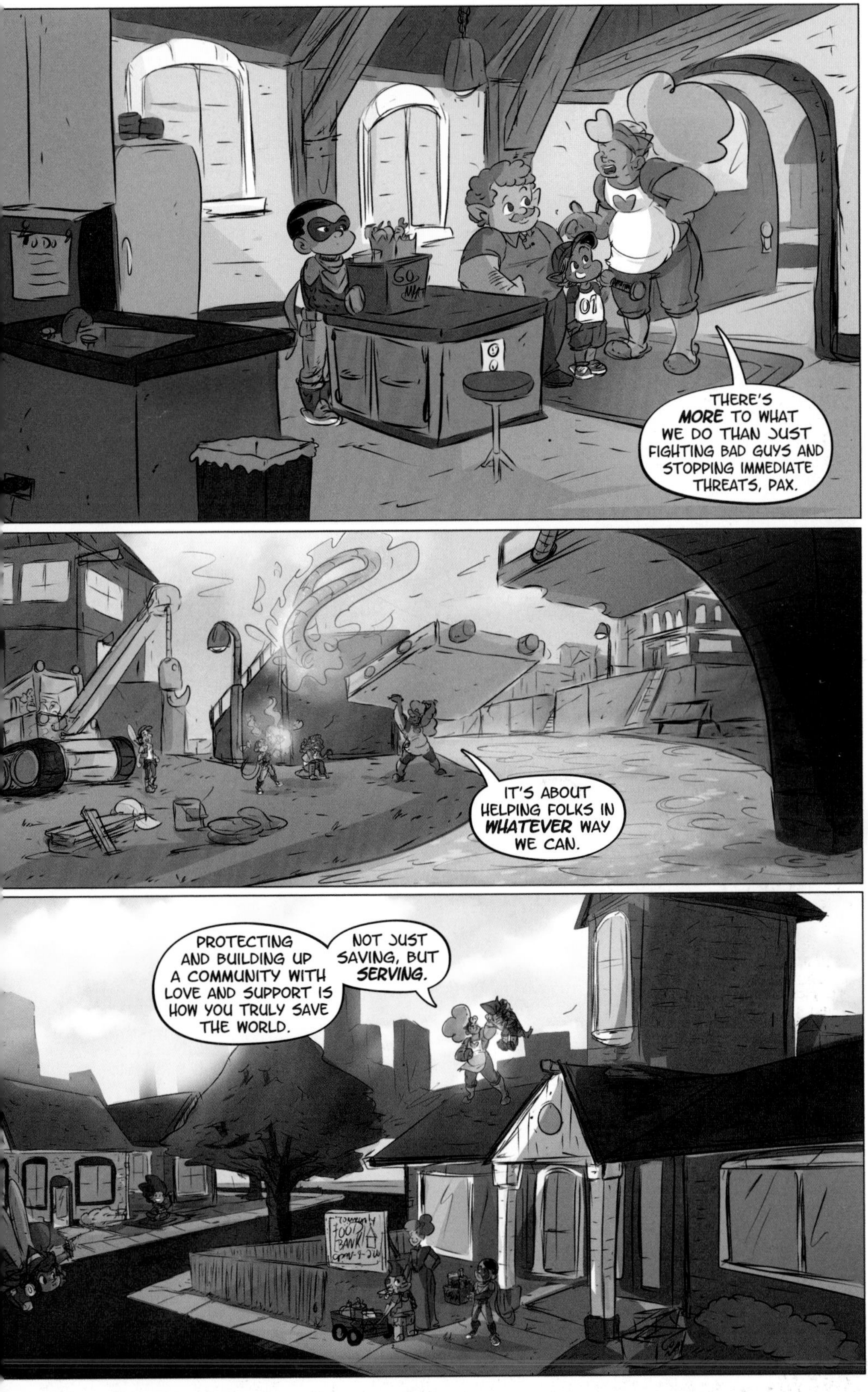
THERE'S MORE TO WHAT WE DO THAN JUST FIGHTING BAD GUYS AND STOPPING IMMEDIATE THREATS, PAX.
IT'S ABOUT HELPING FOLKS IN WHATEVER WAY WE CAN.
PROTECTING AND BUILDING UP A COMMUNITY WITH LOVE AND SUPPORT IS HOW YOU TRULY SAVE THE WORLD.
NOT JUST SAVING, BUT SERVING.

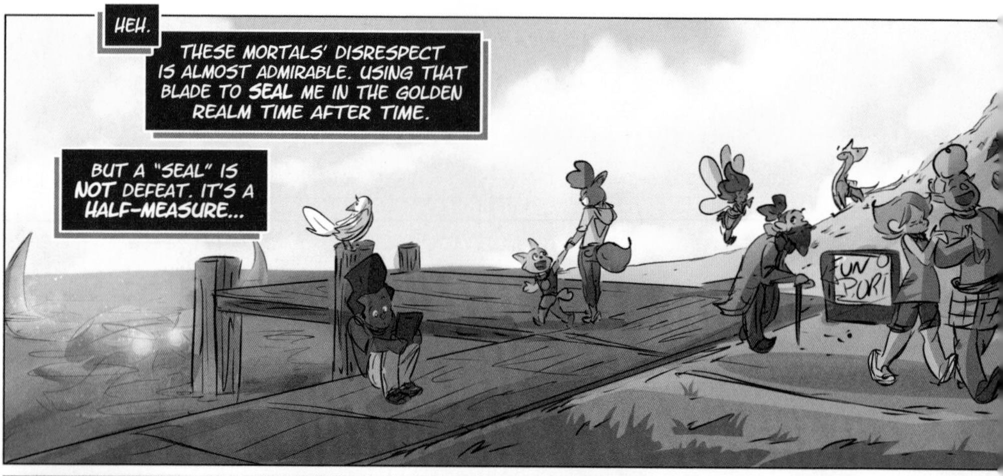
HEH.
THESE MORTALS' DISRESPECT IS ALMOST ADMIRABLE. USING THAT BLADE TO SEAL ME IN THE GOLDEN REALM TIME AFTER TIME.
BUT A "SEAL" IS NOT DEFEAT. IT'S A HALF-MEASURE...

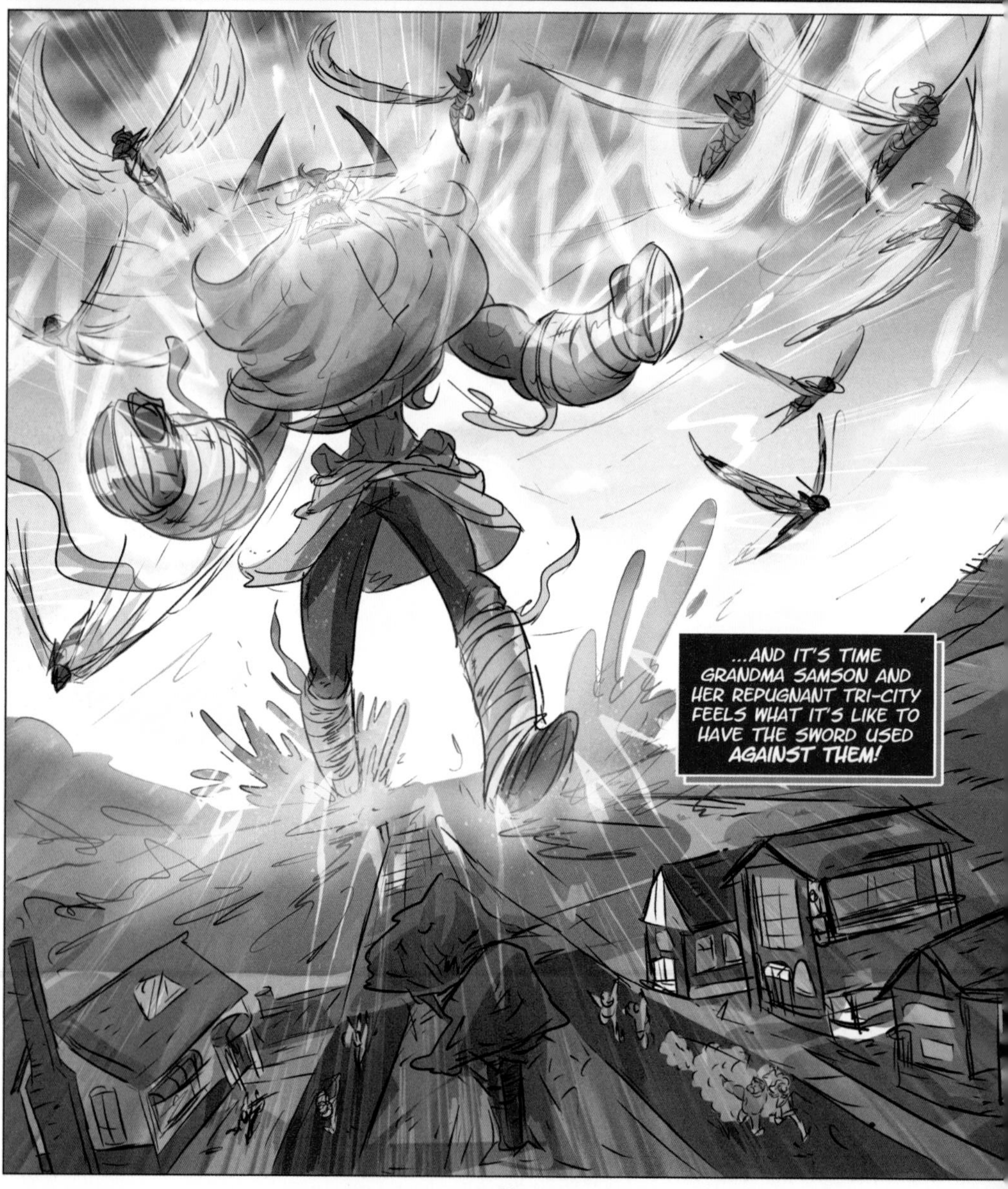
...AND IT'S TIME GRANDMA SAMSON AND HER REPUGNANT TRI-CITY FEELS WHAT IT'S LIKE TO HAVE THE SWORD USED AGAINST THEM!

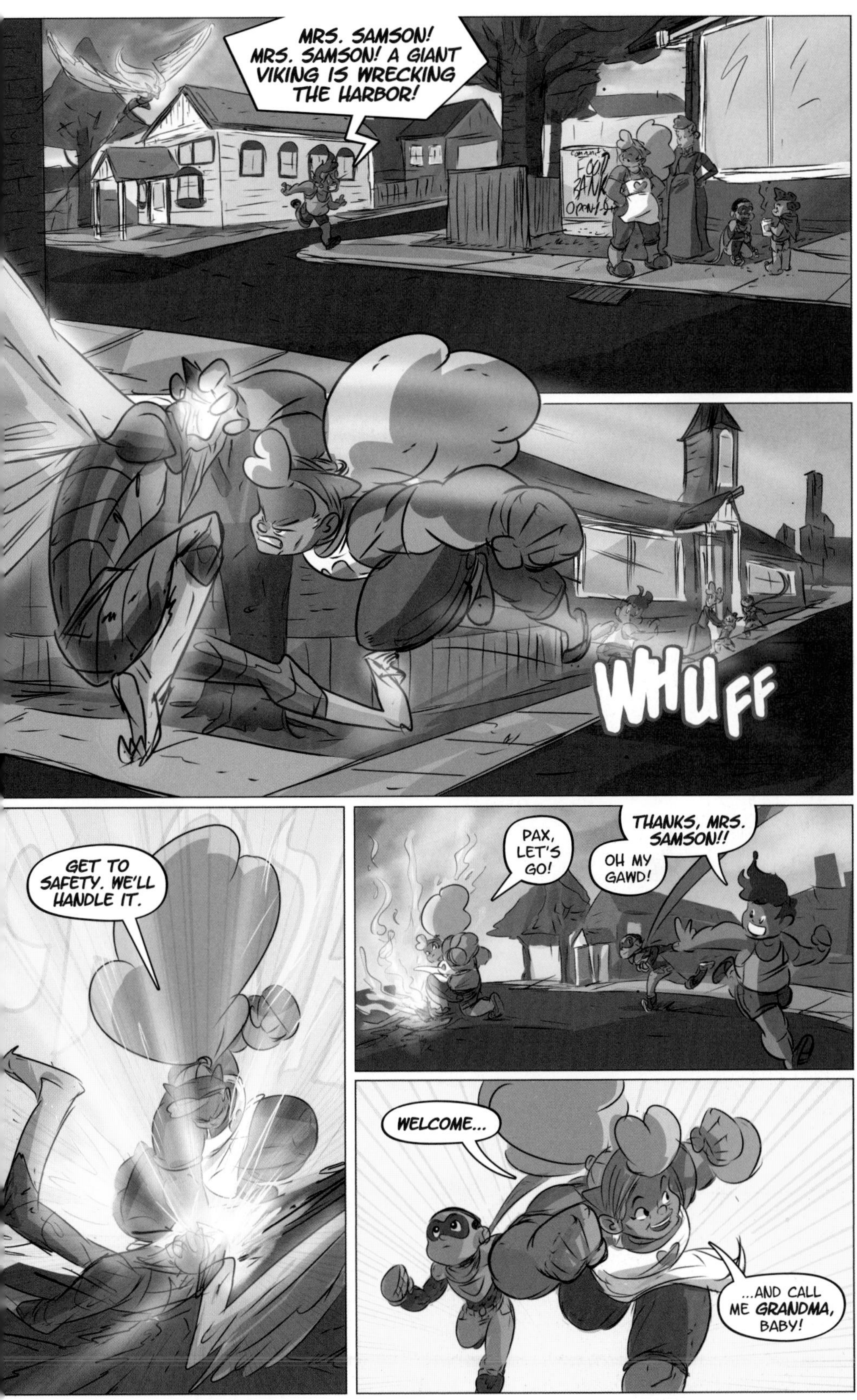
MRS. SAMSON! MRS. SAMSON! A GIANT VIKING IS WRECKING THE HARBOR!
WHUFF
GET TO SAFETY. WE'LL HANDLE IT.
PAX, LET'S GO!
THANKS, MRS. SAMSON!!
OH MY GAWD!
WELCOME...
...AND CALL ME GRANDMA, BABY!

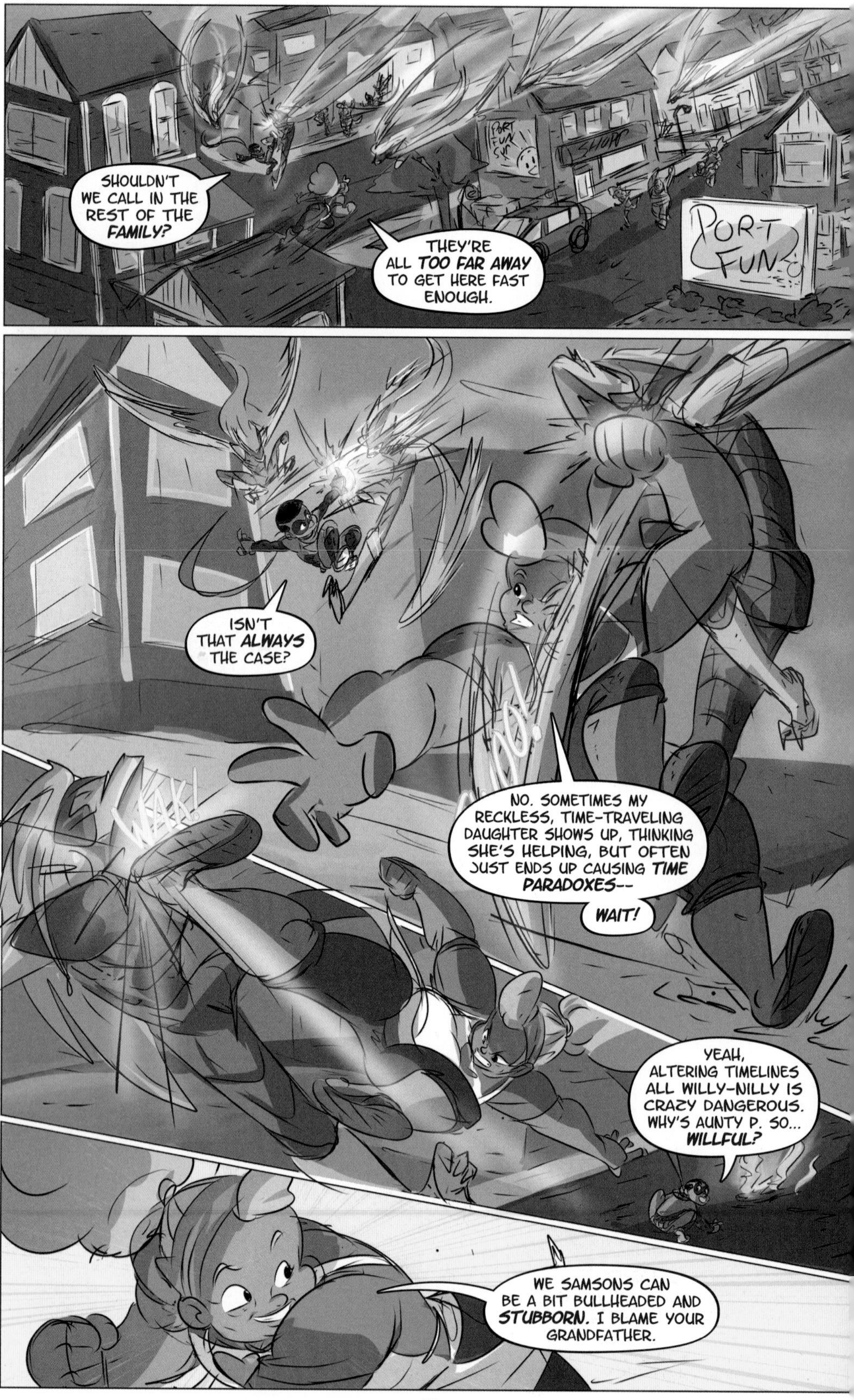
SHOULDN'T WE CALL IN THE REST OF THE FAMILY?
THEY'RE ALL TOO FAR AWAY TO GET HERE FAST ENOUGH.
ISN'T THAT ALWAYS THE CASE?
WAK!
NO. SOMETIMES MY RECKLESS, TIME-TRAVELING DAUGHTER SHOWS UP, THINKING SHE'S HELPING, BUT OFTEN JUST ENDS UP CAUSING TIME PARADOXES--
WAIT!
YEAH, ALTERING TIMELINES ALL WILLY-NILLY IS CRAZY DANGEROUS. WHY'S AUNTY P. SO... WILLFUL?
WE SAMSONS CAN BE A BIT BULLHEADED AND STUBBORN. I BLAME YOUR GRANDFATHER.

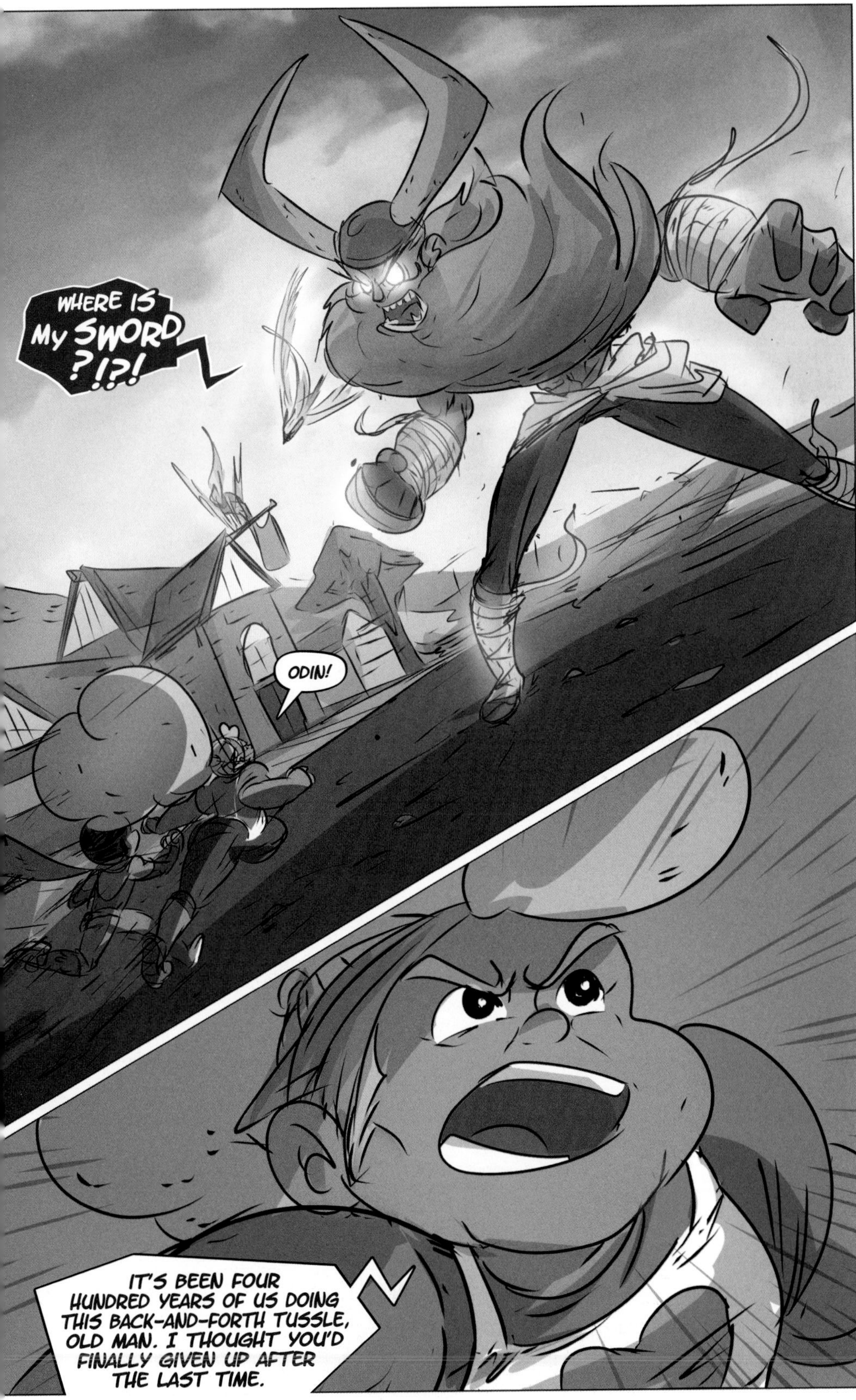
WHERE IS MY SWORD ?!?!
ODIN!
IT'S BEEN FOUR HUNDRED YEARS OF US DOING THIS BACK-AND-FORTH TUSSLE, OLD MAN. I THOUGHT YOU'D FINALLY GIVEN UP AFTER THE LAST TIME.

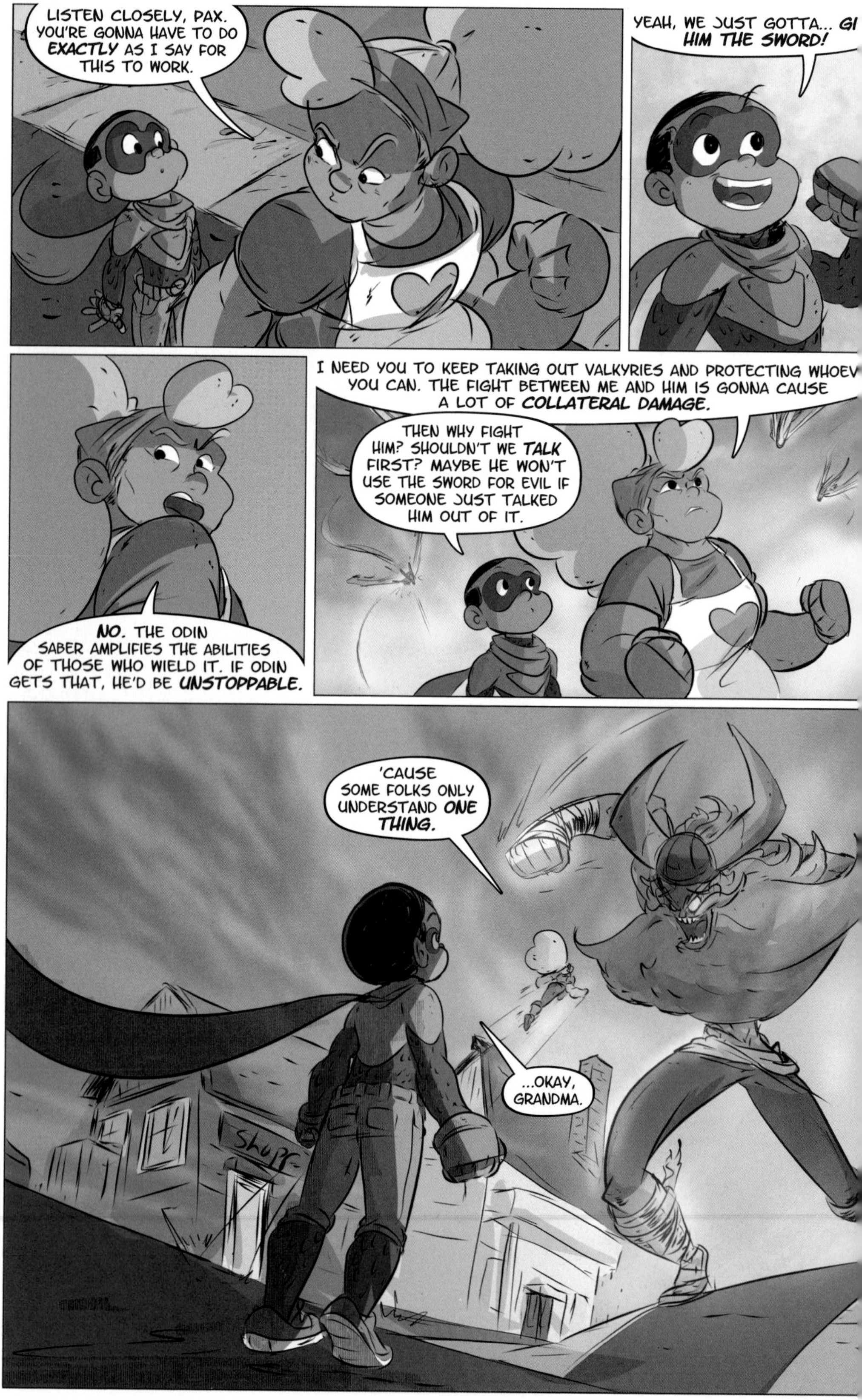
LISTEN CLOSELY, PAX. YOU'RE GONNA HAVE TO DO **EXACTLY** AS I SAY FOR THIS TO WORK.
YEAH, WE JUST GOTTA... **GI HIM THE SWORD!**
NO. THE ODIN SABER AMPLIFIES THE ABILITIES OF THOSE WHO WIELD IT. IF ODIN GETS THAT, HE'D BE **UNSTOPPABLE.**
I NEED YOU TO KEEP TAKING OUT VALKYRIES AND PROTECTING WHOEV YOU CAN. THE FIGHT BETWEEN ME AND HIM IS GONNA CAUSE A LOT OF **COLLATERAL DAMAGE.**
THEN WHY FIGHT HIM? SHOULDN'T WE **TALK** FIRST? MAYBE HE WON'T USE THE SWORD FOR EVIL IF SOMEONE JUST TALKED HIM OUT OF IT.
'CAUSE SOME FOLKS ONLY UNDERSTAND **ONE THING.**
...OKAY, GRANDMA.
SHOPP

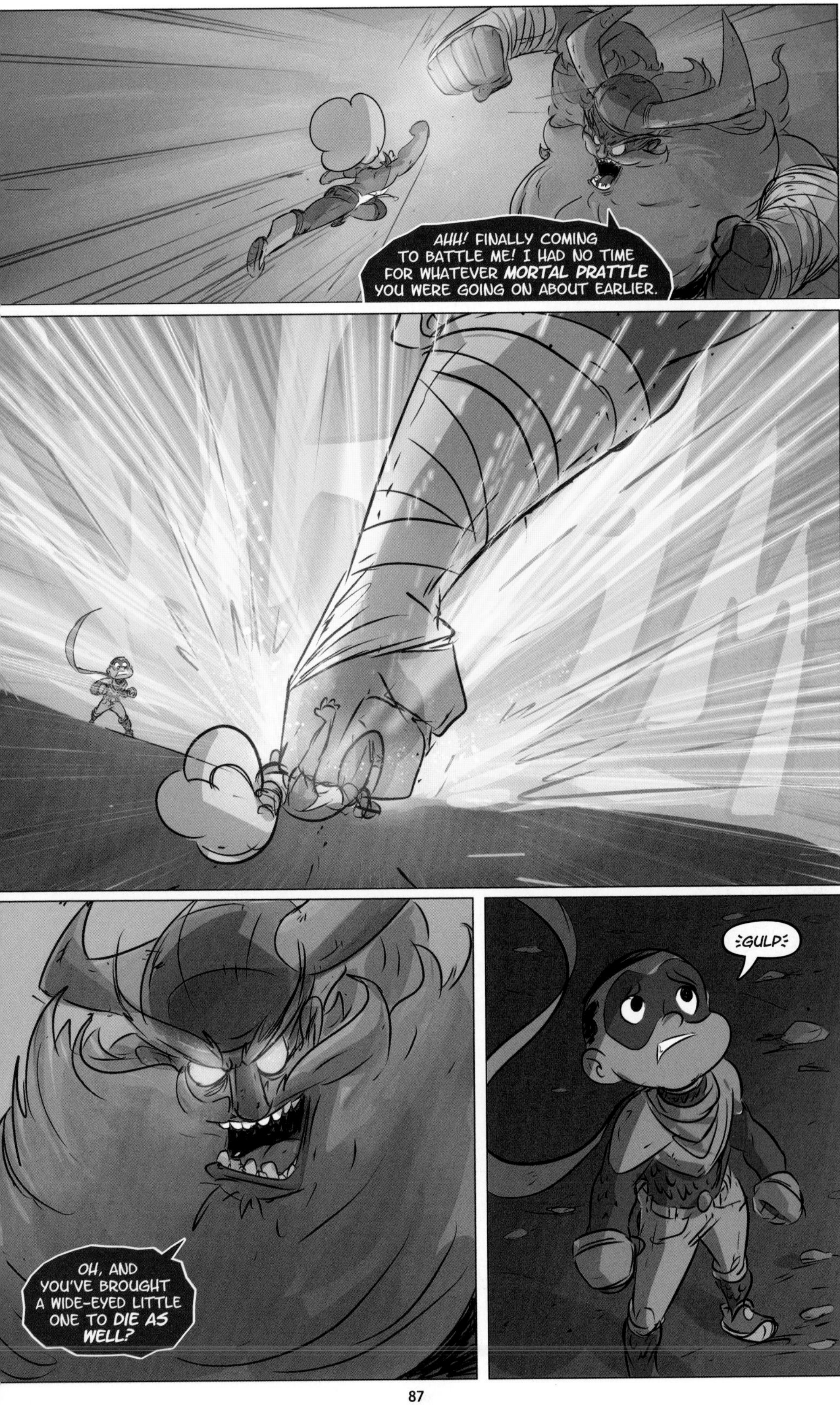
AHH! FINALLY COMING TO BATTLE ME! I HAD NO TIME FOR WHATEVER MORTAL PRATTLE YOU WERE GOING ON ABOUT EARLIER.
OH, AND YOU'VE BROUGHT A WIDE-EYED LITTLE ONE TO DIE AS WELL?
GULP

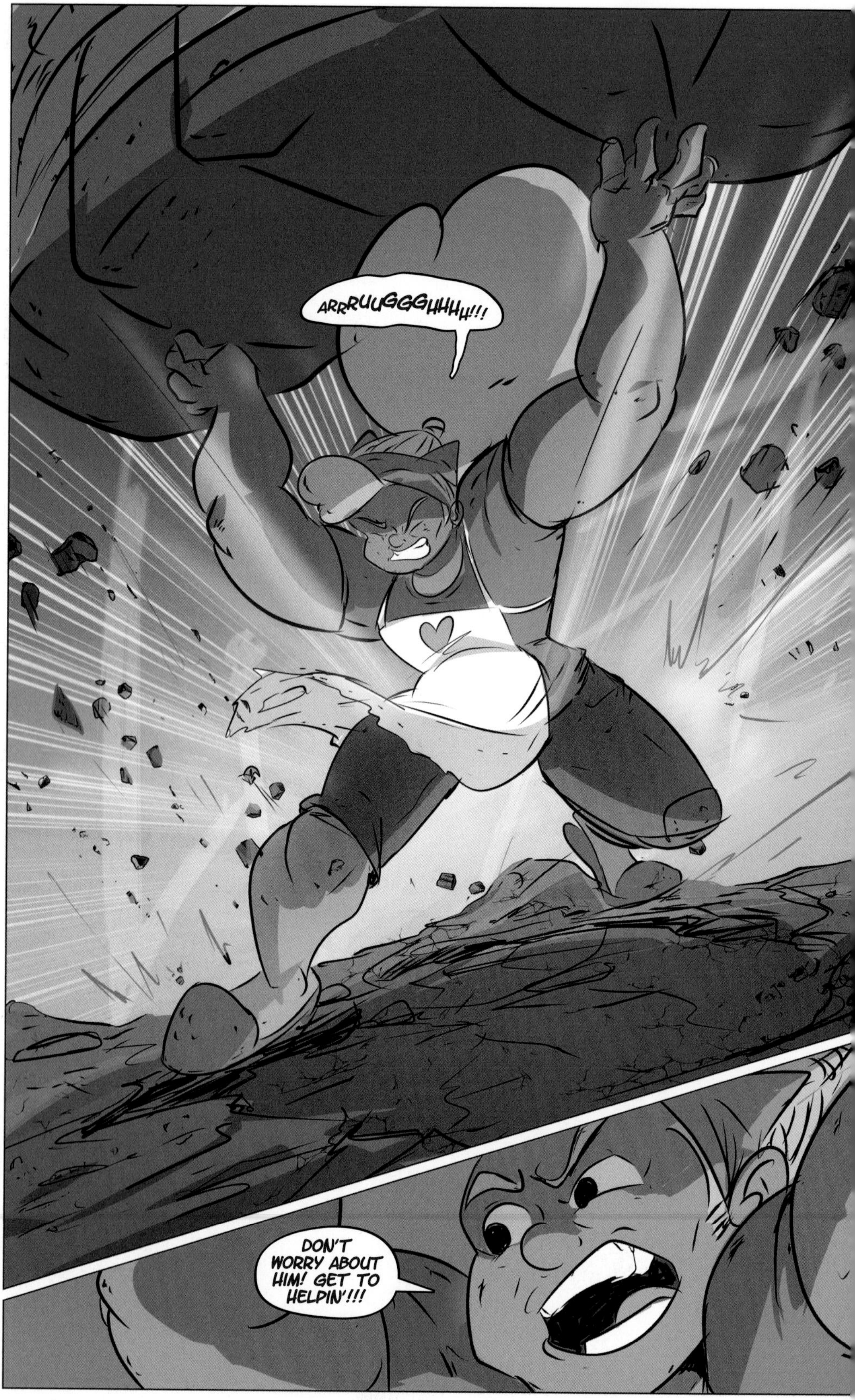
ARRRUUGGGHHHH!!!
DON'T WORRY ABOUT HIM! GET TO HELPIN'!!!

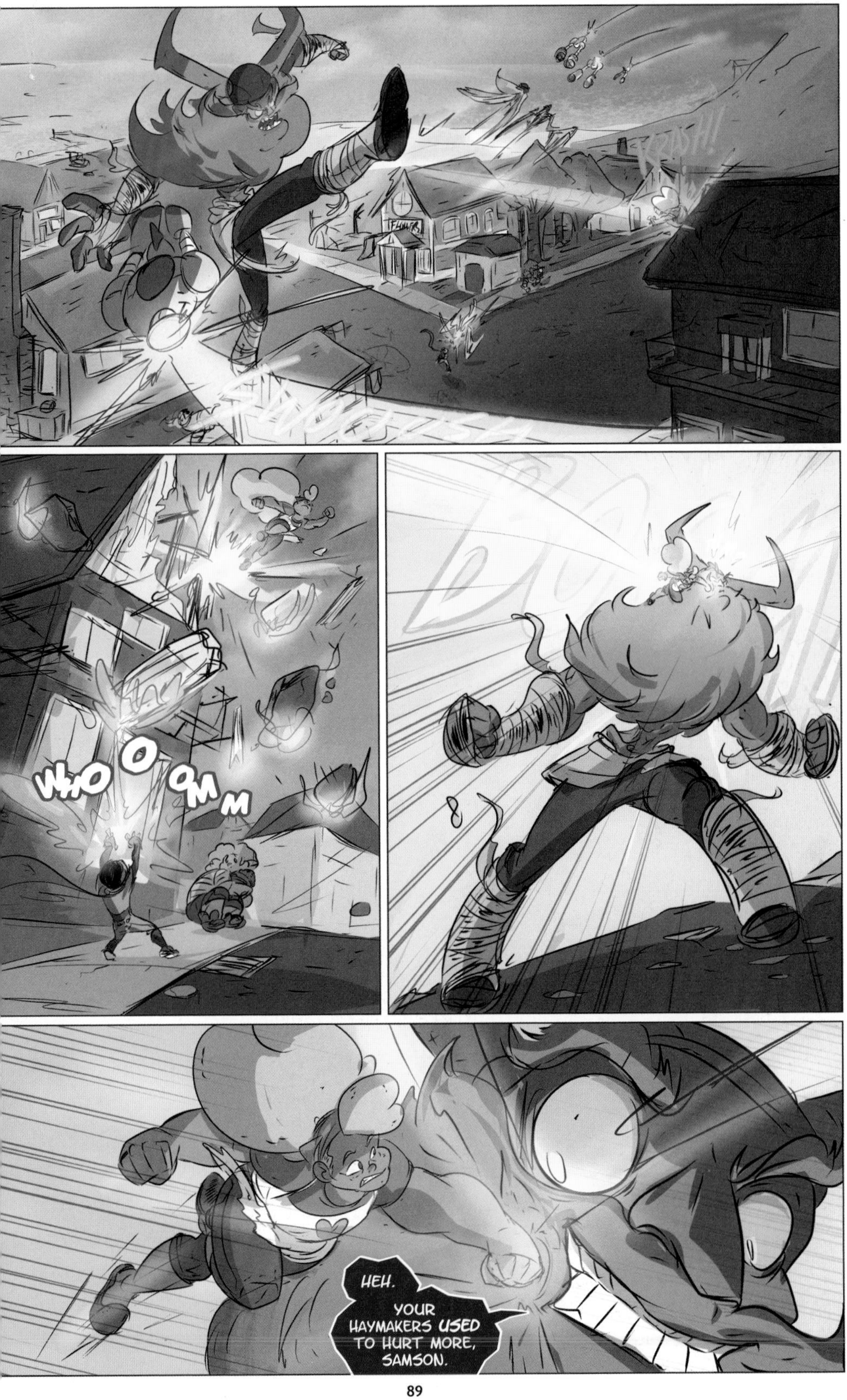
KRASH!
SWOOOSH
WHOOOMM
HEH.
YOUR HAYMAKERS USED TO HURT MORE, SAMSON.

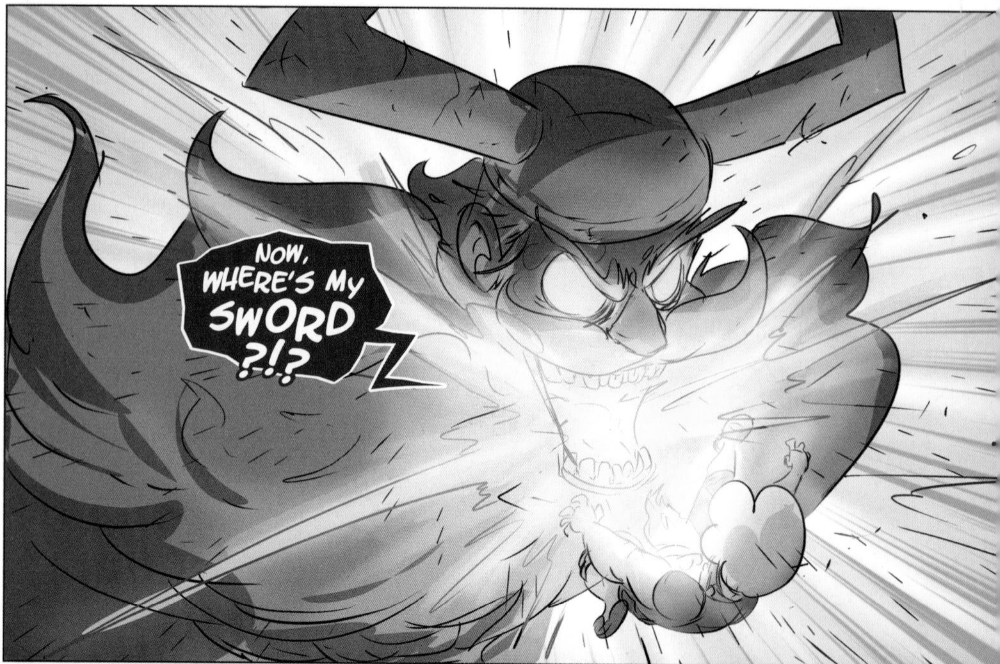
NOW, WHERE'S MY SWORD ?!?

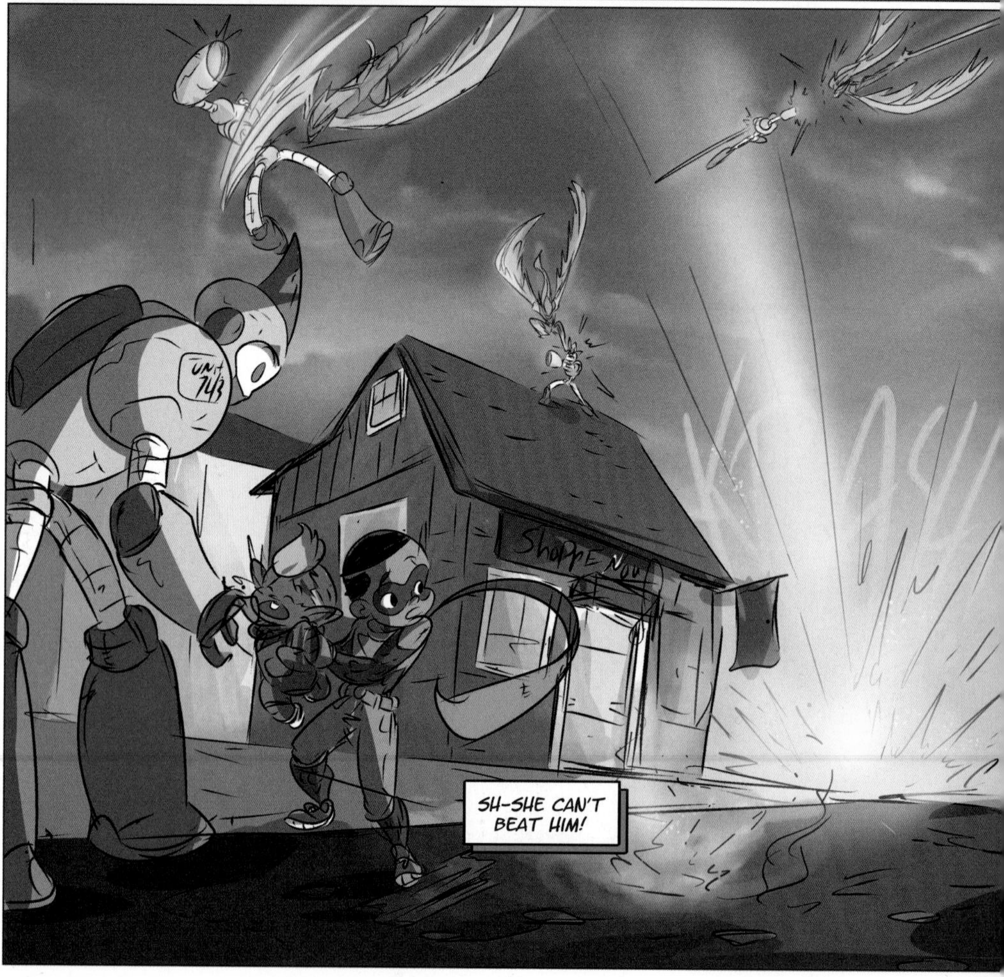
SH-SHE CAN'T BEAT HIM!

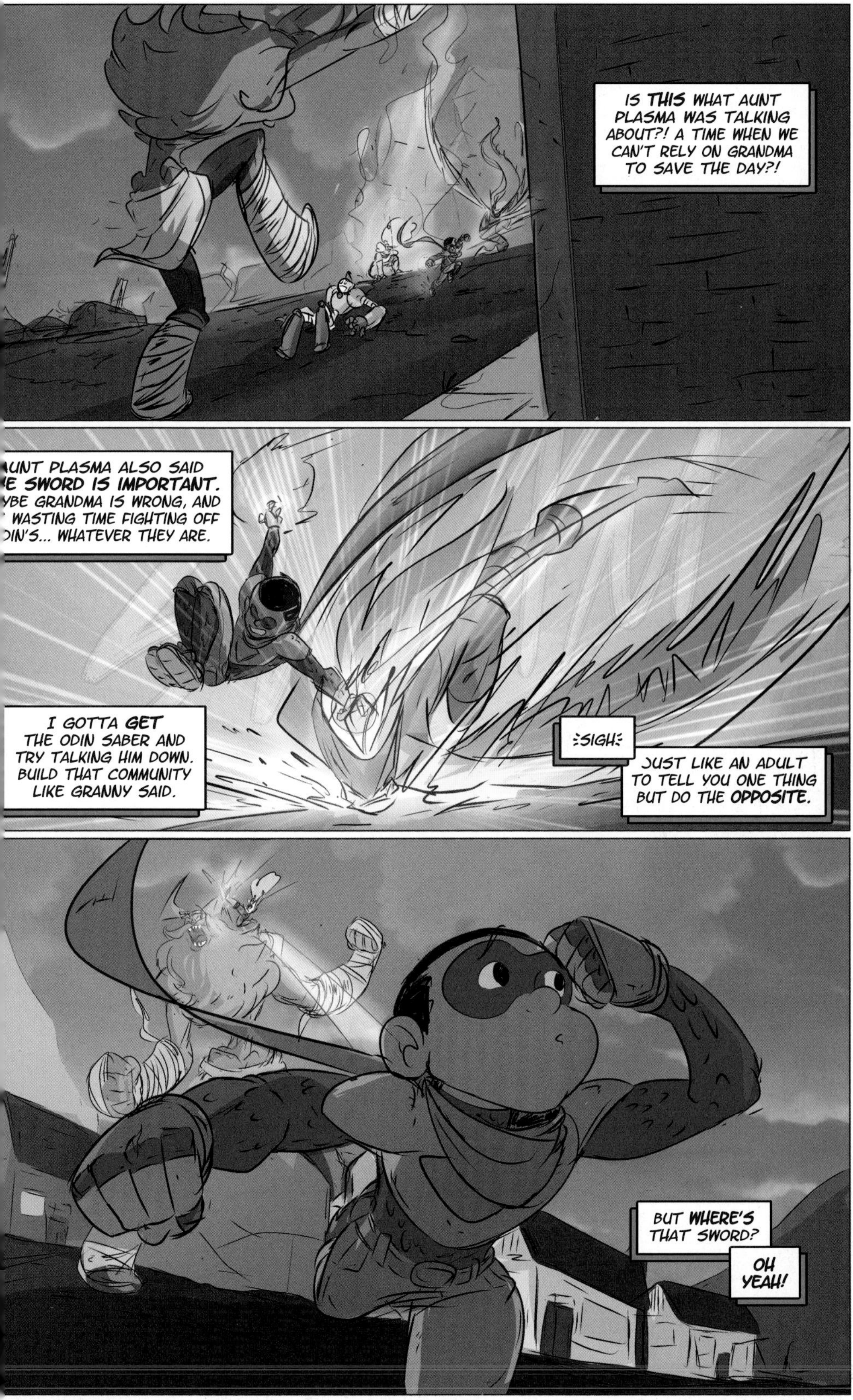

IS THIS WHAT AUNT PLASMA WAS TALKING ABOUT?! A TIME WHEN WE CAN'T RELY ON GRANDMA TO SAVE THE DAY?!
AUNT PLASMA ALSO SAID E SWORD IS IMPORTANT. YBE GRANDMA IS WRONG, AND WASTING TIME FIGHTING OFF DIN'S... WHATEVER THEY ARE.
I GOTTA GET THE ODIN SABER AND TRY TALKING HIM DOWN. BUILD THAT COMMUNITY LIKE GRANNY SAID.
SIGH
JUST LIKE AN ADULT TO TELL YOU ONE THING BUT DO THE OPPOSITE.
BUT WHERE'S THAT SWORD?
OH YEAH!

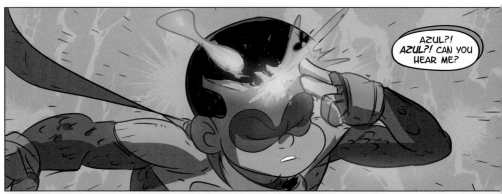

AZUL?! AZUL?! CAN YOU HEAR ME?

YES, MY FRIEND, I CAN. I KNOW ABOUT THE CHAOS. MORE GUARDS ARE ON THE WAY.

SOUNDS GOOD, BUT I GOT A PLAN. I THINK WE SHOULD *GIVE* ODIN THE SWORD--

WHAT?! IT'S A RELIC A AN HEIRLOOM OF MY PEOP LIONSTAR CREATED I TO DEFEAT HIM!!!

YOU DON'T SEE THE *DESTRUCTION* HE'S CAUSING!

THE ANSWER ISN' MORE VIOLEN MAYBE GIVING TO HIM WILL E ALL THIS?!

MY AUNTY PLASMA SAID THE SWORD IS IMPORTANT.

WELL, SHE HAS BEEN TO THE FUTURE...

THIS SEEMS LIKE IT COULD BE A TERRIBLE IDEA, BUT I *TRUST* YOUR INSTINCTS, PAX.

YOU'RE BETTER AT THIS SUPERHERO STUFF THAN YOU THINK. LET'S DO IT.

AWESOME! MEET ME AT THE MUSEUM.

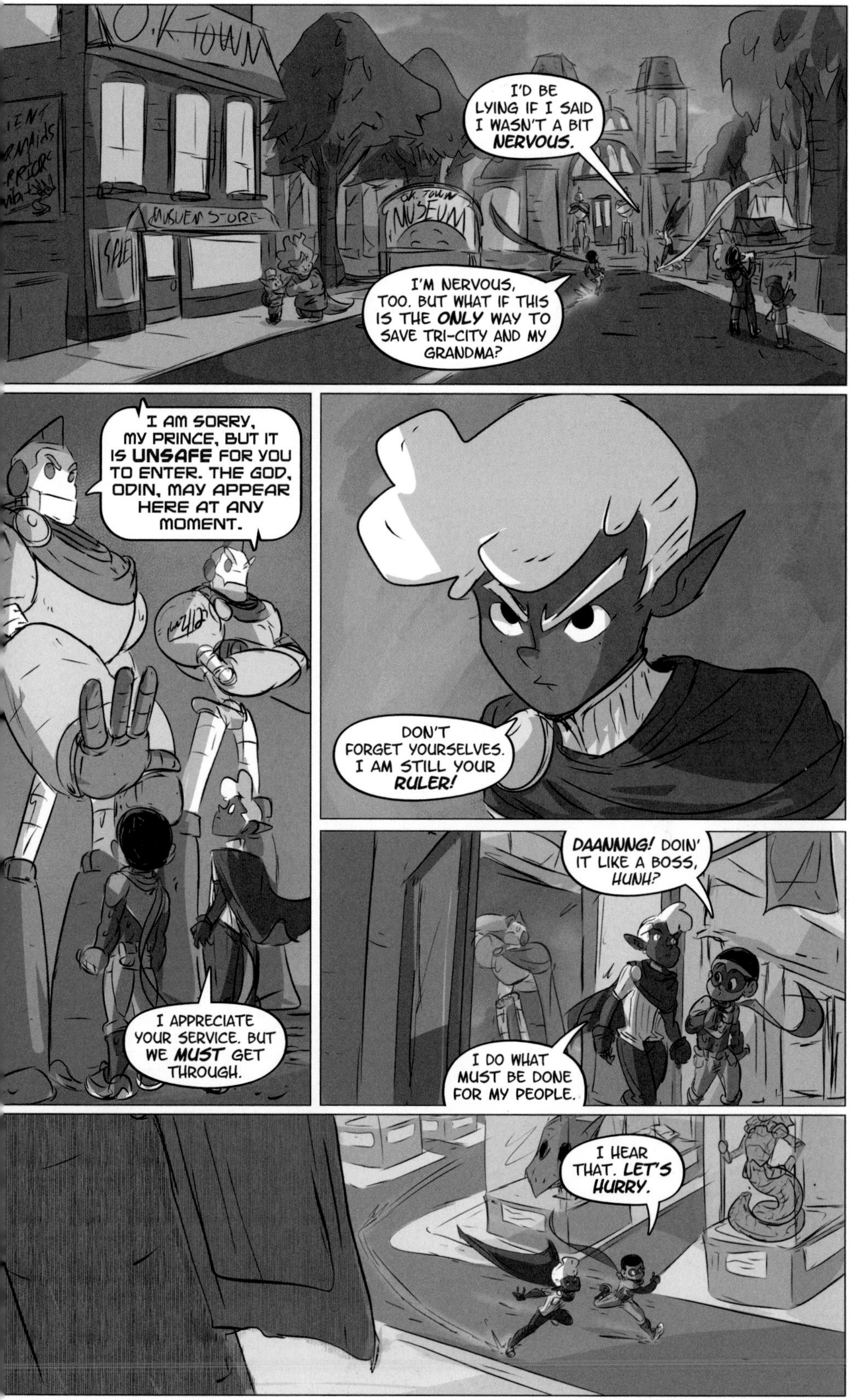
O.K. TOWN
MUSEUM
I'D BE LYING IF I SAID I WASN'T A BIT NERVOUS.
I'M NERVOUS, TOO. BUT WHAT IF THIS IS THE ONLY WAY TO SAVE TRI-CITY AND MY GRANDMA?
I AM SORRY, MY PRINCE, BUT IT IS UNSAFE FOR YOU TO ENTER. THE GOD, ODIN, MAY APPEAR HERE AT ANY MOMENT.
I APPRECIATE YOUR SERVICE. BUT WE MUST GET THROUGH.
DON'T FORGET YOURSELVES. I AM STILL YOUR RULER!
DAANNNG! DOIN' IT LIKE A BOSS, HUNH?
I DO WHAT MUST BE DONE FOR MY PEOPLE.
I HEAR THAT. LET'S HURRY.

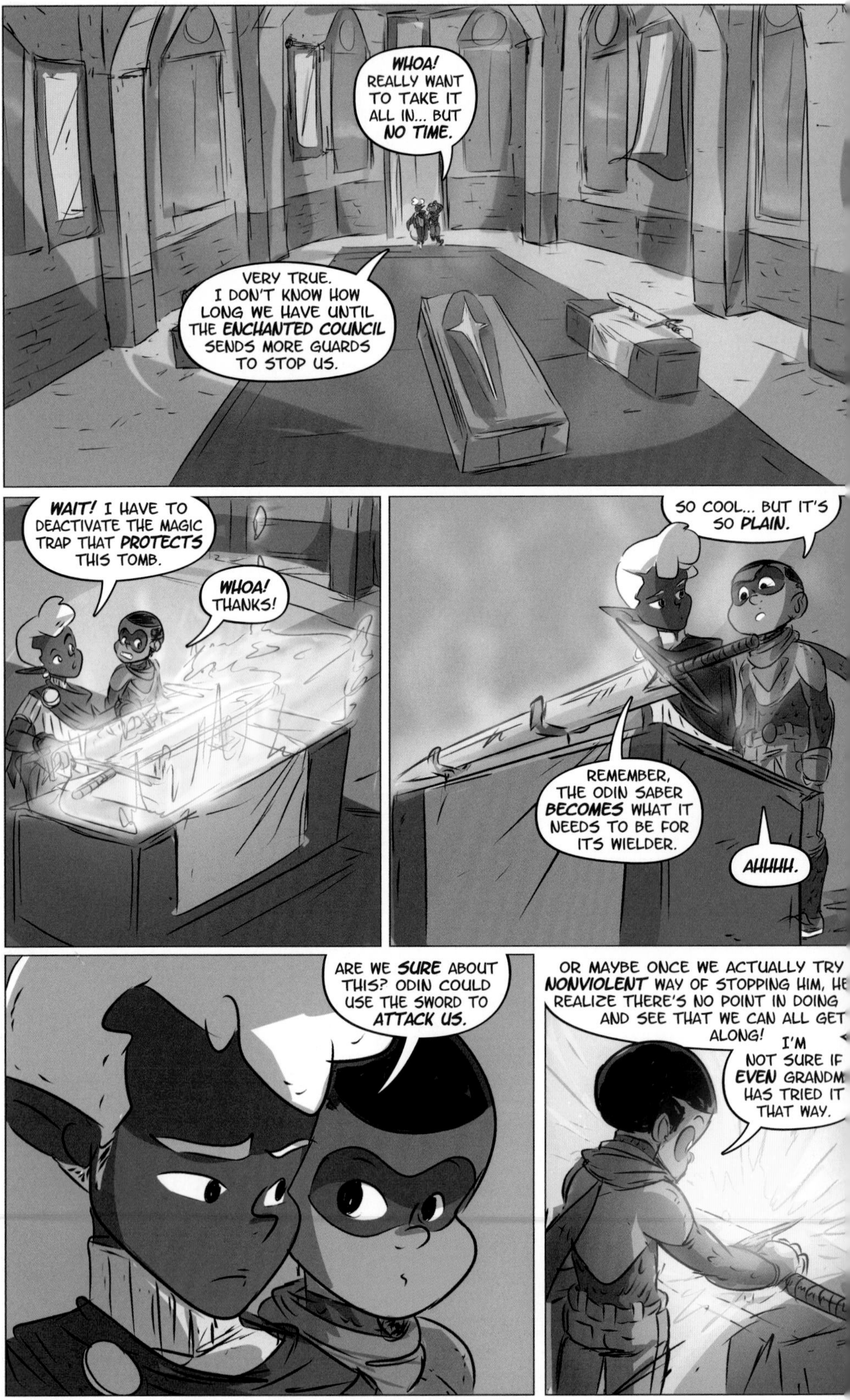
WHOA! REALLY WANT TO TAKE IT ALL IN... BUT NO TIME.
VERY TRUE. I DON'T KNOW HOW LONG WE HAVE UNTIL THE ENCHANTED COUNCIL SENDS MORE GUARDS TO STOP US.
WAIT! I HAVE TO DEACTIVATE THE MAGIC TRAP THAT PROTECTS THIS TOMB.
WHOA! THANKS!
SO COOL... BUT IT'S SO PLAIN.
REMEMBER, THE ODIN SABER BECOMES WHAT IT NEEDS TO BE FOR ITS WIELDER.
AHHHH.
ARE WE SURE ABOUT THIS? ODIN COULD USE THE SWORD TO ATTACK US.
OR MAYBE ONCE WE ACTUALLY TRY NONVIOLENT WAY OF STOPPING HIM, HE REALIZE THERE'S NO POINT IN DOING AND SEE THAT WE CAN ALL GET ALONG!
I'M NOT SURE IF EVEN GRANDM HAS TRIED IT THAT WAY.

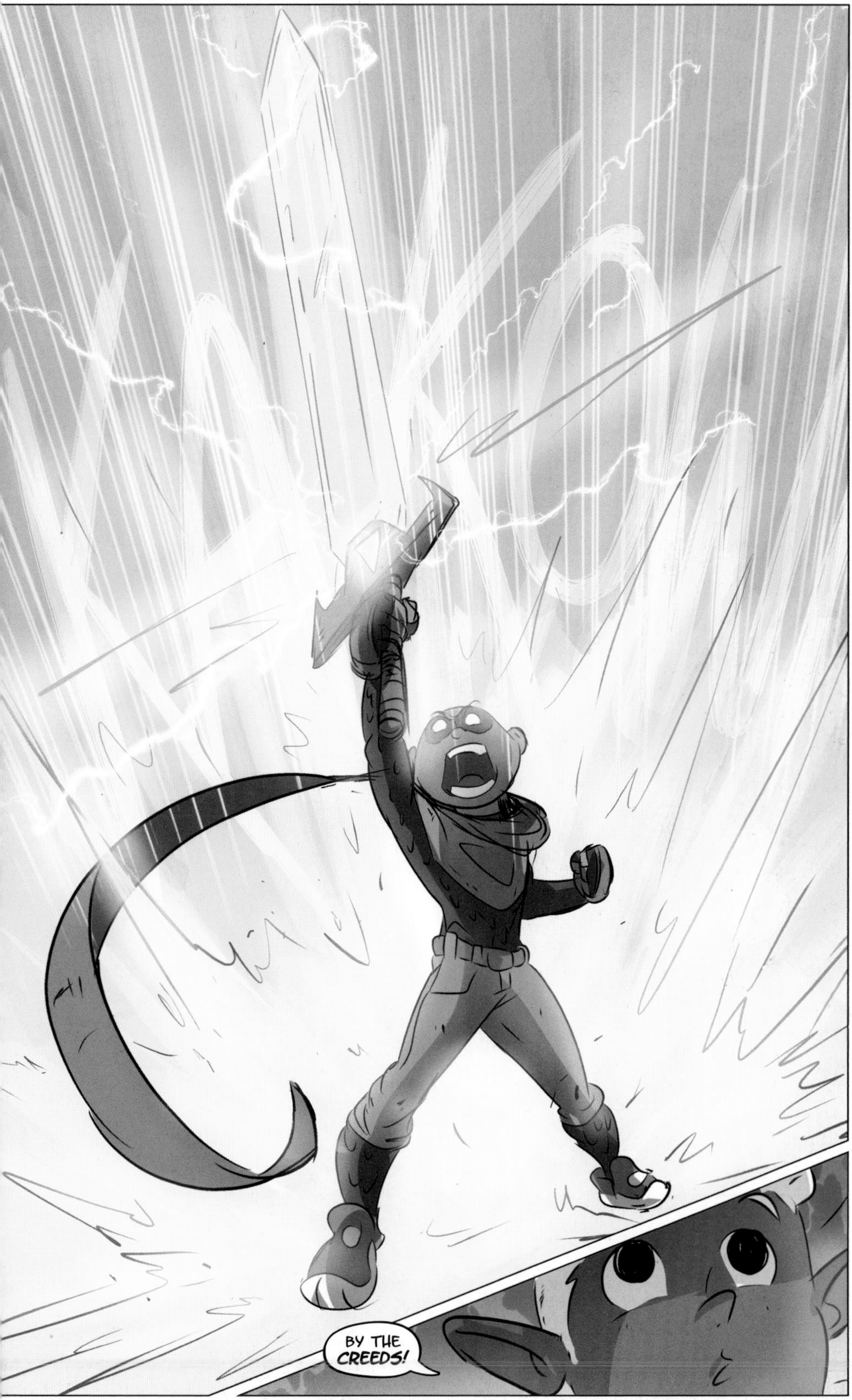
BY THE CREEDS!

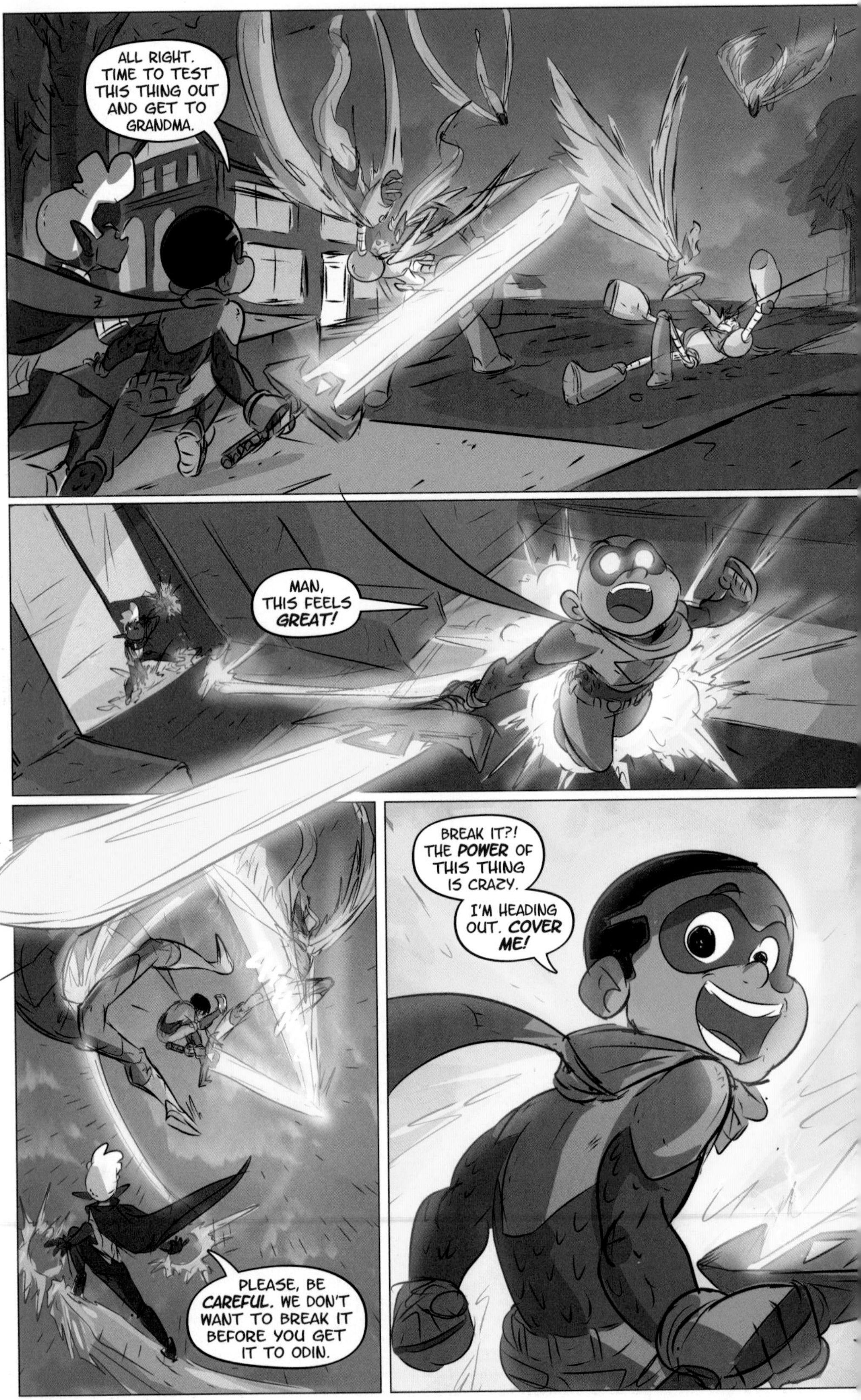
ALL RIGHT. TIME TO TEST THIS THING OUT AND GET TO GRANDMA.
MAN, THIS FEELS **GREAT!**
PLEASE, BE **CAREFUL.** WE DON'T WANT TO BREAK IT BEFORE YOU GET IT TO ODIN.
BREAK IT?! THE **POWER** OF THIS THING IS CRAZY.
I'M HEADING OUT. **COVER ME!**

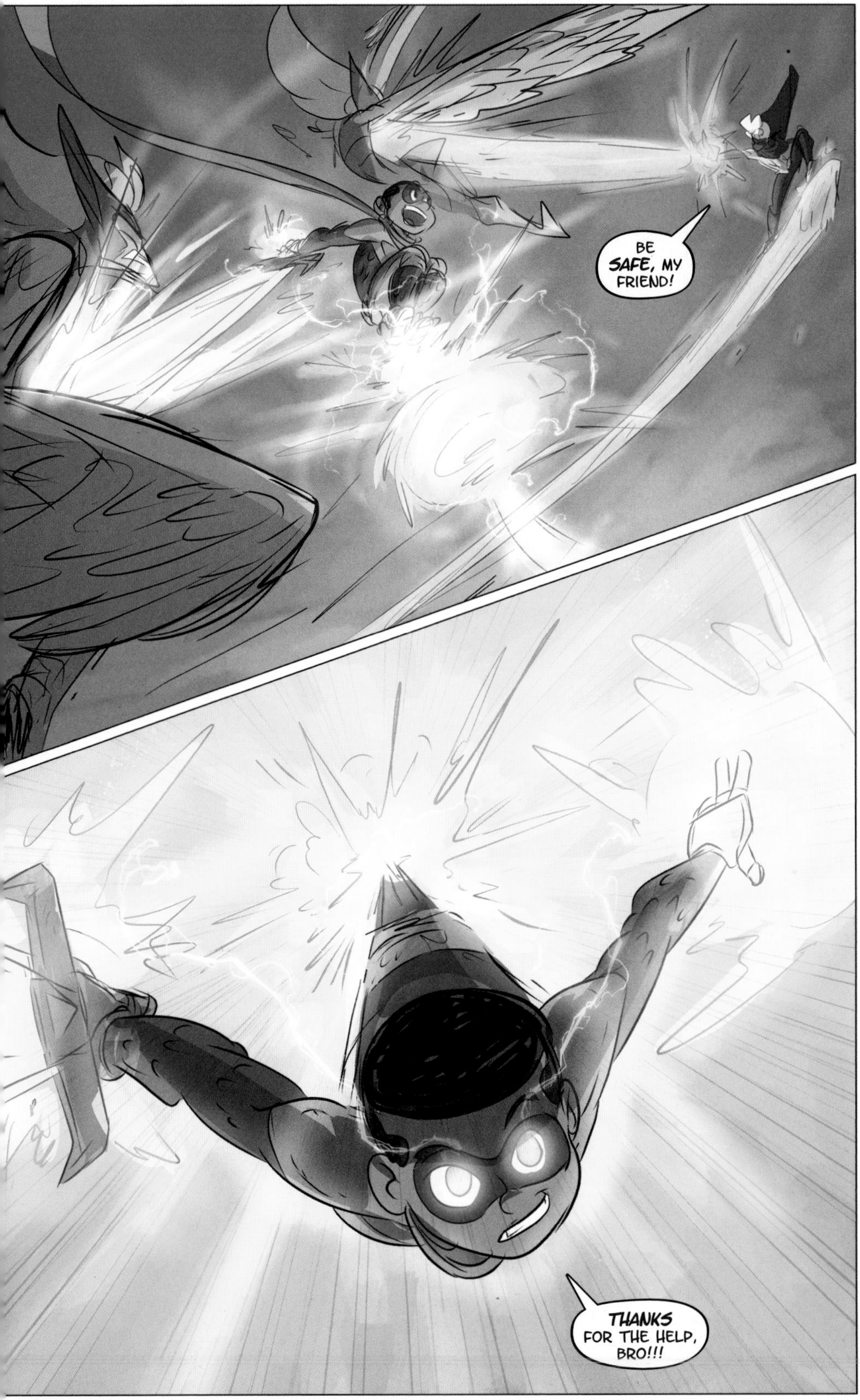

BE SAFE, MY FRIEND!
THANKS FOR THE HELP, BRO!!!

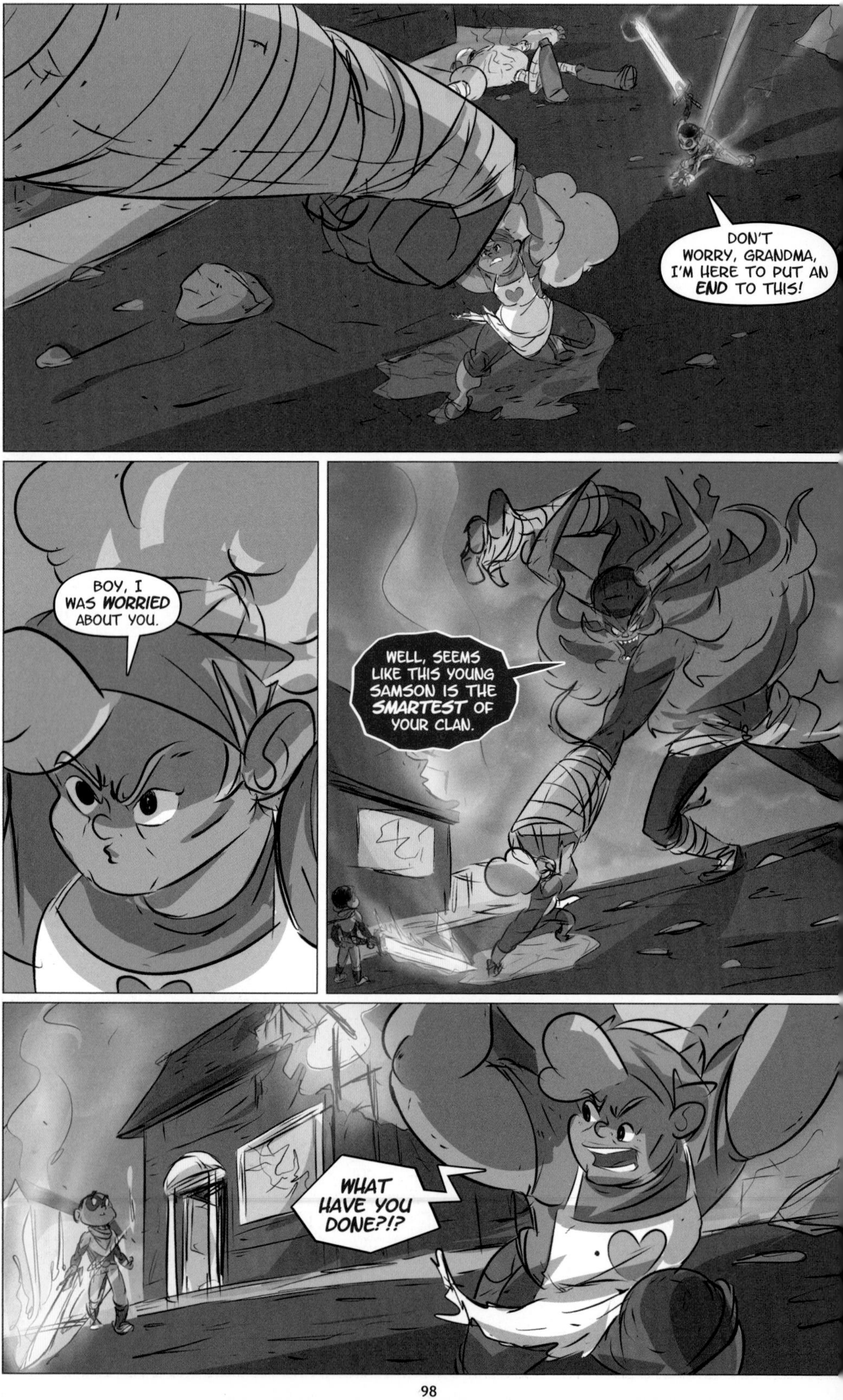
DON'T WORRY, GRANDMA, I'M HERE TO PUT AN END TO THIS!
BOY, I WAS WORRIED ABOUT YOU.
WELL, SEEMS LIKE THIS YOUNG SAMSON IS THE SMARTEST OF YOUR CLAN.
WHAT HAVE YOU DONE?!?

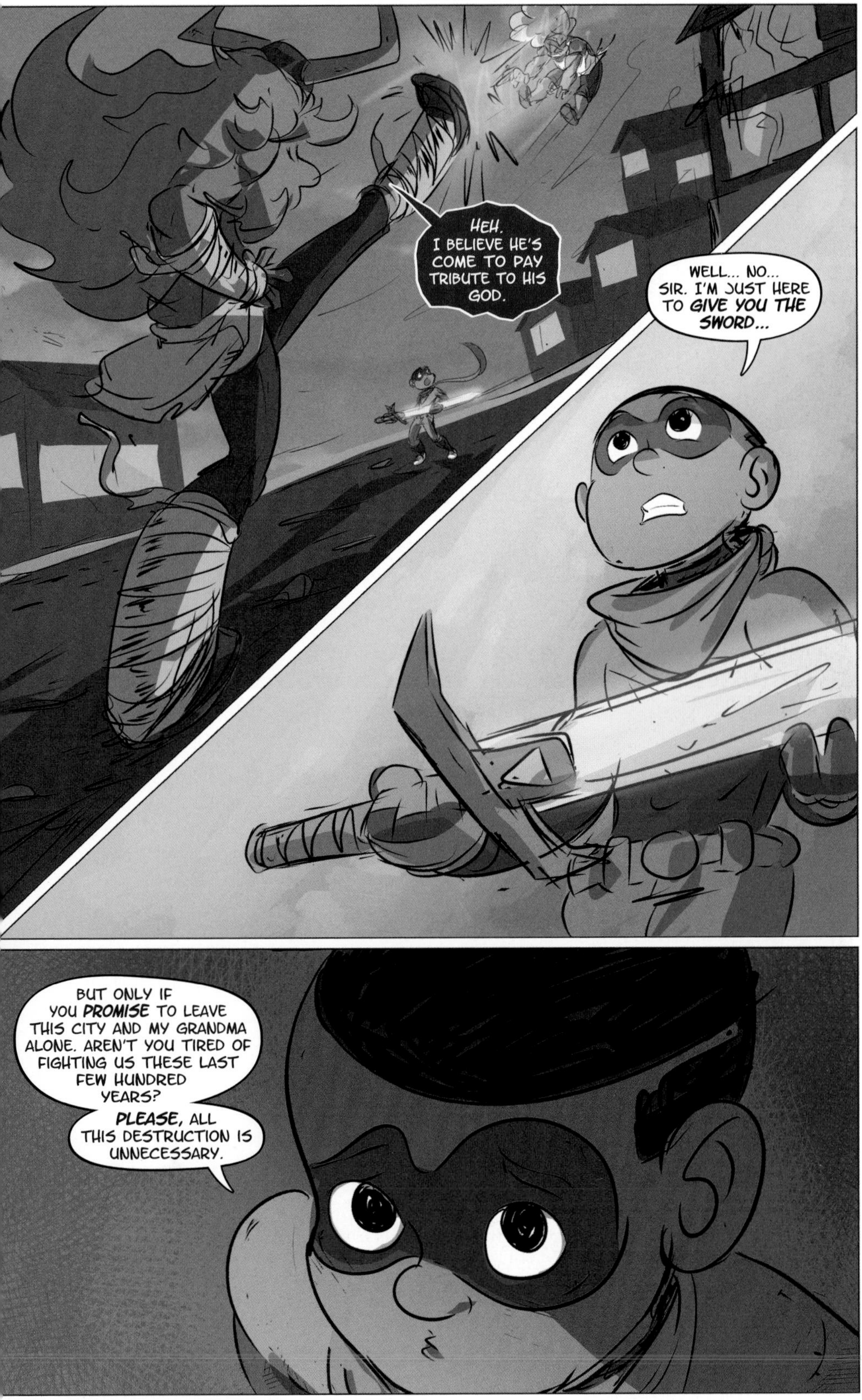
HEH. I BELIEVE HE'S COME TO PAY TRIBUTE TO HIS GOD.
WELL... NO... SIR. I'M JUST HERE TO **GIVE YOU THE SWORD...**
BUT ONLY IF YOU **PROMISE** TO LEAVE THIS CITY AND MY GRANDMA ALONE. AREN'T YOU TIRED OF FIGHTING US THESE LAST FEW HUNDRED YEARS?
PLEASE, ALL THIS DESTRUCTION IS UNNECESSARY.

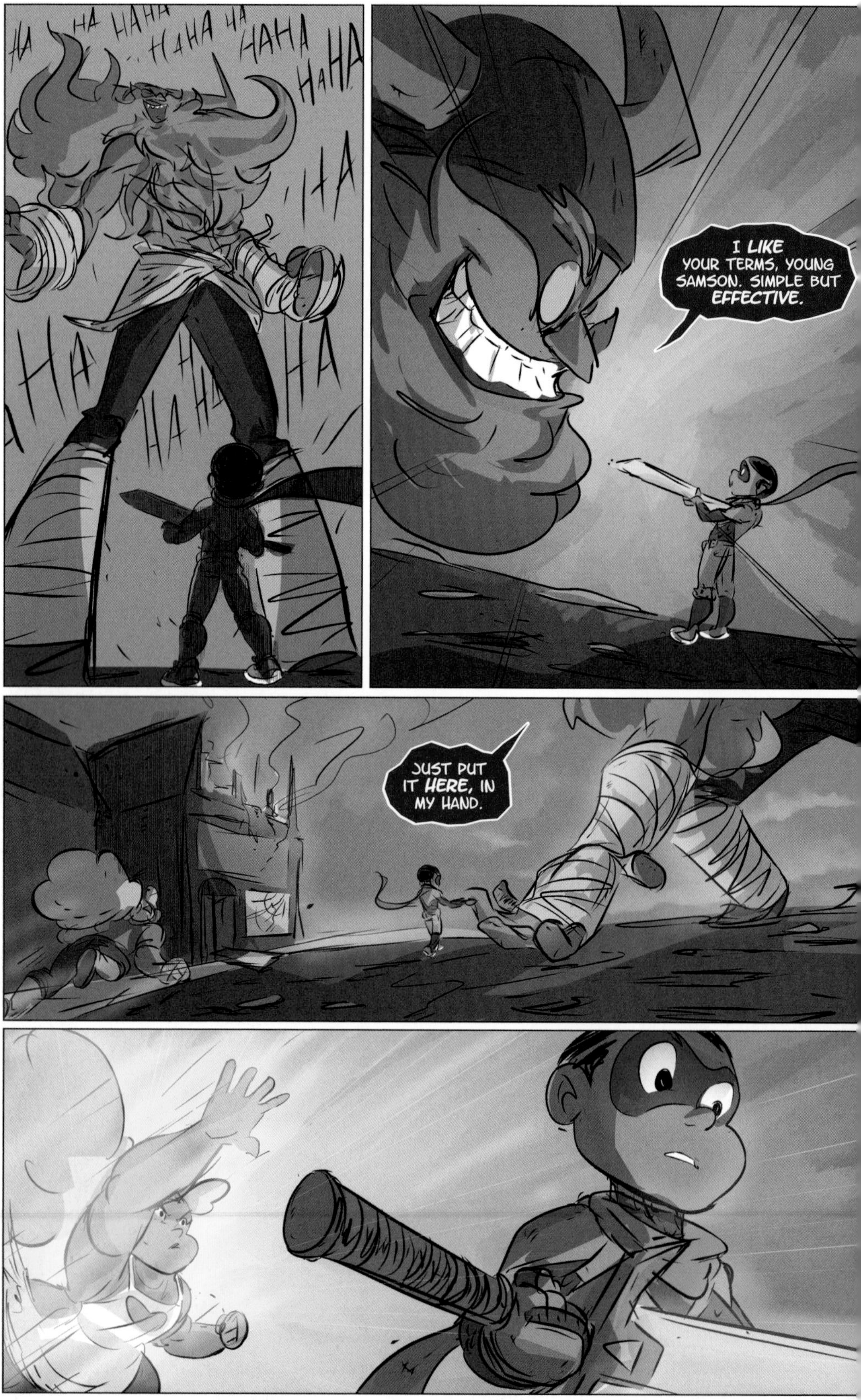
HA HA HAHA HA HA ..HAHA HAHA HAHA
HA
HA HA HA HA HA HA HA HA
I LIKE YOUR TERMS, YOUNG SAMSON. SIMPLE BUT EFFECTIVE.
JUST PUT IT HERE, IN MY HAND.

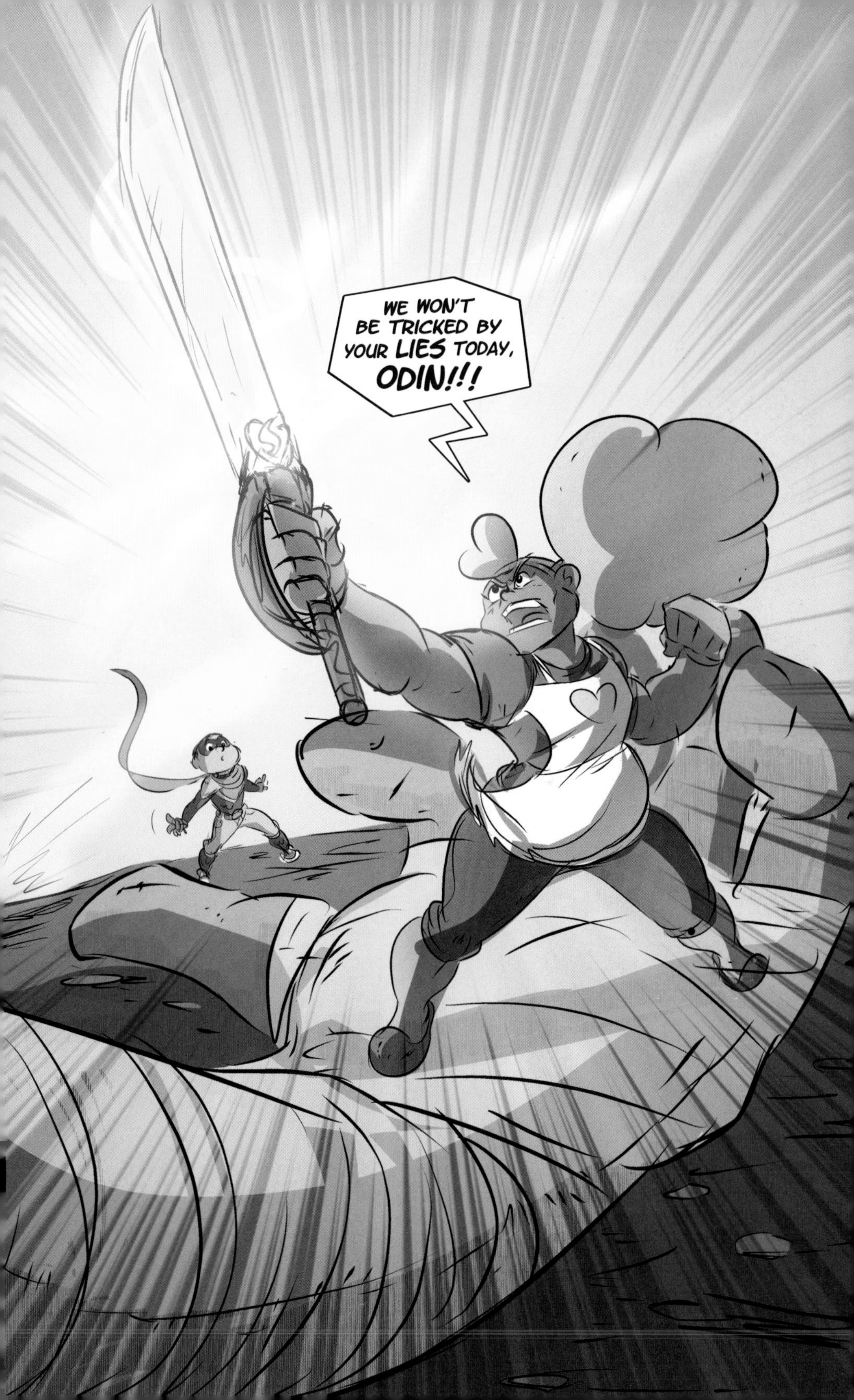
WE WON'T BE TRICKED BY YOUR LIES TODAY, ODIN!!!

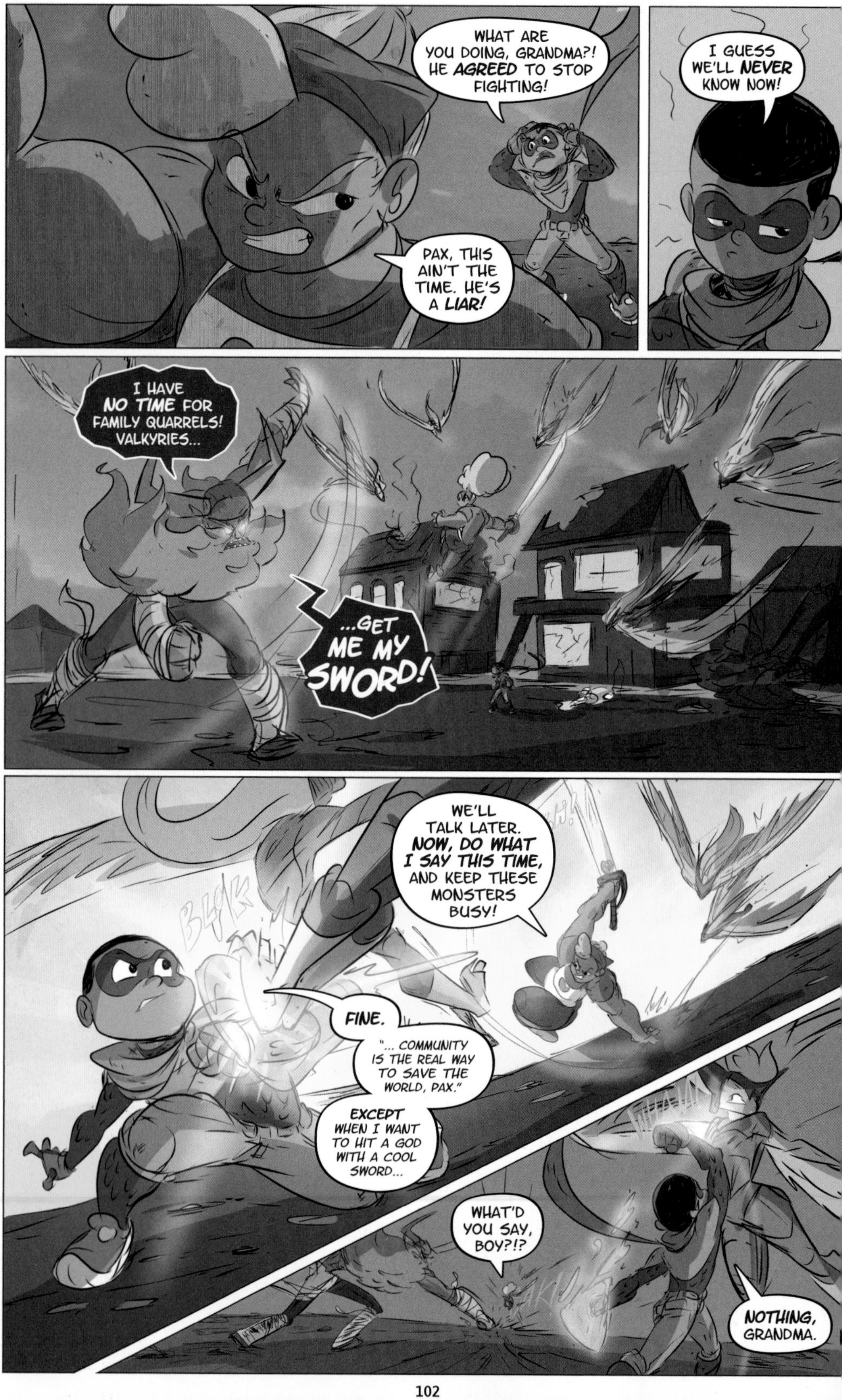
WHAT ARE YOU DOING, GRANDMA?! HE AGREED TO STOP FIGHTING!
PAX, THIS AIN'T THE TIME. HE'S A LIAR!
I GUESS WE'LL NEVER KNOW NOW!
I HAVE NO TIME FOR FAMILY QUARRELS! VALKYRIES...
...GET ME MY SWORD!
WE'LL TALK LATER. NOW, DO WHAT I SAY THIS TIME, AND KEEP THESE MONSTERS BUSY!
FINE.
"... COMMUNITY IS THE REAL WAY TO SAVE THE WORLD, PAX."
EXCEPT WHEN I WANT TO HIT A GOD WITH A COOL SWORD...
WHAT'D YOU SAY, BOY?!?
NOTHING, GRANDMA.

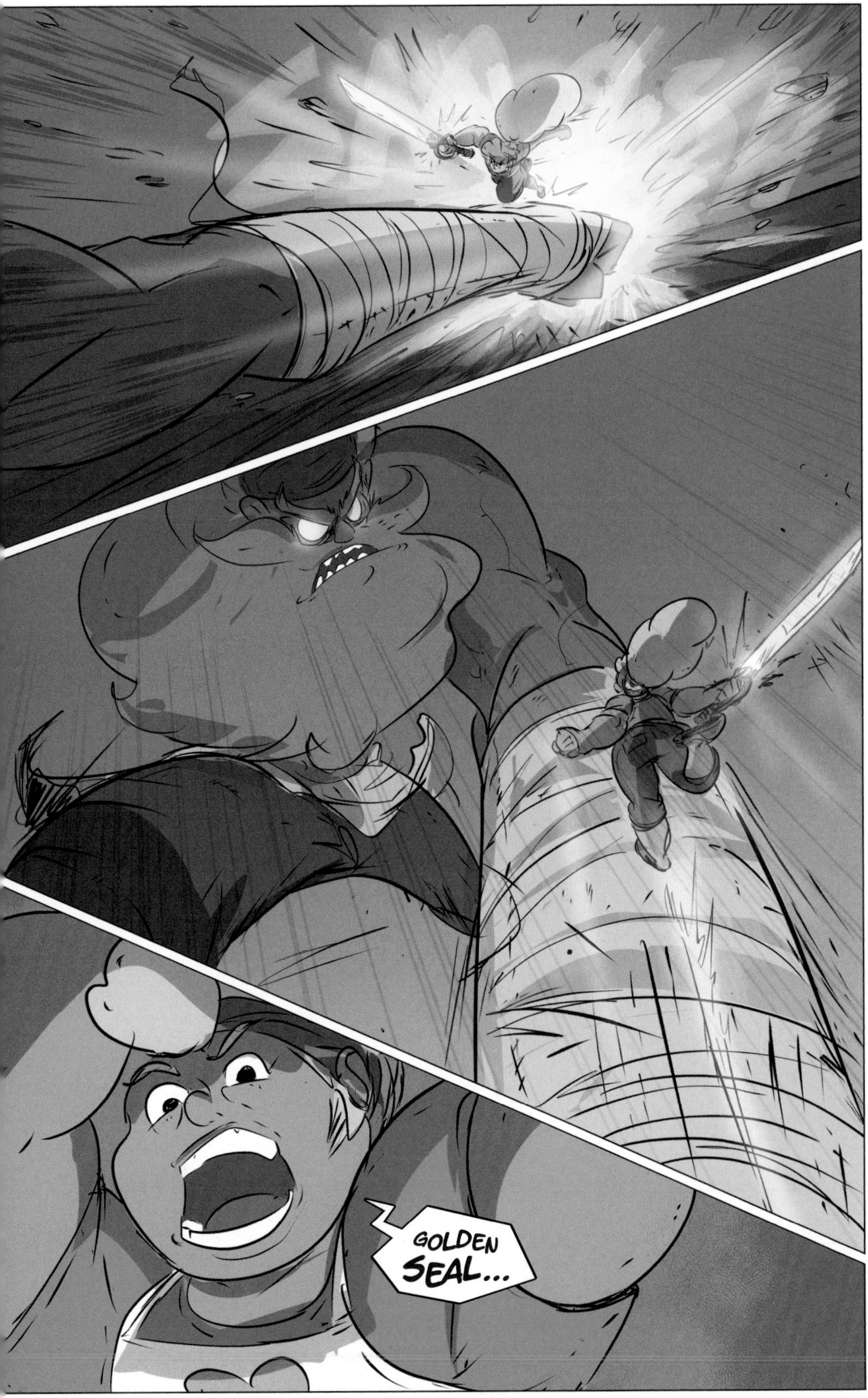
GOLDEN
SEAL...

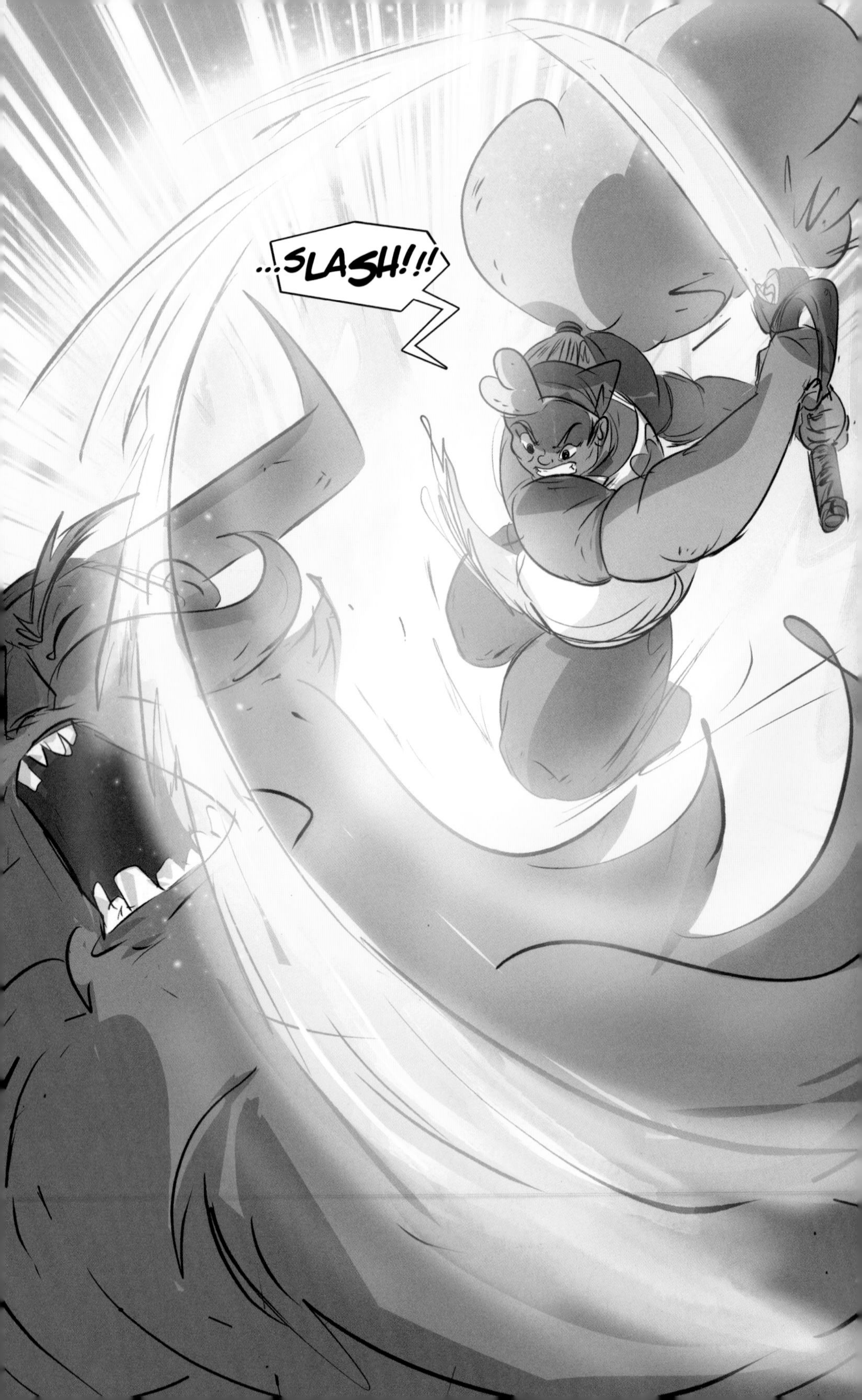
...SLASH!!!

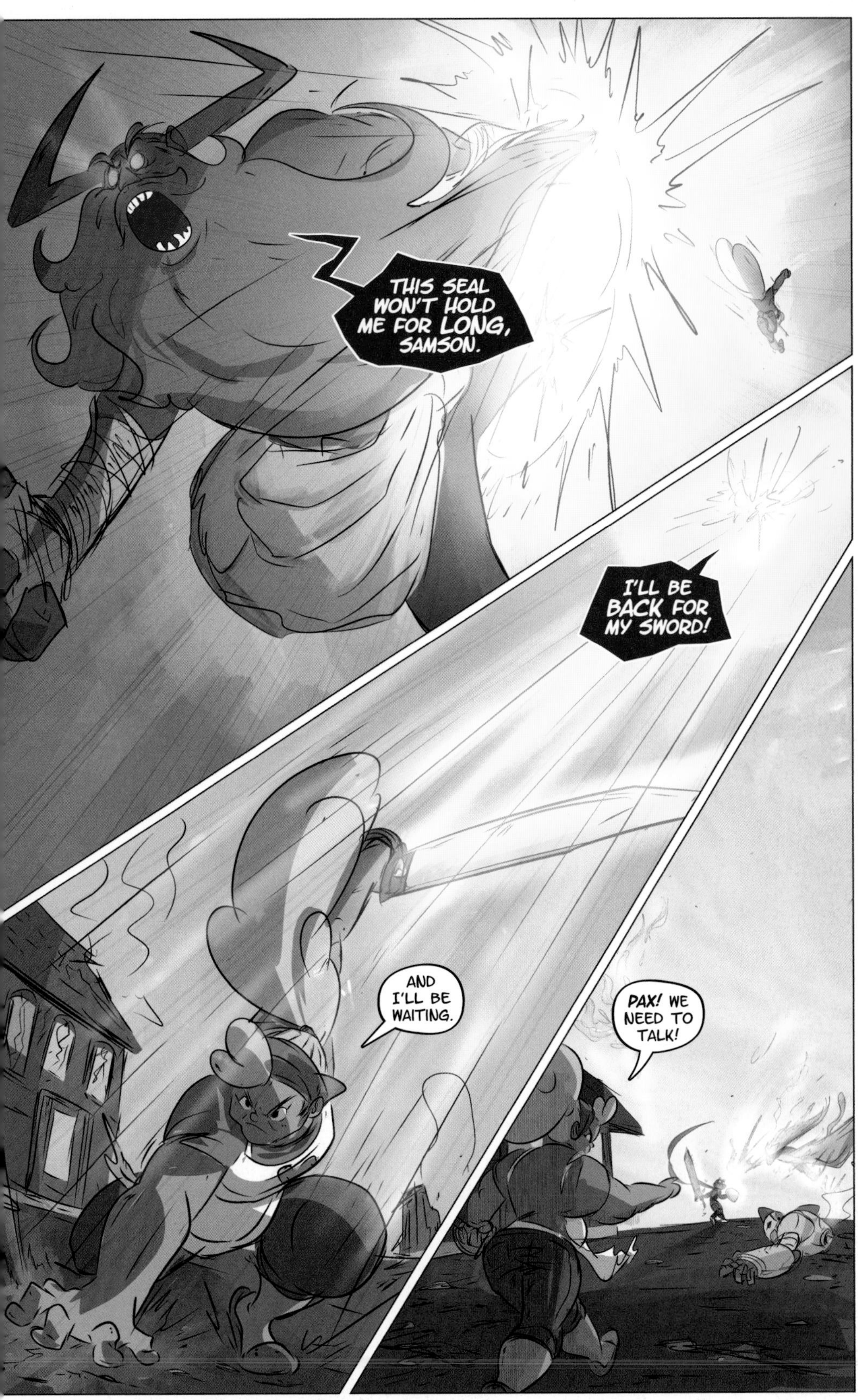

THIS SEAL WON'T HOLD ME FOR LONG, SAMSON.
I'LL BE BACK FOR MY SWORD!
AND I'LL BE WAITING.
PAX! WE NEED TO TALK!

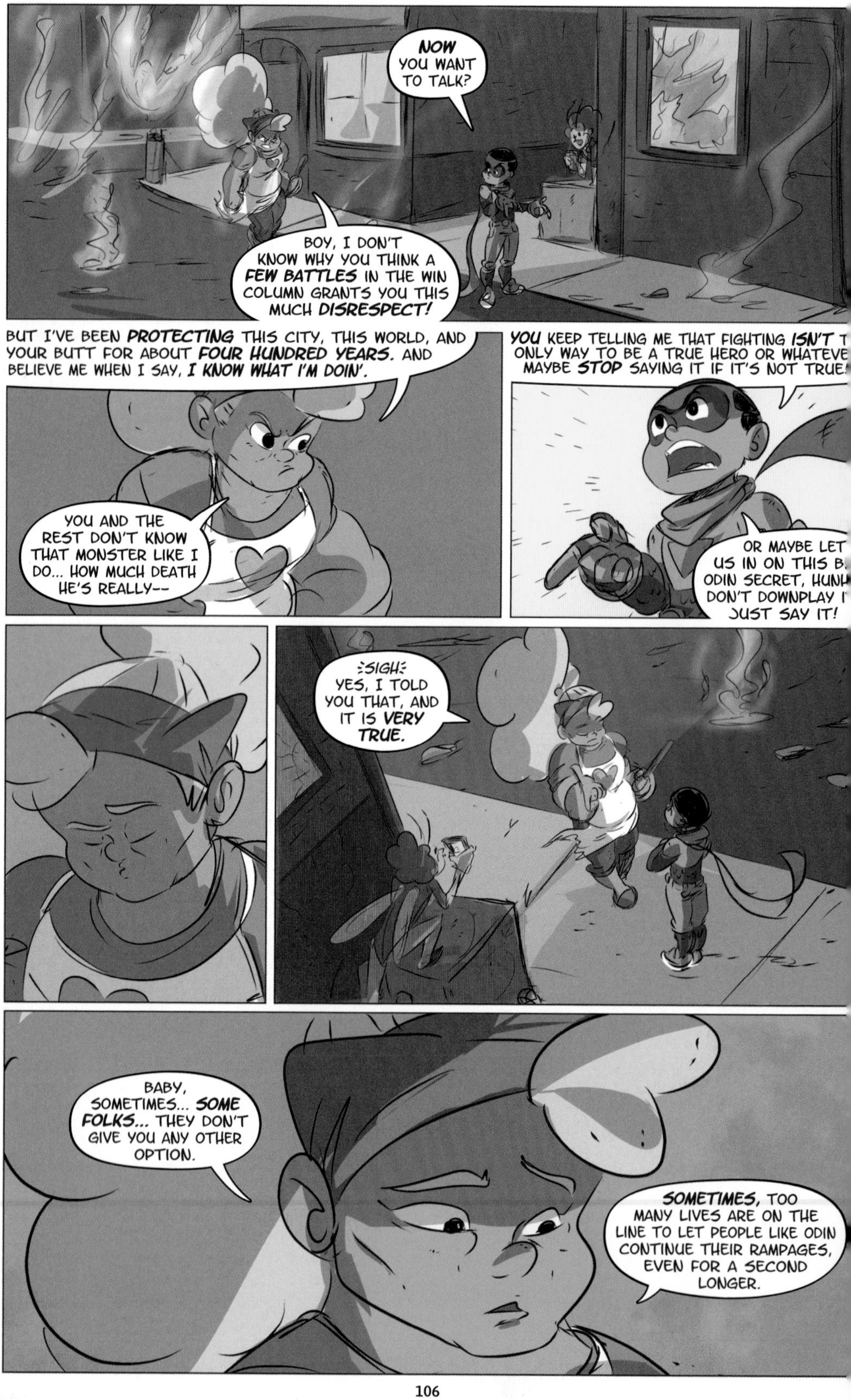
NOW YOU WANT TO TALK?
BOY, I DON'T KNOW WHY YOU THINK A FEW BATTLES IN THE WIN COLUMN GRANTS YOU THIS MUCH DISRESPECT!
BUT I'VE BEEN PROTECTING THIS CITY, THIS WORLD, AND YOUR BUTT FOR ABOUT FOUR HUNDRED YEARS. AND BELIEVE ME WHEN I SAY, I KNOW WHAT I'M DOIN'.
YOU AND THE REST DON'T KNOW THAT MONSTER LIKE I DO... HOW MUCH DEATH HE'S REALLY--
YOU KEEP TELLING ME THAT FIGHTING ISN'T T
ONLY WAY TO BE A TRUE HERO OR WHATEVE
MAYBE STOP SAYING IT IF IT'S NOT TRUE!
OR MAYBE LET US IN ON THIS B
ODIN SECRET, HUNH
DON'T DOWNPLAY I
JUST SAY IT!
SIGH
YES, I TOLD YOU THAT, AND IT IS VERY TRUE.
BABY, SOMETIMES... SOME FOLKS... THEY DON'T GIVE YOU ANY OTHER OPTION.
SOMETIMES, TOO MANY LIVES ARE ON THE LINE TO LET PEOPLE LIKE ODIN CONTINUE THEIR RAMPAGES, EVEN FOR A SECOND LONGER.

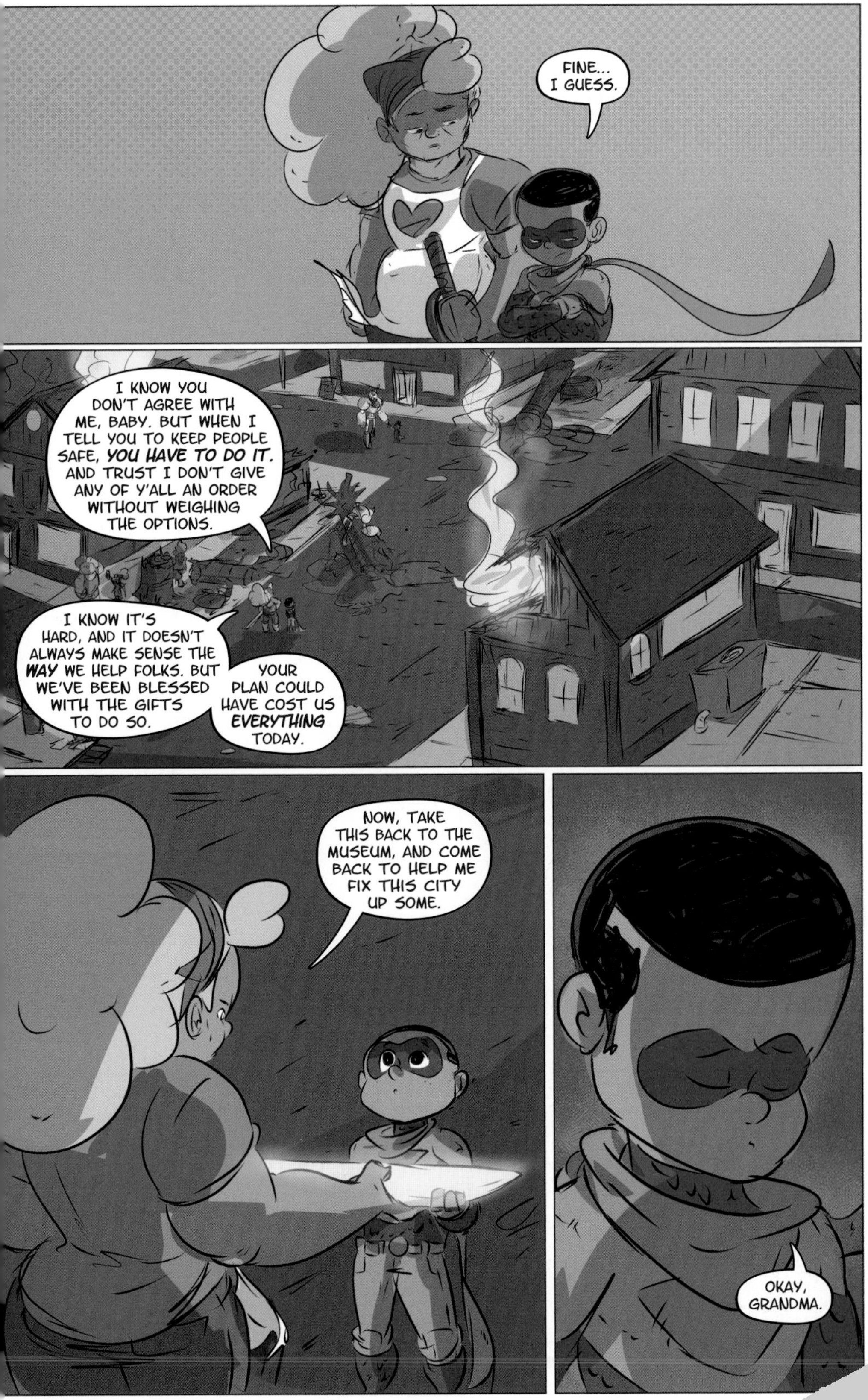
FINE... I GUESS.
I KNOW YOU DON'T AGREE WITH ME, BABY. BUT WHEN I TELL YOU TO KEEP PEOPLE SAFE, YOU HAVE TO DO IT. AND TRUST I DON'T GIVE ANY OF Y'ALL AN ORDER WITHOUT WEIGHING THE OPTIONS.
I KNOW IT'S HARD, AND IT DOESN'T ALWAYS MAKE SENSE THE WAY WE HELP FOLKS. BUT WE'VE BEEN BLESSED WITH THE GIFTS TO DO SO.
YOUR PLAN COULD HAVE COST US EVERYTHING TODAY.
NOW, TAKE THIS BACK TO THE MUSEUM, AND COME BACK TO HELP ME FIX THIS CITY UP SOME.
OKAY, GRANDMA.

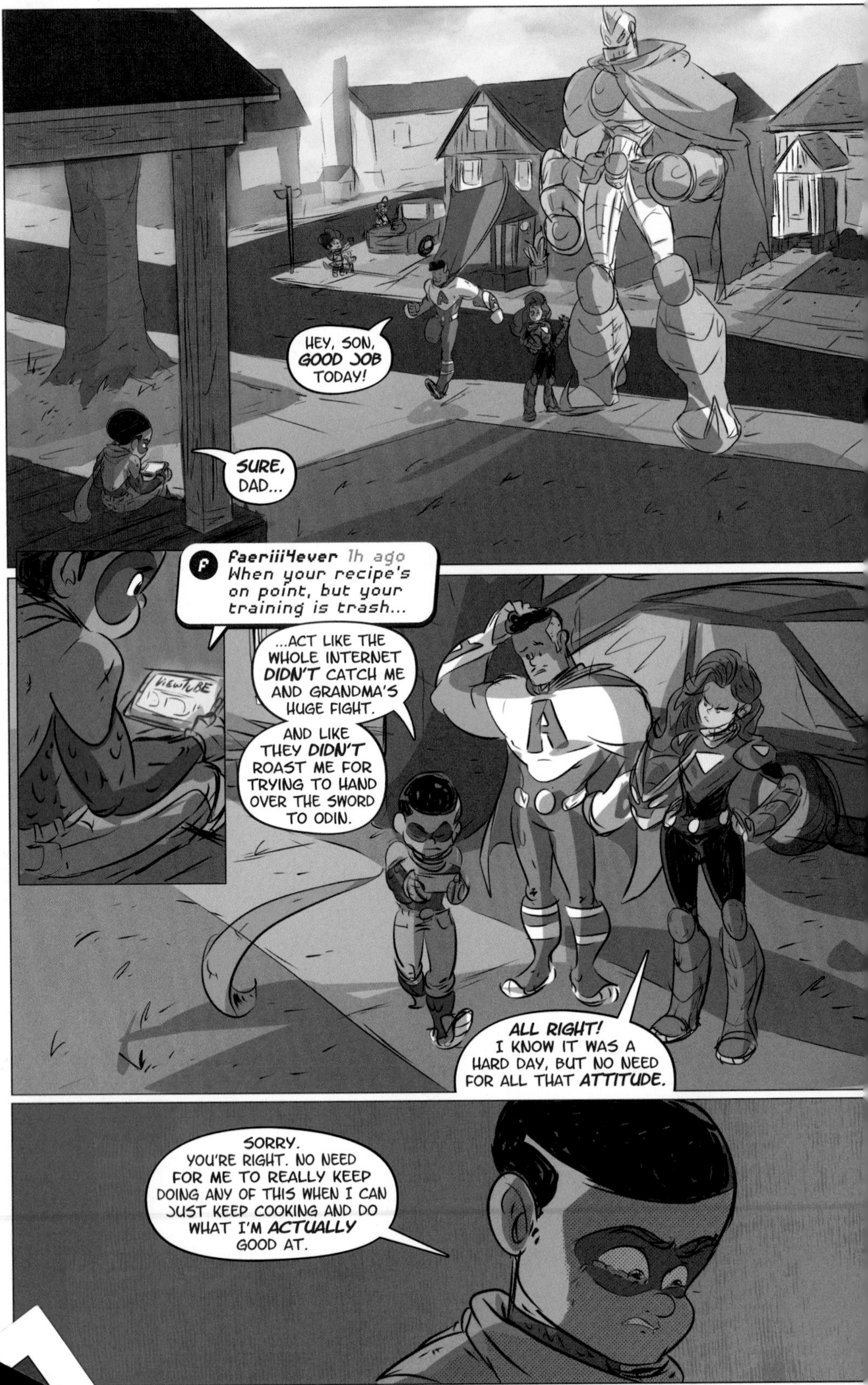
HEY, SON, GOOD JOB TODAY!
SURE, DAD...
Faeriii4ever 1h ago When your recipe's on point, but your training is trash...
VIEWTUBE
...ACT LIKE THE WHOLE INTERNET DIDN'T CATCH ME AND GRANDMA'S HUGE FIGHT.
AND LIKE THEY DIDN'T ROAST ME FOR TRYING TO HAND OVER THE SWORD TO ODIN.
ALL RIGHT! I KNOW IT WAS A HARD DAY, BUT NO NEED FOR ALL THAT ATTITUDE.
SORRY. YOU'RE RIGHT. NO NEED FOR ME TO REALLY KEEP DOING ANY OF THIS WHEN I CAN JUST KEEP COOKING AND DO WHAT I'M ACTUALLY GOOD AT.

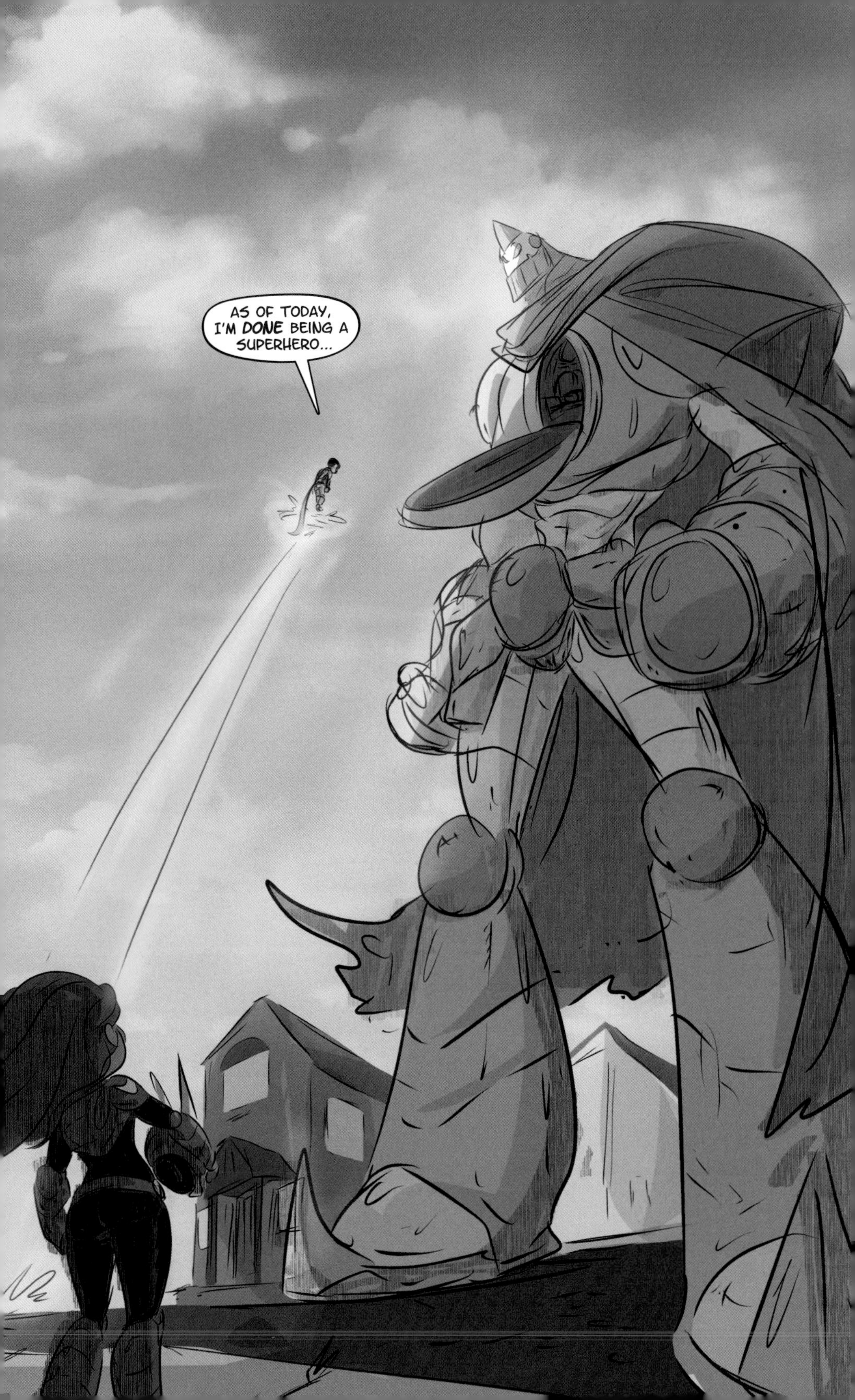
AS OF TODAY, I'M DONE BEING A SUPERHERO...

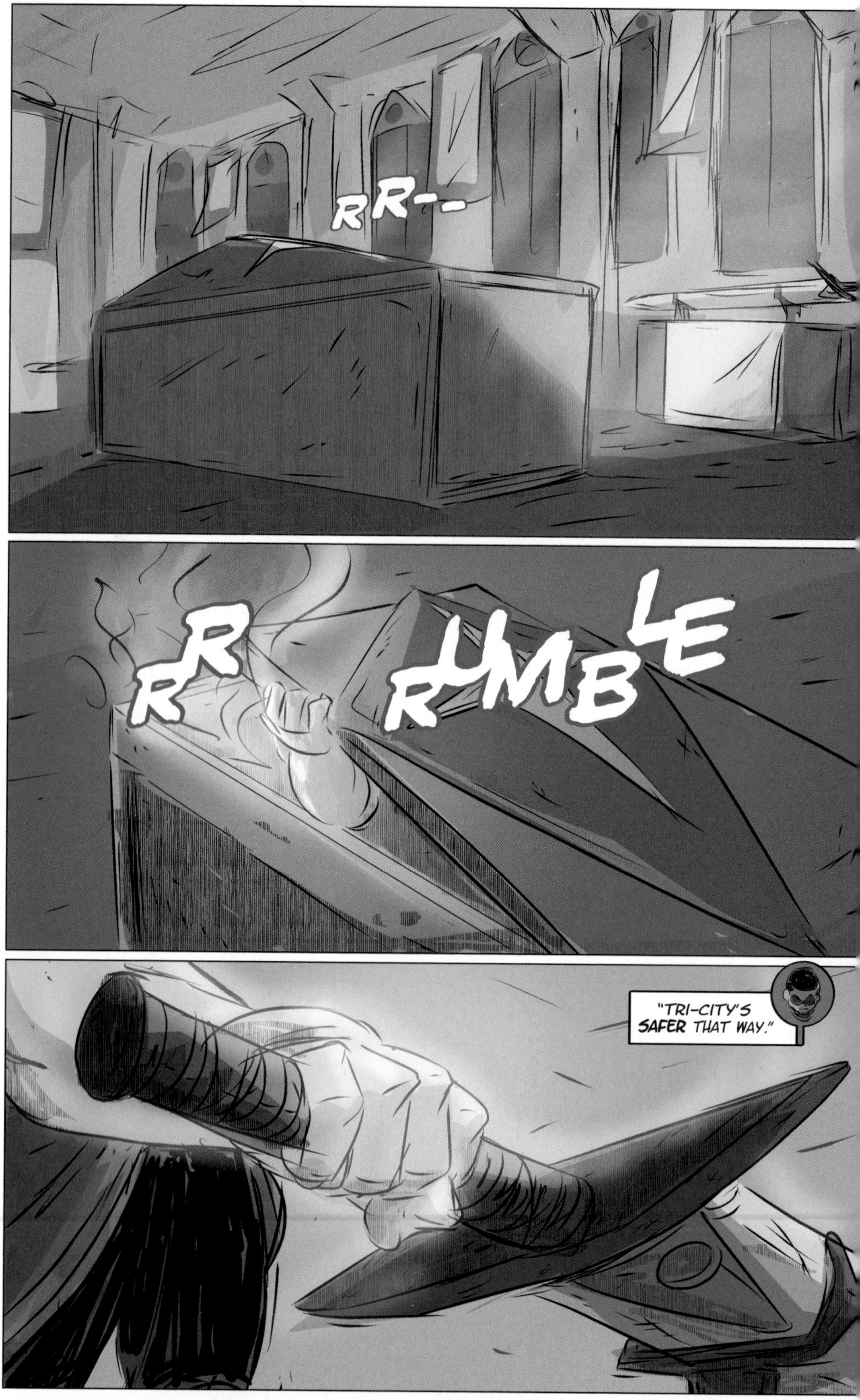
RR---
RRRUMBLE
"TRI-CITY'S SAFER THAT WAY."

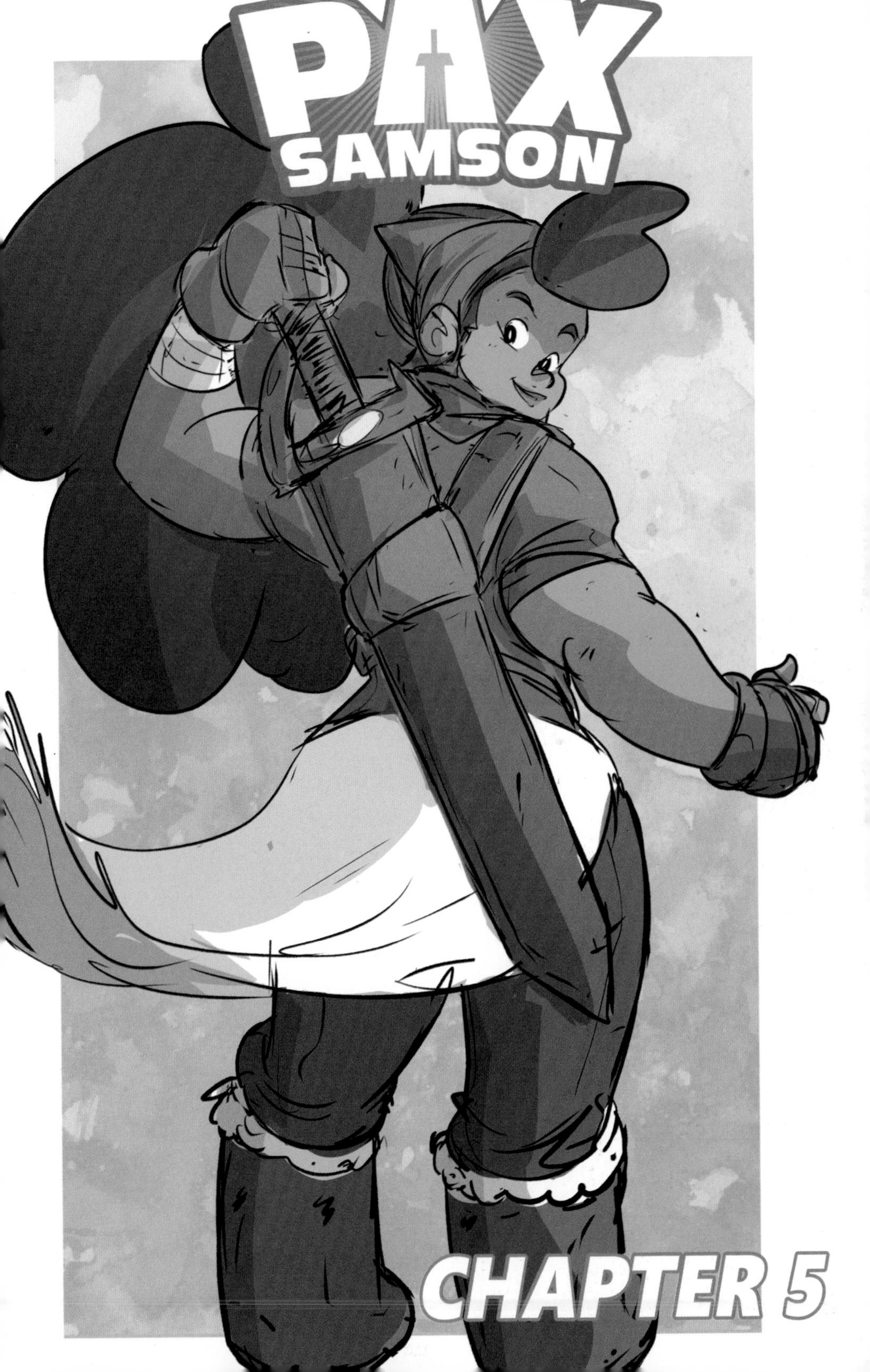
PAX
SAMSON
CHAPTER 5

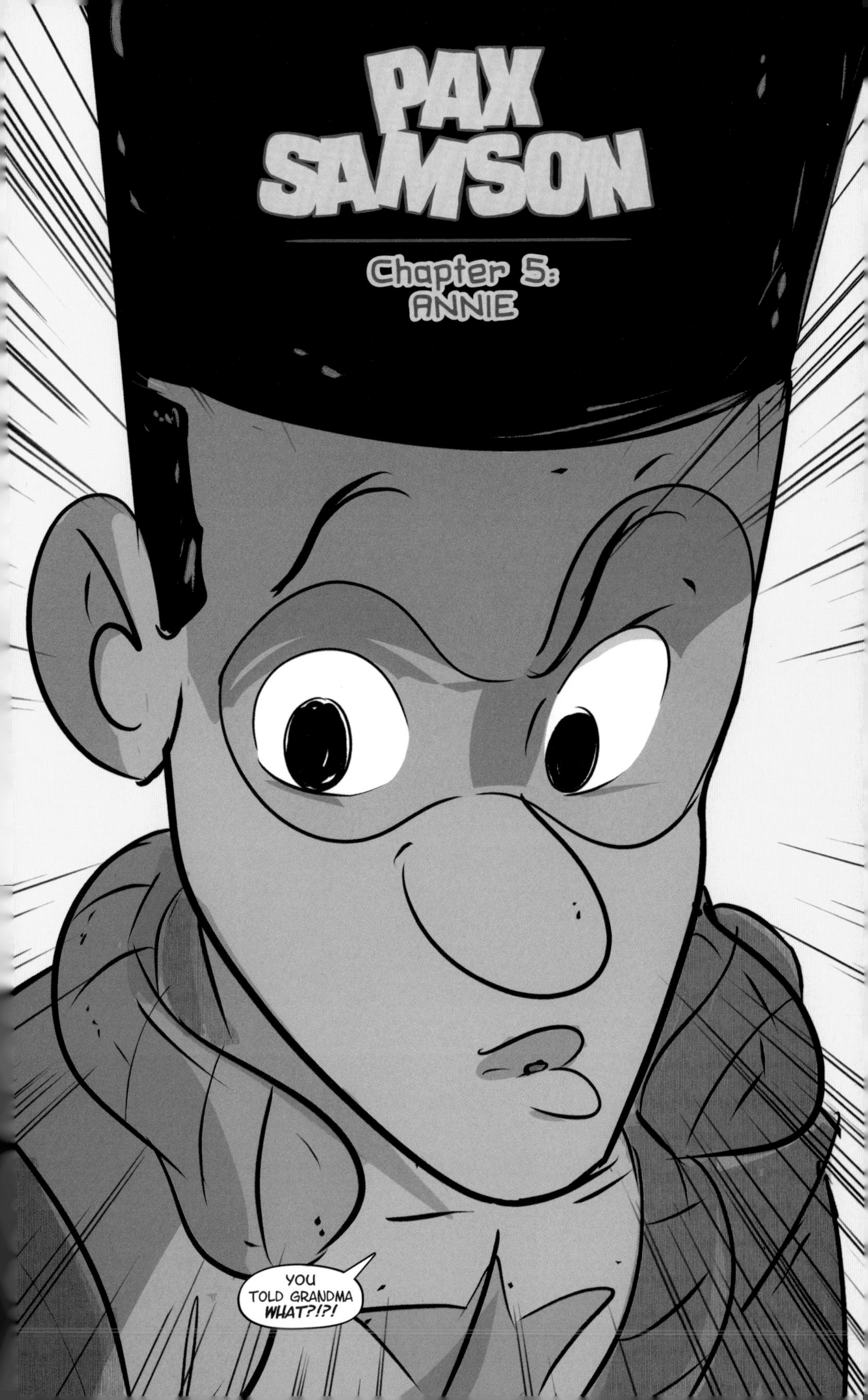
PAX SAMSON
Chapter 5: ANNIE
YOU TOLD GRANDMA WHAT?!?!

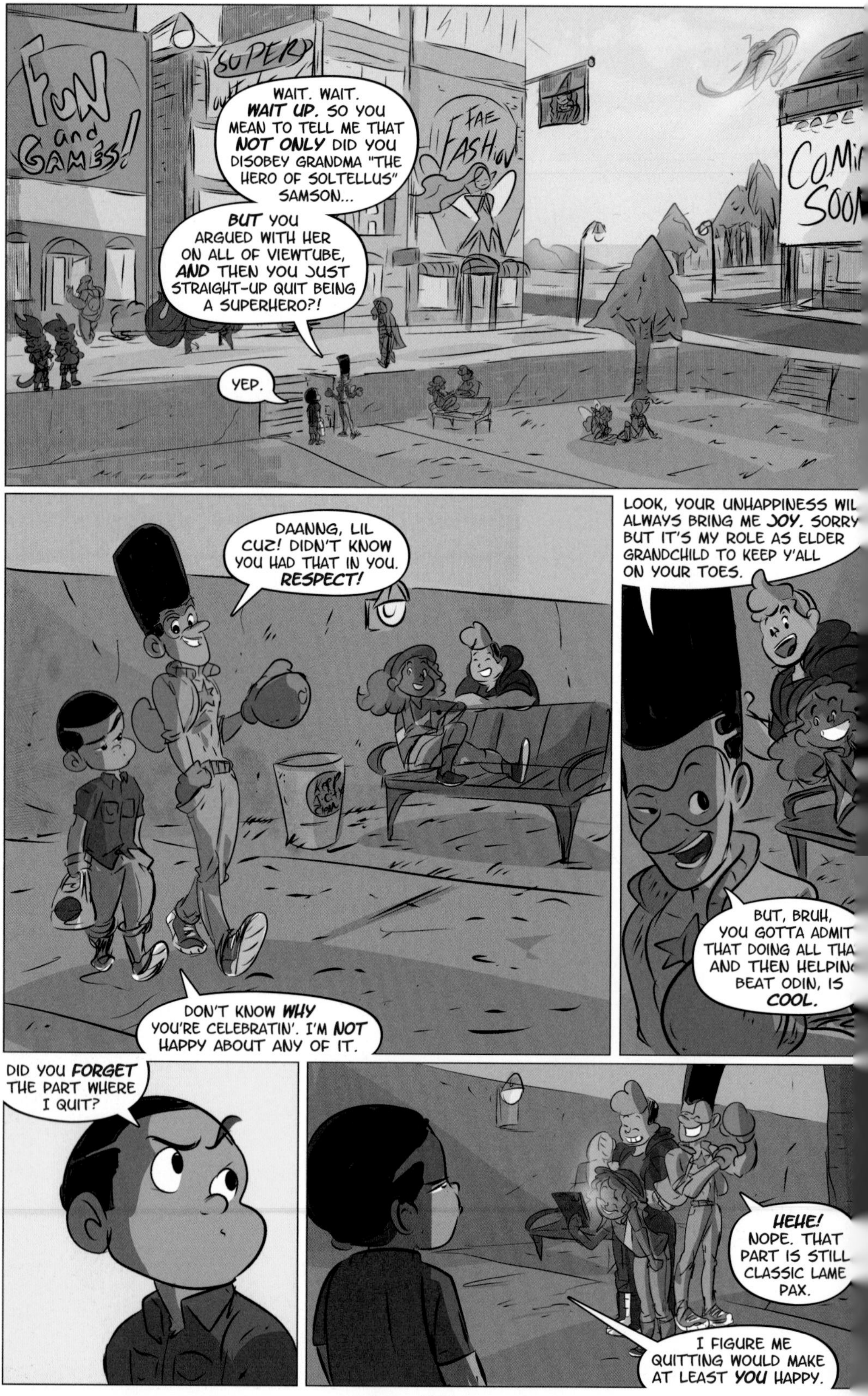
FUN and GAMES!
SUPER
FAE FASHION
COMING SOON
WAIT. WAIT. WAIT UP. SO YOU MEAN TO TELL ME THAT NOT ONLY DID YOU DISOBEY GRANDMA "THE HERO OF SOLTELLUS" SAMSON...
BUT YOU ARGUED WITH HER ON ALL OF VIEWTUBE, AND THEN YOU JUST STRAIGHT-UP QUIT BEING A SUPERHERO?!
YEP.
DAANNG, LIL CUZ! DIDN'T KNOW YOU HAD THAT IN YOU. RESPECT!
DON'T KNOW WHY YOU'RE CELEBRATIN'. I'M NOT HAPPY ABOUT ANY OF IT.
LOOK, YOUR UNHAPPINESS WIL ALWAYS BRING ME JOY. SORRY BUT IT'S MY ROLE AS ELDER GRANDCHILD TO KEEP Y'ALL ON YOUR TOES.
BUT, BRUH, YOU GOTTA ADMIT THAT DOING ALL THA AND THEN HELPIN BEAT ODIN, IS COOL.
DID YOU FORGET THE PART WHERE I QUIT?
HEHE! NOPE. THAT PART IS STILL CLASSIC LAME PAX.
I FIGURE ME QUITTING WOULD MAKE AT LEAST YOU HAPPY.

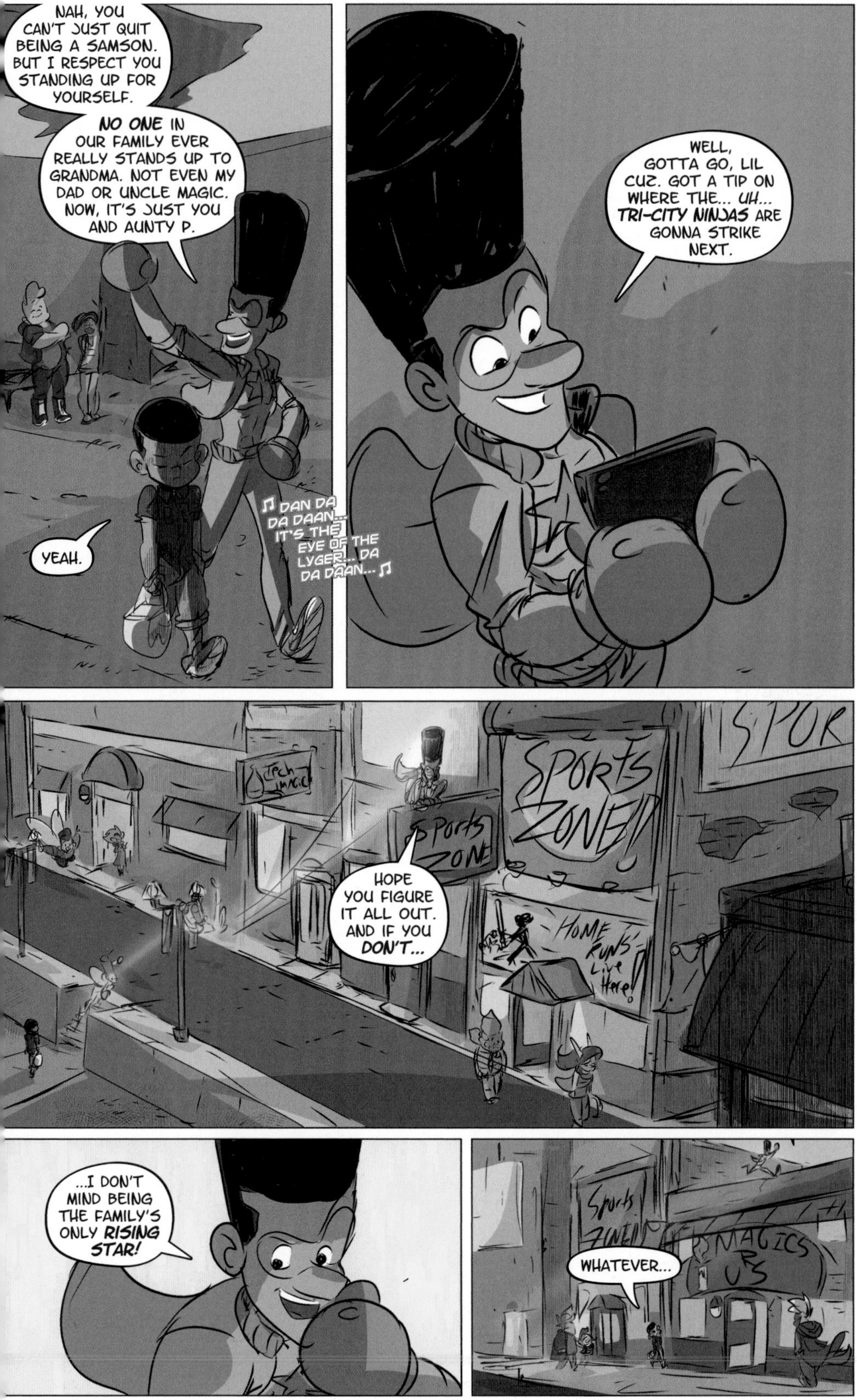
NAH, YOU CAN'T JUST QUIT BEING A SAMSON. BUT I RESPECT YOU STANDING UP FOR YOURSELF.
NO ONE IN OUR FAMILY EVER REALLY STANDS UP TO GRANDMA. NOT EVEN MY DAD OR UNCLE MAGIC. NOW, IT'S JUST YOU AND AUNTY P.
YEAH.
♫ DAN DA DA DAAN... IT'S THE EYE OF THE LYGER... DA DA DAAN... ♫
WELL, GOTTA GO, LIL CUZ. GOT A TIP ON WHERE THE... UH... TRI-CITY NINJAS ARE GONNA STRIKE NEXT.
SPOR
Sports ZONE!
Tech Magic
Sports ZONE
HOPE YOU FIGURE IT ALL OUT. AND IF YOU DON'T...
HOME RUNS Live Here!
...I DON'T MIND BEING THE FAMILY'S ONLY RISING STAR!
Sports ZONE
MAGICS R US
WHATEVER...

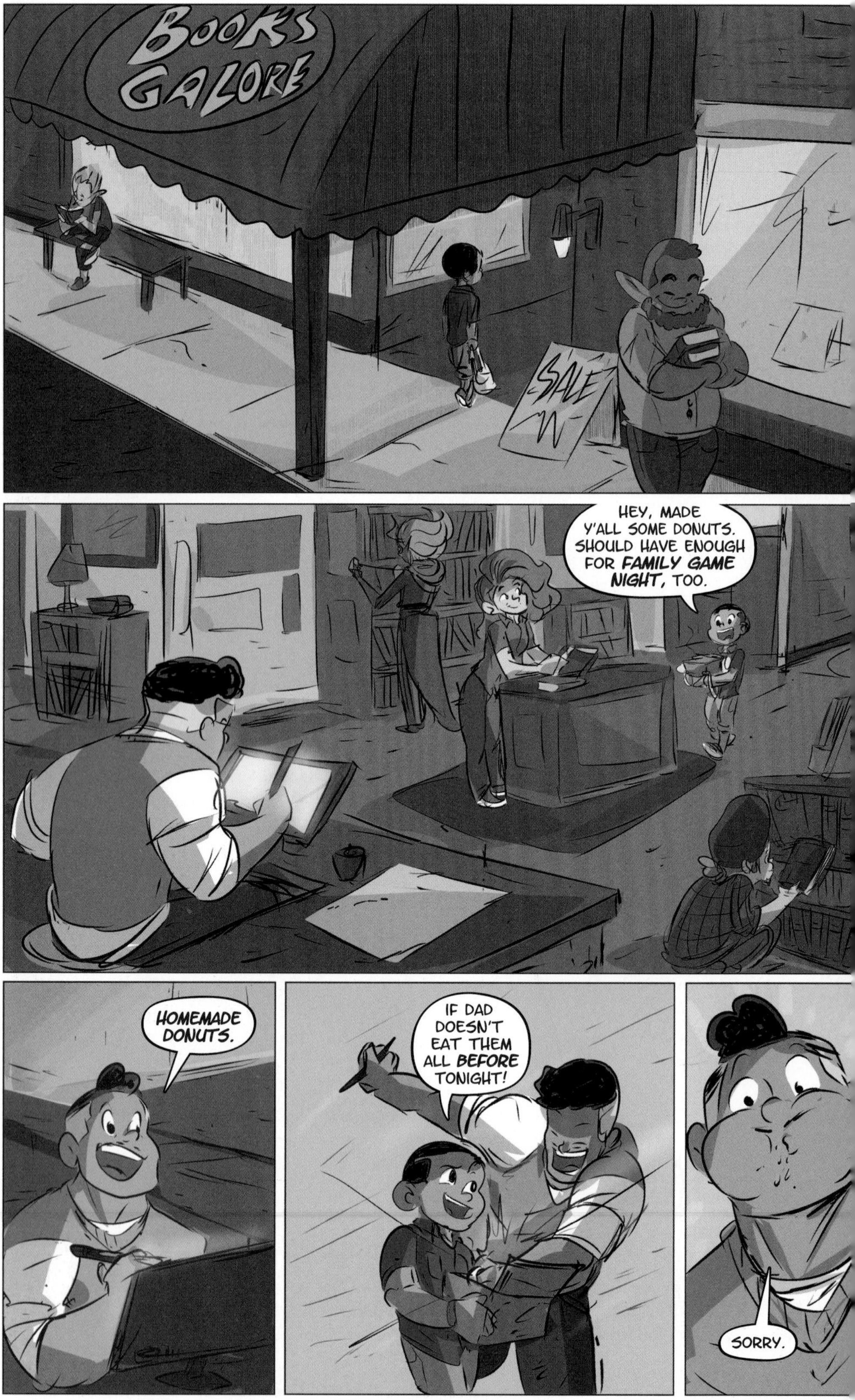
BOOKS GALORE
SALE
HEY, MADE Y'ALL SOME DONUTS. SHOULD HAVE ENOUGH FOR **FAMILY GAME NIGHT**, TOO.
HOMEMADE DONUTS.
IF DAD DOESN'T EAT THEM ALL **BEFORE** TONIGHT!
SORRY.

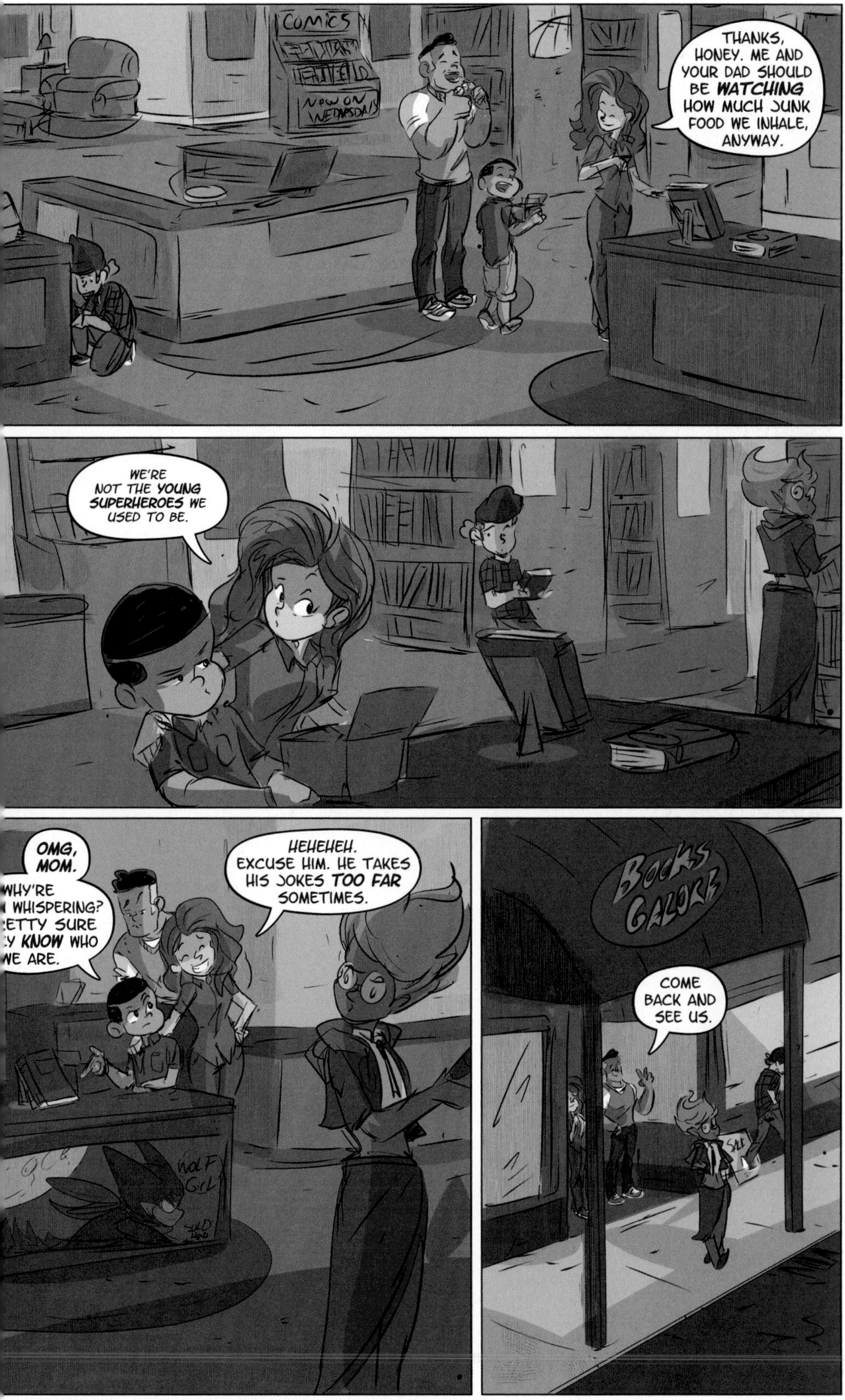
COMICS
THANKS, HONEY. ME AND YOUR DAD SHOULD BE **WATCHING** HOW MUCH JUNK FOOD WE INHALE, ANYWAY.
WE'RE NOT THE **YOUNG SUPERHEROES** WE USED TO BE.
OMG, MOM.
WHY'RE
WHISPERING?
ETTY SURE
Y **KNOW** WHO
WE ARE.
HEHEHEH. EXCUSE HIM. HE TAKES HIS JOKES **TOO FAR** SOMETIMES.
BOOKS GALORE
COME BACK AND SEE US.

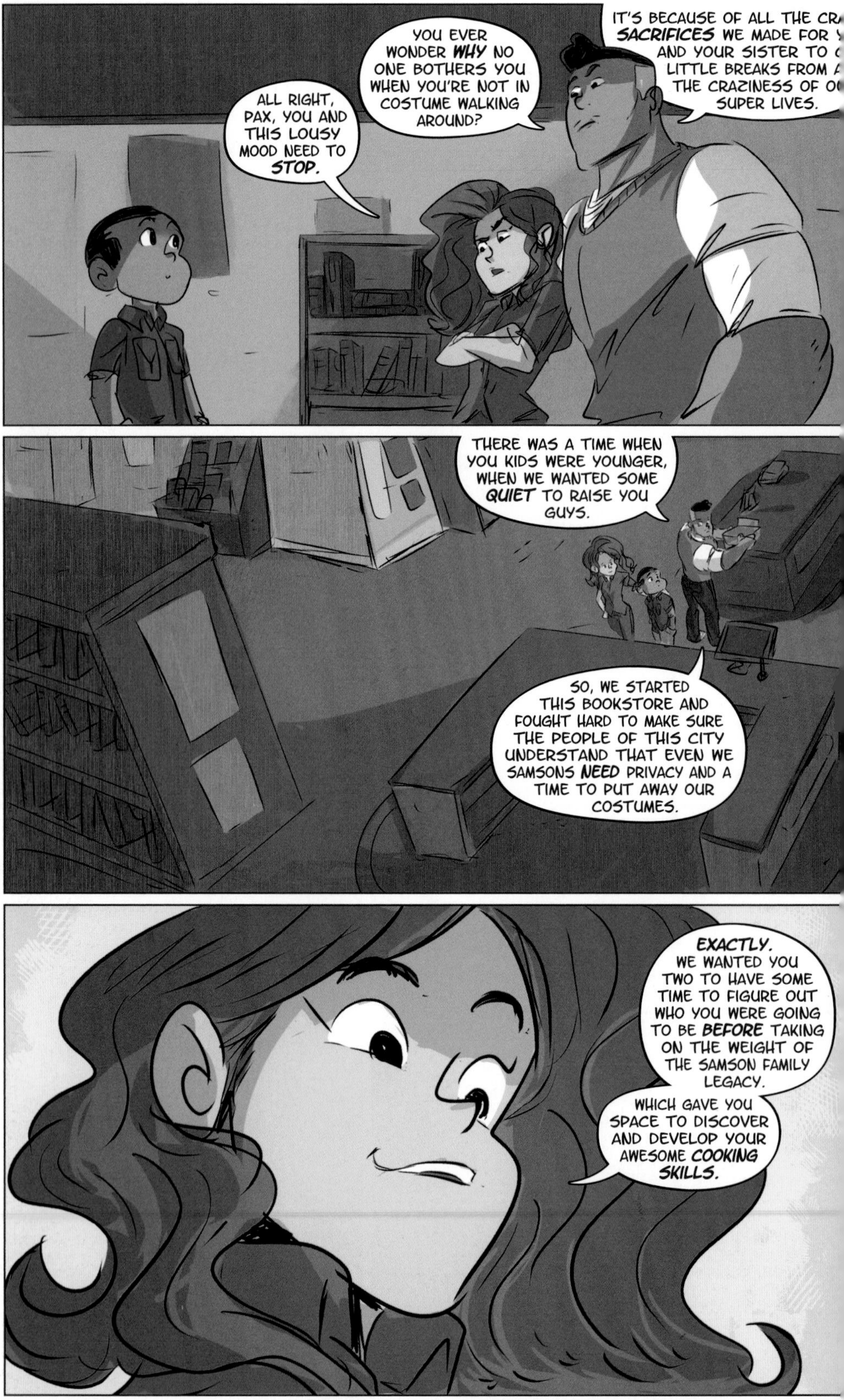
ALL RIGHT, PAX, YOU AND THIS LOUSY MOOD NEED TO STOP.
YOU EVER WONDER WHY NO ONE BOTHERS YOU WHEN YOU'RE NOT IN COSTUME WALKING AROUND?
IT'S BECAUSE OF ALL THE CRA SACRIFICES WE MADE FOR Y AND YOUR SISTER TO LITTLE BREAKS FROM THE CRAZINESS OF O SUPER LIVES.
THERE WAS A TIME WHEN YOU KIDS WERE YOUNGER, WHEN WE WANTED SOME QUIET TO RAISE YOU GUYS.
SO, WE STARTED THIS BOOKSTORE AND FOUGHT HARD TO MAKE SURE THE PEOPLE OF THIS CITY UNDERSTAND THAT EVEN WE SAMSONS NEED PRIVACY AND A TIME TO PUT AWAY OUR COSTUMES.
EXACTLY. WE WANTED YOU TWO TO HAVE SOME TIME TO FIGURE OUT WHO YOU WERE GOING TO BE BEFORE TAKING ON THE WEIGHT OF THE SAMSON FAMILY LEGACY.
WHICH GAVE YOU SPACE TO DISCOVER AND DEVELOP YOUR AWESOME COOKING SKILLS.

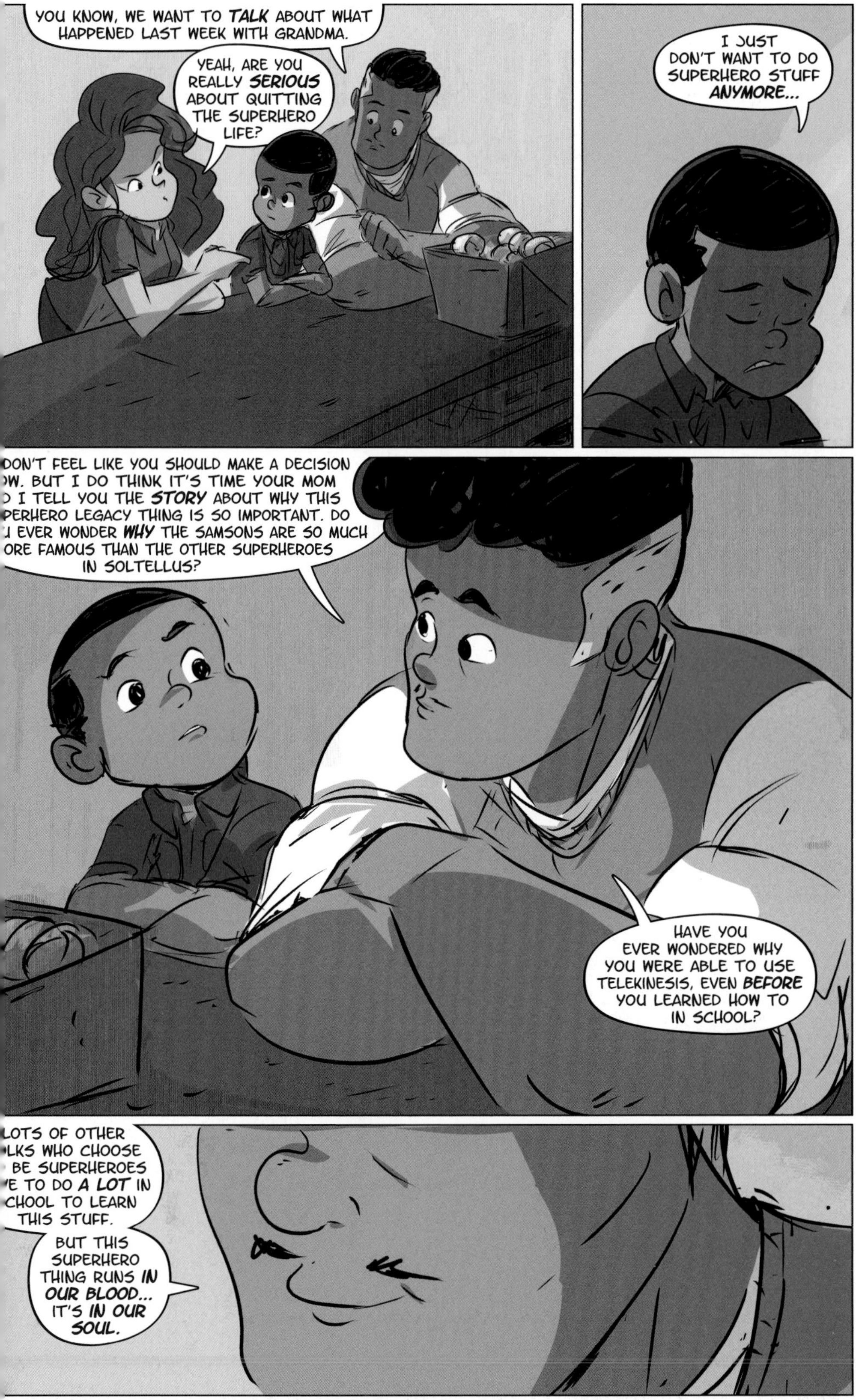
YOU KNOW, WE WANT TO TALK ABOUT WHAT HAPPENED LAST WEEK WITH GRANDMA.
YEAH, ARE YOU REALLY SERIOUS ABOUT QUITTING THE SUPERHERO LIFE?
I JUST DON'T WANT TO DO SUPERHERO STUFF ANYMORE...
DON'T FEEL LIKE YOU SHOULD MAKE A DECISION OW. BUT I DO THINK IT'S TIME YOUR MOM D I TELL YOU THE STORY ABOUT WHY THIS PERHERO LEGACY THING IS SO IMPORTANT. DO U EVER WONDER WHY THE SAMSONS ARE SO MUCH ORE FAMOUS THAN THE OTHER SUPERHEROES IN SOLTELLUS?
HAVE YOU EVER WONDERED WHY YOU WERE ABLE TO USE TELEKINESIS, EVEN BEFORE YOU LEARNED HOW TO IN SCHOOL?
LOTS OF OTHER LKS WHO CHOOSE BE SUPERHEROES E TO DO A LOT IN CHOOL TO LEARN THIS STUFF.
BUT THIS SUPERHERO THING RUNS IN OUR BLOOD... IT'S IN OUR SOUL.

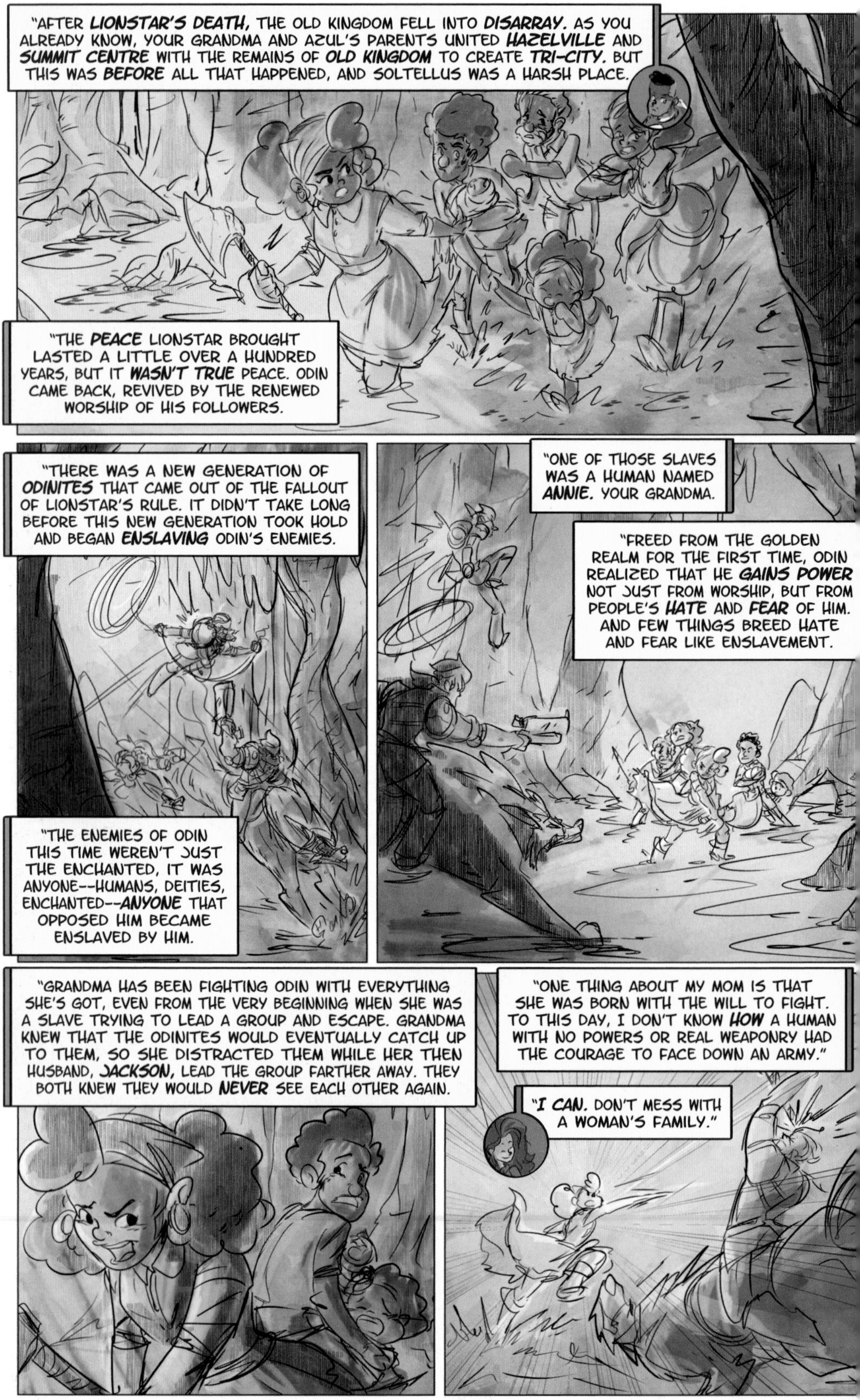
"AFTER LIONSTAR'S DEATH, THE OLD KINGDOM FELL INTO DISARRAY. AS YOU ALREADY KNOW, YOUR GRANDMA AND AZUL'S PARENTS UNITED HAZELVILLE AND SUMMIT CENTRE WITH THE REMAINS OF OLD KINGDOM TO CREATE TRI-CITY. BUT THIS WAS BEFORE ALL THAT HAPPENED, AND SOLTELLUS WAS A HARSH PLACE.
"THE PEACE LIONSTAR BROUGHT LASTED A LITTLE OVER A HUNDRED YEARS, BUT IT WASN'T TRUE PEACE. ODIN CAME BACK, REVIVED BY THE RENEWED WORSHIP OF HIS FOLLOWERS.
"THERE WAS A NEW GENERATION OF ODINITES THAT CAME OUT OF THE FALLOUT OF LIONSTAR'S RULE. IT DIDN'T TAKE LONG BEFORE THIS NEW GENERATION TOOK HOLD AND BEGAN ENSLAVING ODIN'S ENEMIES.
"THE ENEMIES OF ODIN THIS TIME WEREN'T JUST THE ENCHANTED, IT WAS ANYONE--HUMANS, DEITIES, ENCHANTED--ANYONE THAT OPPOSED HIM BECAME ENSLAVED BY HIM.
"ONE OF THOSE SLAVES WAS A HUMAN NAMED ANNIE. YOUR GRANDMA.
"FREED FROM THE GOLDEN REALM FOR THE FIRST TIME, ODIN REALIZED THAT HE GAINS POWER NOT JUST FROM WORSHIP, BUT FROM PEOPLE'S HATE AND FEAR OF HIM. AND FEW THINGS BREED HATE AND FEAR LIKE ENSLAVEMENT.
"GRANDMA HAS BEEN FIGHTING ODIN WITH EVERYTHING SHE'S GOT, EVEN FROM THE VERY BEGINNING WHEN SHE WAS A SLAVE TRYING TO LEAD A GROUP AND ESCAPE. GRANDMA KNEW THAT THE ODINITES WOULD EVENTUALLY CATCH UP TO THEM, SO SHE DISTRACTED THEM WHILE HER THEN HUSBAND, JACKSON, LEAD THE GROUP FARTHER AWAY. THEY BOTH KNEW THEY WOULD NEVER SEE EACH OTHER AGAIN.
"ONE THING ABOUT MY MOM IS THAT SHE WAS BORN WITH THE WILL TO FIGHT. TO THIS DAY, I DON'T KNOW HOW A HUMAN WITH NO POWERS OR REAL WEAPONRY HAD THE COURAGE TO FACE DOWN AN ARMY."
"I CAN. DON'T MESS WITH A WOMAN'S FAMILY."

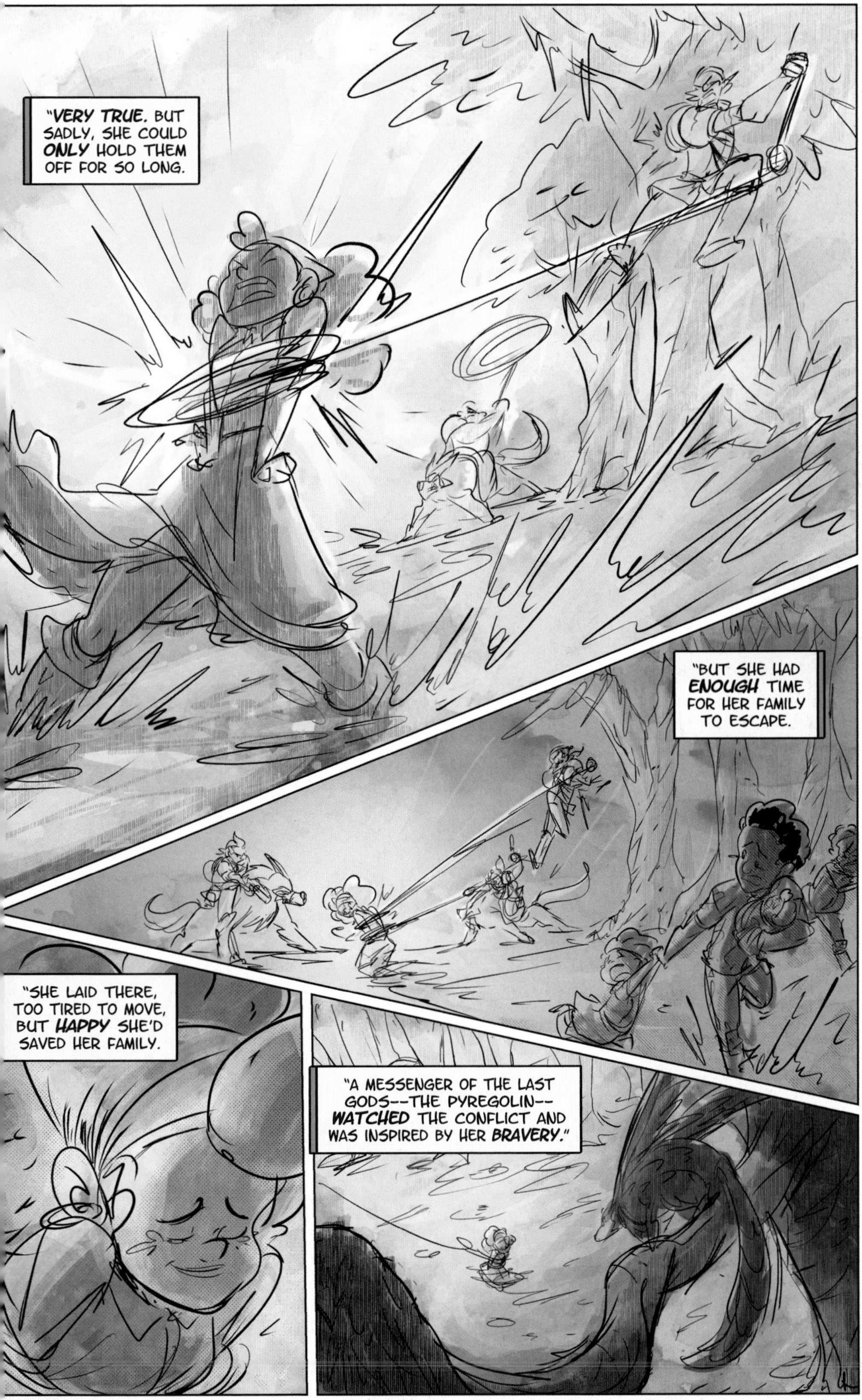
"VERY TRUE. BUT SADLY, SHE COULD ONLY HOLD THEM OFF FOR SO LONG.
"BUT SHE HAD ENOUGH TIME FOR HER FAMILY TO ESCAPE.
"SHE LAID THERE, TOO TIRED TO MOVE, BUT HAPPY SHE'D SAVED HER FAMILY.
"A MESSENGER OF THE LAST GODS--THE PYREGOLIN--WATCHED THE CONFLICT AND WAS INSPIRED BY HER BRAVERY."

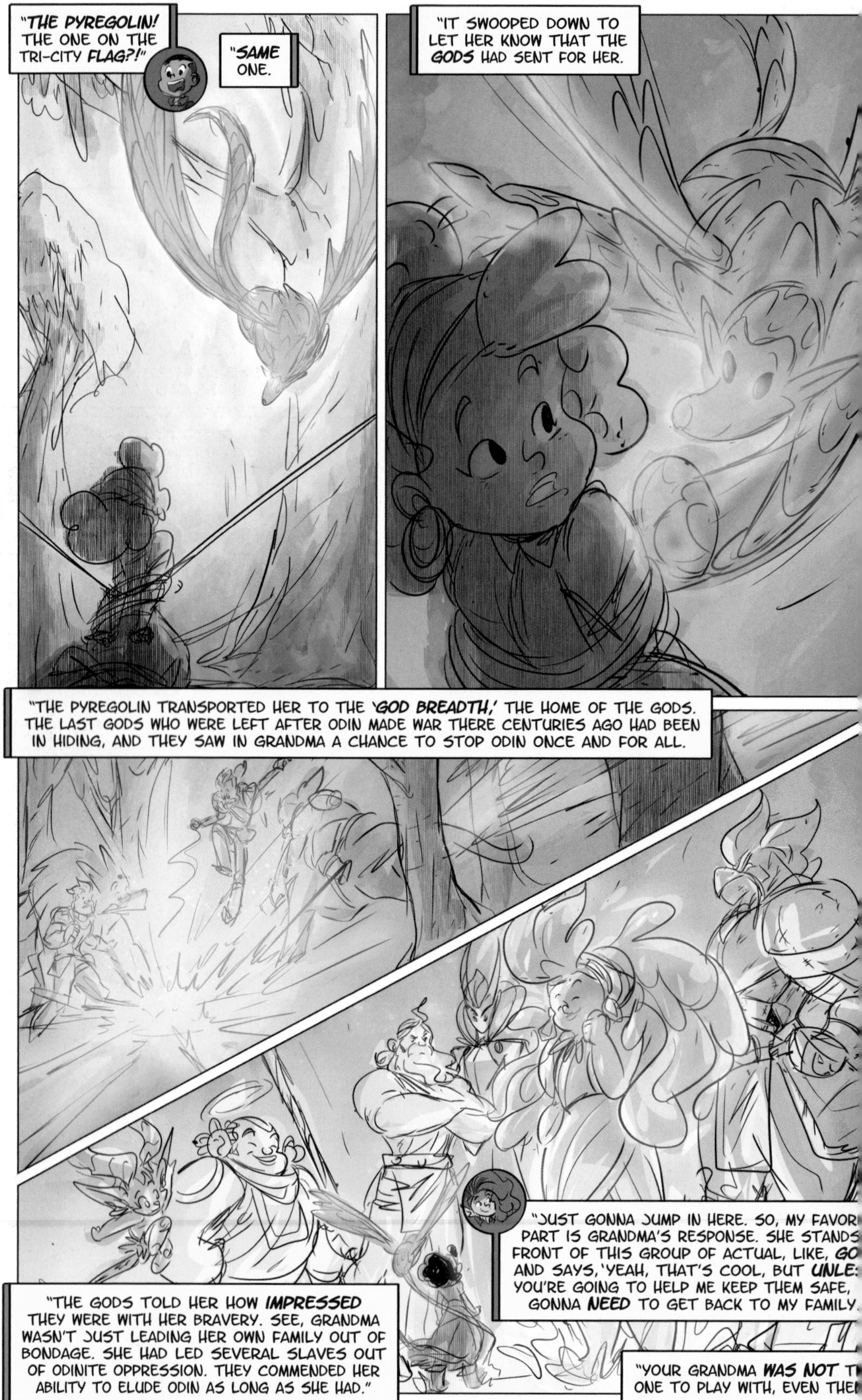
"THE PYREGOLIN! THE ONE ON THE TRI-CITY FLAG?!"
"SAME ONE.
"IT SWOOPED DOWN TO LET HER KNOW THAT THE GODS HAD SENT FOR HER.
"THE PYREGOLIN TRANSPORTED HER TO THE 'GOD BREADTH,' THE HOME OF THE GODS. THE LAST GODS WHO WERE LEFT AFTER ODIN MADE WAR THERE CENTURIES AGO HAD BEEN IN HIDING, AND THEY SAW IN GRANDMA A CHANCE TO STOP ODIN ONCE AND FOR ALL.
"THE GODS TOLD HER HOW IMPRESSED THEY WERE WITH HER BRAVERY. SEE, GRANDMA WASN'T JUST LEADING HER OWN FAMILY OUT OF BONDAGE. SHE HAD LED SEVERAL SLAVES OUT OF ODINITE OPPRESSION. THEY COMMENDED HER ABILITY TO ELUDE ODIN AS LONG AS SHE HAD."
"JUST GONNA JUMP IN HERE. SO, MY FAVORI PART IS GRANDMA'S RESPONSE. SHE STANDS FRONT OF THIS GROUP OF ACTUAL, LIKE, GO AND SAYS, 'YEAH, THAT'S COOL, BUT UNLE YOU'RE GOING TO HELP ME KEEP THEM SAFE, GONNA NEED TO GET BACK TO MY FAMILY.
"YOUR GRANDMA WAS NOT T ONE TO PLAY WITH, EVEN THE

ABSOLUTELY NOT!"

"SEE, IF THE GODS CAME OUT OF THEIR HIDING PLACES, ODIN WOULD BE ABLE TO *TRACK* THEM AND *WIPE* THEM OUT.

"SO, THEY *NEEDED* YOUR GRANDMA TO GET THE SABER, UNDETECTED, TO SAVE THEM."

"BUT IN ORDER TO COMPLETE THE QUEST AND DEFEAT HIM, SHE WOULD NEED THE *POWER* OF A GOD. *YEMOJA*, IN ALL HER WISDOM, OFFERED HER *THE POWER OF THE LAST GODS*."

"BUT I DON'T GET THE STUFF ABOUT *SEALING* AND *ODIN*, 'CAUSE GRANDMA BEATS HIM PRETTY REGULARLY THESE DAYS."

"THE ODIN YOU GUYS KNOW IS A PUSHOVER, A GOON. YOU'VE NEVER ACTUALLY EXPERIENCED THE *REAL* MAD GOD. ACCORDING TO GRANDMA, ALL WE'VE SEEN ARE... PIECES OF HIM. WE HAVEN'T PUT TOGETHER HOW THEY CROP UP FROM TIME TO TIME, BUT SHE THINKS SHE KNOWS WHY: TO KEEP HIS MEMORY *ALIVE*. AS I SAID, ADORATION OR EVEN HATE POWERS HIM, SO IT'S LIKE HE NEEDS TO REMIND THE WORLD HE EXISTS AND THE CHAOS HE'S CAPABLE OF IN ORDER TO STAY ALIVE. MAYBE HE HOPES THAT, ONE DAY, HE CAN GAIN ENOUGH POWER TO FULLY RETURN. SEALING IS THE ONLY WAY WE'VE BEEN ABLE TO STOP THE MORE POWERFUL PIECES OF ODIN. I THINK HIS POWER MAY BE *TOO* GREAT TO BE ELIMINATED. EVEN HIS FELLOW GODS DIDN'T KNOW HOW TO KILL HIM."

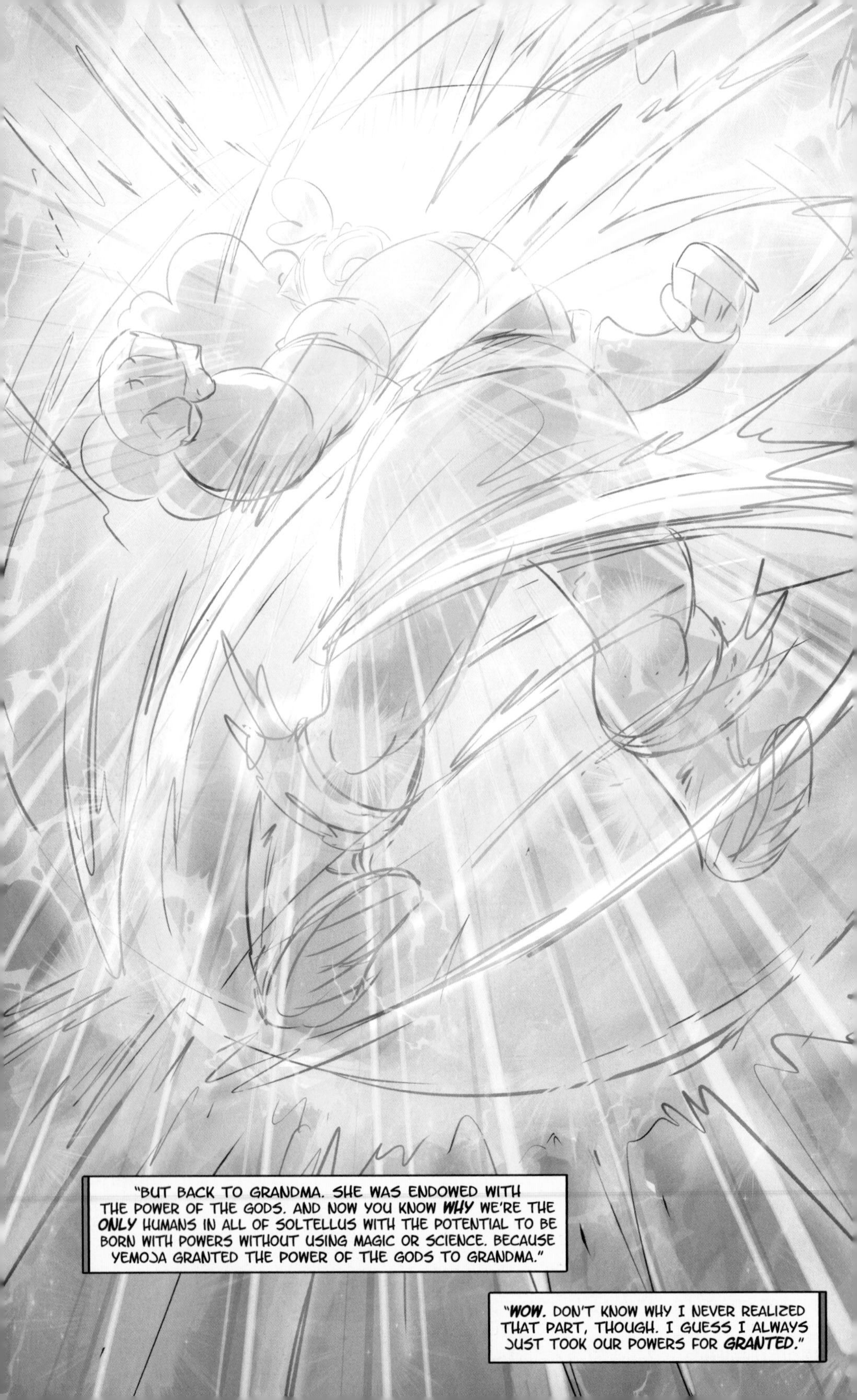
"BUT BACK TO GRANDMA. SHE WAS ENDOWED WITH THE POWER OF THE GODS. AND NOW YOU KNOW **WHY** WE'RE THE **ONLY** HUMANS IN ALL OF SOLTELLUS WITH THE POTENTIAL TO BE BORN WITH POWERS WITHOUT USING MAGIC OR SCIENCE. BECAUSE YEMOJA GRANTED THE POWER OF THE GODS TO GRANDMA."
"**WOW.** DON'T KNOW WHY I NEVER REALIZED THAT PART, THOUGH. I GUESS I ALWAYS JUST TOOK OUR POWERS FOR **GRANTED**."

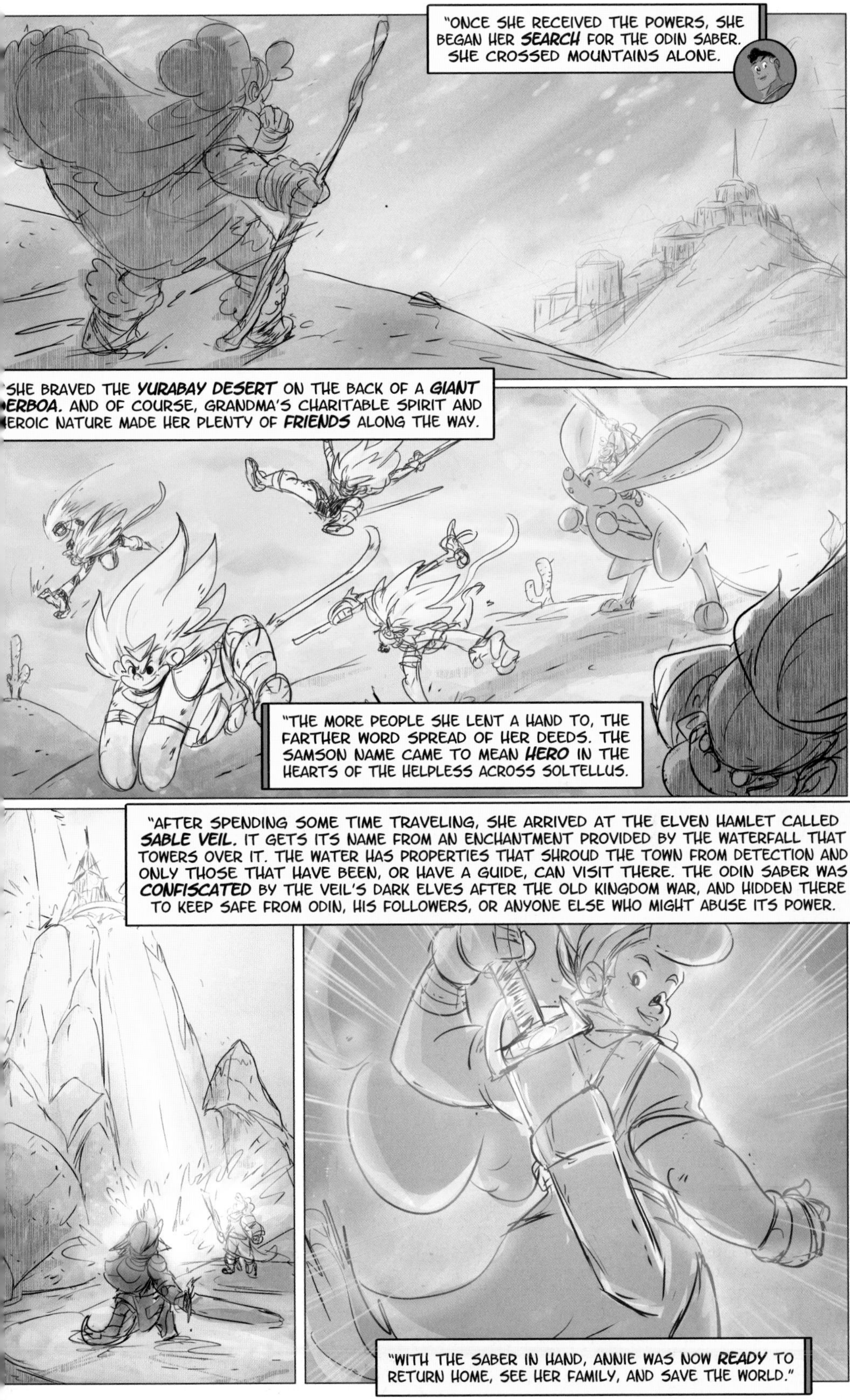
"ONCE SHE RECEIVED THE POWERS, SHE BEGAN HER SEARCH FOR THE ODIN SABER. SHE CROSSED MOUNTAINS ALONE.
"SHE BRAVED THE YURABAY DESERT ON THE BACK OF A GIANT ERBOA. AND OF COURSE, GRANDMA'S CHARITABLE SPIRIT AND EROIC NATURE MADE HER PLENTY OF FRIENDS ALONG THE WAY.
"THE MORE PEOPLE SHE LENT A HAND TO, THE FARTHER WORD SPREAD OF HER DEEDS. THE SAMSON NAME CAME TO MEAN HERO IN THE HEARTS OF THE HELPLESS ACROSS SOLTELLUS.
"AFTER SPENDING SOME TIME TRAVELING, SHE ARRIVED AT THE ELVEN HAMLET CALLED SABLE VEIL. IT GETS ITS NAME FROM AN ENCHANTMENT PROVIDED BY THE WATERFALL THAT TOWERS OVER IT. THE WATER HAS PROPERTIES THAT SHROUD THE TOWN FROM DETECTION AND ONLY THOSE THAT HAVE BEEN, OR HAVE A GUIDE, CAN VISIT THERE. THE ODIN SABER WAS CONFISCATED BY THE VEIL'S DARK ELVES AFTER THE OLD KINGDOM WAR, AND HIDDEN THERE TO KEEP SAFE FROM ODIN, HIS FOLLOWERS, OR ANYONE ELSE WHO MIGHT ABUSE ITS POWER.
"WITH THE SABER IN HAND, ANNIE WAS NOW READY TO RETURN HOME, SEE HER FAMILY, AND SAVE THE WORLD."

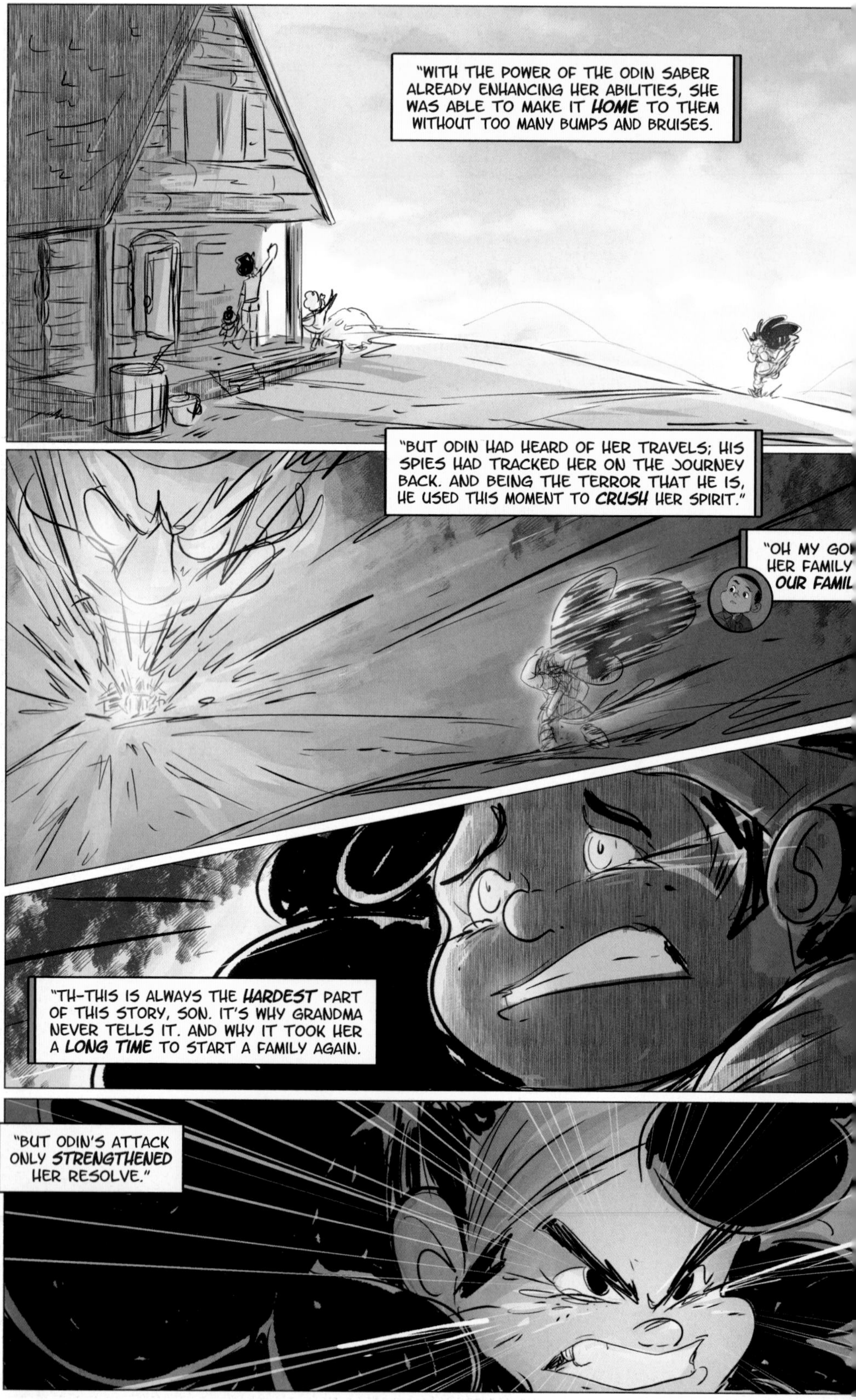
"WITH THE POWER OF THE ODIN SABER ALREADY ENHANCING HER ABILITIES, SHE WAS ABLE TO MAKE IT HOME TO THEM WITHOUT TOO MANY BUMPS AND BRUISES.
"BUT ODIN HAD HEARD OF HER TRAVELS; HIS SPIES HAD TRACKED HER ON THE JOURNEY BACK. AND BEING THE TERROR THAT HE IS, HE USED THIS MOMENT TO CRUSH HER SPIRIT."
"OH MY GO HER FAMILY OUR FAMIL
"TH-THIS IS ALWAYS THE HARDEST PART OF THIS STORY, SON. IT'S WHY GRANDMA NEVER TELLS IT. AND WHY IT TOOK HER A LONG TIME TO START A FAMILY AGAIN.
"BUT ODIN'S ATTACK ONLY STRENGTHENED HER RESOLVE."

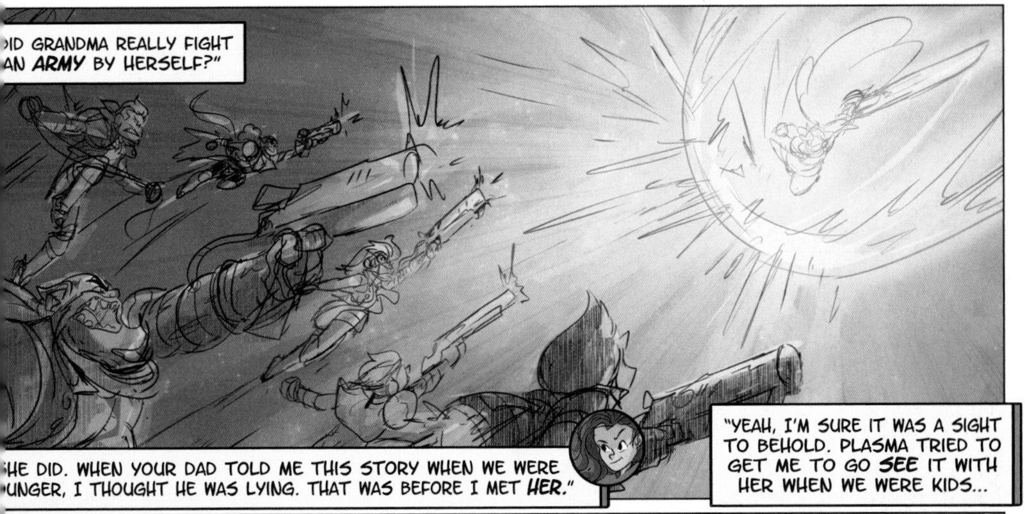
ID GRANDMA REALLY FIGHT AN **ARMY** BY HERSELF?"
HE DID. WHEN YOUR DAD TOLD ME THIS STORY WHEN WE WERE UNGER, I THOUGHT HE WAS LYING. THAT WAS BEFORE I MET **HER.**"
"YEAH, I'M SURE IT WAS A SIGHT TO BEHOLD. PLASMA TRIED TO GET ME TO GO **SEE** IT WITH HER WHEN WE WERE KIDS...

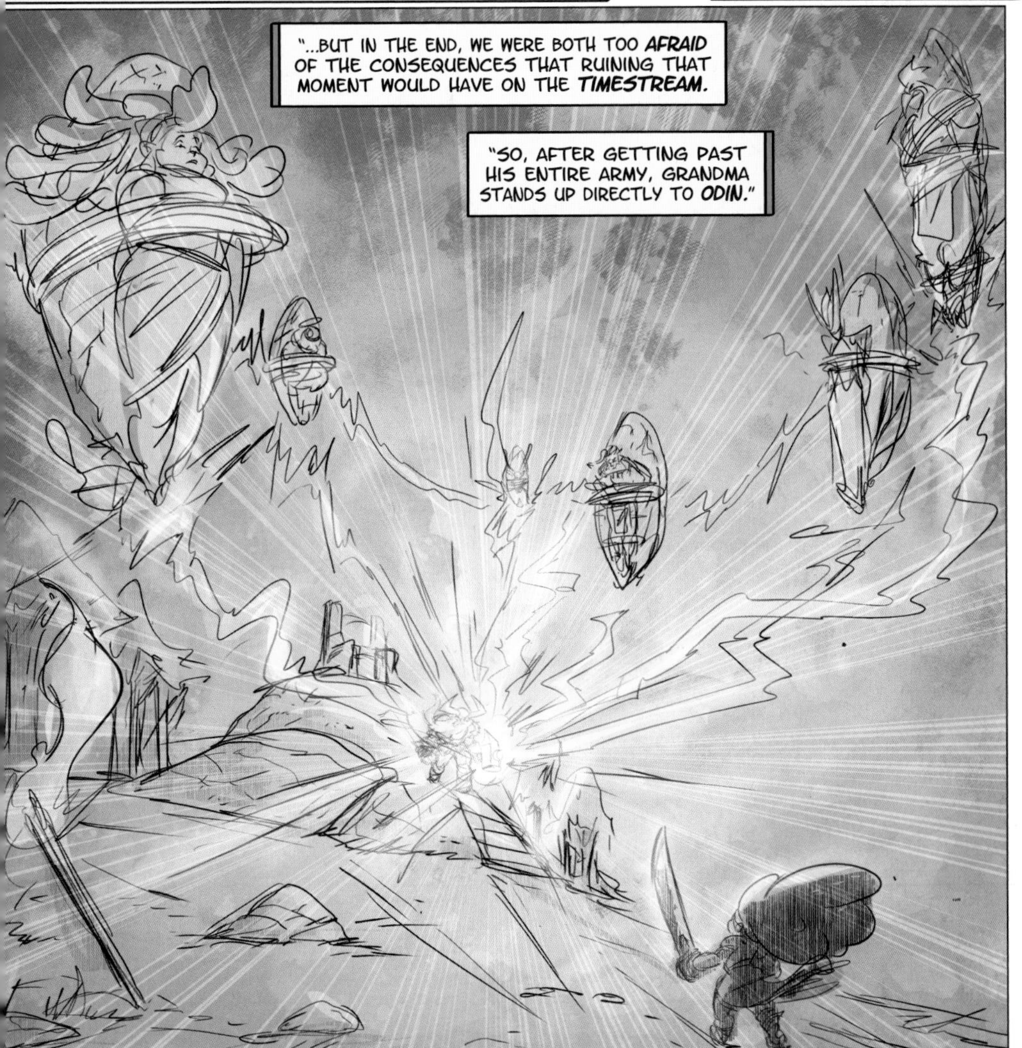
"...BUT IN THE END, WE WERE BOTH TOO **AFRAID** OF THE CONSEQUENCES THAT RUINING THAT MOMENT WOULD HAVE ON THE **TIMESTREAM.**
"SO, AFTER GETTING PAST HIS ENTIRE ARMY, GRANDMA STANDS UP DIRECTLY TO **ODIN.**"

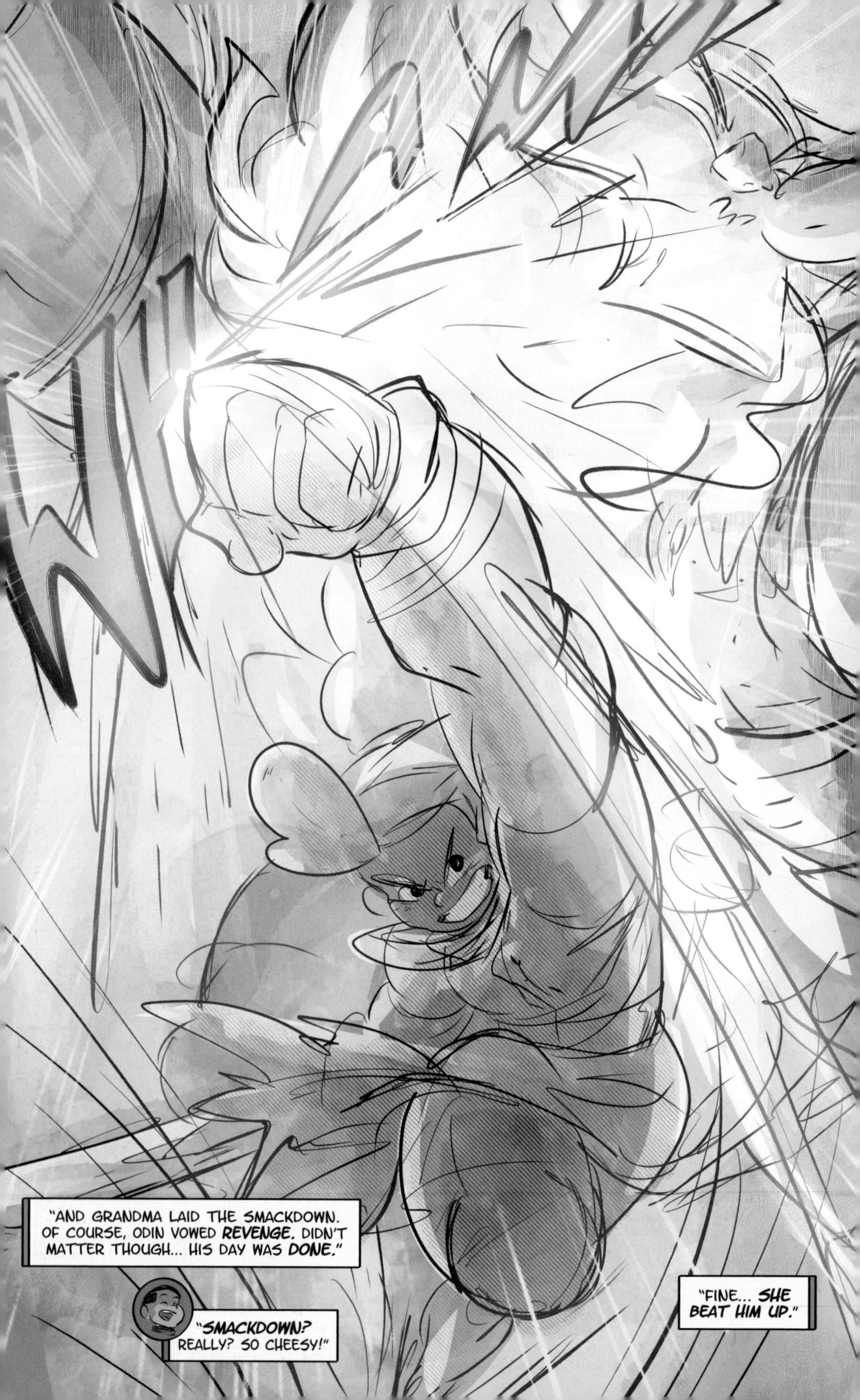
"AND GRANDMA LAID THE SMACKDOWN. OF COURSE, ODIN VOWED **REVENGE.** DIDN'T MATTER THOUGH... HIS DAY WAS **DONE.**"
"**SMACKDOWN?** REALLY? SO CHEESY!"
"FINE... **SHE** BEAT HIM UP."

SHE **FREED** THE LAST GODS, INCLUDING MOJA, WHO HAD BEEN CAPTURED SINCE GRANDMA HAD BEEN ON HER QUEST.

"THE LOSS OF HER FAMILY WEIGHED **HEAVILY** ON HER, THOUGH. THE GODS TRIED TO COMFORT HER, SAYING HER SACRIFICE MADE SURE MANY MORE COULD PROSPER AND LIVE FREELY.

AS THEY FADED AWAY, THEY REMINDED HER THAT WHILE THE HEARTS OF HUMANITY WILL ALWAYS SWING BETWEEN GOOD AND EVIL, ON THAT DAY, SHE ENDED THE INFLUENCE OF A MAD GOD. OR SO SHE THOUGHT.

"NOW WE KNOW THAT PIECES OF ODIN CAN **RETURN**, LIKE THE OTHER DAY WITH YOU AND HER FIGHTING HIM.

"GRANDMA WAS PROUD OF HER NEW ROLE AS THE WORLD'S **CHAMPION**."

"BUT WAIT, WHAT ABOUT **US?** I MEAN, WHAT MADE HER WANT TO HAVE A FAMILY **AGAIN?**"

"WELL, SINCE YOUR GRANDMA HAS THE POWERS OF THE GODS FLOWING INSIDE OF HER, SHE'S VERY LONG-LIVED, AND I SUPPOSE THAT'S A THING THAT CAN GET VERY **LONELY**. BUT THAT'S... A STORY FOR HER AND YOUR GRANDPA TO TELL."

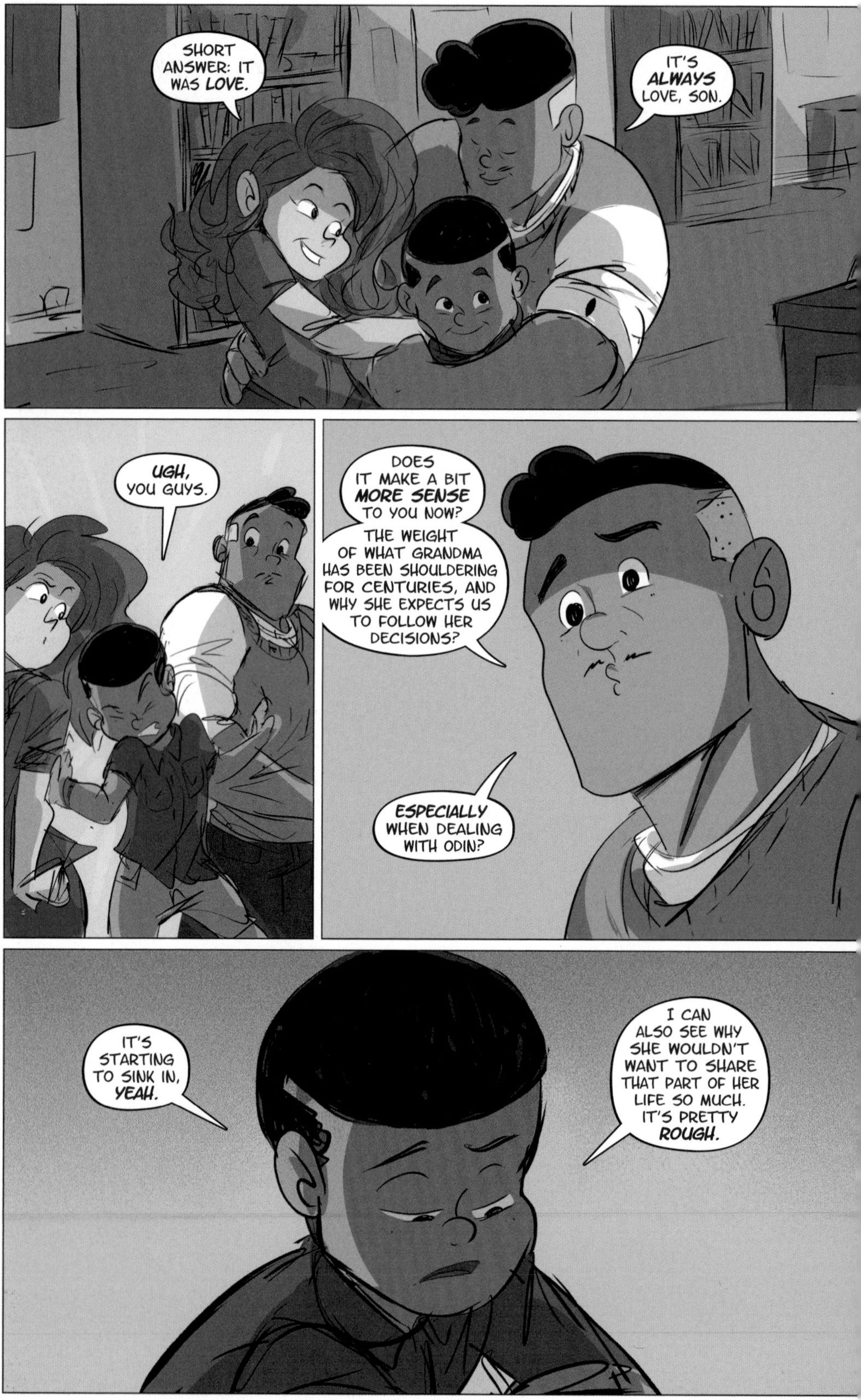
SHORT ANSWER: IT WAS LOVE.
IT'S ALWAYS LOVE, SON.
UGH, YOU GUYS.
DOES IT MAKE A BIT MORE SENSE TO YOU NOW?
THE WEIGHT OF WHAT GRANDMA HAS BEEN SHOULDERING FOR CENTURIES, AND WHY SHE EXPECTS US TO FOLLOW HER DECISIONS?
ESPECIALLY WHEN DEALING WITH ODIN?
IT'S STARTING TO SINK IN, YEAH.
I CAN ALSO SEE WHY SHE WOULDN'T WANT TO SHARE THAT PART OF HER LIFE SO MUCH. IT'S PRETTY ROUGH.

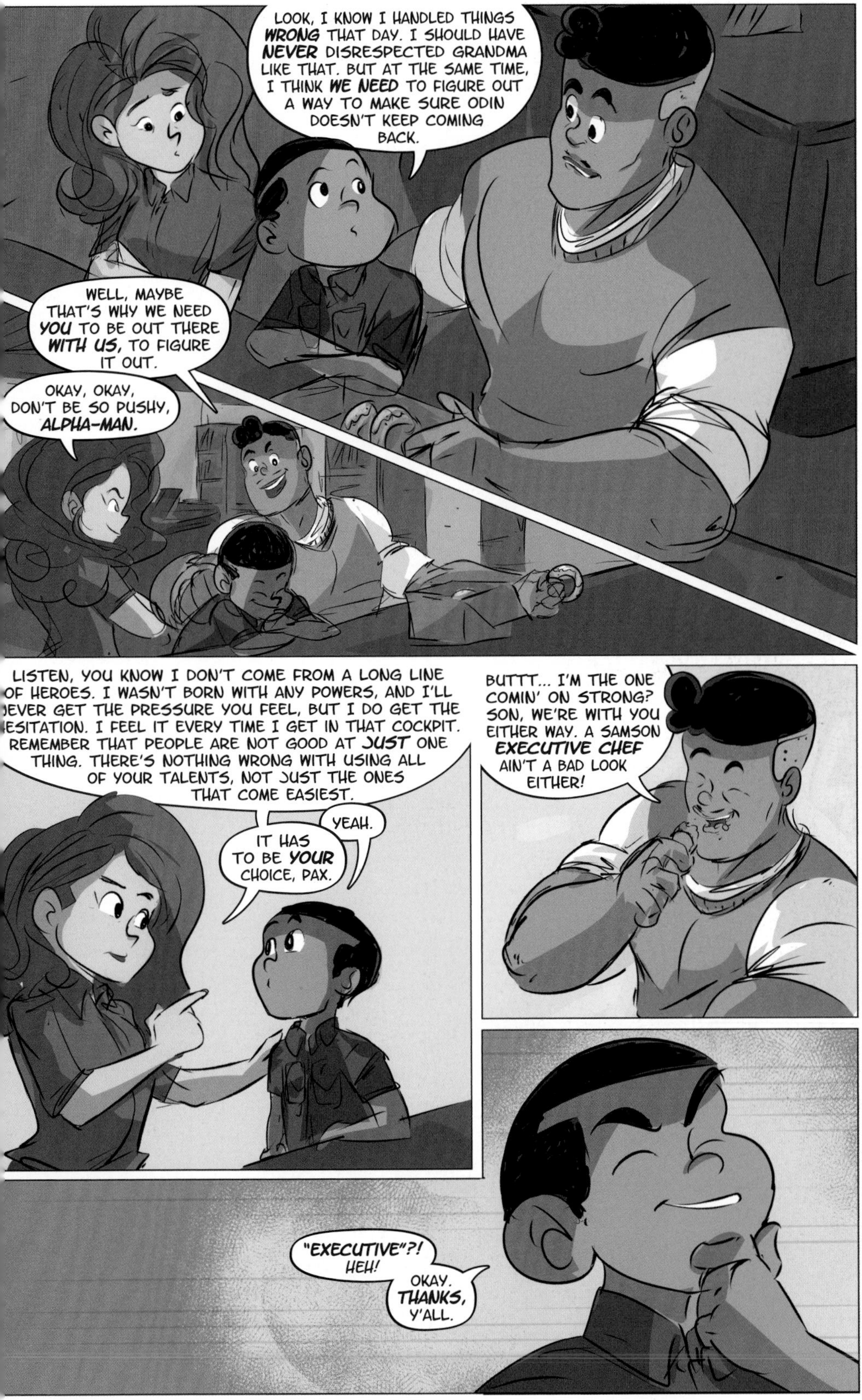
LOOK, I KNOW I HANDLED THINGS **WRONG** THAT DAY. I SHOULD HAVE **NEVER** DISRESPECTED GRANDMA LIKE THAT. BUT AT THE SAME TIME, I THINK **WE NEED** TO FIGURE OUT A WAY TO MAKE SURE ODIN DOESN'T KEEP COMING BACK.
WELL, MAYBE THAT'S WHY WE NEED **YOU** TO BE OUT THERE **WITH US,** TO FIGURE IT OUT.
OKAY, OKAY, DON'T BE SO PUSHY, **ALPHA-MAN.**
LISTEN, YOU KNOW I DON'T COME FROM A LONG LINE OF HEROES. I WASN'T BORN WITH ANY POWERS, AND I'LL NEVER GET THE PRESSURE YOU FEEL, BUT I DO GET THE HESITATION. I FEEL IT EVERY TIME I GET IN THAT COCKPIT. REMEMBER THAT PEOPLE ARE NOT GOOD AT **JUST** ONE THING. THERE'S NOTHING WRONG WITH USING ALL OF YOUR TALENTS, NOT JUST THE ONES THAT COME EASIEST.
IT HAS TO BE **YOUR** CHOICE, PAX.
YEAH.
BUTTT... I'M THE ONE COMIN' ON STRONG? SON, WE'RE WITH YOU EITHER WAY. A SAMSON **EXECUTIVE CHEF** AIN'T A BAD LOOK EITHER!
"EXECUTIVE"?! HEH!
OKAY. **THANKS,** Y'ALL.

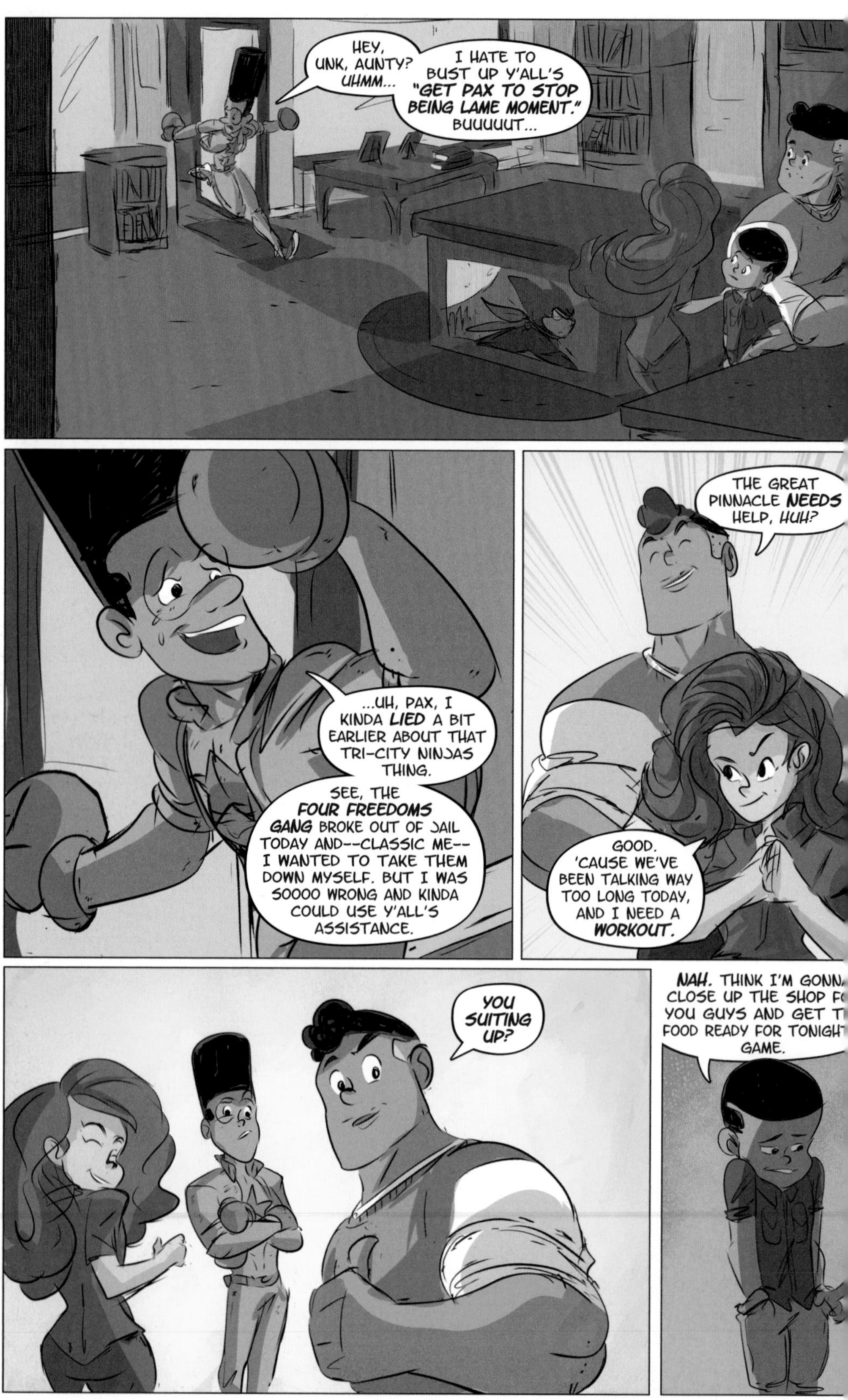
HEY, UNK, AUNTY? UHMM...
I HATE TO BUST UP Y'ALL'S **"GET PAX TO STOP BEING LAME MOMENT."** BUUUUUT...
...UH, PAX, I KINDA **LIED** A BIT EARLIER ABOUT THAT TRI-CITY NINJAS THING.
SEE, THE **FOUR FREEDOMS GANG** BROKE OUT OF JAIL TODAY AND--CLASSIC ME--I WANTED TO TAKE THEM DOWN MYSELF. BUT I WAS SOOOO WRONG AND KINDA COULD USE Y'ALL'S ASSISTANCE.
THE GREAT PINNACLE **NEEDS** HELP, HUH?
GOOD. 'CAUSE WE'VE BEEN TALKING WAY TOO LONG TODAY, AND I NEED A **WORKOUT**.
YOU SUITING UP?
NAH. THINK I'M GONN CLOSE UP THE SHOP F YOU GUYS AND GET T FOOD READY FOR TONIGHT GAME.

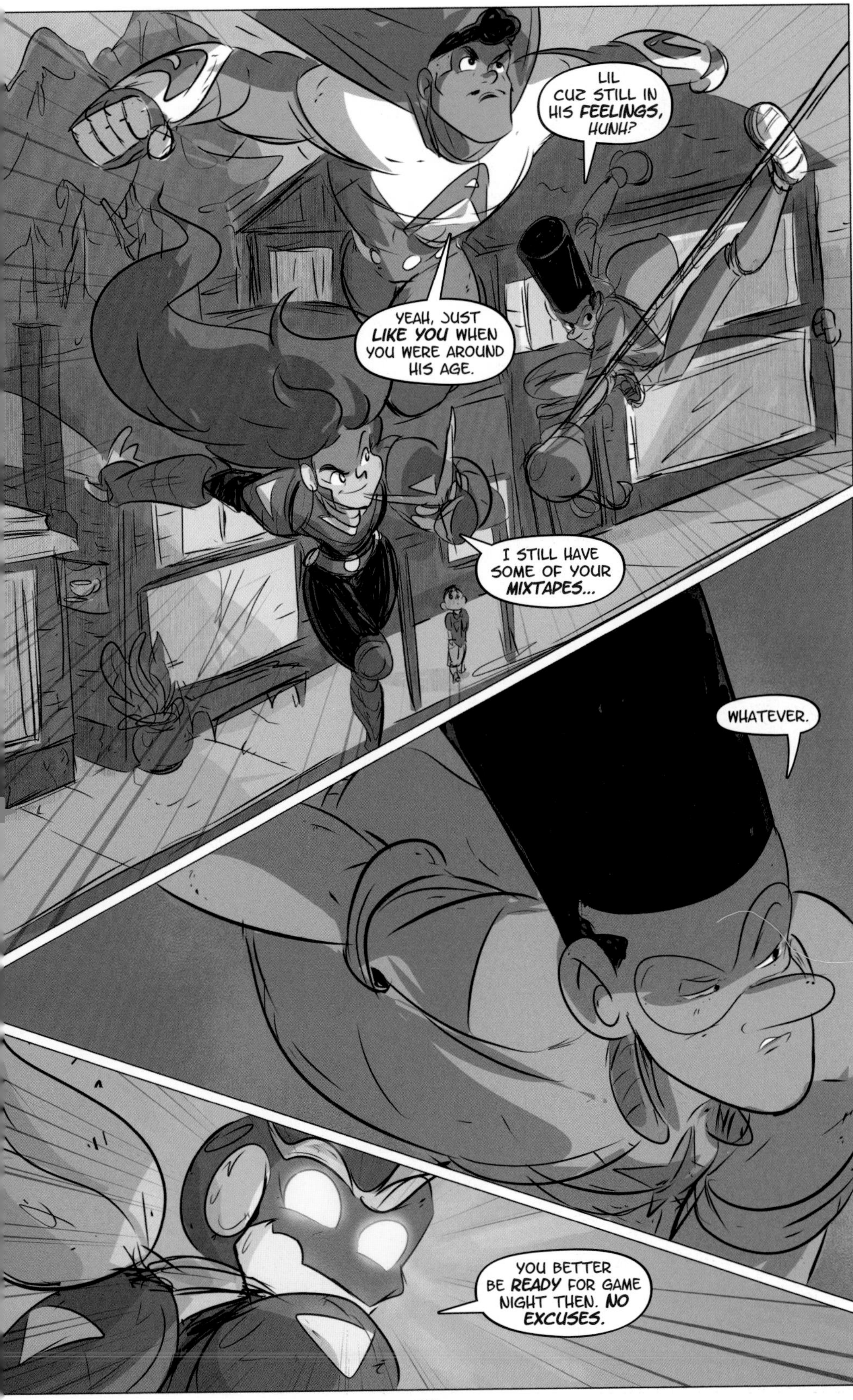
LIL CUZ STILL IN HIS FEELINGS, HUNH?
YEAH, JUST LIKE YOU WHEN YOU WERE AROUND HIS AGE.
I STILL HAVE SOME OF YOUR MIXTAPES...
WHATEVER.
YOU BETTER BE READY FOR GAME NIGHT THEN. NO EXCUSES.

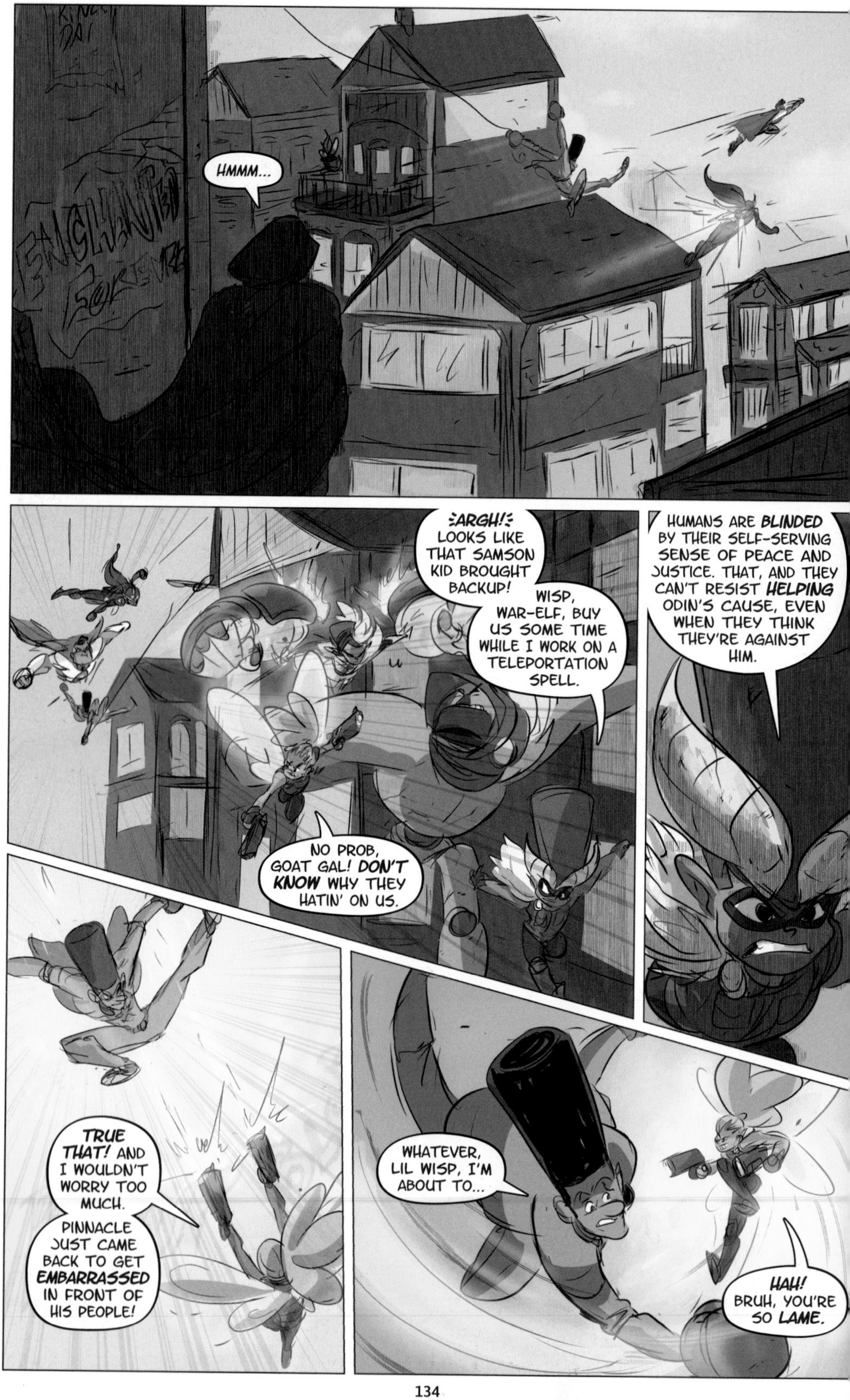

HMMM...
ARGH! LOOKS LIKE THAT SAMSON KID BROUGHT BACKUP!
WISP, WAR-ELF, BUY US SOME TIME WHILE I WORK ON A TELEPORTATION SPELL.
NO PROB, GOAT GAL! **DON'T KNOW** WHY THEY HATIN' ON US.
HUMANS ARE **BLINDED** BY THEIR SELF-SERVING SENSE OF PEACE AND JUSTICE. THAT, AND THEY CAN'T RESIST **HELPING** ODIN'S CAUSE, EVEN WHEN THEY THINK THEY'RE AGAINST HIM.
TRUE THAT! AND I WOULDN'T WORRY TOO MUCH.
PINNACLE JUST CAME BACK TO GET **EMBARRASSED** IN FRONT OF HIS PEOPLE!
WHATEVER, LIL WISP, I'M ABOUT TO...
HAH! BRUH, YOU'RE SO **LAME.**

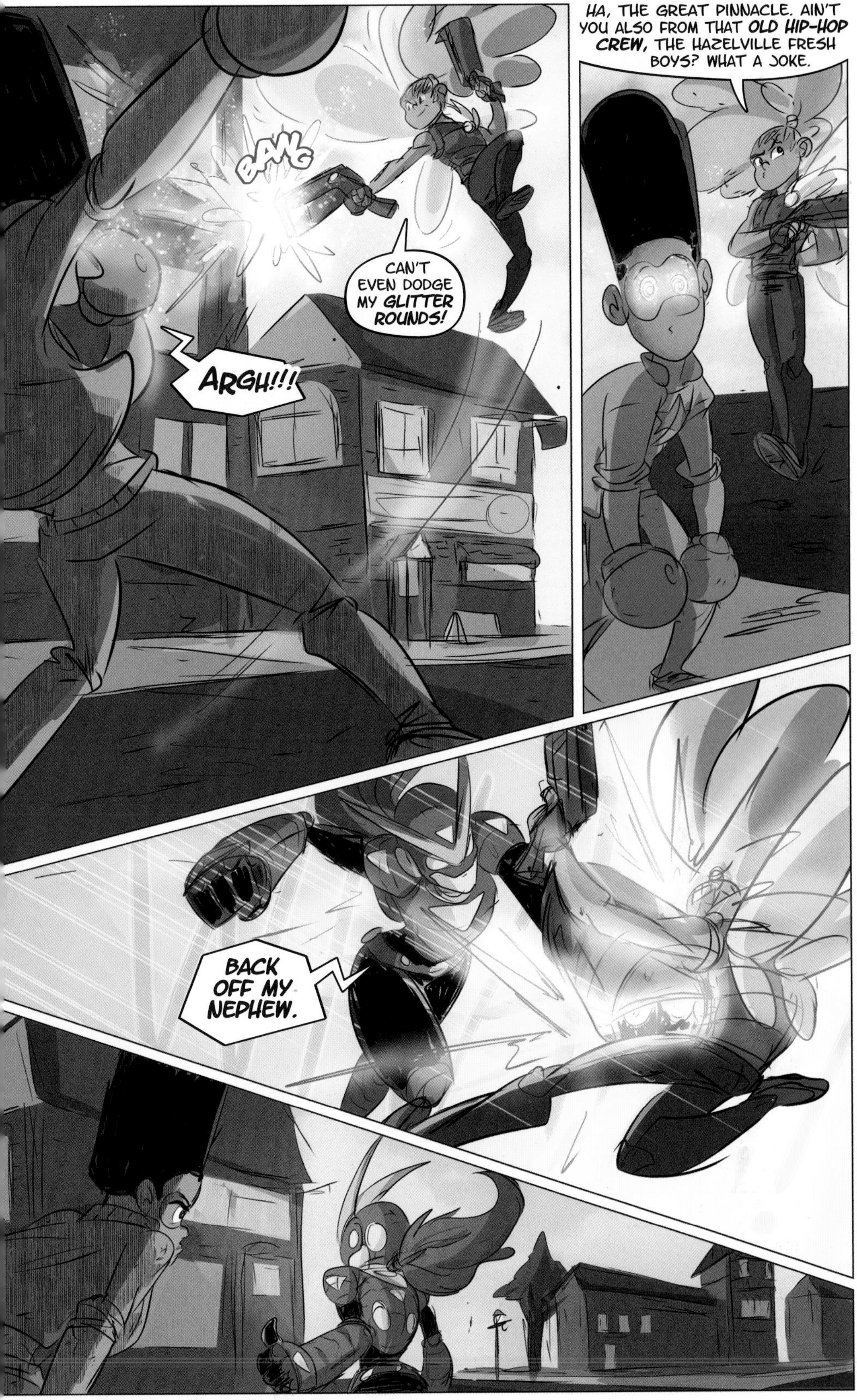
BANG
CAN'T EVEN DODGE MY GLITTER ROUNDS!
ARGH!!!
HA, THE GREAT PINNACLE. AIN'T YOU ALSO FROM THAT OLD HIP-HOP CREW, THE HAZELVILLE FRESH BOYS? WHAT A JOKE.
BACK OFF MY NEPHEW.

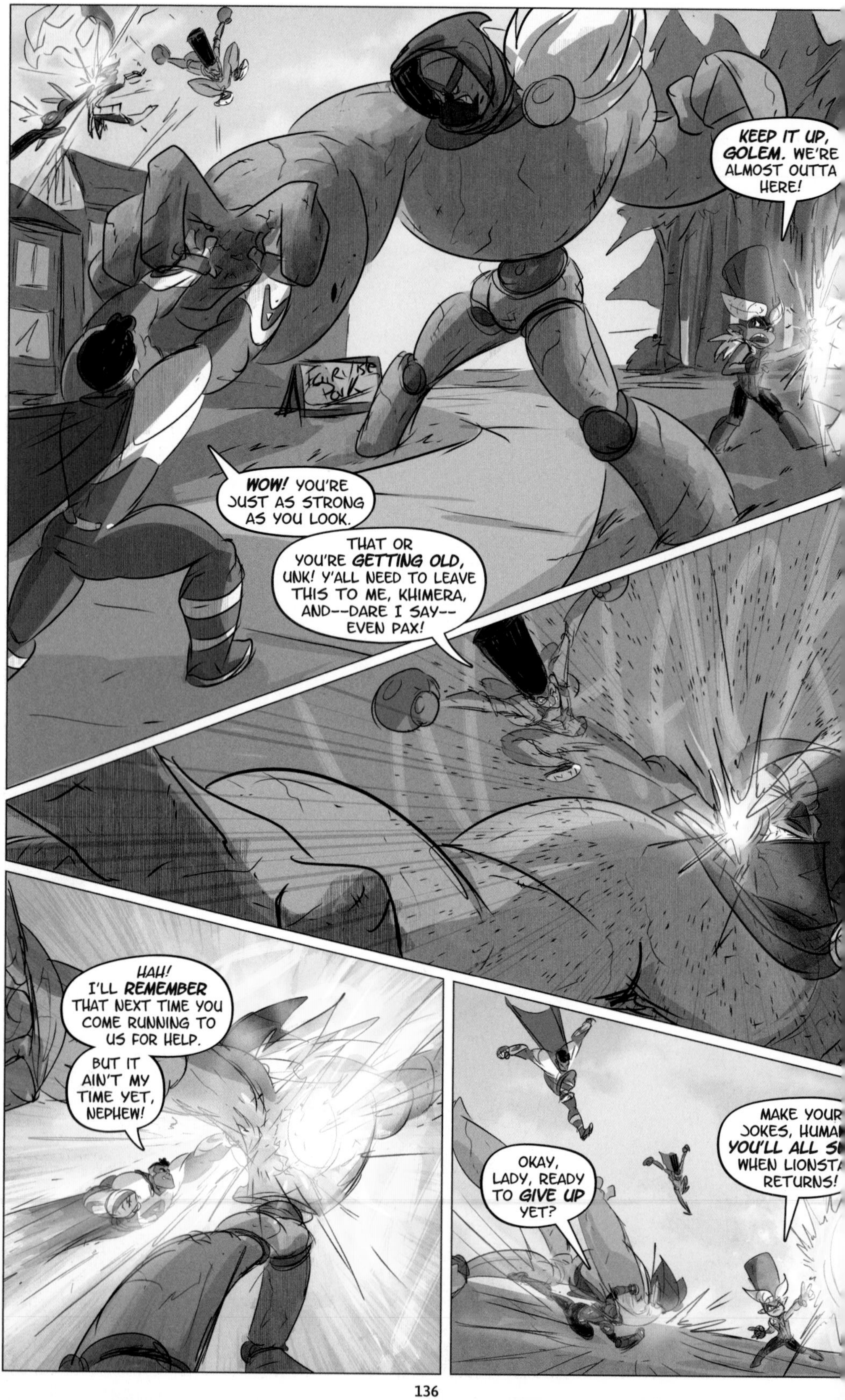
KEEP IT UP, GOLEM. WE'RE ALMOST OUTTA HERE!
WOW! YOU'RE JUST AS STRONG AS YOU LOOK.
THAT OR YOU'RE GETTING OLD, UNK! Y'ALL NEED TO LEAVE THIS TO ME, KHIMERA, AND--DARE I SAY--EVEN PAX!
HAH! I'LL REMEMBER THAT NEXT TIME YOU COME RUNNING TO US FOR HELP.
BUT IT AIN'T MY TIME YET, NEPHEW!
OKAY, LADY, READY TO GIVE UP YET?
MAKE YOUR JOKES, HUMA YOU'LL ALL S WHEN LIONSTA RETURNS!

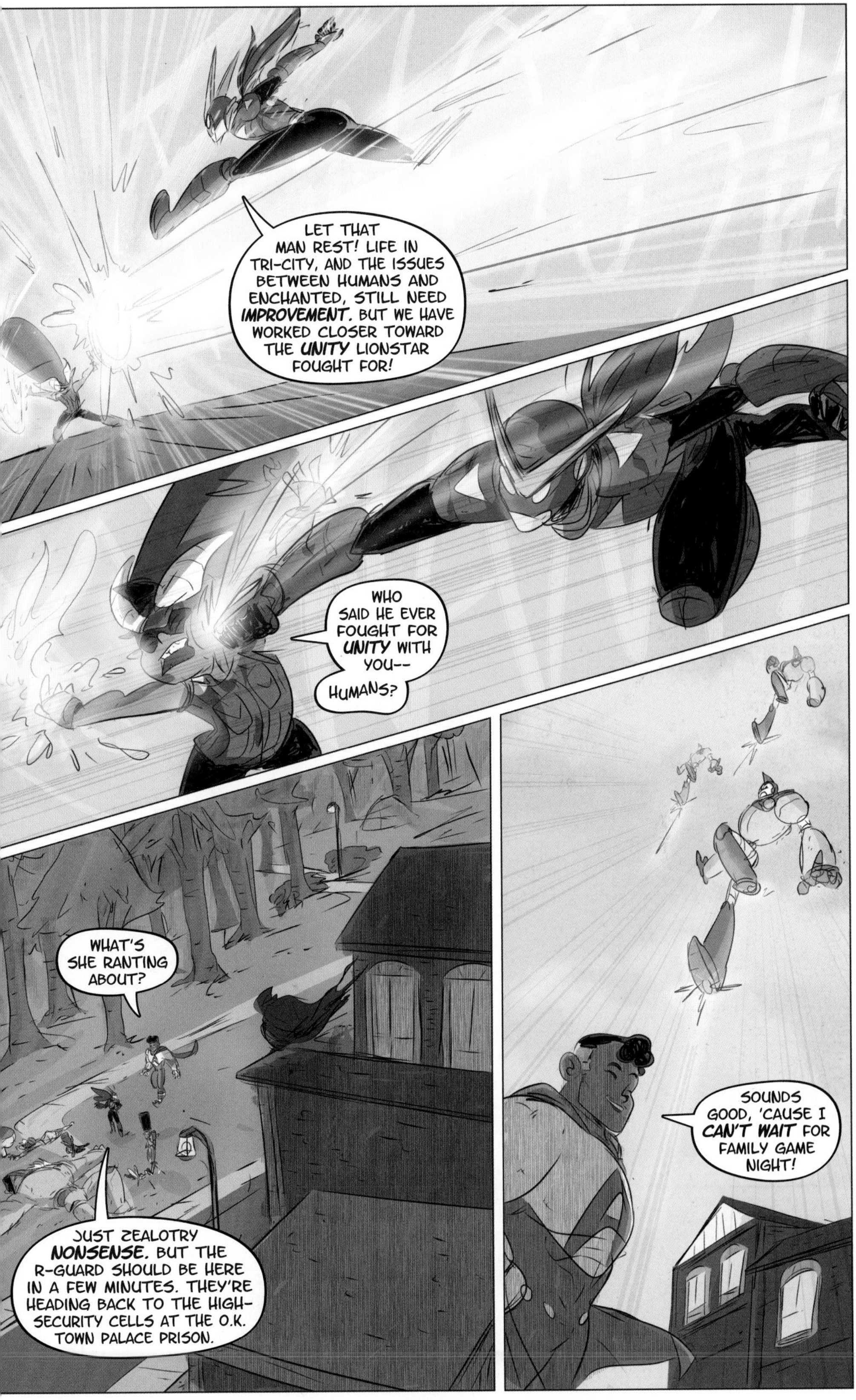
LET THAT MAN REST! LIFE IN TRI-CITY, AND THE ISSUES BETWEEN HUMANS AND ENCHANTED, STILL NEED **IMPROVEMENT.** BUT WE HAVE WORKED CLOSER TOWARD THE **UNITY** LIONSTAR FOUGHT FOR!
WHO SAID HE EVER FOUGHT FOR **UNITY** WITH YOU--
HUMANS?
WHAT'S SHE RANTING ABOUT?
JUST ZEALOTRY **NONSENSE.** BUT THE R-GUARD SHOULD BE HERE IN A FEW MINUTES. THEY'RE HEADING BACK TO THE HIGH-SECURITY CELLS AT THE O.K. TOWN PALACE PRISON.
SOUNDS GOOD, 'CAUSE I **CAN'T WAIT** FOR FAMILY GAME NIGHT!

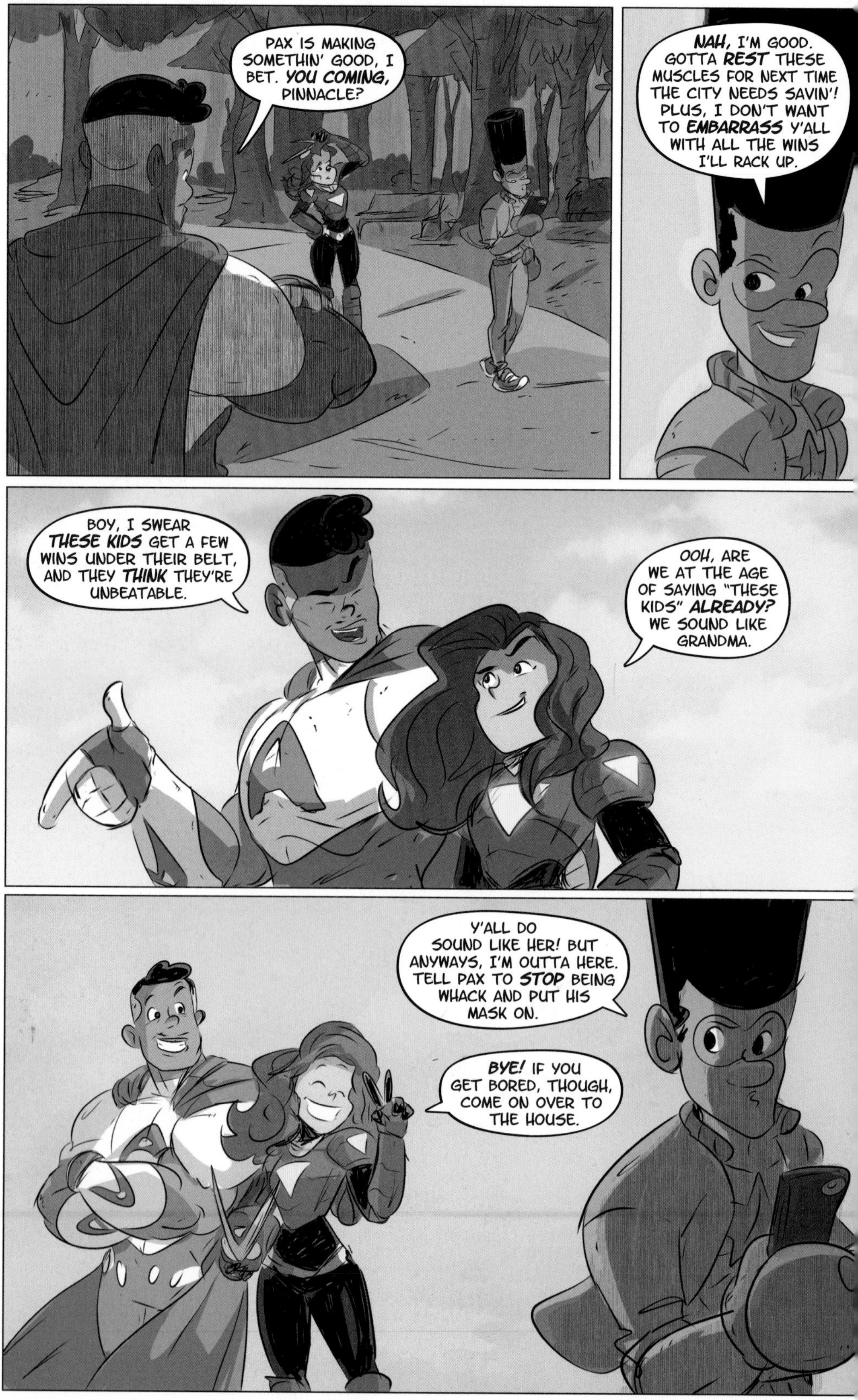
PAX IS MAKING SOMETHIN' GOOD, I BET. YOU COMING, PINNACLE?
NAH, I'M GOOD. GOTTA REST THESE MUSCLES FOR NEXT TIME THE CITY NEEDS SAVIN'! PLUS, I DON'T WANT TO EMBARRASS Y'ALL WITH ALL THE WINS I'LL RACK UP.
BOY, I SWEAR THESE KIDS GET A FEW WINS UNDER THEIR BELT, AND THEY THINK THEY'RE UNBEATABLE.
OOH, ARE WE AT THE AGE OF SAYING "THESE KIDS" ALREADY? WE SOUND LIKE GRANDMA.
Y'ALL DO SOUND LIKE HER! BUT ANYWAYS, I'M OUTTA HERE. TELL PAX TO STOP BEING WHACK AND PUT HIS MASK ON.
BYE! IF YOU GET BORED, THOUGH, COME ON OVER TO THE HOUSE.

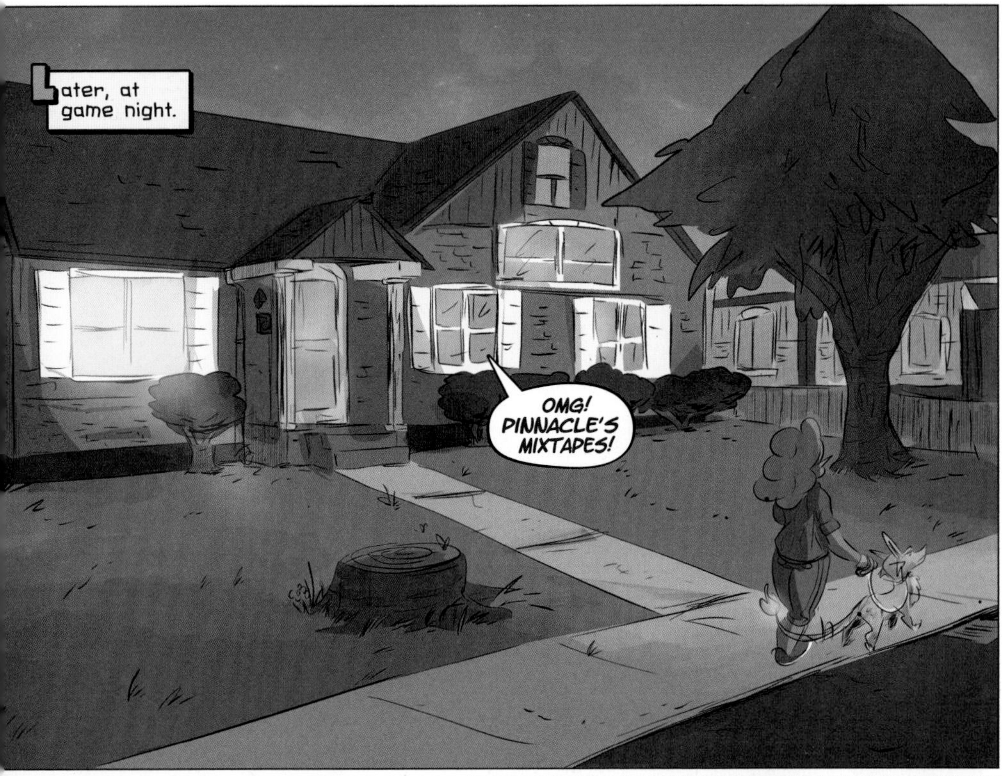
Later, at game night.
OMG! PINNACLE'S MIXTAPES!

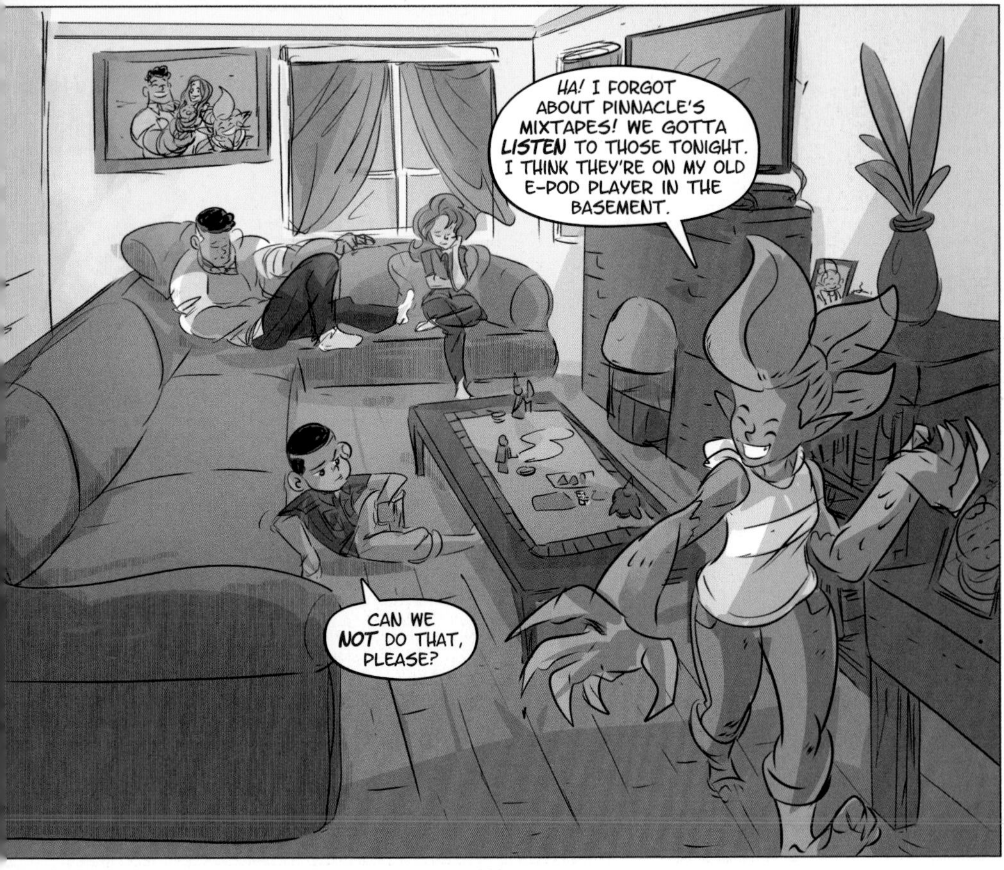
HA! I FORGOT ABOUT PINNACLE'S MIXTAPES! WE GOTTA LISTEN TO THOSE TONIGHT. I THINK THEY'RE ON MY OLD E-POD PLAYER IN THE BASEMENT.
CAN WE NOT DO THAT, PLEASE?

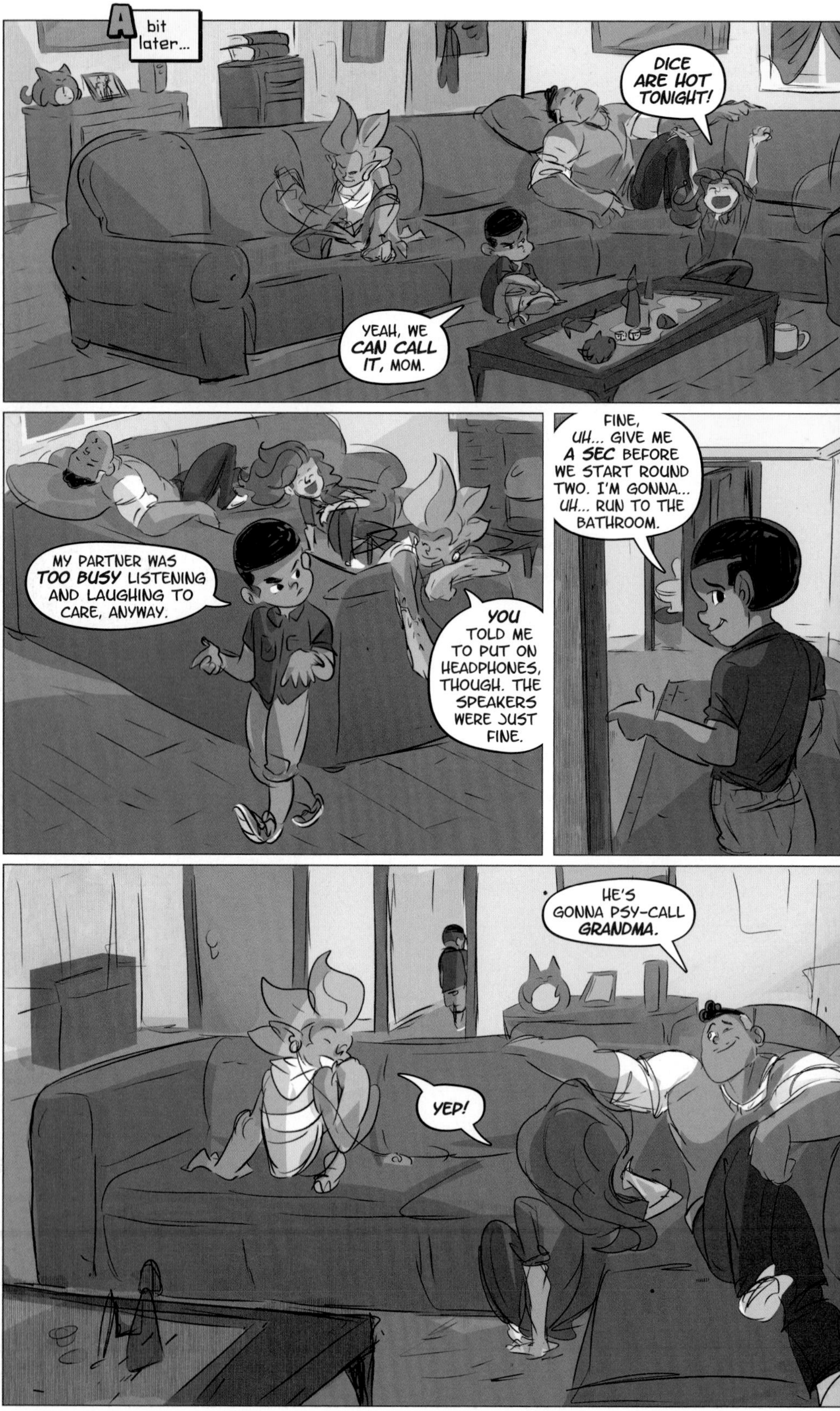
A bit later...
DICE ARE HOT TONIGHT!
YEAH, WE CAN CALL IT, MOM.
MY PARTNER WAS TOO BUSY LISTENING AND LAUGHING TO CARE, ANYWAY.
YOU TOLD ME TO PUT ON HEADPHONES, THOUGH. THE SPEAKERS WERE JUST FINE.
FINE, UH... GIVE ME A SEC BEFORE WE START ROUND TWO. I'M GONNA... UH... RUN TO THE BATHROOM.
HE'S GONNA PSY-CALL GRANDMA.
YEP!

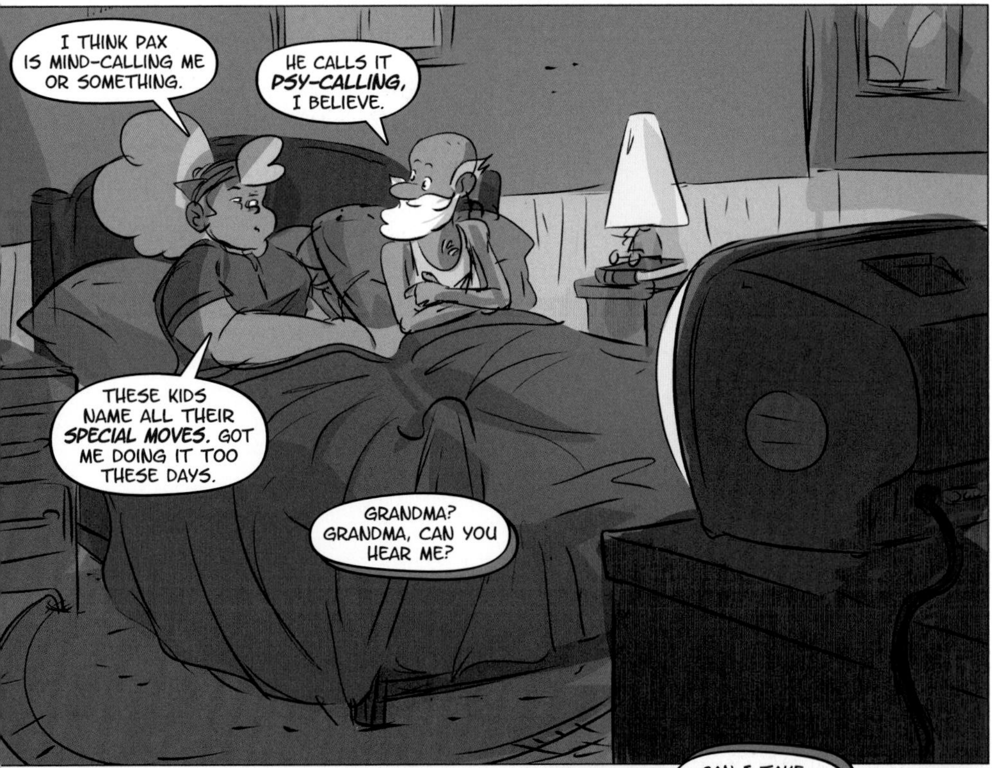
I THINK PAX IS MIND-CALLING ME OR SOMETHING.
HE CALLS IT PSY-CALLING, I BELIEVE.
THESE KIDS NAME ALL THEIR SPECIAL MOVES. GOT ME DOING IT TOO THESE DAYS.
GRANDMA? GRANDMA, CAN YOU HEAR ME?

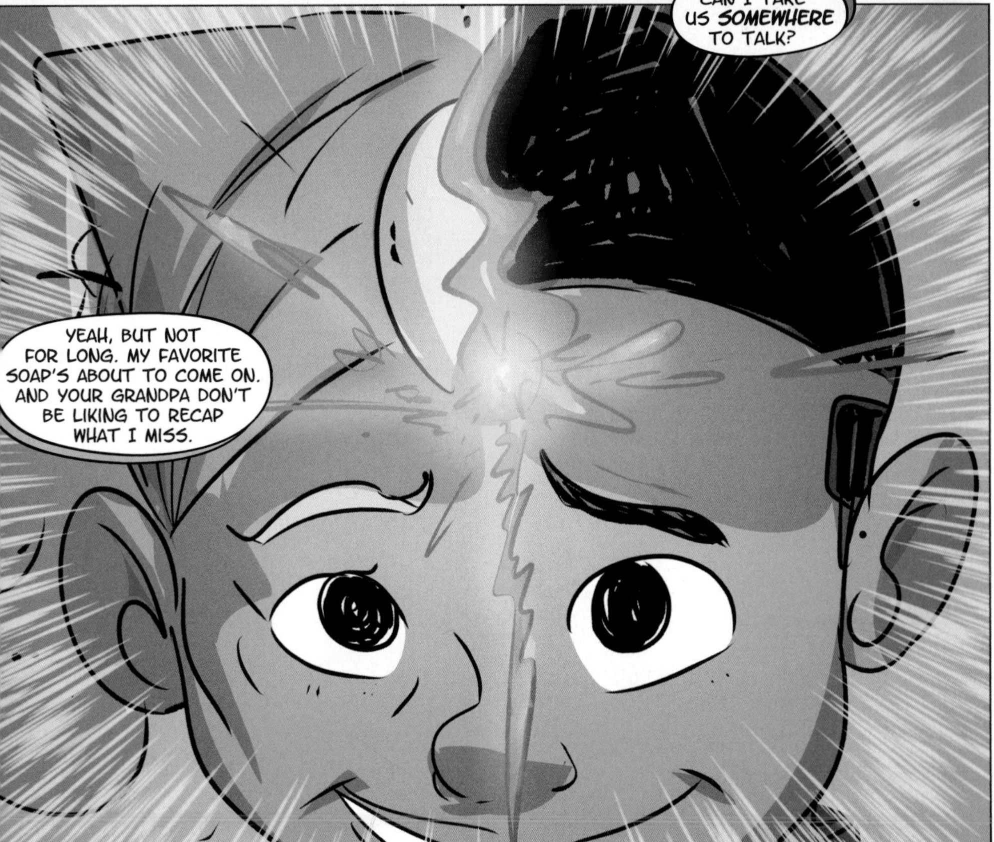
CAN I TAKE US SOMEWHERE TO TALK?
YEAH, BUT NOT FOR LONG. MY FAVORITE SOAP'S ABOUT TO COME ON. AND YOUR GRANDPA DON'T BE LIKING TO RECAP WHAT I MISS.

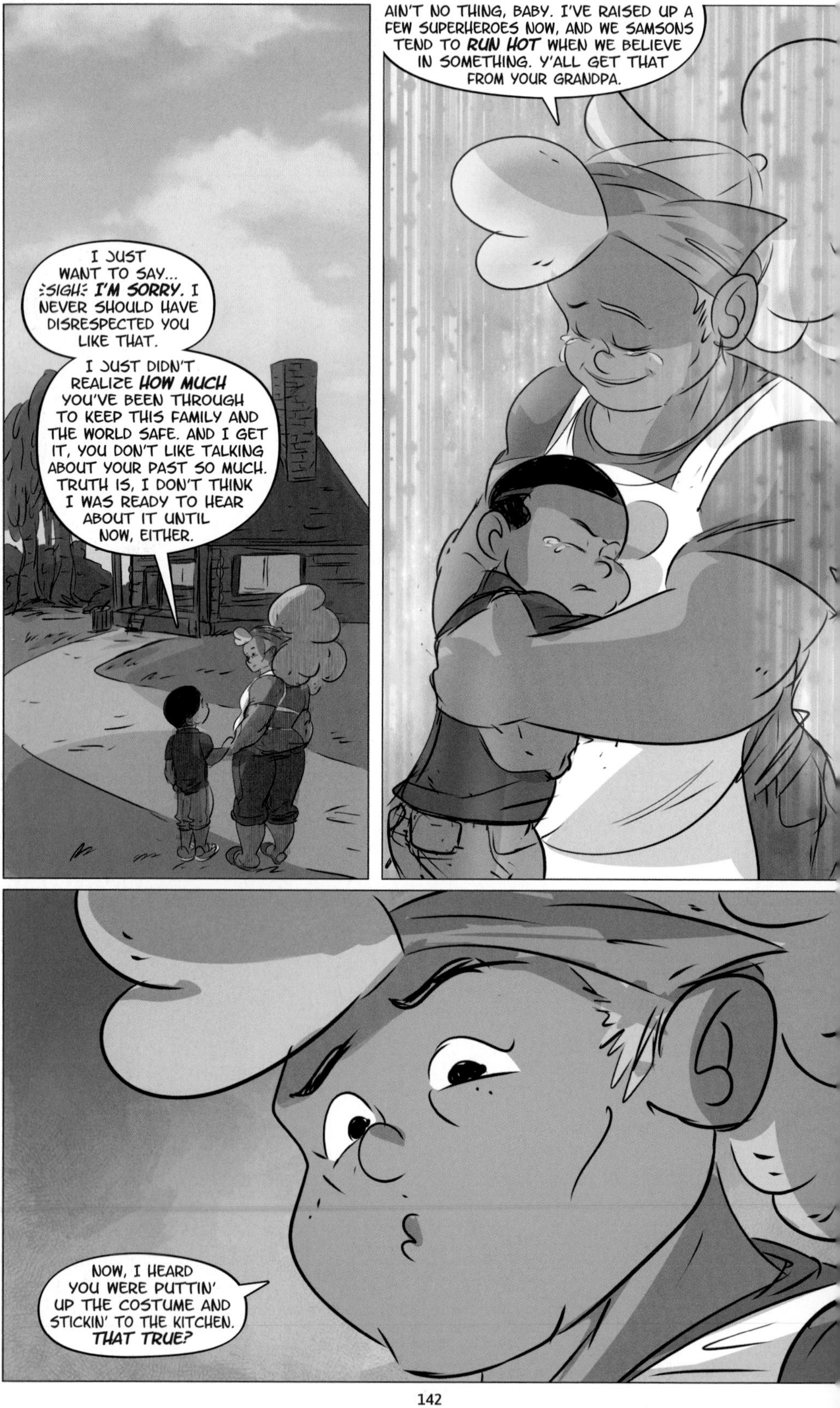
I JUST WANT TO SAY... :SIGH: I'M SORRY. I NEVER SHOULD HAVE DISRESPECTED YOU LIKE THAT.
I JUST DIDN'T REALIZE HOW MUCH YOU'VE BEEN THROUGH TO KEEP THIS FAMILY AND THE WORLD SAFE. AND I GET IT, YOU DON'T LIKE TALKING ABOUT YOUR PAST SO MUCH. TRUTH IS, I DON'T THINK I WAS READY TO HEAR ABOUT IT UNTIL NOW, EITHER.
AIN'T NO THING, BABY. I'VE RAISED UP A FEW SUPERHEROES NOW, AND WE SAMSONS TEND TO RUN HOT WHEN WE BELIEVE IN SOMETHING. Y'ALL GET THAT FROM YOUR GRANDPA.
NOW, I HEARD YOU WERE PUTTIN' UP THE COSTUME AND STICKIN' TO THE KITCHEN. THAT TRUE?

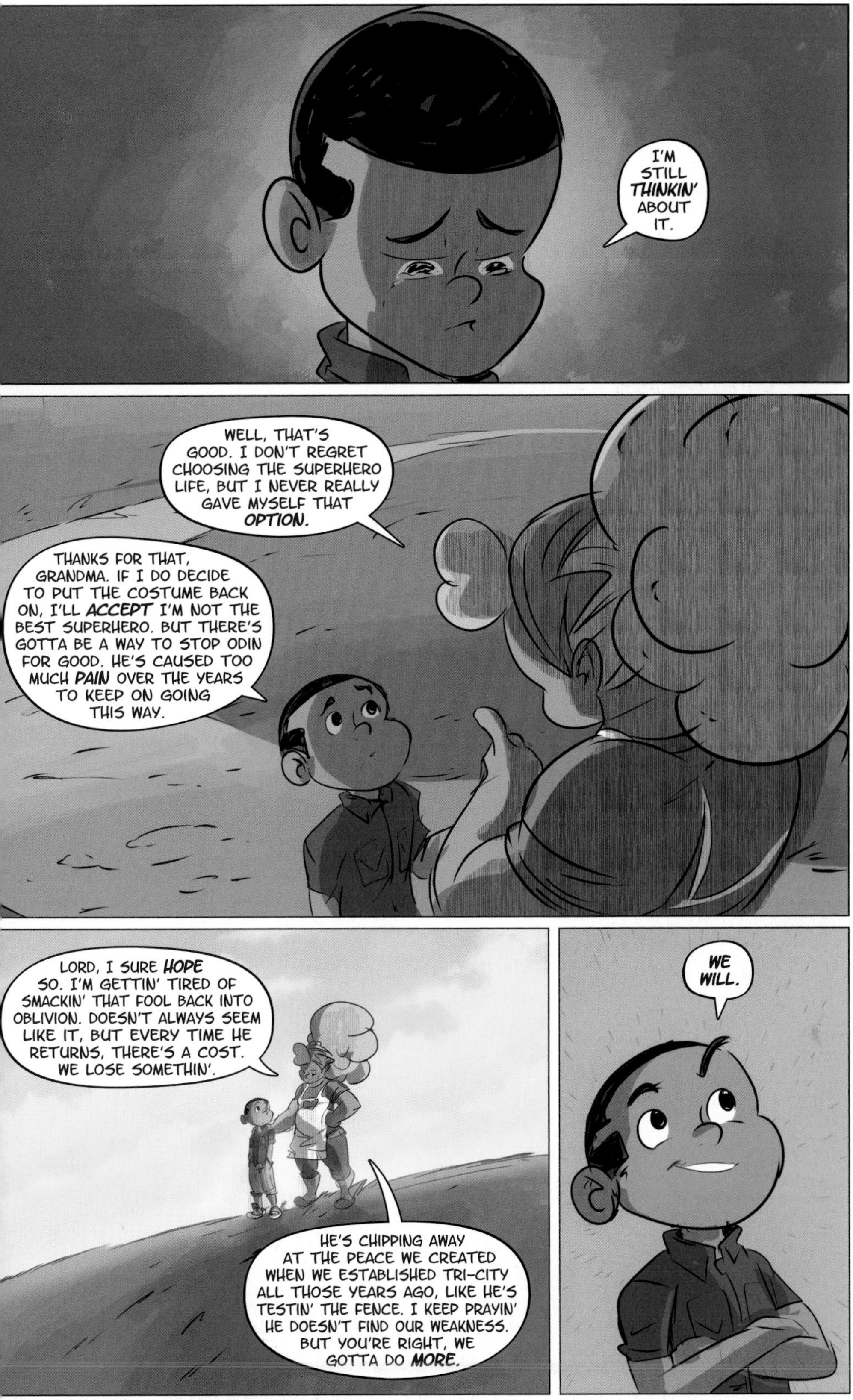
I'M STILL THINKIN' ABOUT IT.
WELL, THAT'S GOOD. I DON'T REGRET CHOOSING THE SUPERHERO LIFE, BUT I NEVER REALLY GAVE MYSELF THAT OPTION.
THANKS FOR THAT, GRANDMA. IF I DO DECIDE TO PUT THE COSTUME BACK ON, I'LL ACCEPT I'M NOT THE BEST SUPERHERO. BUT THERE'S GOTTA BE A WAY TO STOP ODIN FOR GOOD. HE'S CAUSED TOO MUCH PAIN OVER THE YEARS TO KEEP ON GOING THIS WAY.
LORD, I SURE HOPE SO. I'M GETTIN' TIRED OF SMACKIN' THAT FOOL BACK INTO OBLIVION. DOESN'T ALWAYS SEEM LIKE IT, BUT EVERY TIME HE RETURNS, THERE'S A COST. WE LOSE SOMETHIN'.
HE'S CHIPPING AWAY AT THE PEACE WE CREATED WHEN WE ESTABLISHED TRI-CITY ALL THOSE YEARS AGO, LIKE HE'S TESTIN' THE FENCE. I KEEP PRAYIN' HE DOESN'T FIND OUR WEAKNESS. BUT YOU'RE RIGHT, WE GOTTA DO MORE.
WE WILL.

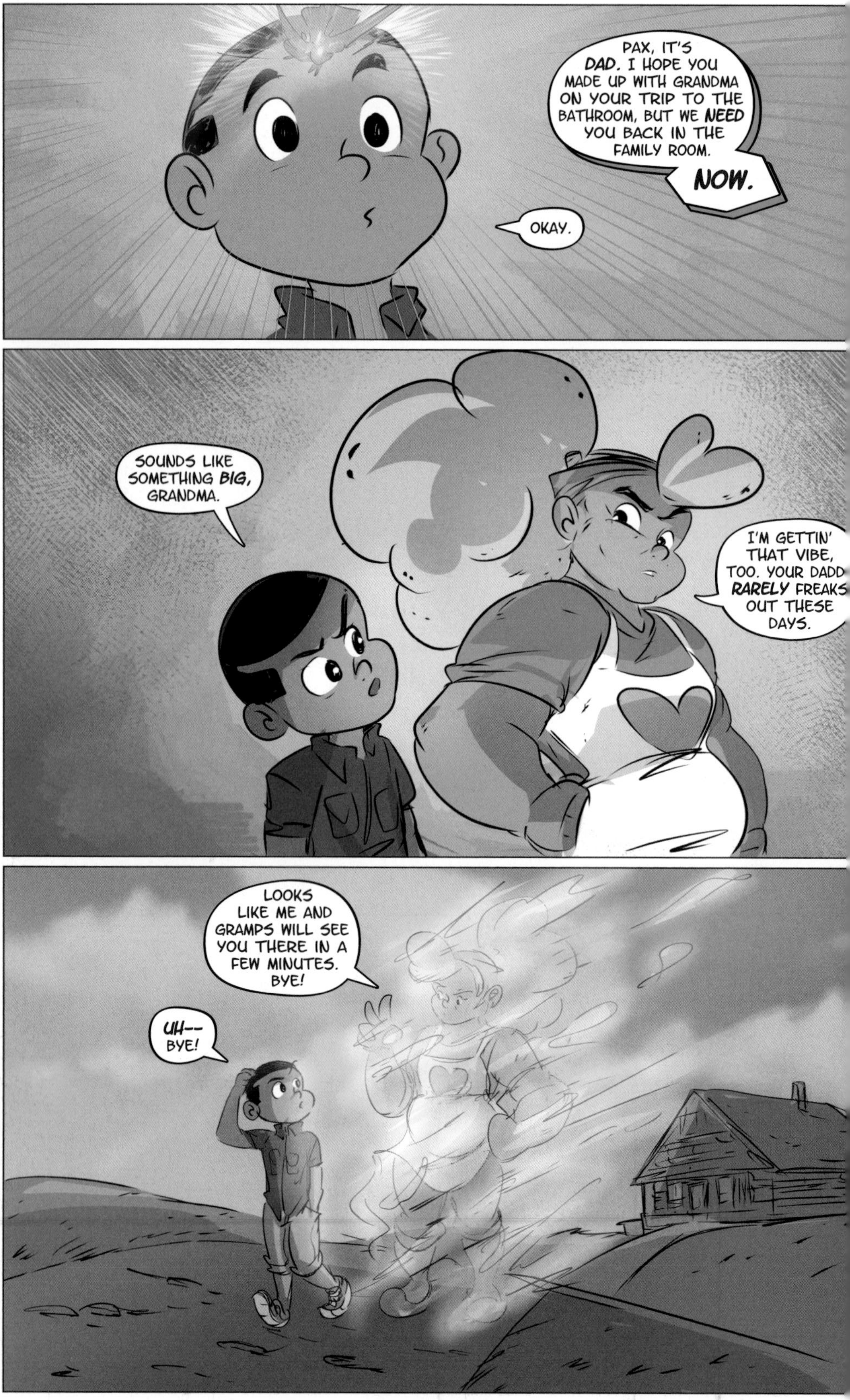
PAX, IT'S DAD. I HOPE YOU MADE UP WITH GRANDMA ON YOUR TRIP TO THE BATHROOM, BUT WE NEED YOU BACK IN THE FAMILY ROOM.
NOW.
OKAY.
SOUNDS LIKE SOMETHING BIG, GRANDMA.
I'M GETTIN' THAT VIBE, TOO. YOUR DADD RARELY FREAKS OUT THESE DAYS.
LOOKS LIKE ME AND GRAMPS WILL SEE YOU THERE IN A FEW MINUTES. BYE!
UH-- BYE!

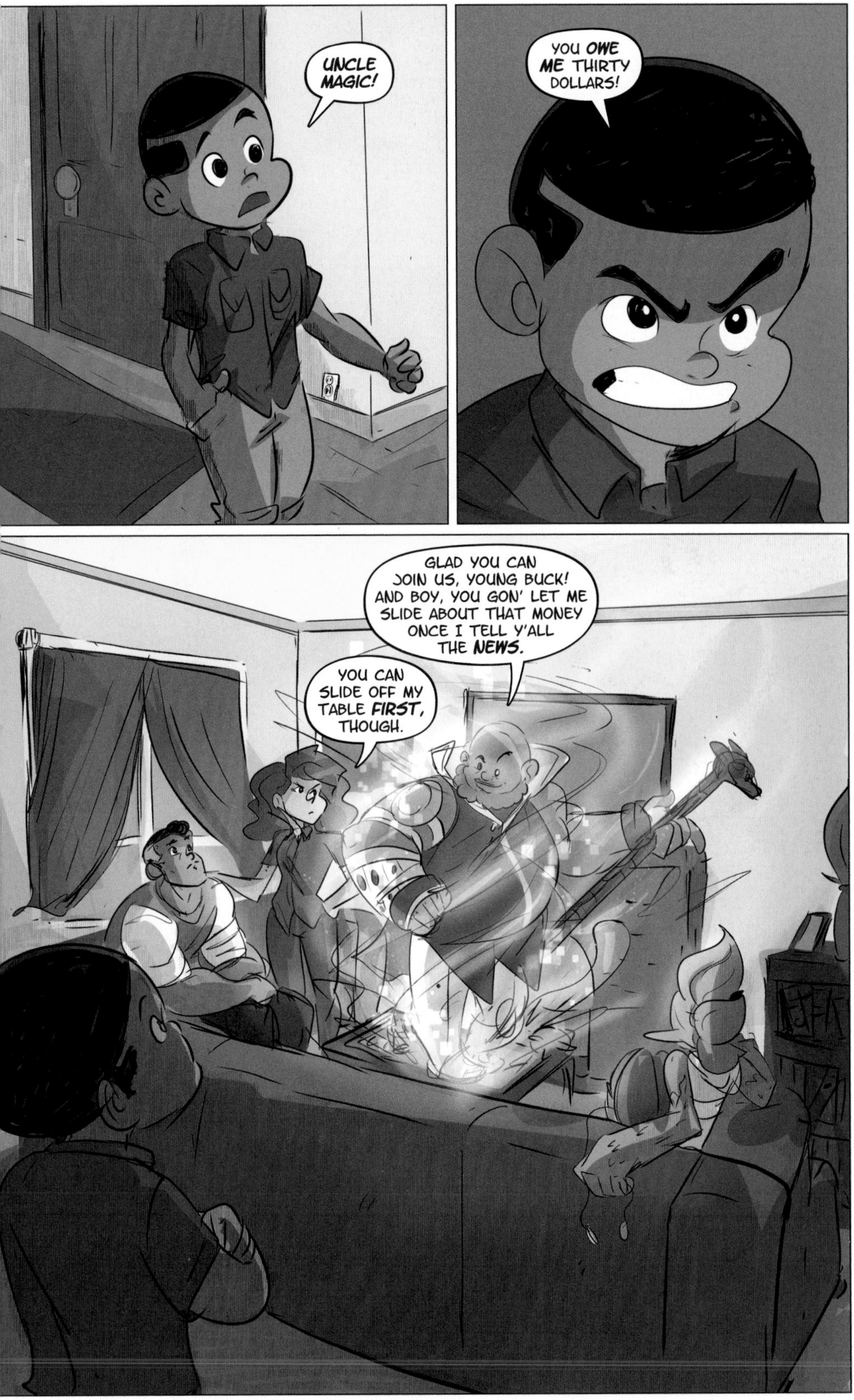
UNCLE MAGIC!
YOU OWE ME THIRTY DOLLARS!
GLAD YOU CAN JOIN US, YOUNG BUCK! AND BOY, YOU GON' LET ME SLIDE ABOUT THAT MONEY ONCE I TELL Y'ALL THE NEWS.
YOU CAN SLIDE OFF MY TABLE FIRST, THOUGH.

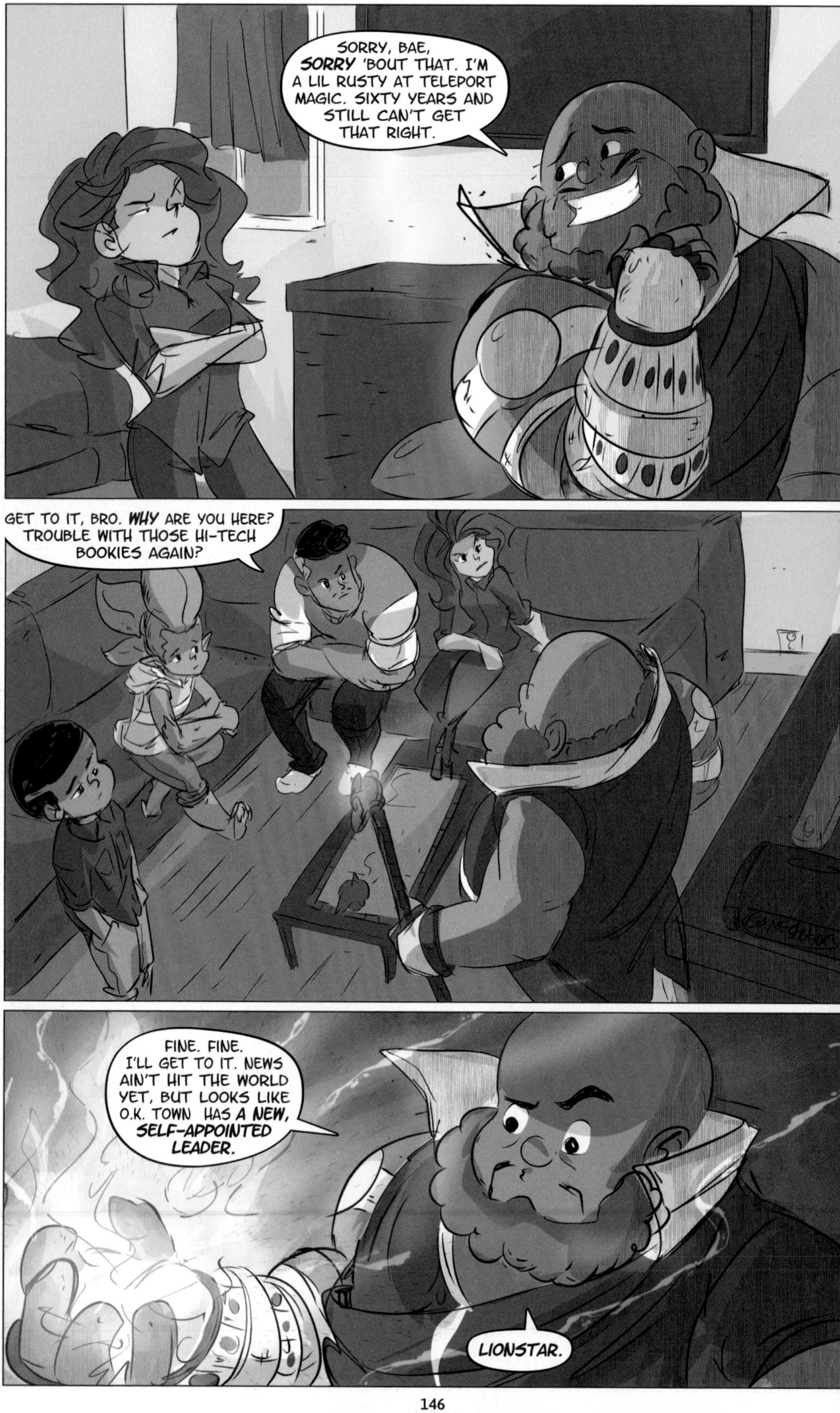
SORRY, BAE, SORRY 'BOUT THAT. I'M A LIL RUSTY AT TELEPORT MAGIC. SIXTY YEARS AND STILL CAN'T GET THAT RIGHT.
GET TO IT, BRO. WHY ARE YOU HERE? TROUBLE WITH THOSE HI-TECH BOOKIES AGAIN?
FINE. FINE. I'LL GET TO IT. NEWS AIN'T HIT THE WORLD YET, BUT LOOKS LIKE O.K. TOWN HAS A NEW, SELF-APPOINTED LEADER.
LIONSTAR.

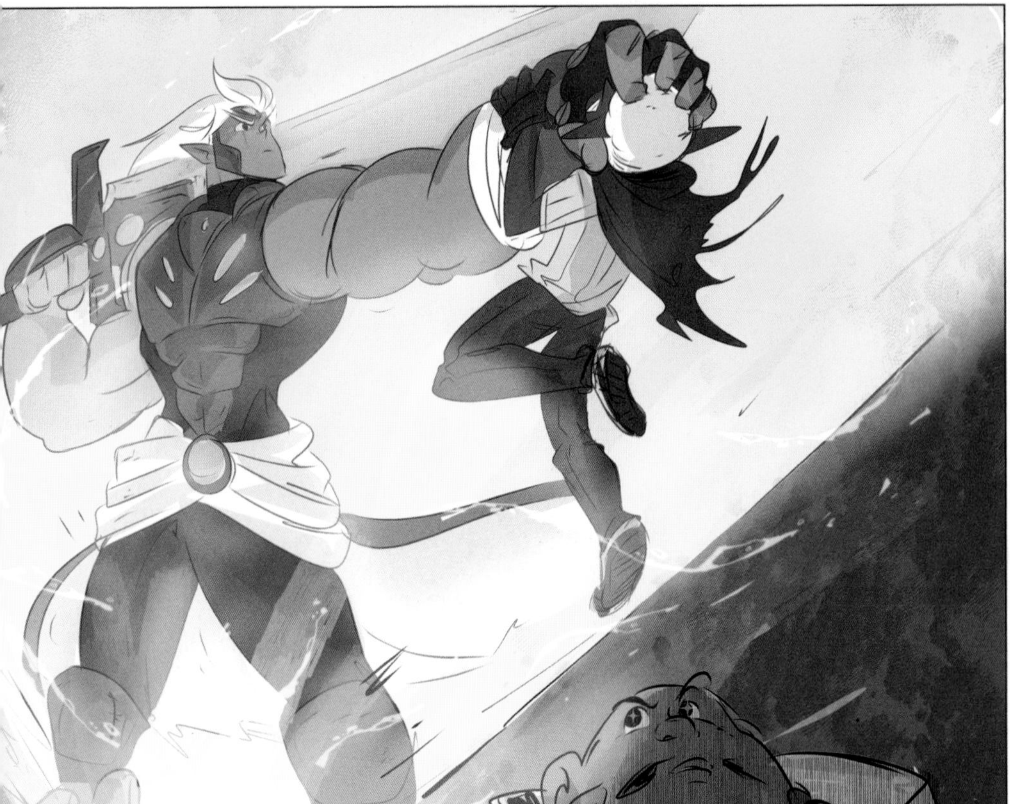

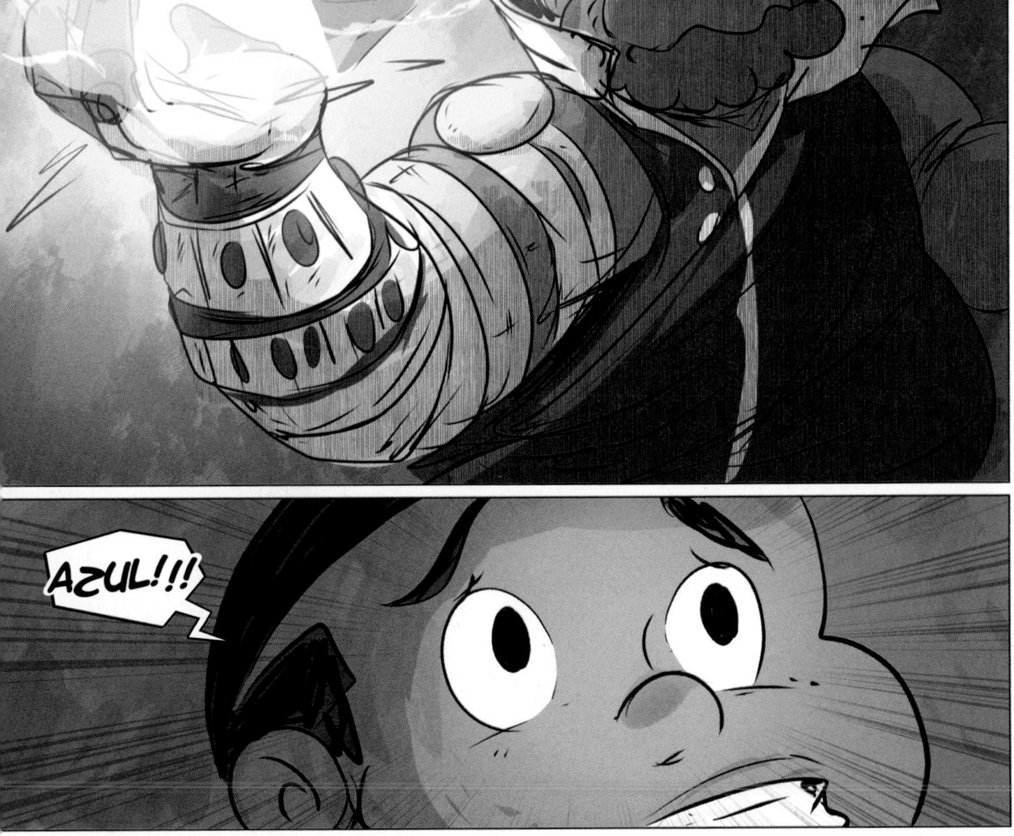
AZUL!!!

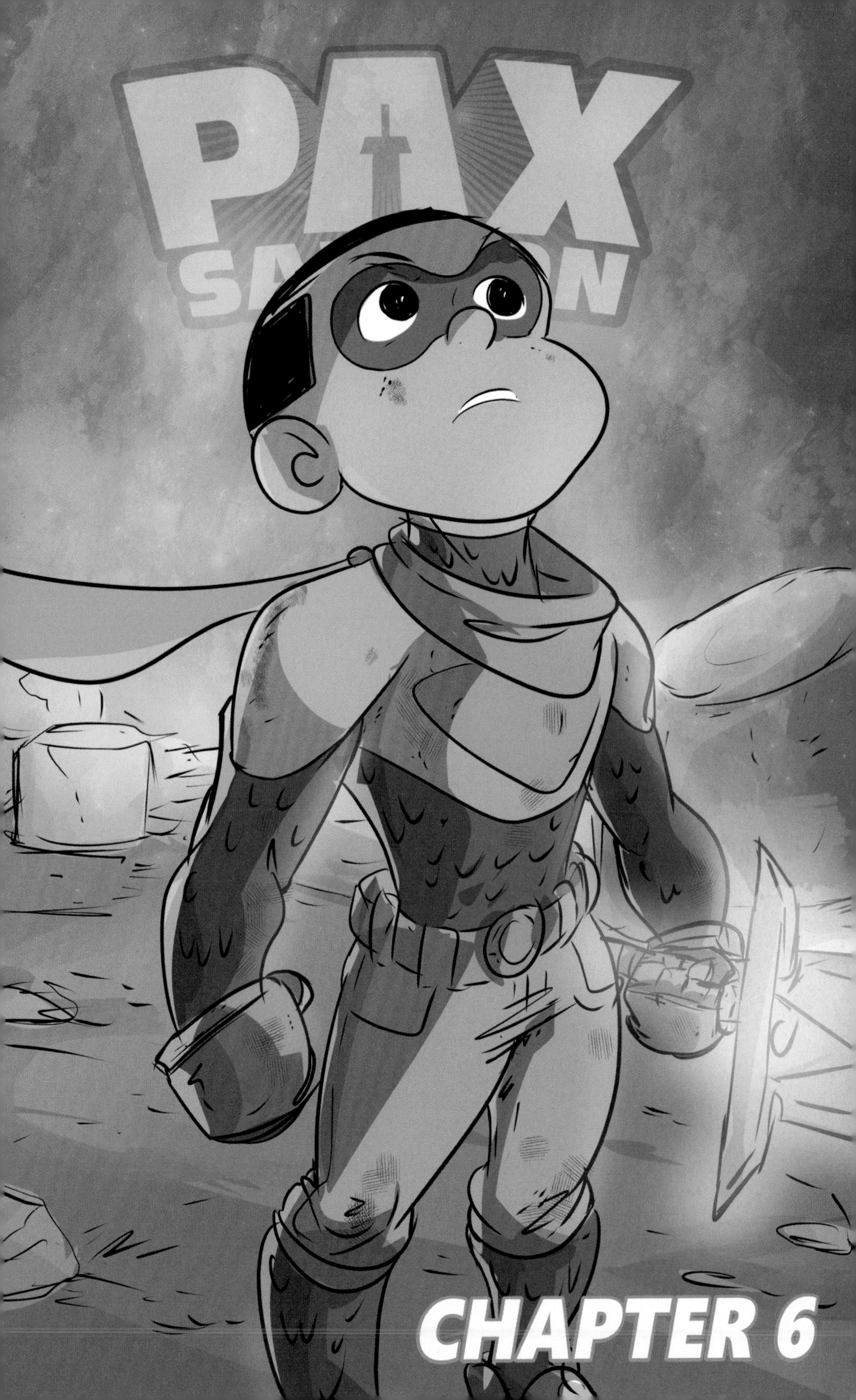
PAX

CHAPTER 6

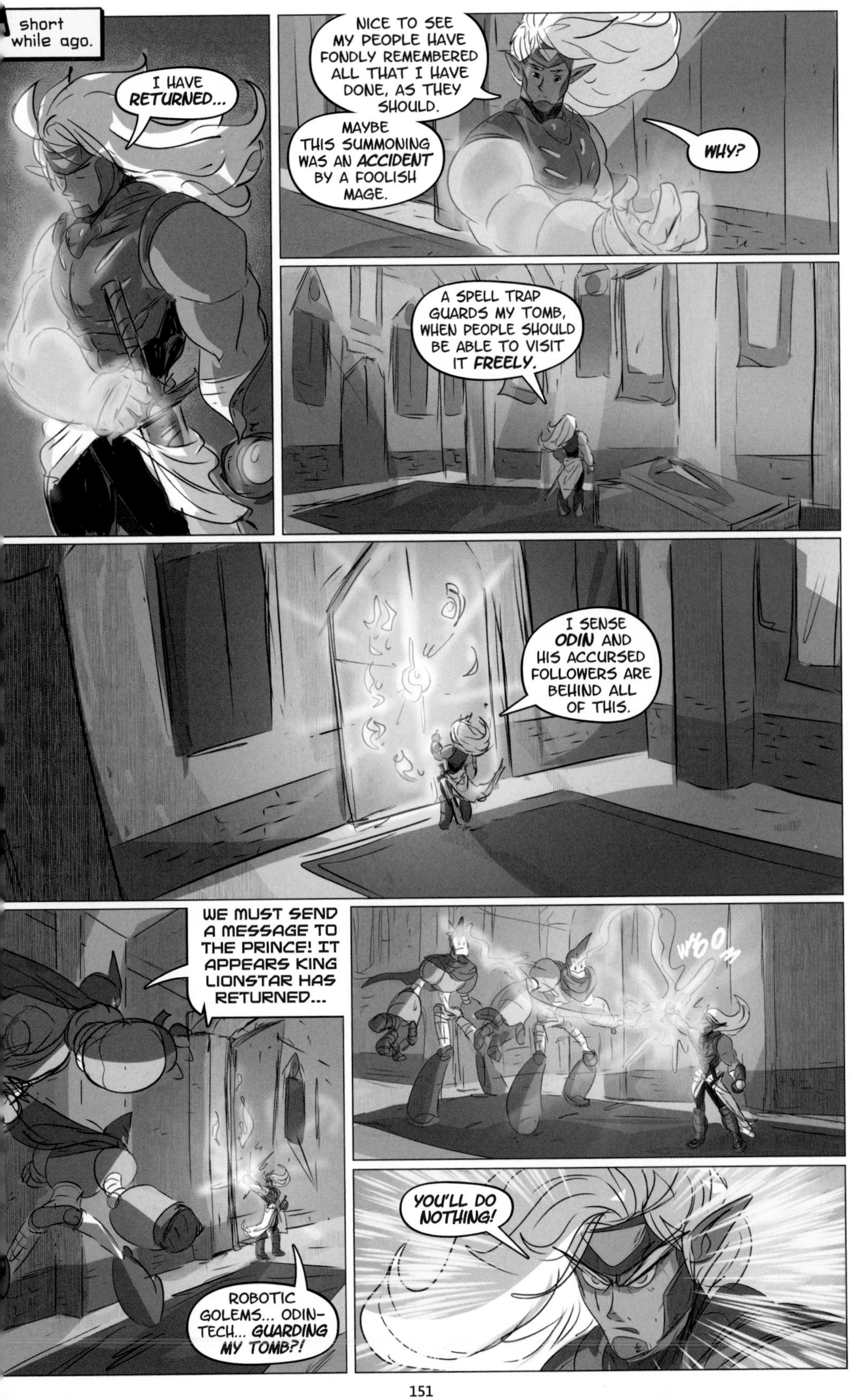

short while ago.
I HAVE RETURNED...
NICE TO SEE MY PEOPLE HAVE FONDLY REMEMBERED ALL THAT I HAVE DONE, AS THEY SHOULD.
MAYBE THIS SUMMONING WAS AN ACCIDENT BY A FOOLISH MAGE.
WHY?
A SPELL TRAP GUARDS MY TOMB, WHEN PEOPLE SHOULD BE ABLE TO VISIT IT FREELY.
I SENSE ODIN AND HIS ACCURSED FOLLOWERS ARE BEHIND ALL OF THIS.
WE MUST SEND A MESSAGE TO THE PRINCE! IT APPEARS KING LIONSTAR HAS RETURNED...
ROBOTIC GOLEMS... ODIN-TECH... GUARDING MY TOMB?!
WHOOM
YOU'LL DO NOTHING!

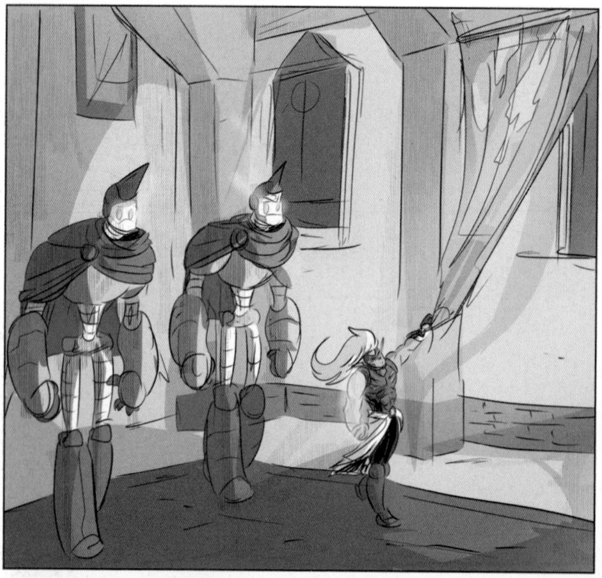

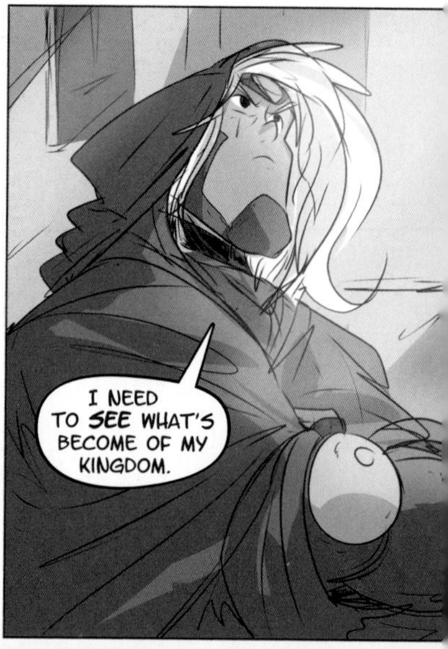
I NEED TO SEE WHAT'S BECOME OF MY KINGDOM.

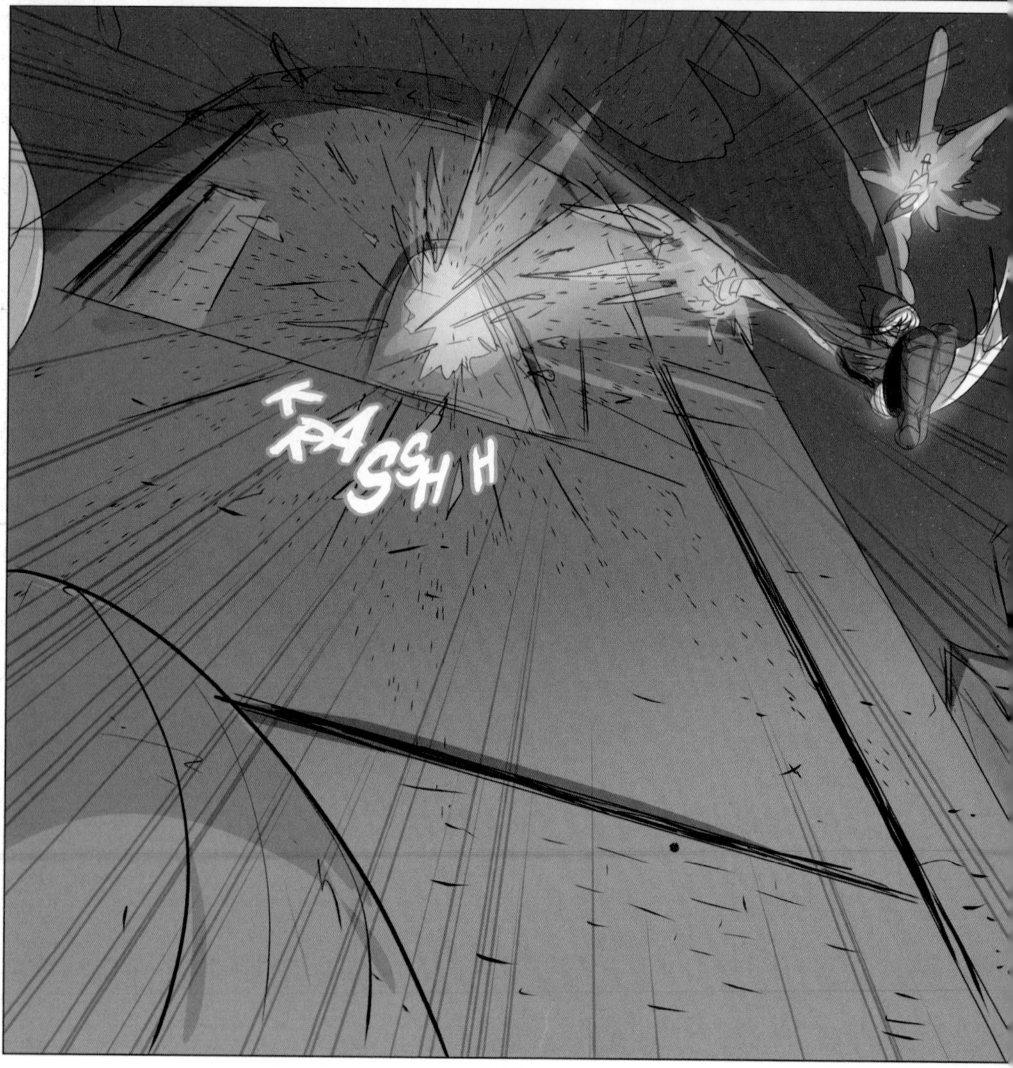
KRASSHH

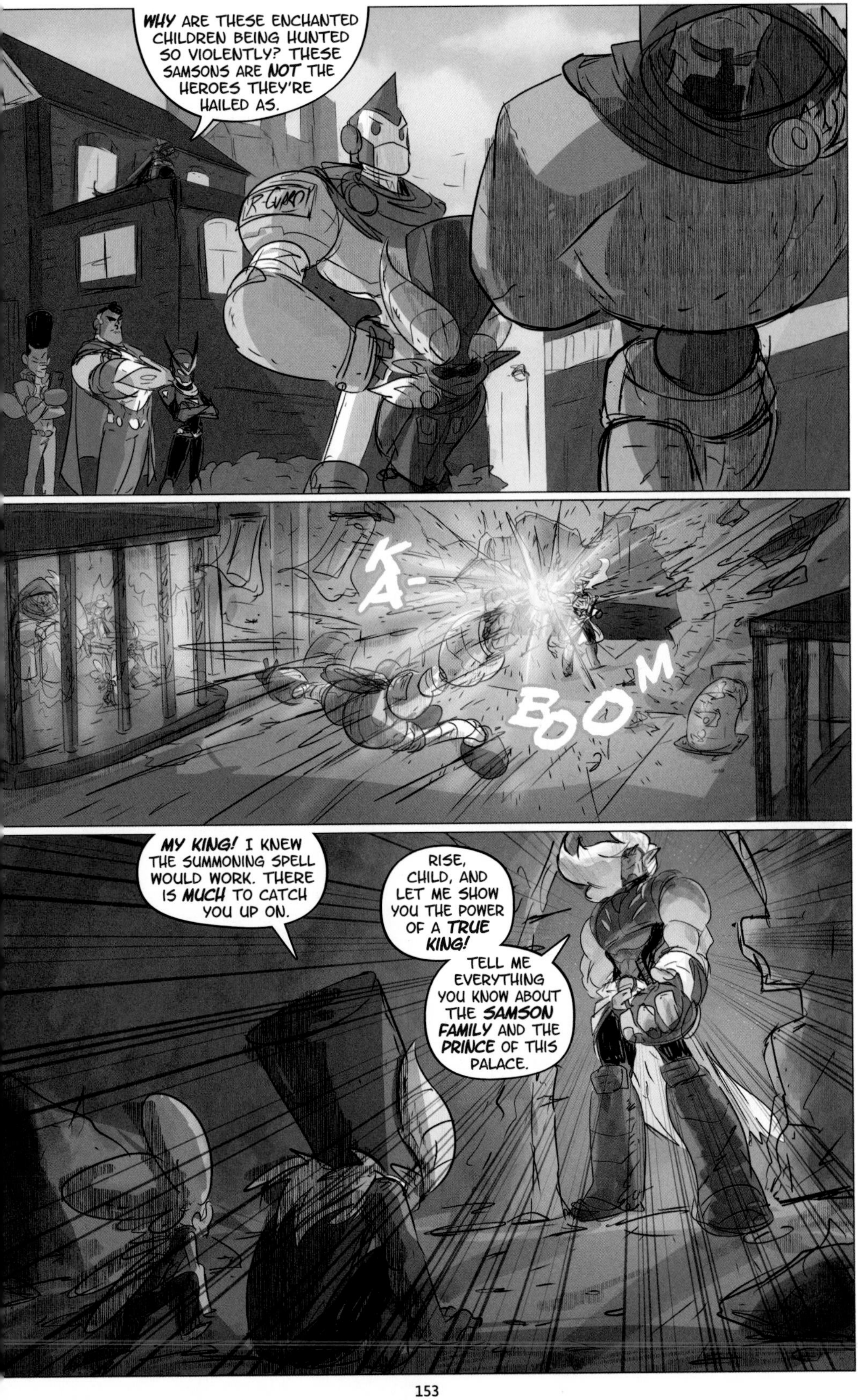
WHY ARE THESE ENCHANTED CHILDREN BEING HUNTED SO VIOLENTLY? THESE SAMSONS ARE NOT THE HEROES THEY'RE HAILED AS.
R-GUARD
KA-
BOOM
MY KING! I KNEW THE SUMMONING SPELL WOULD WORK. THERE IS MUCH TO CATCH YOU UP ON.
RISE, CHILD, AND LET ME SHOW YOU THE POWER OF A TRUE KING!
TELL ME EVERYTHING YOU KNOW ABOUT THE SAMSON FAMILY AND THE PRINCE OF THIS PALACE.

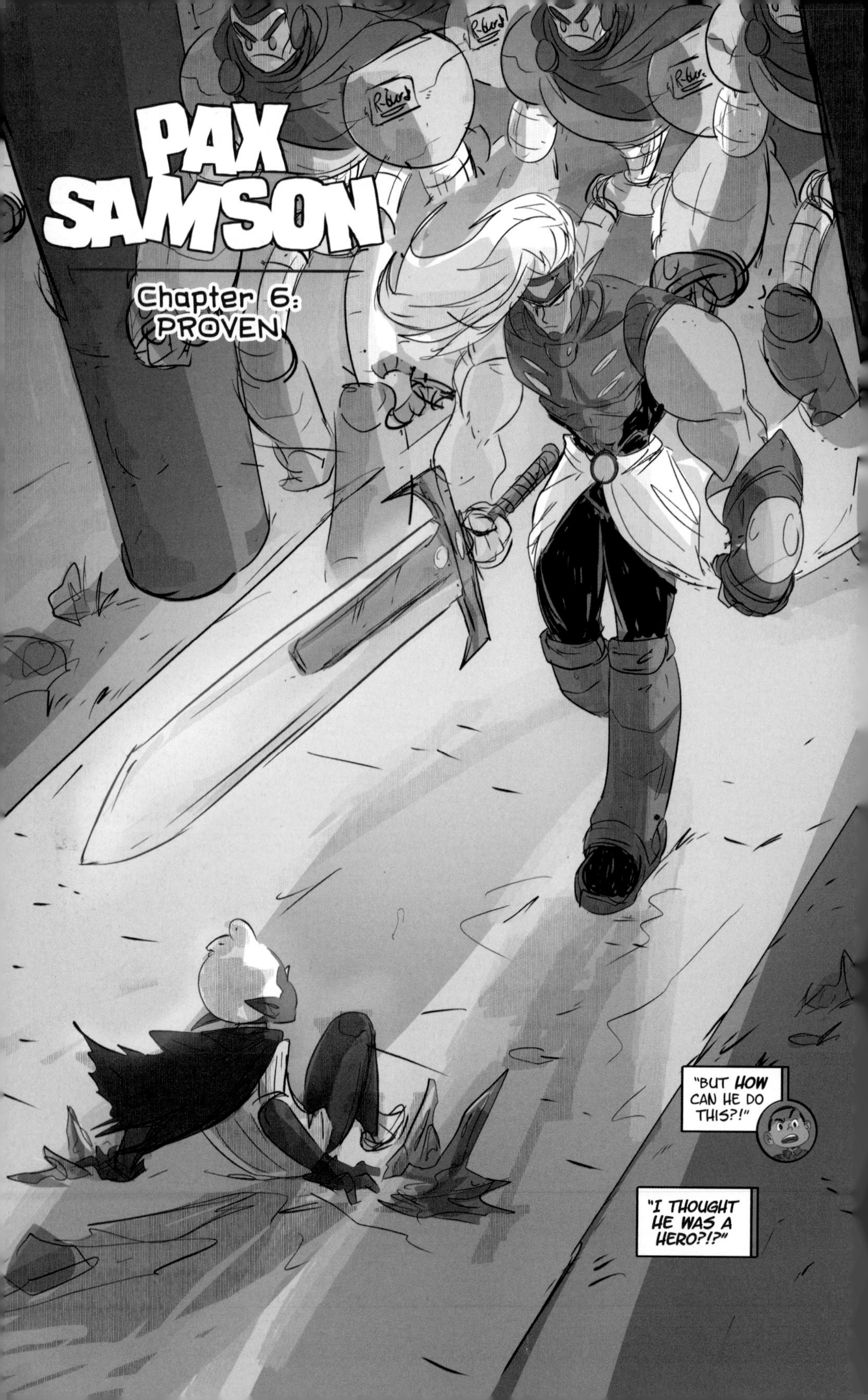
PAX SAMSON
Chapter 6: PROVEN
"BUT HOW CAN HE DO THIS?!"
"I THOUGHT HE WAS A HERO?!?"

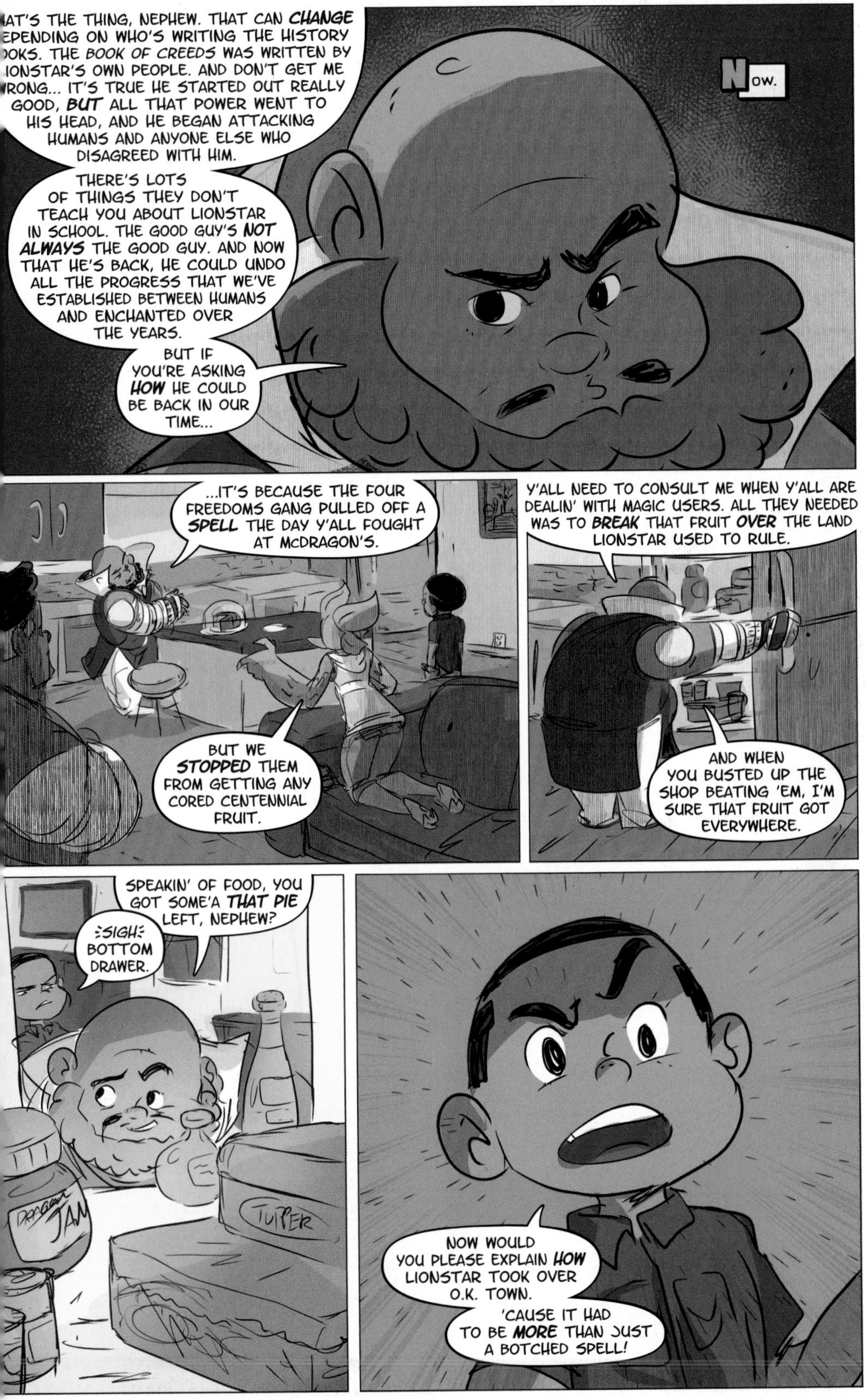
AT'S THE THING, NEPHEW. THAT CAN CHANGE EPENDING ON WHO'S WRITING THE HISTORY OOKS. THE BOOK OF CREEDS WAS WRITTEN BY IONSTAR'S OWN PEOPLE. AND DON'T GET ME RONG... IT'S TRUE HE STARTED OUT REALLY GOOD, BUT ALL THAT POWER WENT TO HIS HEAD, AND HE BEGAN ATTACKING HUMANS AND ANYONE ELSE WHO DISAGREED WITH HIM.
THERE'S LOTS OF THINGS THEY DON'T TEACH YOU ABOUT LIONSTAR IN SCHOOL. THE GOOD GUY'S NOT ALWAYS THE GOOD GUY. AND NOW THAT HE'S BACK, HE COULD UNDO ALL THE PROGRESS THAT WE'VE ESTABLISHED BETWEEN HUMANS AND ENCHANTED OVER THE YEARS.
BUT IF YOU'RE ASKING HOW HE COULD BE BACK IN OUR TIME...
NOW.
...IT'S BECAUSE THE FOUR FREEDOMS GANG PULLED OFF A SPELL THE DAY Y'ALL FOUGHT AT McDRAGON'S.
BUT WE STOPPED THEM FROM GETTING ANY CORED CENTENNIAL FRUIT.
Y'ALL NEED TO CONSULT ME WHEN Y'ALL ARE DEALIN' WITH MAGIC USERS. ALL THEY NEEDED WAS TO BREAK THAT FRUIT OVER THE LAND LIONSTAR USED TO RULE.
AND WHEN YOU BUSTED UP THE SHOP BEATING 'EM, I'M SURE THAT FRUIT GOT EVERYWHERE.
SPEAKIN' OF FOOD, YOU GOT SOME'A THAT PIE LEFT, NEPHEW?
SIGH BOTTOM DRAWER.
DRAGON JAM
TUPPER
NOW WOULD YOU PLEASE EXPLAIN HOW LIONSTAR TOOK OVER O.K. TOWN.
'CAUSE IT HAD TO BE MORE THAN JUST A BOTCHED SPELL!

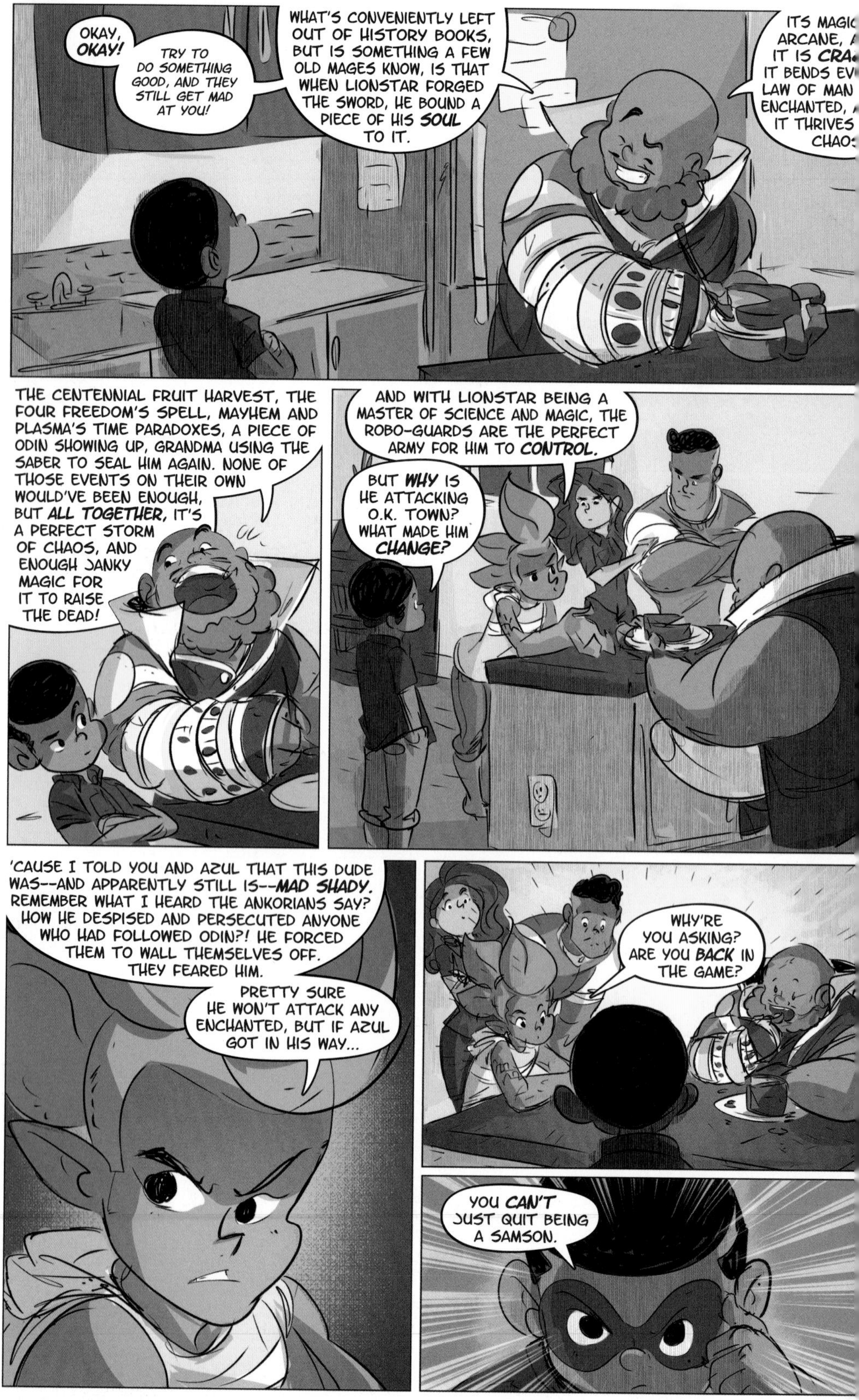

OKAY, OKAY!
TRY TO DO SOMETHING GOOD, AND THEY STILL GET MAD AT YOU!
WHAT'S CONVENIENTLY LEFT OUT OF HISTORY BOOKS, BUT IS SOMETHING A FEW OLD MAGES KNOW, IS THAT WHEN LIONSTAR FORGED THE SWORD, HE BOUND A PIECE OF HIS SOUL TO IT.
ITS MAGIC ARCANE, IT IS IT BENDS LAW OF MAN ENCHANTED, IT THRIVES
THE CENTENNIAL FRUIT HARVEST, THE FOUR FREEDOM'S SPELL, MAYHEM AND PLASMA'S TIME PARADOXES, A PIECE OF ODIN SHOWING UP, GRANDMA USING THE SABER TO SEAL HIM AGAIN. NONE OF THOSE EVENTS ON THEIR OWN WOULD'VE BEEN ENOUGH, BUT ALL TOGETHER, IT'S A PERFECT STORM OF CHAOS, AND ENOUGH JANKY MAGIC FOR IT TO RAISE THE DEAD!
AND WITH LIONSTAR BEING A MASTER OF SCIENCE AND MAGIC, THE ROBO-GUARDS ARE THE PERFECT ARMY FOR HIM TO CONTROL.
BUT WHY IS HE ATTACKING O.K. TOWN? WHAT MADE HIM CHANGE?
'CAUSE I TOLD YOU AND AZUL THAT THIS DUDE WAS--AND APPARENTLY STILL IS--MAD SHADY. REMEMBER WHAT I HEARD THE ANKORIANS SAY? HOW HE DESPISED AND PERSECUTED ANYONE WHO HAD FOLLOWED ODIN?! HE FORCED THEM TO WALL THEMSELVES OFF. THEY FEARED HIM.
PRETTY SURE HE WON'T ATTACK ANY ENCHANTED, BUT IF AZUL GOT IN HIS WAY...
WHY'RE YOU ASKING? ARE YOU BACK IN THE GAME?
YOU CAN'T JUST QUIT BEING A SAMSON.

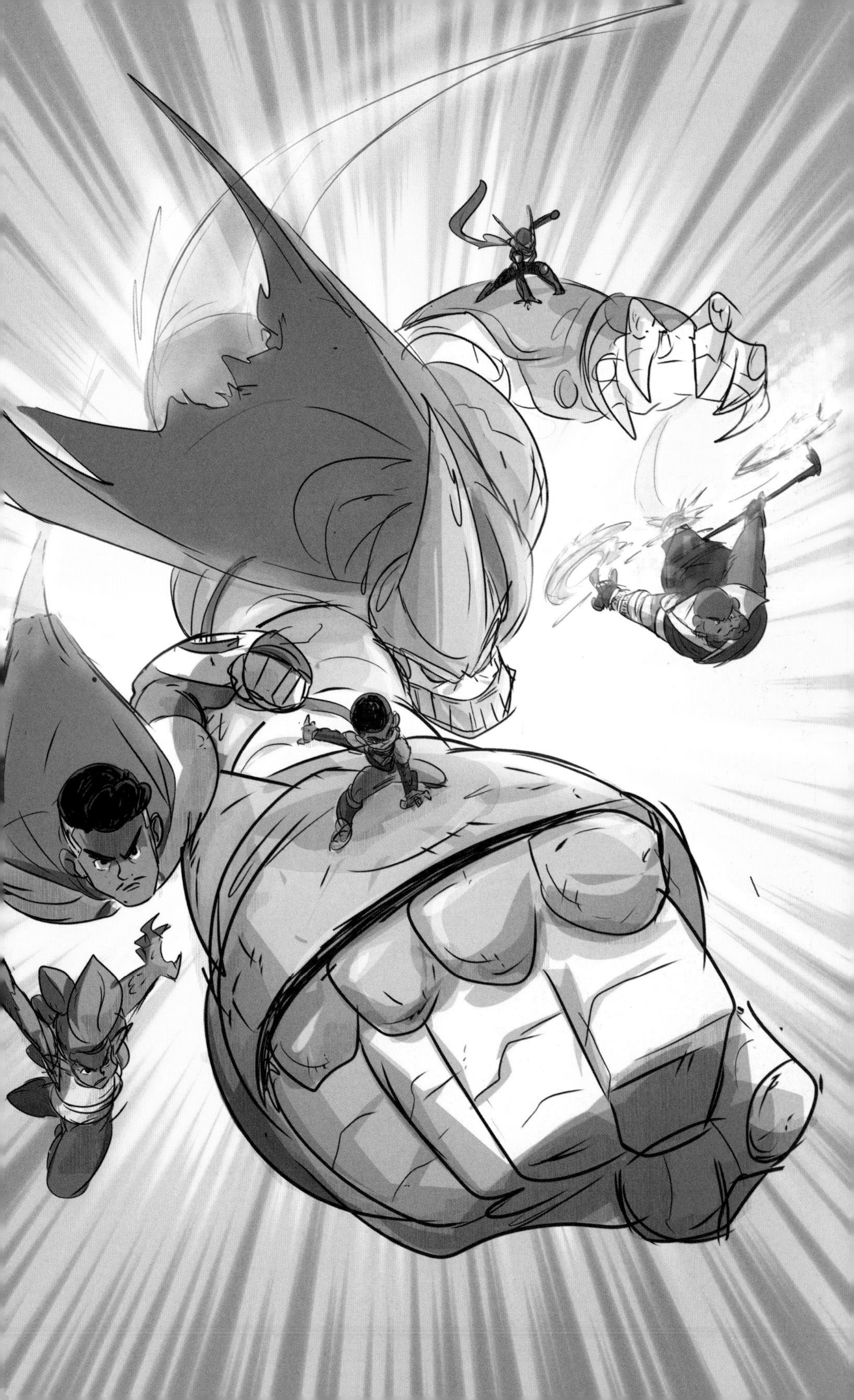

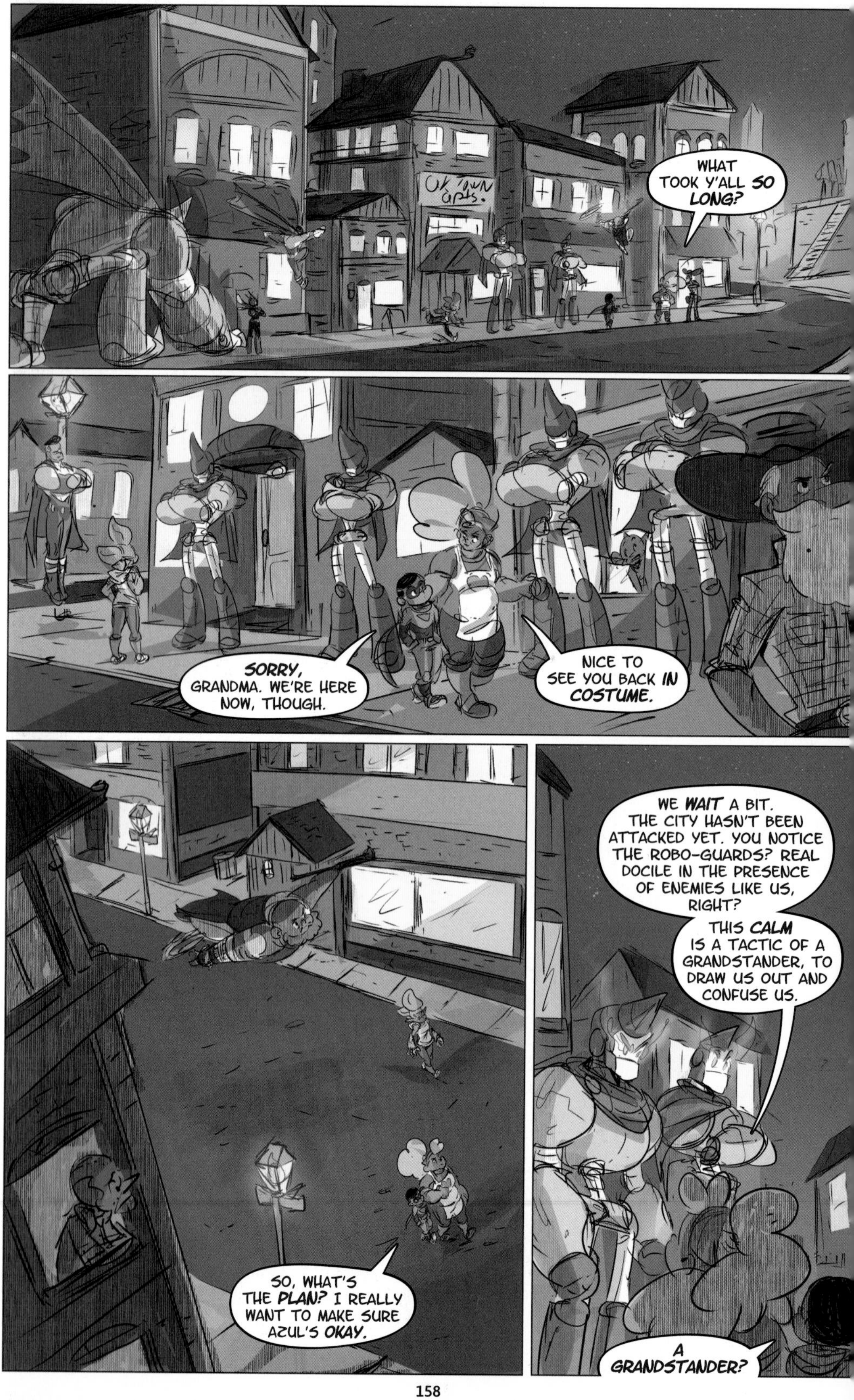
WHAT TOOK Y'ALL **SO LONG?**
SORRY, GRANDMA. WE'RE HERE NOW, THOUGH.
NICE TO SEE YOU BACK **IN COSTUME.**
SO, WHAT'S THE **PLAN?** I REALLY WANT TO MAKE SURE AZUL'S **OKAY.**
WE **WAIT** A BIT. THE CITY HASN'T BEEN ATTACKED YET. YOU NOTICE THE ROBO-GUARDS? REAL DOCILE IN THE PRESENCE OF ENEMIES LIKE US, RIGHT?
THIS **CALM** IS A TACTIC OF A GRANDSTANDER, TO DRAW US OUT AND CONFUSE US.
A **GRANDSTANDER?**

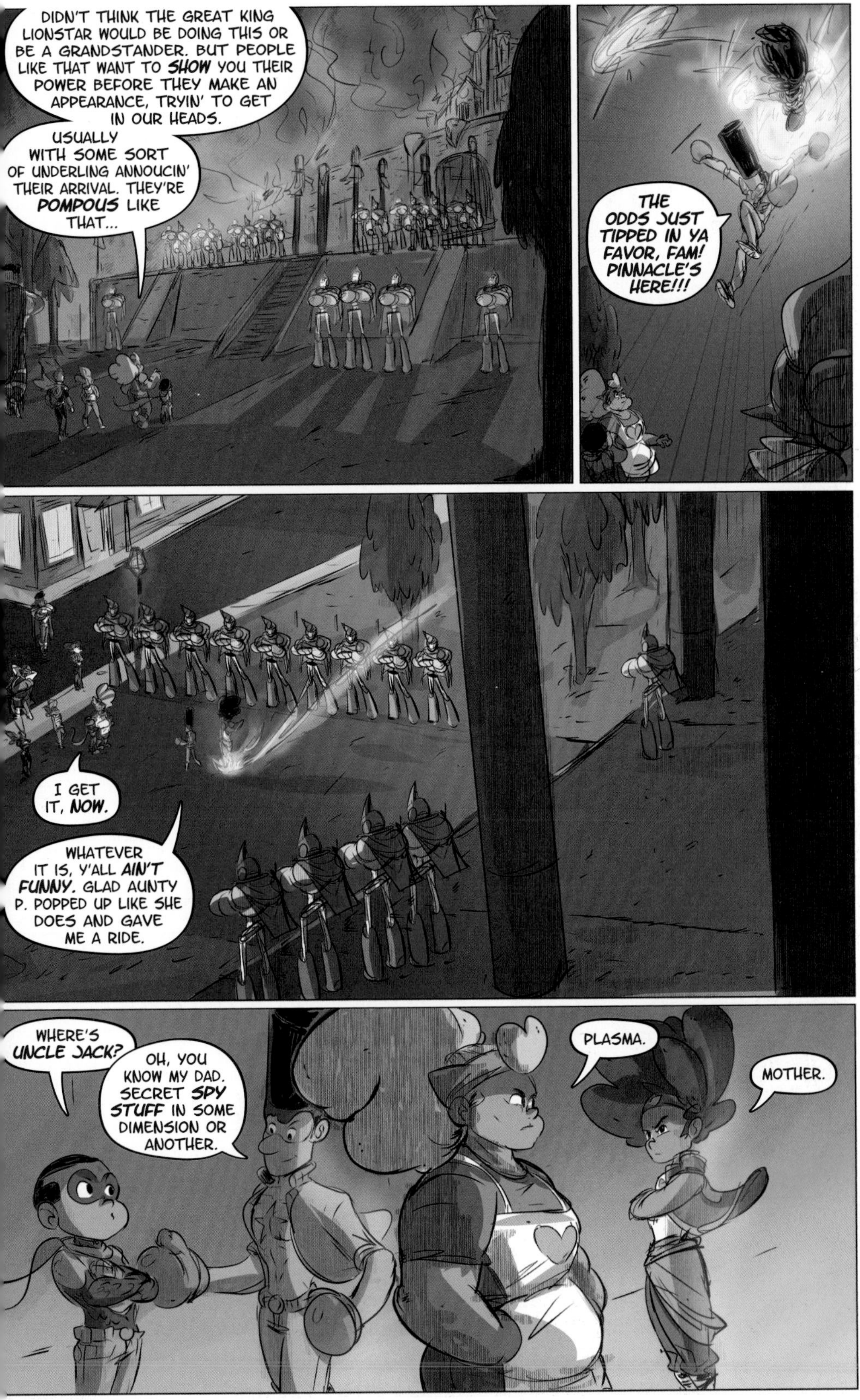
DIDN'T THINK THE GREAT KING LIONSTAR WOULD BE DOING THIS OR BE A GRANDSTANDER. BUT PEOPLE LIKE THAT WANT TO SHOW YOU THEIR POWER BEFORE THEY MAKE AN APPEARANCE, TRYIN' TO GET IN OUR HEADS.
USUALLY WITH SOME SORT OF UNDERLING ANNOUCIN' THEIR ARRIVAL. THEY'RE POMPOUS LIKE THAT...
THE ODDS JUST TIPPED IN YA FAVOR, FAM! PINNACLE'S HERE!!!
I GET IT, NOW.
WHATEVER IT IS, Y'ALL AIN'T FUNNY. GLAD AUNTY P. POPPED UP LIKE SHE DOES AND GAVE ME A RIDE.
WHERE'S UNCLE JACK?
OH, YOU KNOW MY DAD. SECRET SPY STUFF IN SOME DIMENSION OR ANOTHER.
PLASMA.
MOTHER.

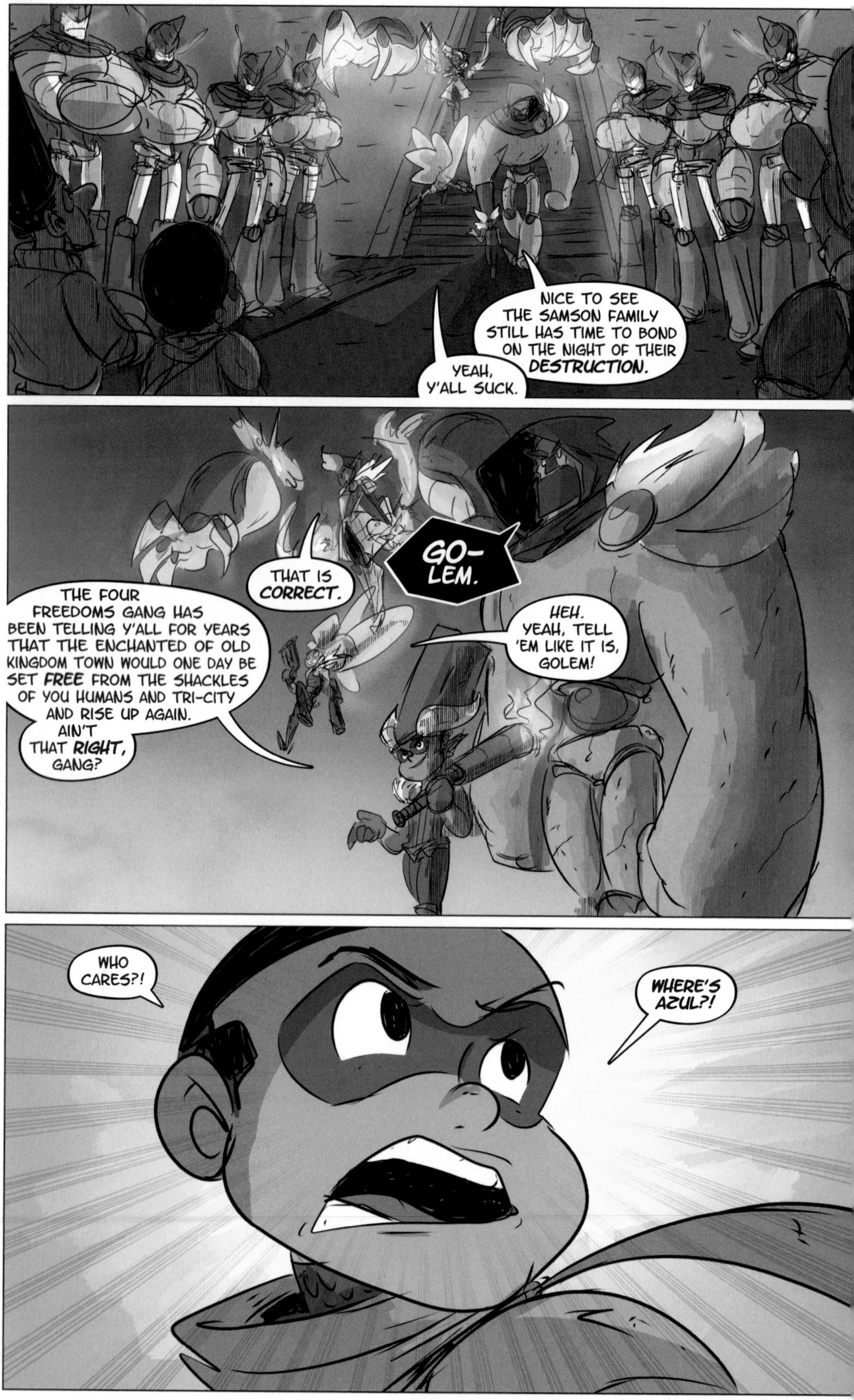

NICE TO SEE THE SAMSON FAMILY STILL HAS TIME TO BOND ON THE NIGHT OF THEIR **DESTRUCTION.**
YEAH, Y'ALL SUCK.
GO-LEM.
THAT IS **CORRECT.**
THE FOUR FREEDOMS GANG HAS BEEN TELLING Y'ALL FOR YEARS THAT THE ENCHANTED OF OLD KINGDOM TOWN WOULD ONE DAY BE SET **FREE** FROM THE SHACKLES OF YOU HUMANS AND TRI-CITY AND RISE UP AGAIN. AIN'T THAT **RIGHT,** GANG?
HEH. YEAH, TELL 'EM LIKE IT IS, GOLEM!
WHO CARES?!
WHERE'S AZUL?!

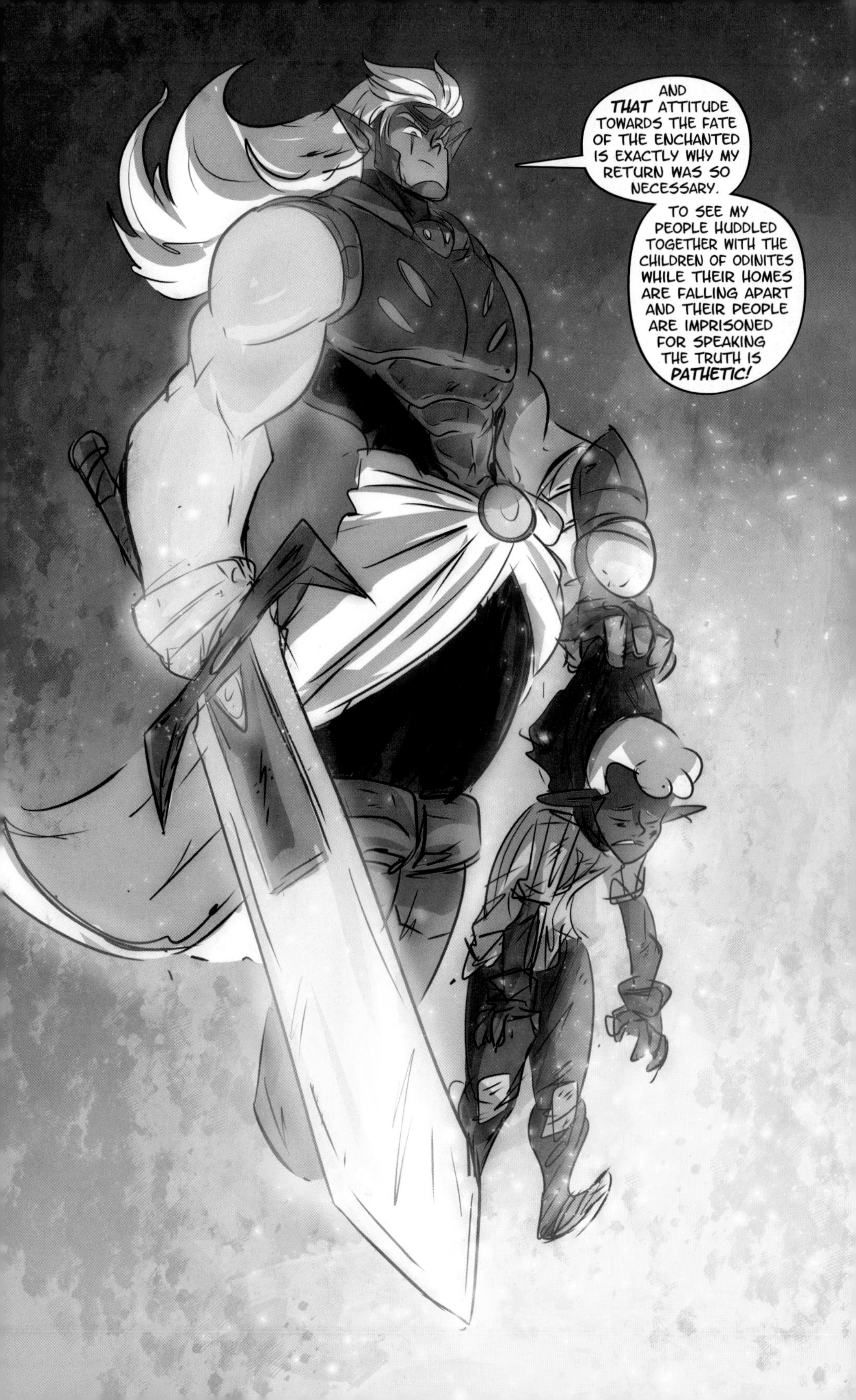
AND **THAT** ATTITUDE TOWARDS THE FATE OF THE ENCHANTED IS EXACTLY WHY MY RETURN WAS SO NECESSARY.
TO SEE MY PEOPLE HUDDLED TOGETHER WITH THE CHILDREN OF ODINITES WHILE THEIR HOMES ARE FALLING APART AND THEIR PEOPLE ARE IMPRISONED FOR SPEAKING THE TRUTH IS **PATHETIC!**

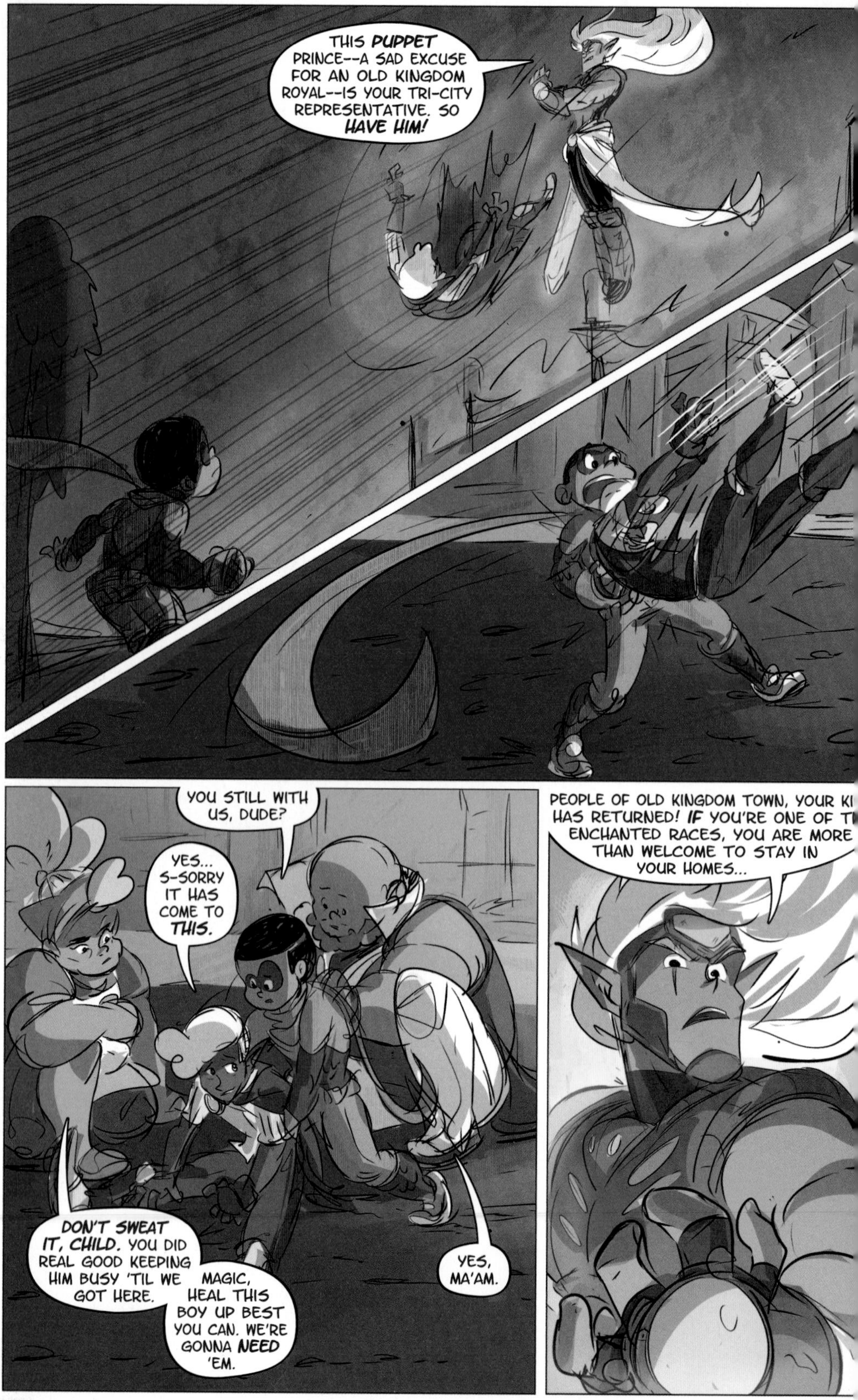
THIS PUPPET PRINCE--A SAD EXCUSE FOR AN OLD KINGDOM ROYAL--IS YOUR TRI-CITY REPRESENTATIVE. SO HAVE HIM!
YOU STILL WITH US, DUDE?
YES... S-SORRY IT HAS COME TO THIS.
DON'T SWEAT IT, CHILD. YOU DID REAL GOOD KEEPING HIM BUSY 'TIL WE GOT HERE.
MAGIC, HEAL THIS BOY UP BEST YOU CAN. WE'RE GONNA NEED 'EM.
YES, MA'AM.
PEOPLE OF OLD KINGDOM TOWN, YOUR KI HAS RETURNED! IF YOU'RE ONE OF TI ENCHANTED RACES, YOU ARE MORE THAN WELCOME TO STAY IN YOUR HOMES...

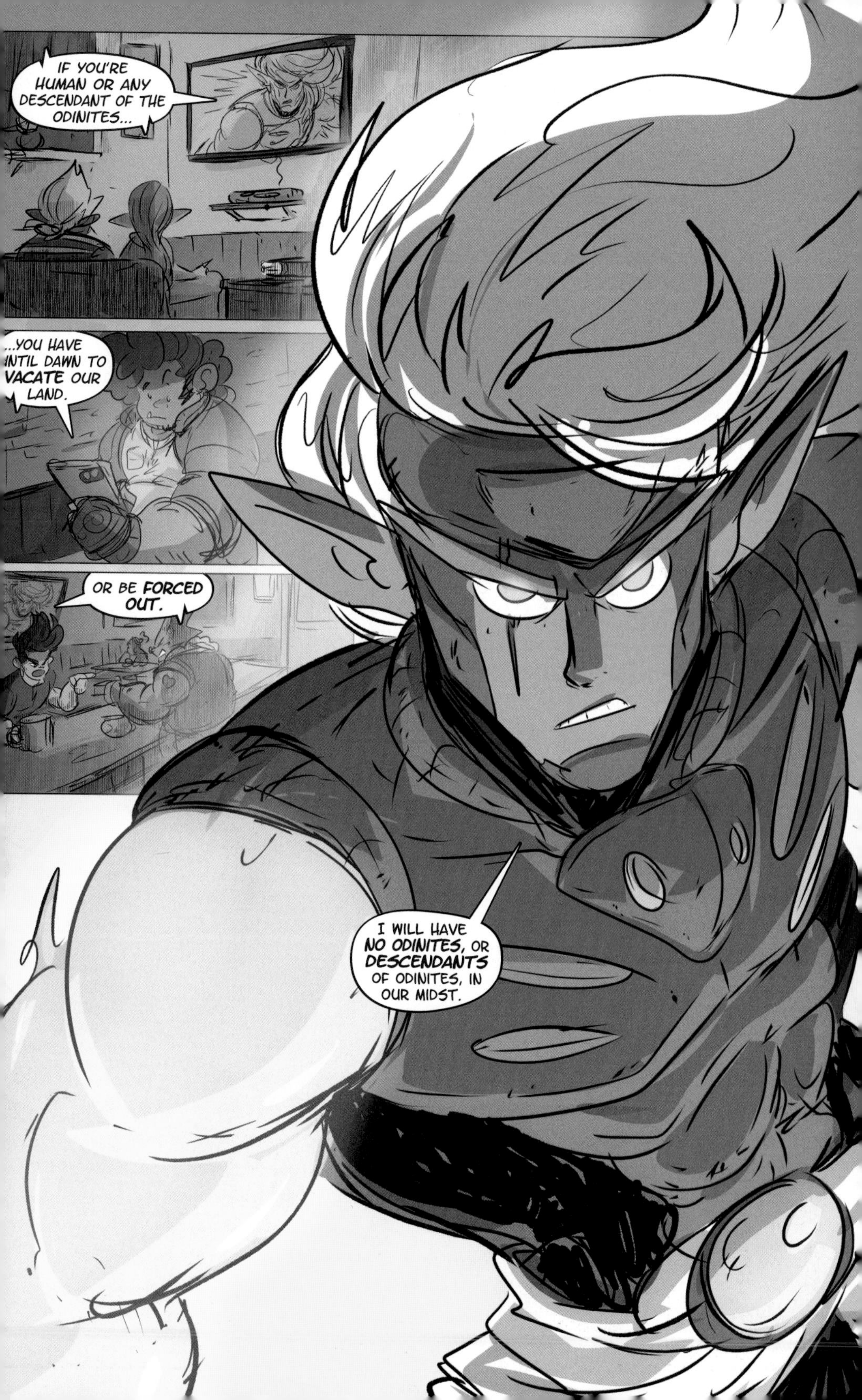
IF YOU'RE HUMAN OR ANY DESCENDANT OF THE ODINITES...
...YOU HAVE UNTIL DAWN TO VACATE OUR LAND.
OR BE FORCED OUT.
I WILL HAVE NO ODINITES, OR DESCENDANTS OF ODINITES, IN OUR MIDST.

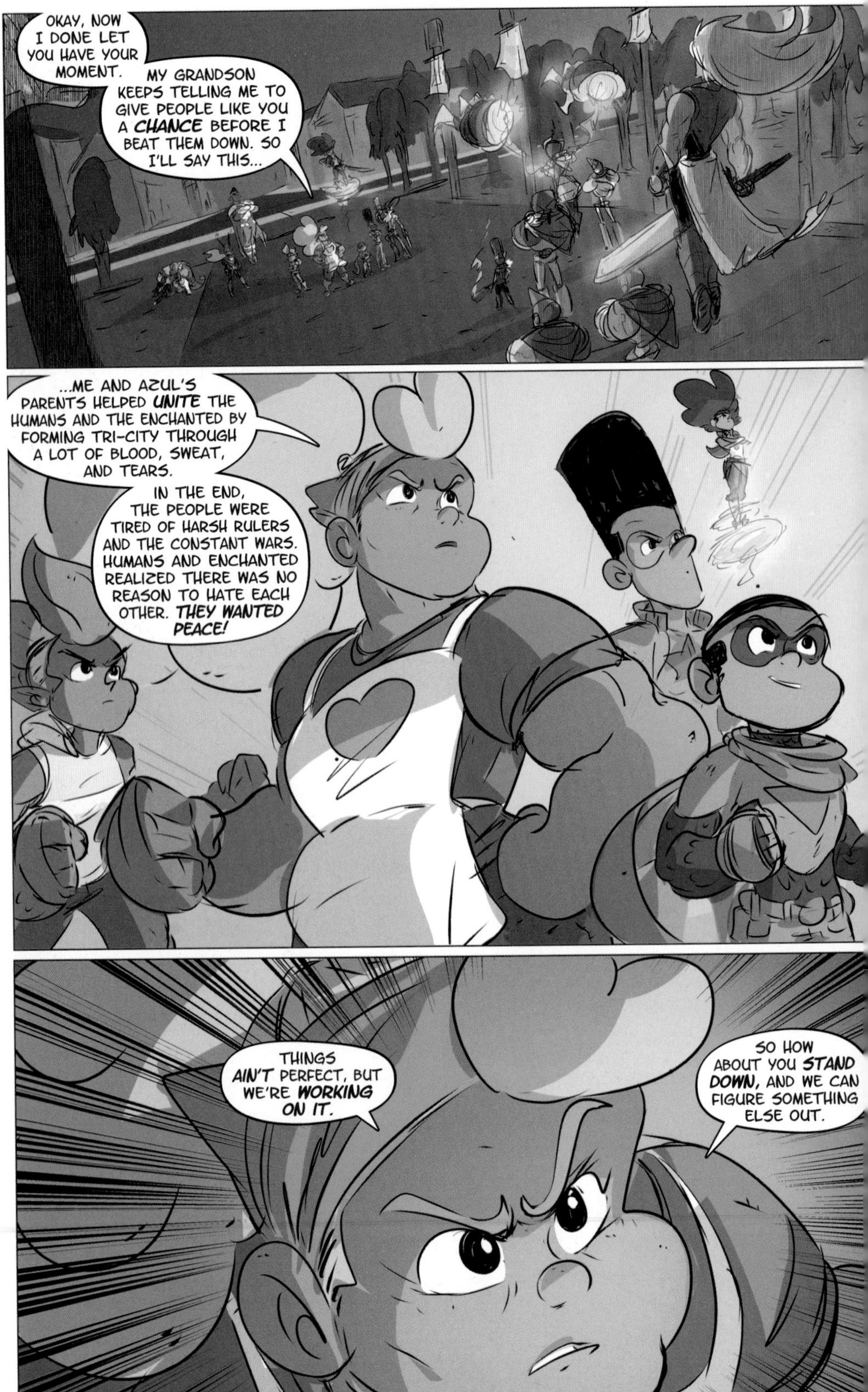
OKAY, NOW I DONE LET YOU HAVE YOUR MOMENT.
MY GRANDSON KEEPS TELLING ME TO GIVE PEOPLE LIKE YOU A CHANCE BEFORE I BEAT THEM DOWN. SO I'LL SAY THIS...
...ME AND AZUL'S PARENTS HELPED UNITE THE HUMANS AND THE ENCHANTED BY FORMING TRI-CITY THROUGH A LOT OF BLOOD, SWEAT, AND TEARS.
IN THE END, THE PEOPLE WERE TIRED OF HARSH RULERS AND THE CONSTANT WARS. HUMANS AND ENCHANTED REALIZED THERE WAS NO REASON TO HATE EACH OTHER. THEY WANTED PEACE!
THINGS AIN'T PERFECT, BUT WE'RE WORKING ON IT.
SO HOW ABOUT YOU STAND DOWN, AND WE CAN FIGURE SOMETHING ELSE OUT.

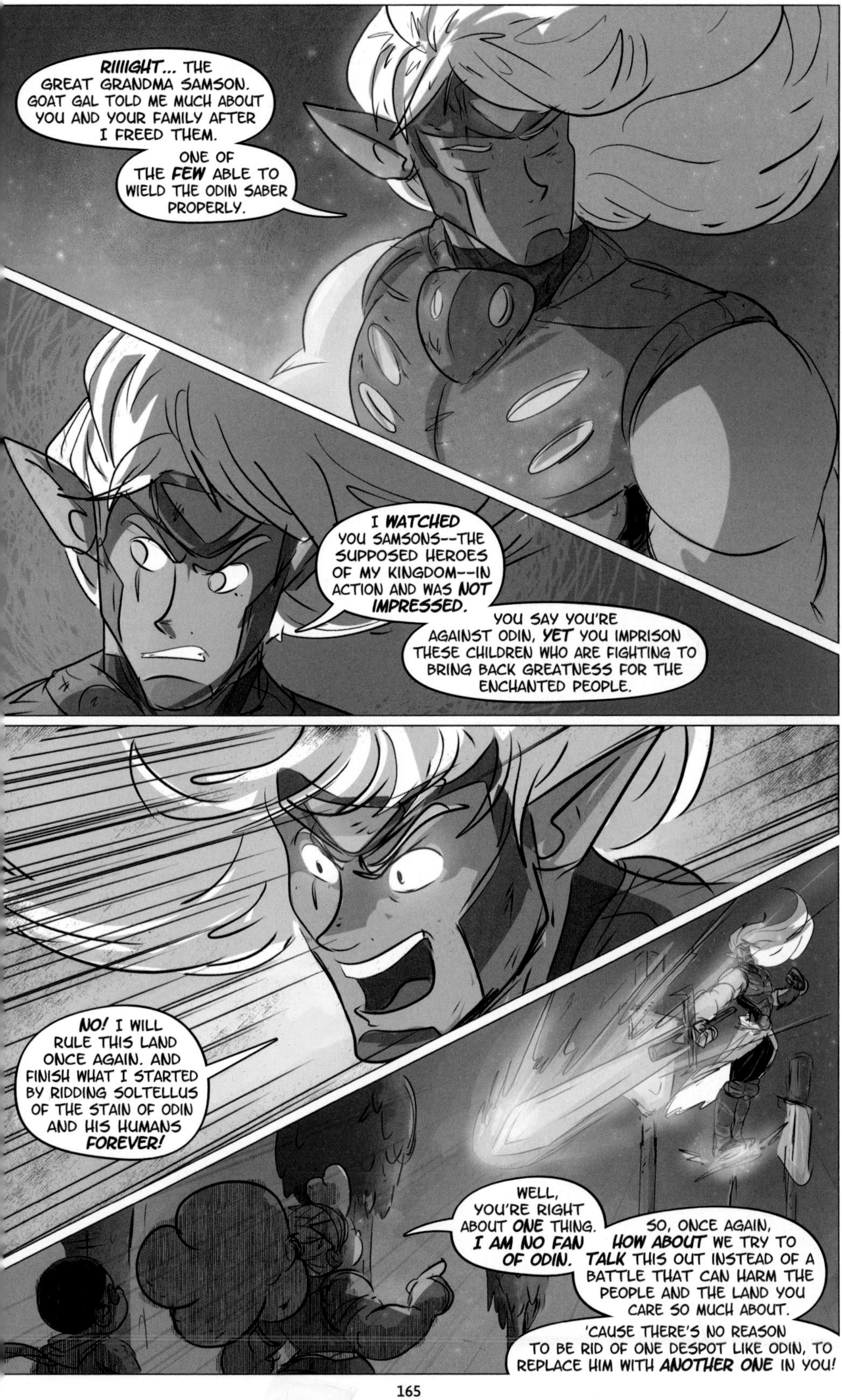
RIIIIGHT... THE GREAT GRANDMA SAMSON. GOAT GAL TOLD ME MUCH ABOUT YOU AND YOUR FAMILY AFTER I FREED THEM.
ONE OF THE FEW ABLE TO WIELD THE ODIN SABER PROPERLY.
I WATCHED YOU SAMSONS--THE SUPPOSED HEROES OF MY KINGDOM--IN ACTION AND WAS NOT IMPRESSED.
YOU SAY YOU'RE AGAINST ODIN, YET YOU IMPRISON THESE CHILDREN WHO ARE FIGHTING TO BRING BACK GREATNESS FOR THE ENCHANTED PEOPLE.
NO! I WILL RULE THIS LAND ONCE AGAIN. AND FINISH WHAT I STARTED BY RIDDING SOLTELLUS OF THE STAIN OF ODIN AND HIS HUMANS FOREVER!
WELL, YOU'RE RIGHT ABOUT ONE THING. I AM NO FAN OF ODIN.
SO, ONCE AGAIN, HOW ABOUT WE TRY TO TALK THIS OUT INSTEAD OF A BATTLE THAT CAN HARM THE PEOPLE AND THE LAND YOU CARE SO MUCH ABOUT.
'CAUSE THERE'S NO REASON TO BE RID OF ONE DESPOT LIKE ODIN, TO REPLACE HIM WITH ANOTHER ONE IN YOU!

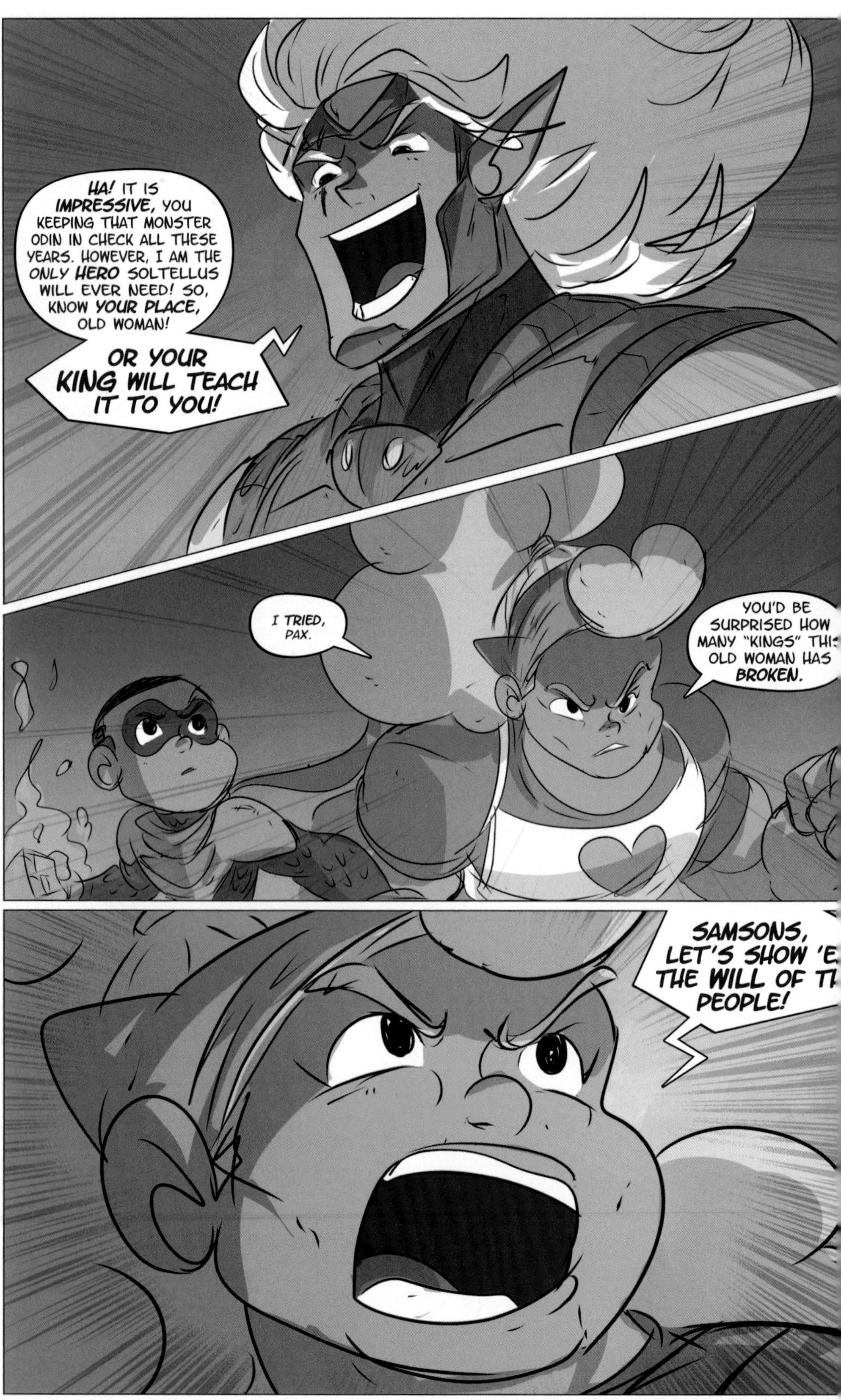
HA! IT IS IMPRESSIVE, YOU KEEPING THAT MONSTER ODIN IN CHECK ALL THESE YEARS. HOWEVER, I AM THE ONLY HERO SOLTELLUS WILL EVER NEED! SO, KNOW YOUR PLACE, OLD WOMAN!
OR YOUR KING WILL TEACH IT TO YOU!
I TRIED, PAX.
YOU'D BE SURPRISED HOW MANY "KINGS" THI OLD WOMAN HAS BROKEN.
SAMSONS, LET'S SHOW 'E THE WILL OF TH PEOPLE!

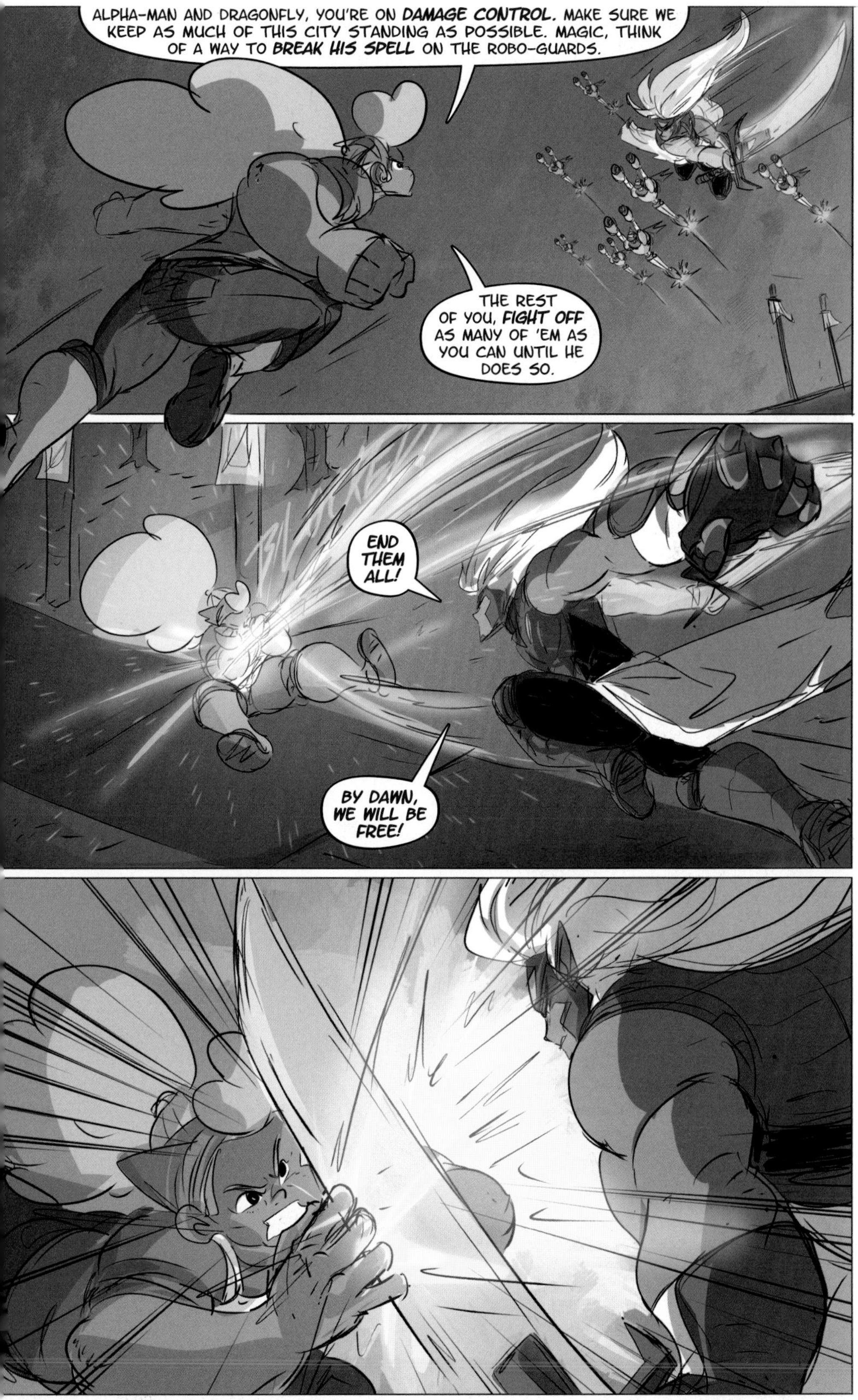
ALPHA-MAN AND DRAGONFLY, YOU'RE ON DAMAGE CONTROL. MAKE SURE WE KEEP AS MUCH OF THIS CITY STANDING AS POSSIBLE. MAGIC, THINK OF A WAY TO BREAK HIS SPELL ON THE ROBO-GUARDS.
THE REST OF YOU, FIGHT OFF AS MANY OF 'EM AS YOU CAN UNTIL HE DOES SO.
END THEM ALL!
BY DAWN, WE WILL BE FREE!

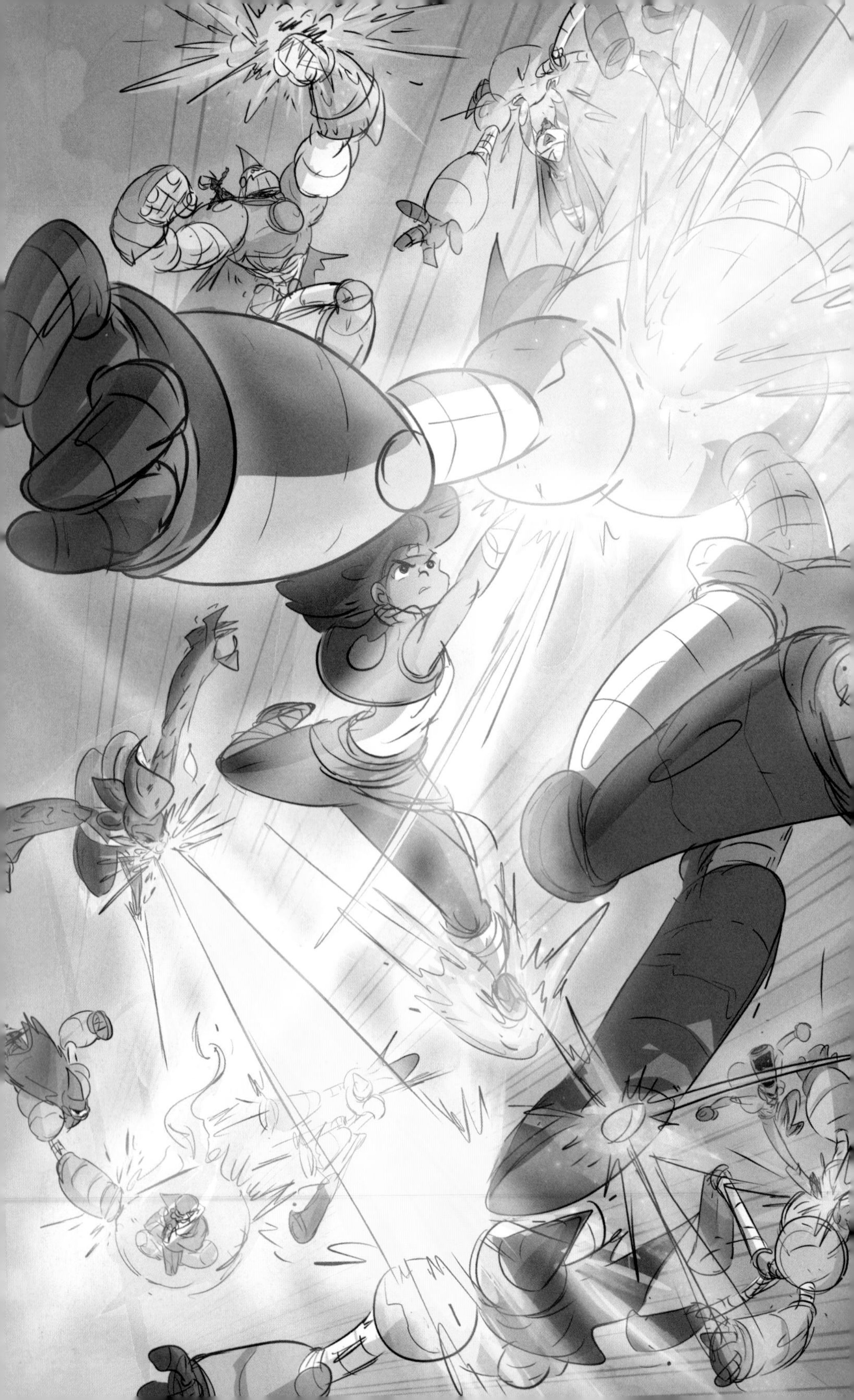

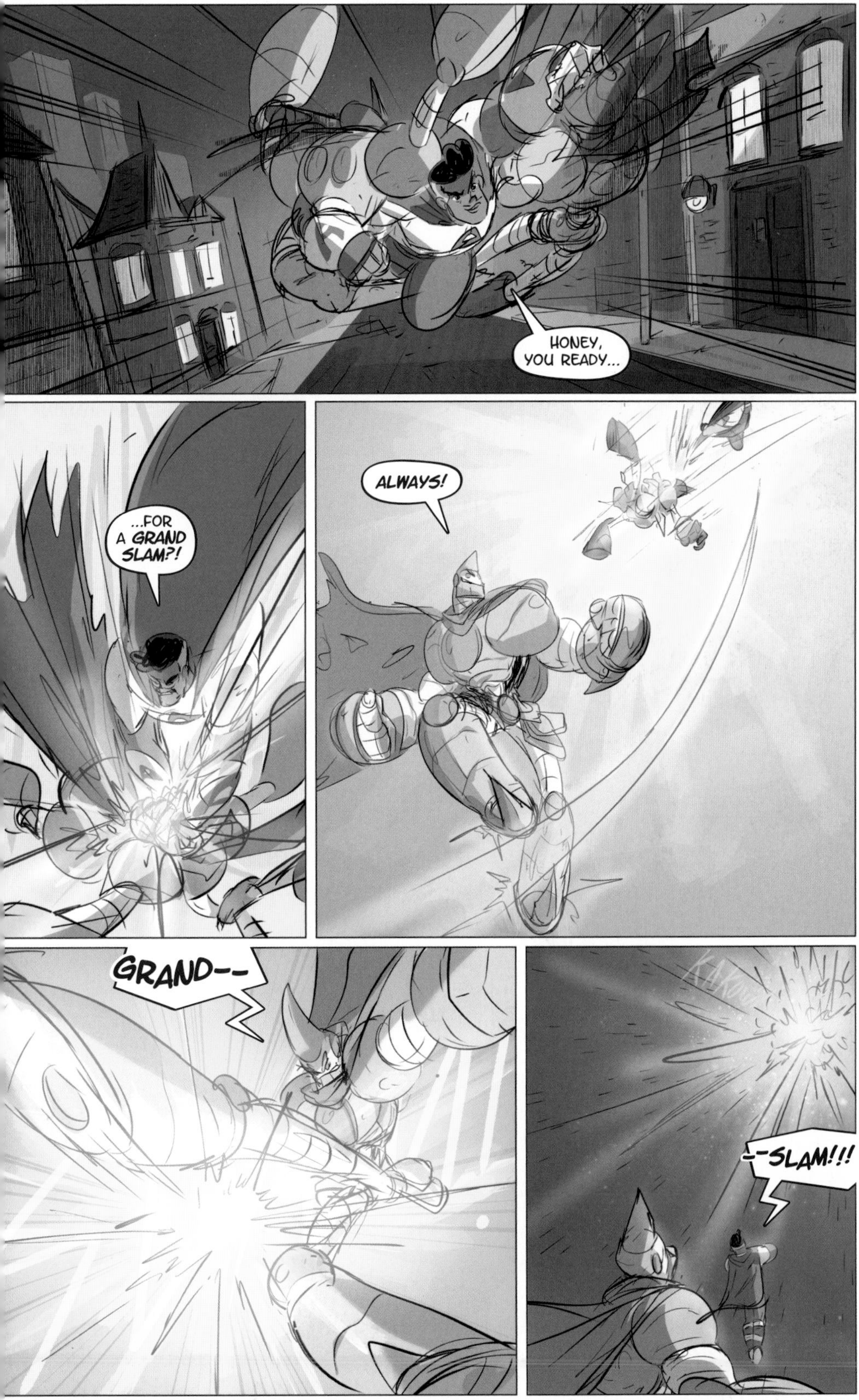
HONEY, YOU READY...
...FOR A GRAND SLAM?!
ALWAYS!
GRAND--
--SLAM!!!

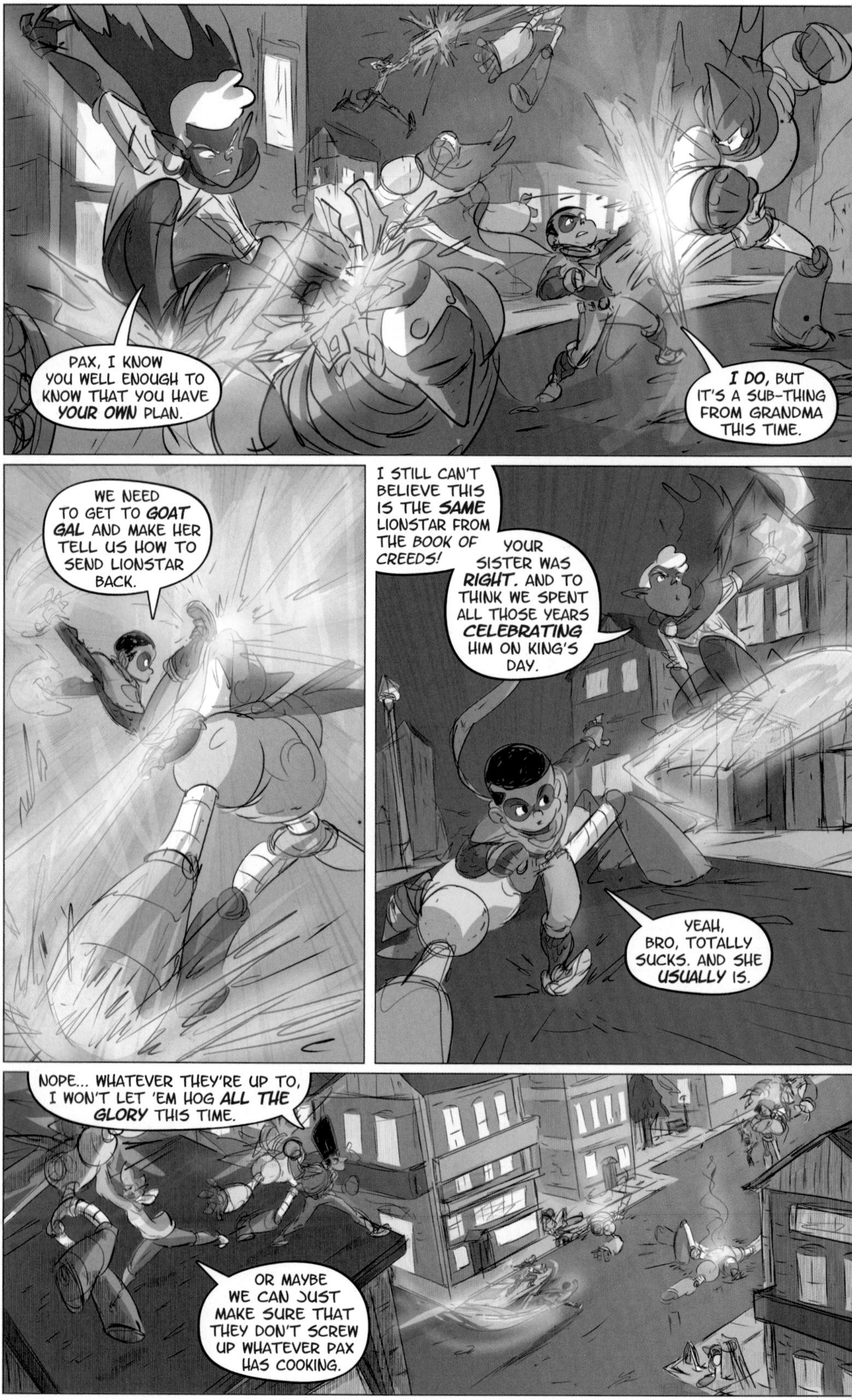

PAX, I KNOW YOU WELL ENOUGH TO KNOW THAT YOU HAVE **YOUR OWN** PLAN.
I DO, BUT IT'S A SUB-THING FROM GRANDMA THIS TIME.
WE NEED TO GET TO **GOAT GAL** AND MAKE HER TELL US HOW TO SEND LIONSTAR BACK.
I STILL CAN'T BELIEVE THIS IS THE **SAME** LIONSTAR FROM THE *BOOK OF CREEDS!*
YOUR SISTER WAS **RIGHT.** AND TO THINK WE SPENT ALL THOSE YEARS **CELEBRATING** HIM ON KING'S DAY.
YEAH, BRO, TOTALLY SUCKS. AND SHE **USUALLY** IS.
NOPE... WHATEVER THEY'RE UP TO, I WON'T LET 'EM HOG **ALL THE GLORY** THIS TIME.
OR MAYBE WE CAN JUST MAKE SURE THAT THEY DON'T SCREW UP WHATEVER PAX HAS COOKING.

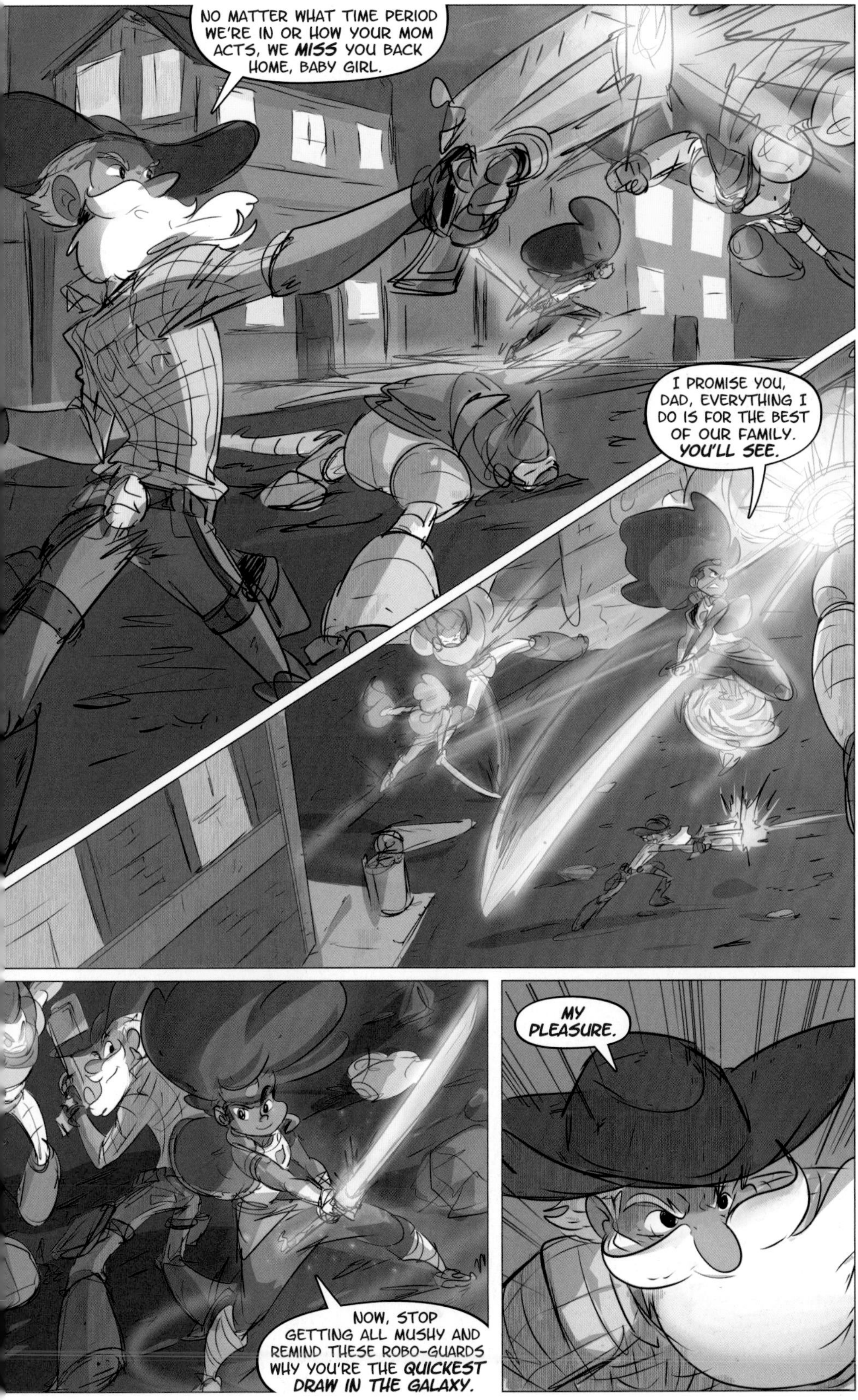
NO MATTER WHAT TIME PERIOD WE'RE IN OR HOW YOUR MOM ACTS, WE MISS YOU BACK HOME, BABY GIRL.
I PROMISE YOU, DAD, EVERYTHING I DO IS FOR THE BEST OF OUR FAMILY. YOU'LL SEE.
NOW, STOP GETTING ALL MUSHY AND REMIND THESE ROBO-GUARDS WHY YOU'RE THE QUICKEST DRAW IN THE GALAXY.
MY PLEASURE.

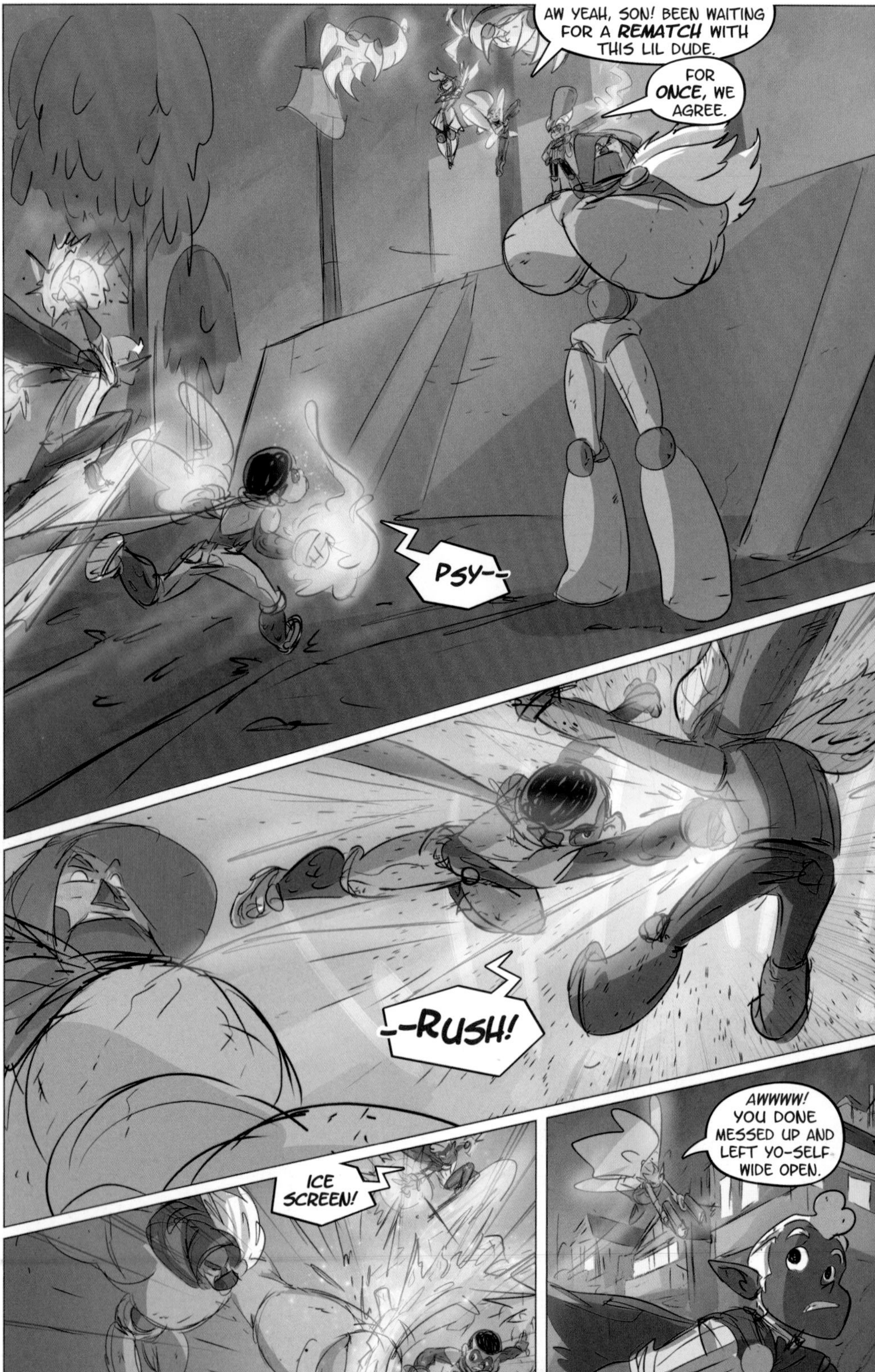
AW YEAH, SON! BEEN WAITING FOR A REMATCH WITH THIS LIL DUDE.
FOR ONCE, WE AGREE.
PSY--
--RUSH!
ICE SCREEN!
AWWWW! YOU DONE MESSED UP AND LEFT YO-SELF WIDE OPEN.

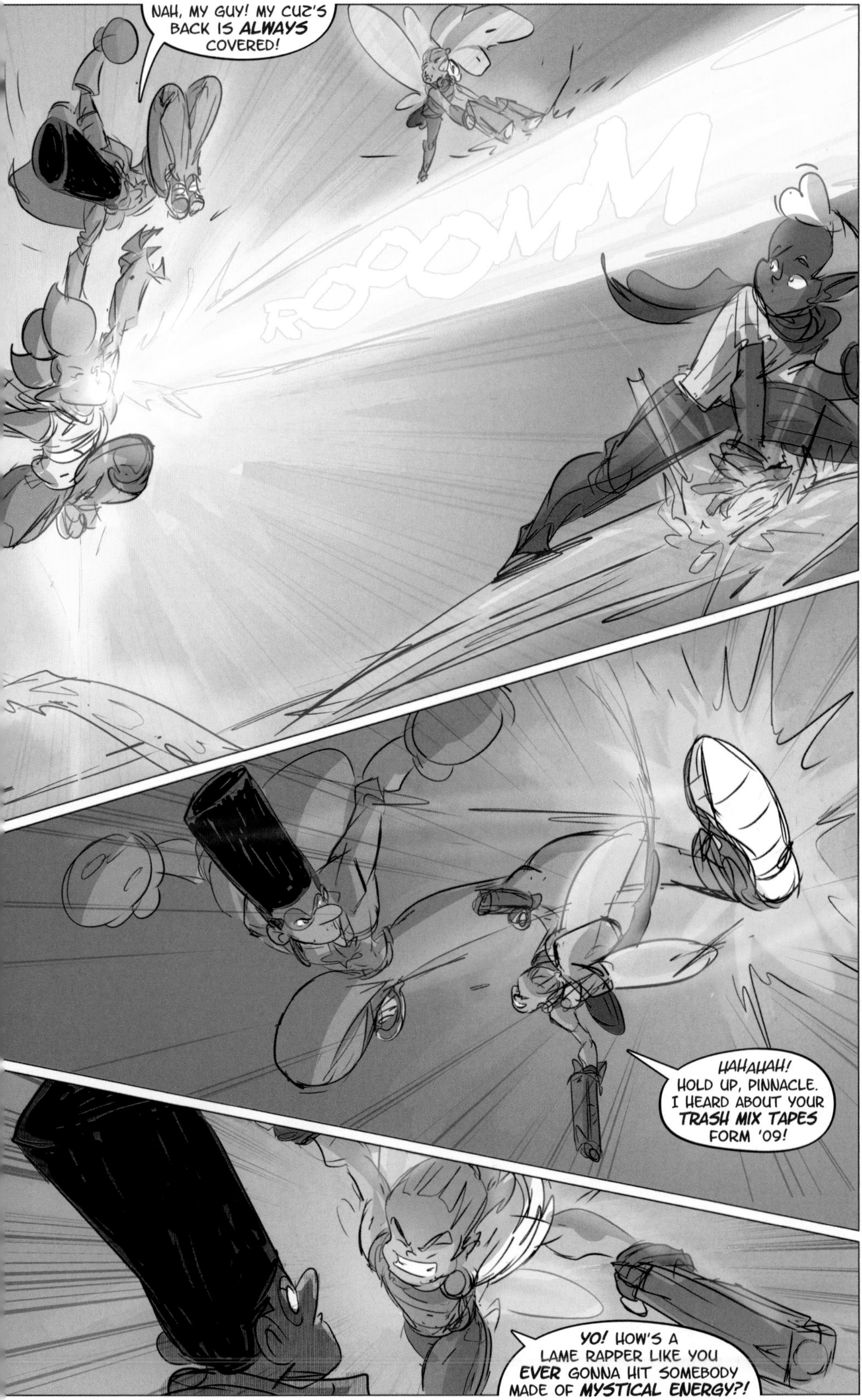
NAH, MY GUY! MY CUZ'S BACK IS ALWAYS COVERED!
ROOOMM
HAHAHAH! HOLD UP, PINNACLE. I HEARD ABOUT YOUR TRASH MIX TAPES FORM '09!
YO! HOW'S A LAME RAPPER LIKE YOU EVER GONNA HIT SOMEBODY MADE OF MYSTICAL ENERGY?!

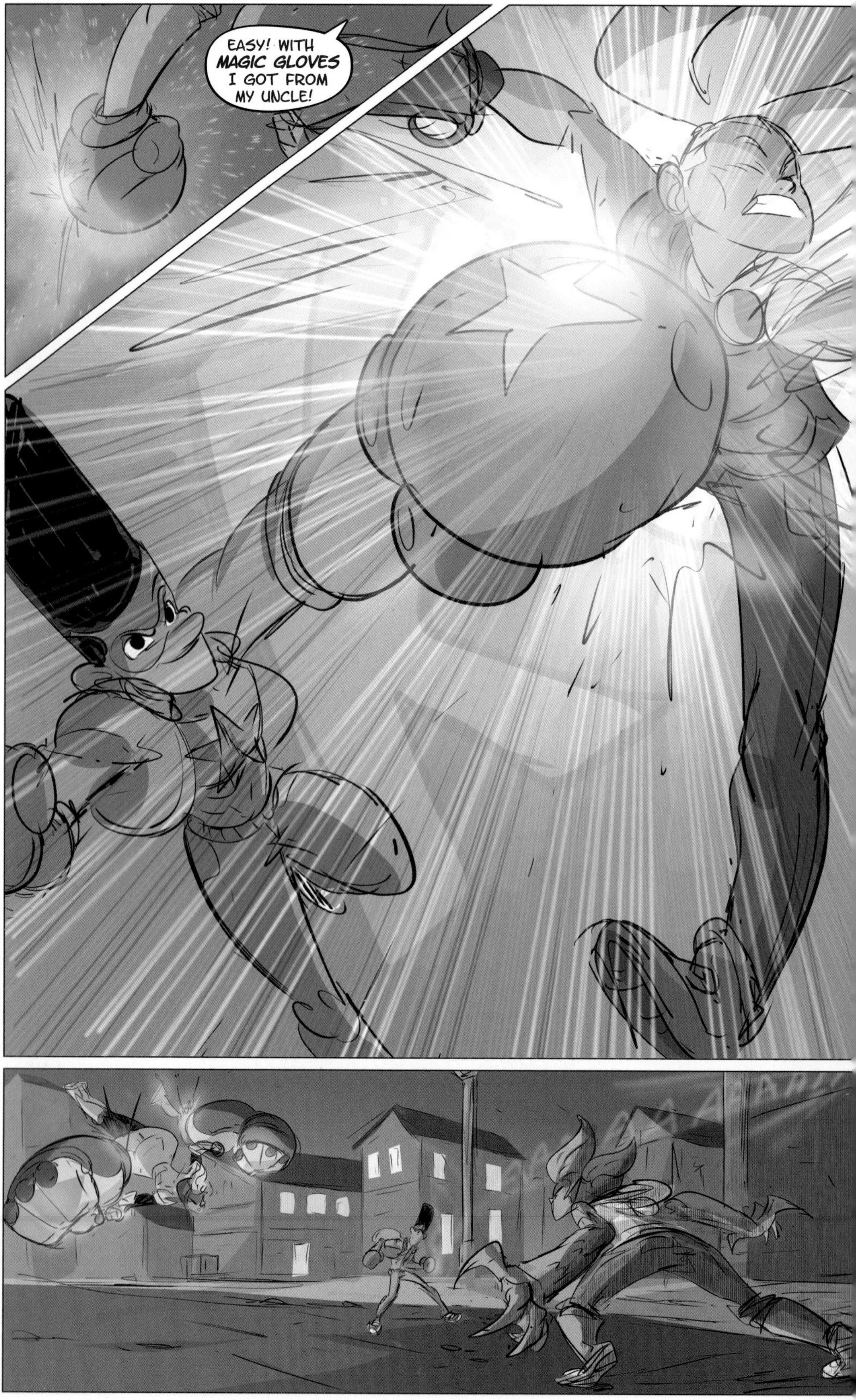
EASY! WITH MAGIC GLOVES I GOT FROM MY UNCLE!

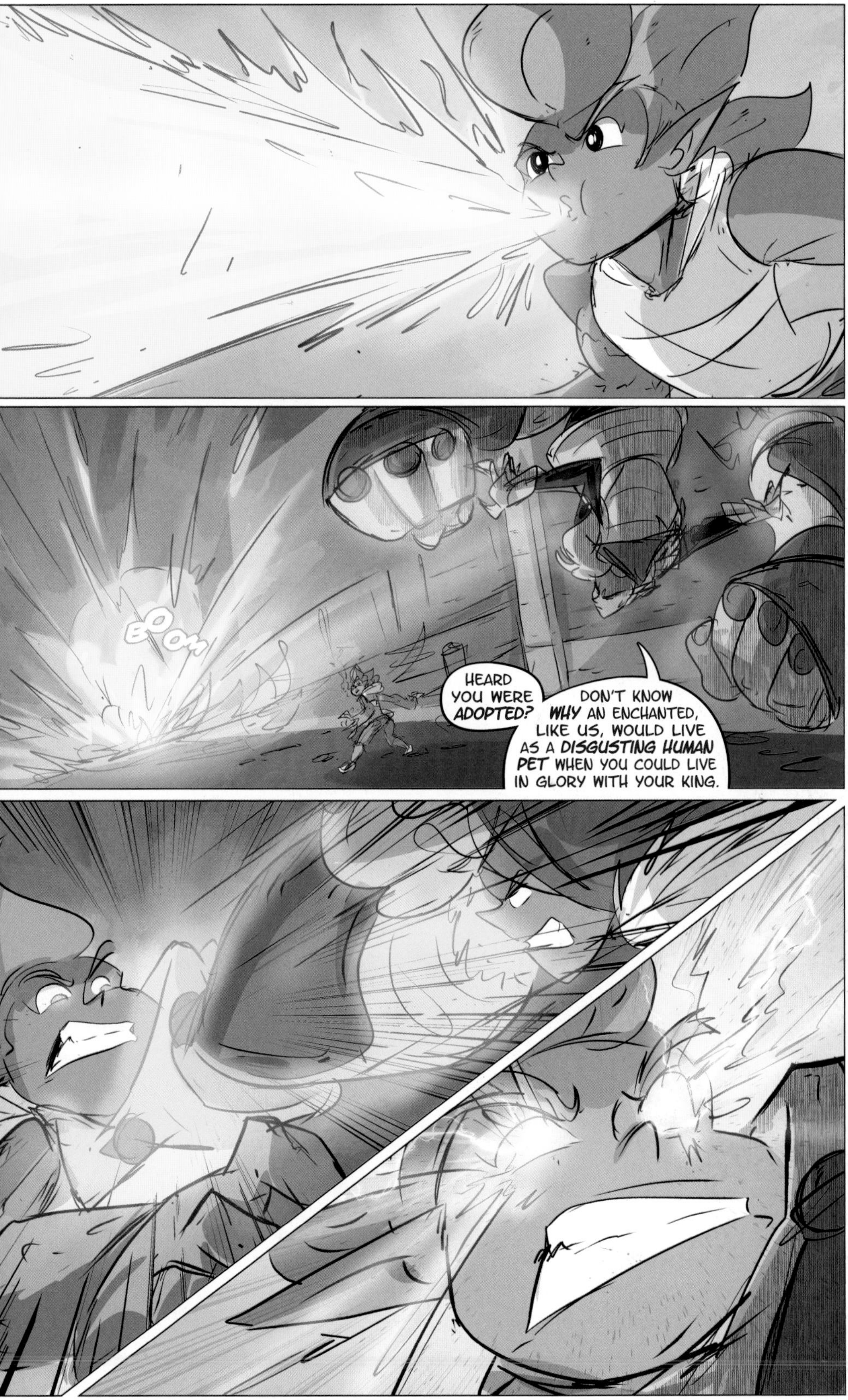
BOOM
HEARD YOU WERE ADOPTED?
DON'T KNOW WHY AN ENCHANTED, LIKE US, WOULD LIVE AS A DISGUSTING HUMAN PET WHEN YOU COULD LIVE IN GLORY WITH YOUR KING.

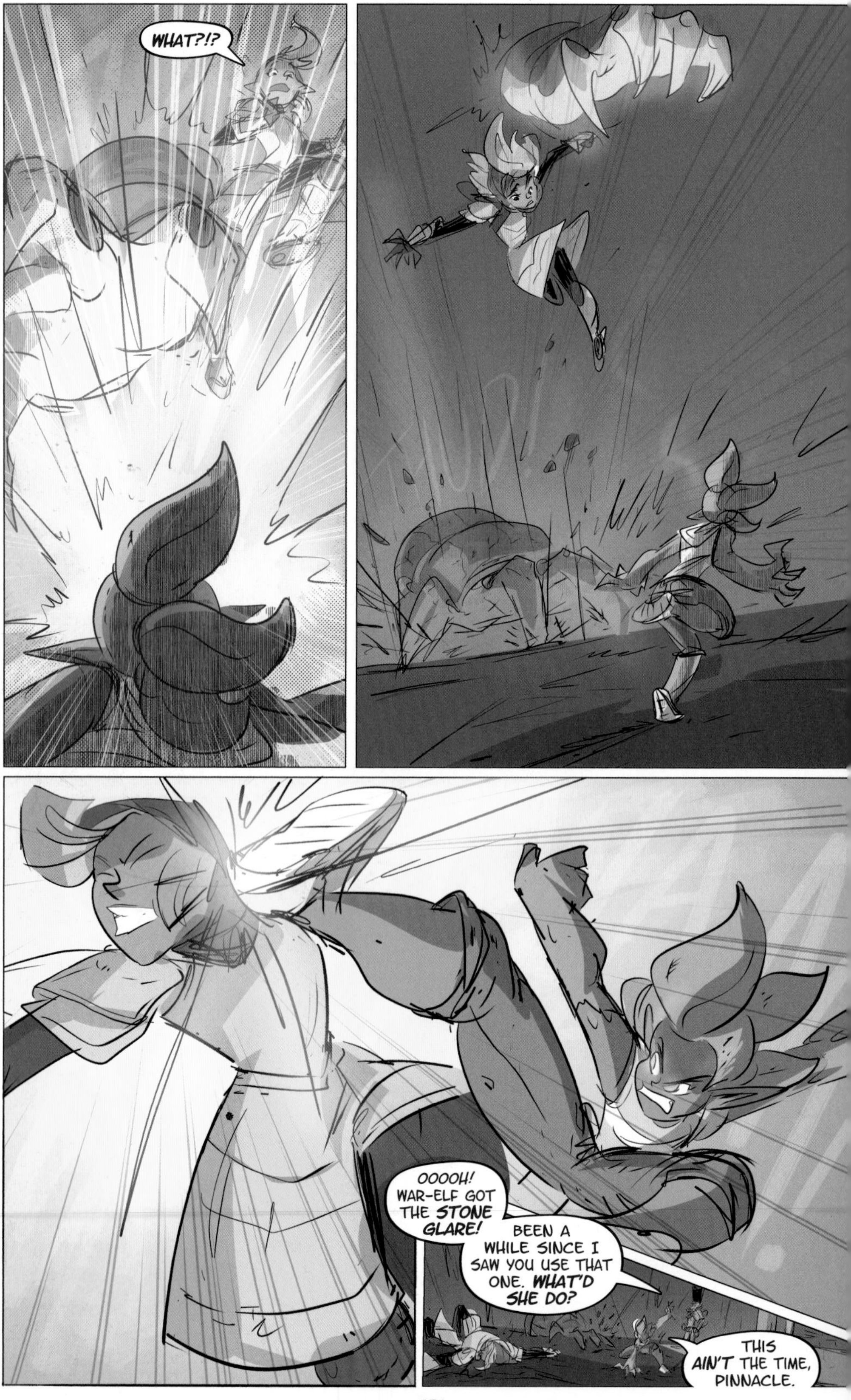
WHAT?!?
OOOOH! WAR-ELF GOT THE STONE GLARE!
BEEN A WHILE SINCE I SAW YOU USE THAT ONE. WHAT'D SHE DO?
THIS AIN'T THE TIME, PINNACLE.

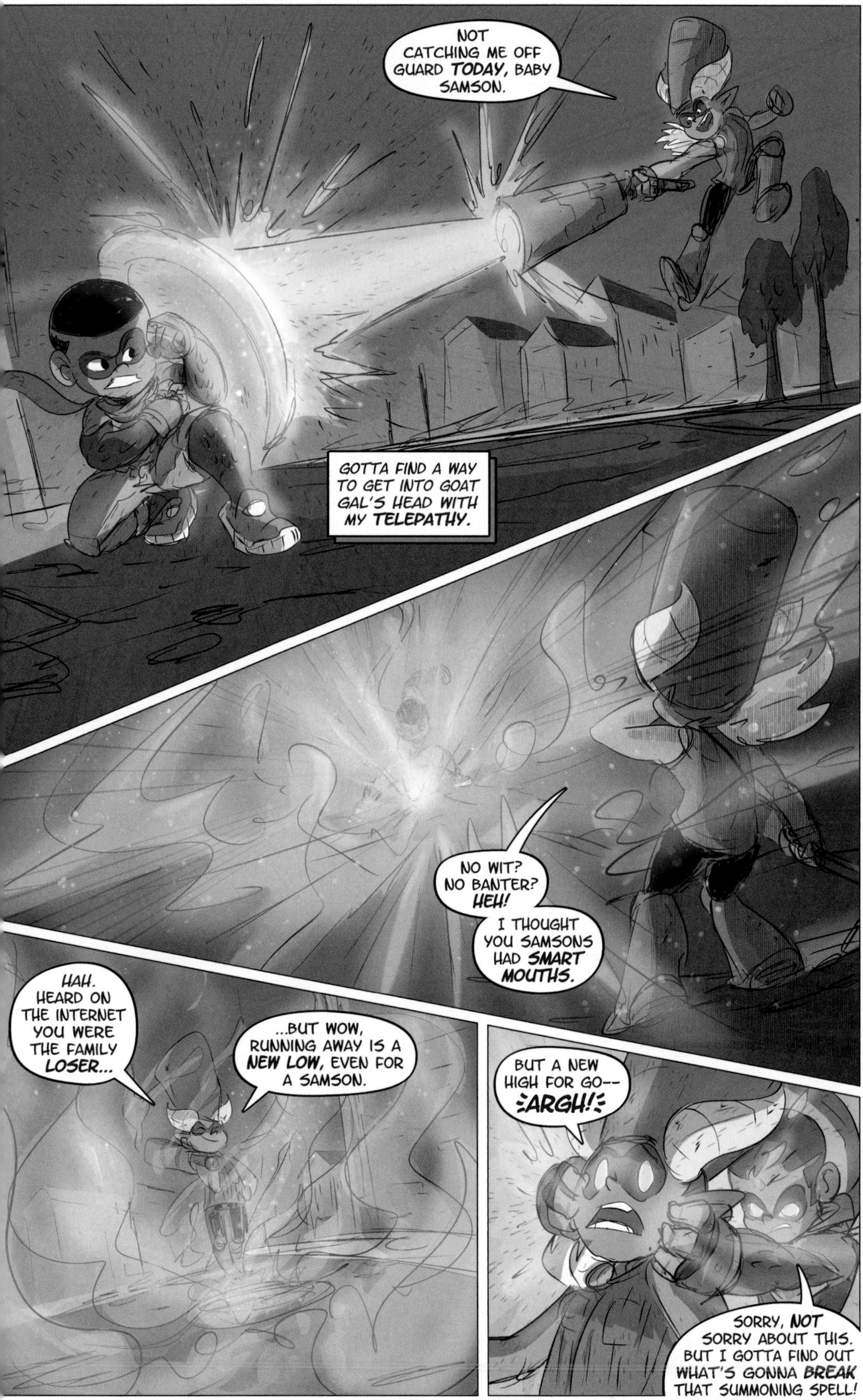
NOT CATCHING ME OFF GUARD TODAY, BABY SAMSON.
GOTTA FIND A WAY TO GET INTO GOAT GAL'S HEAD WITH MY TELEPATHY.
NO WIT? NO BANTER? HEH!
I THOUGHT YOU SAMSONS HAD SMART MOUTHS.
HAH. HEARD ON THE INTERNET YOU WERE THE FAMILY LOSER...
...BUT WOW, RUNNING AWAY IS A NEW LOW, EVEN FOR A SAMSON.
BUT A NEW HIGH FOR GO-- ARGH!
SORRY, NOT SORRY ABOUT THIS. BUT I GOTTA FIND OUT WHAT'S GONNA BREAK THAT SUMMONING SPELL!

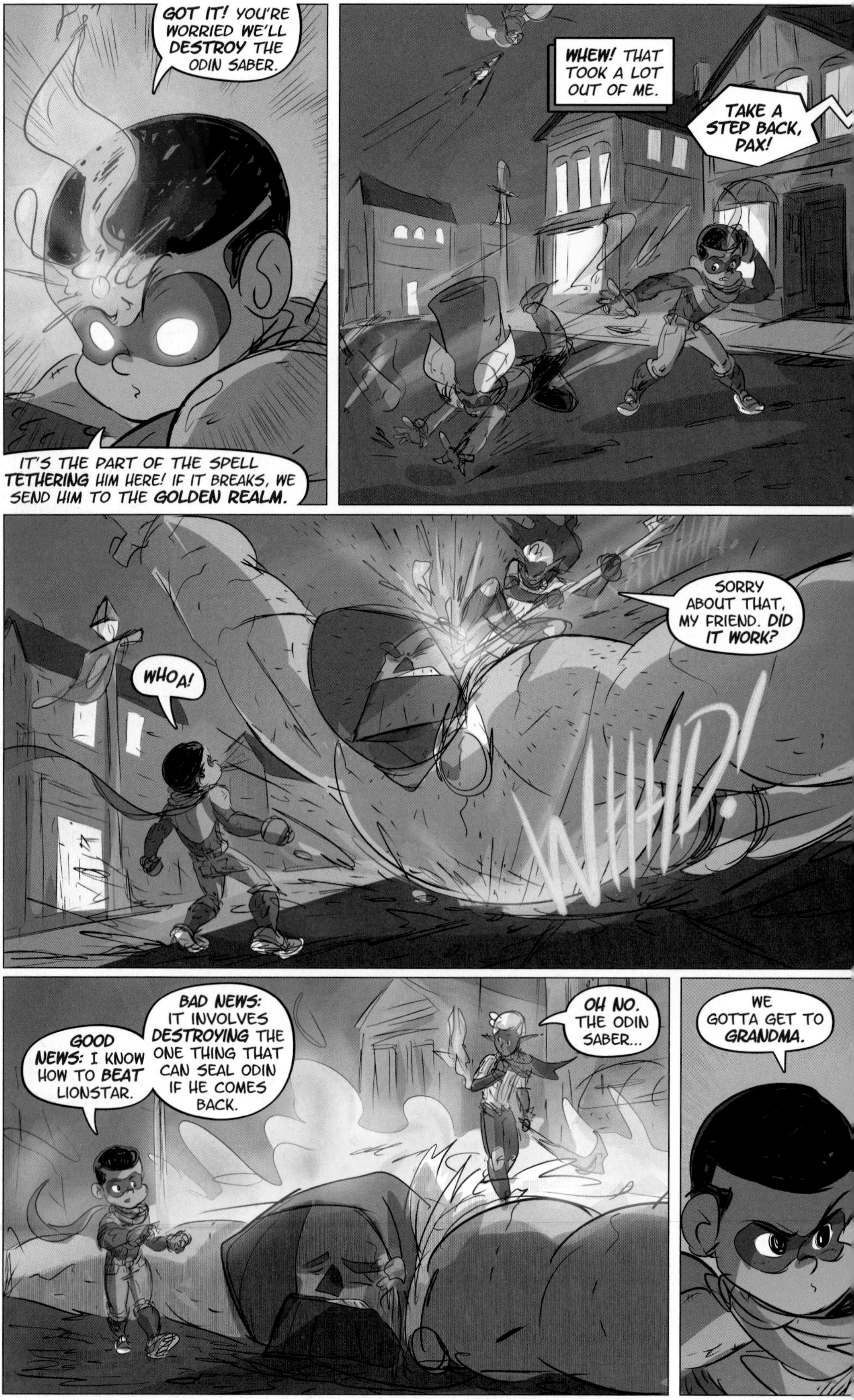
GOT IT! YOU'RE WORRIED WE'LL DESTROY THE ODIN SABER.
IT'S THE PART OF THE SPELL TETHERING HIM HERE! IF IT BREAKS, WE SEND HIM TO THE GOLDEN REALM.
WHEW! THAT TOOK A LOT OUT OF ME.
TAKE A STEP BACK, PAX!
WHOA!
SORRY ABOUT THAT, MY FRIEND. DID IT WORK?
WHUD!
GOOD NEWS: I KNOW HOW TO BEAT LIONSTAR.
BAD NEWS: IT INVOLVES DESTROYING THE ONE THING THAT CAN SEAL ODIN IF HE COMES BACK.
OH NO. THE ODIN SABER...
WE GOTTA GET TO GRANDMA.

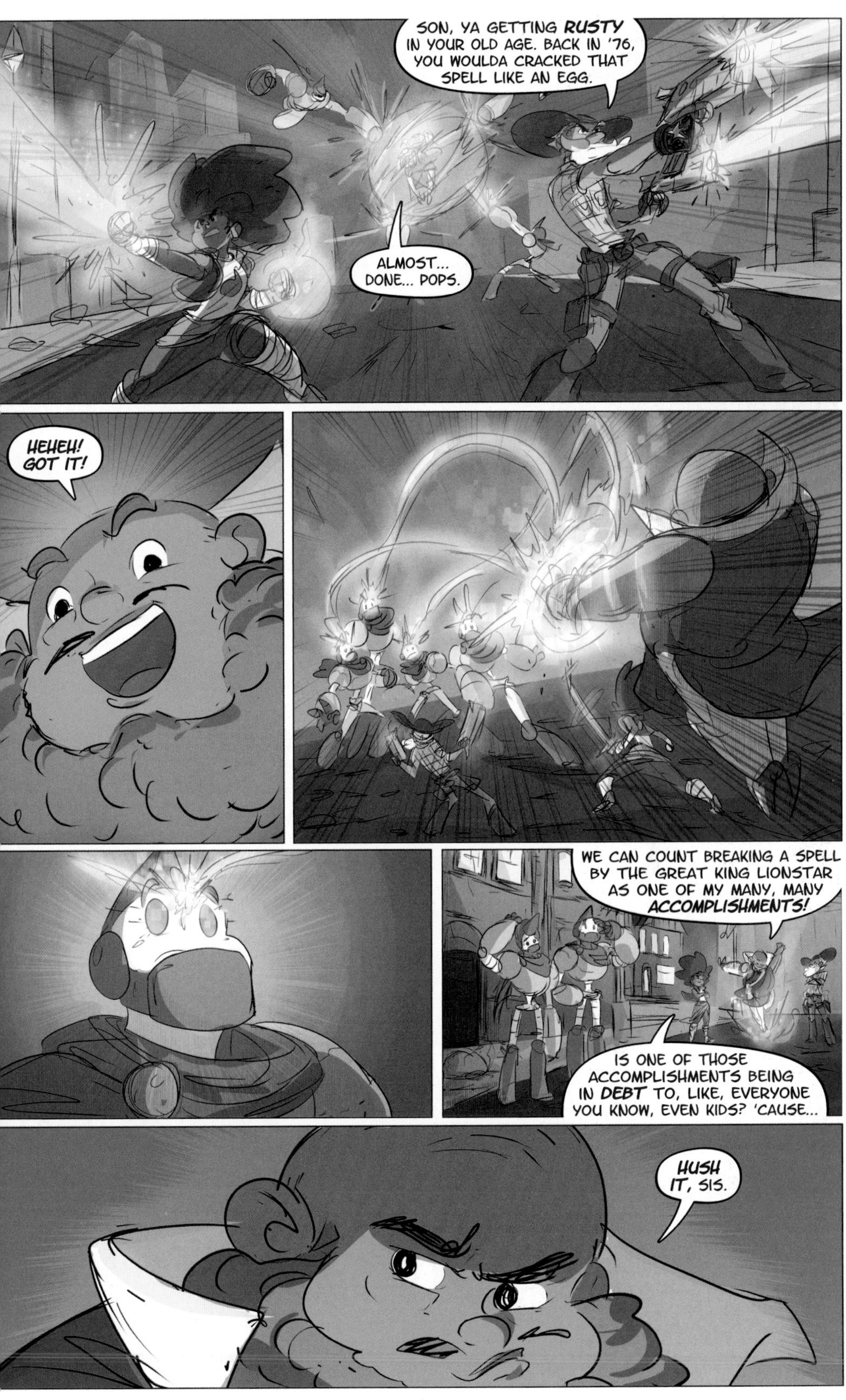
SON, YA GETTING RUSTY IN YOUR OLD AGE. BACK IN '76, YOU WOULDA CRACKED THAT SPELL LIKE AN EGG.
ALMOST... DONE... POPS.
HEHEH! GOT IT!
WE CAN COUNT BREAKING A SPELL BY THE GREAT KING LIONSTAR AS ONE OF MY MANY, MANY ACCOMPLISHMENTS!
IS ONE OF THOSE ACCOMPLISHMENTS BEING IN DEBT TO, LIKE, EVERYONE YOU KNOW, EVEN KIDS? 'CAUSE...
HUSH IT, SIS.

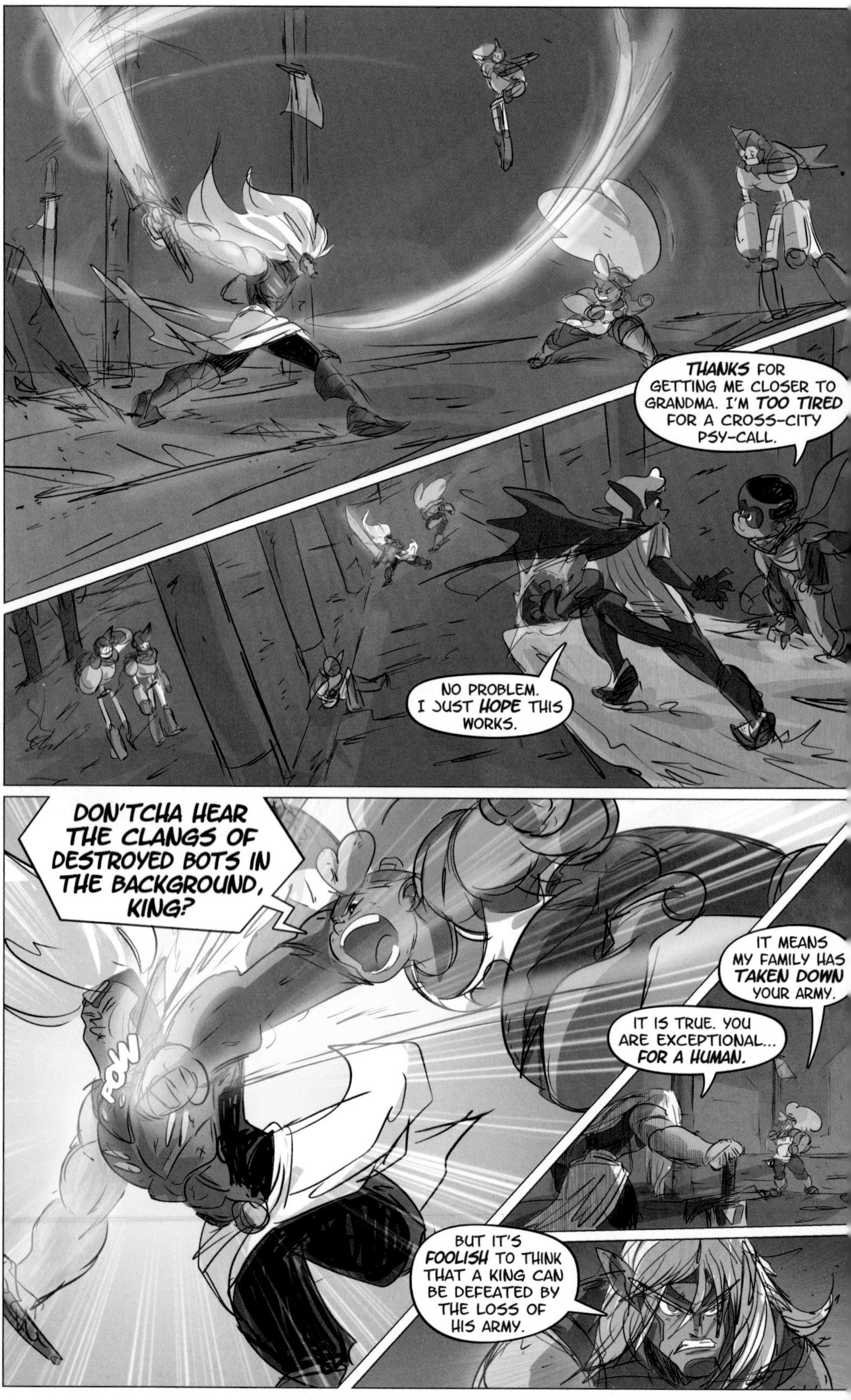
THANKS FOR GETTING ME CLOSER TO GRANDMA. I'M TOO TIRED FOR A CROSS-CITY PSY-CALL.
NO PROBLEM. I JUST HOPE THIS WORKS.
DON'TCHA HEAR THE CLANGS OF DESTROYED BOTS IN THE BACKGROUND, KING?
POW
IT MEANS MY FAMILY HAS TAKEN DOWN YOUR ARMY.
IT IS TRUE. YOU ARE EXCEPTIONAL... FOR A HUMAN.
BUT IT'S FOOLISH TO THINK THAT A KING CAN BE DEFEATED BY THE LOSS OF HIS ARMY.

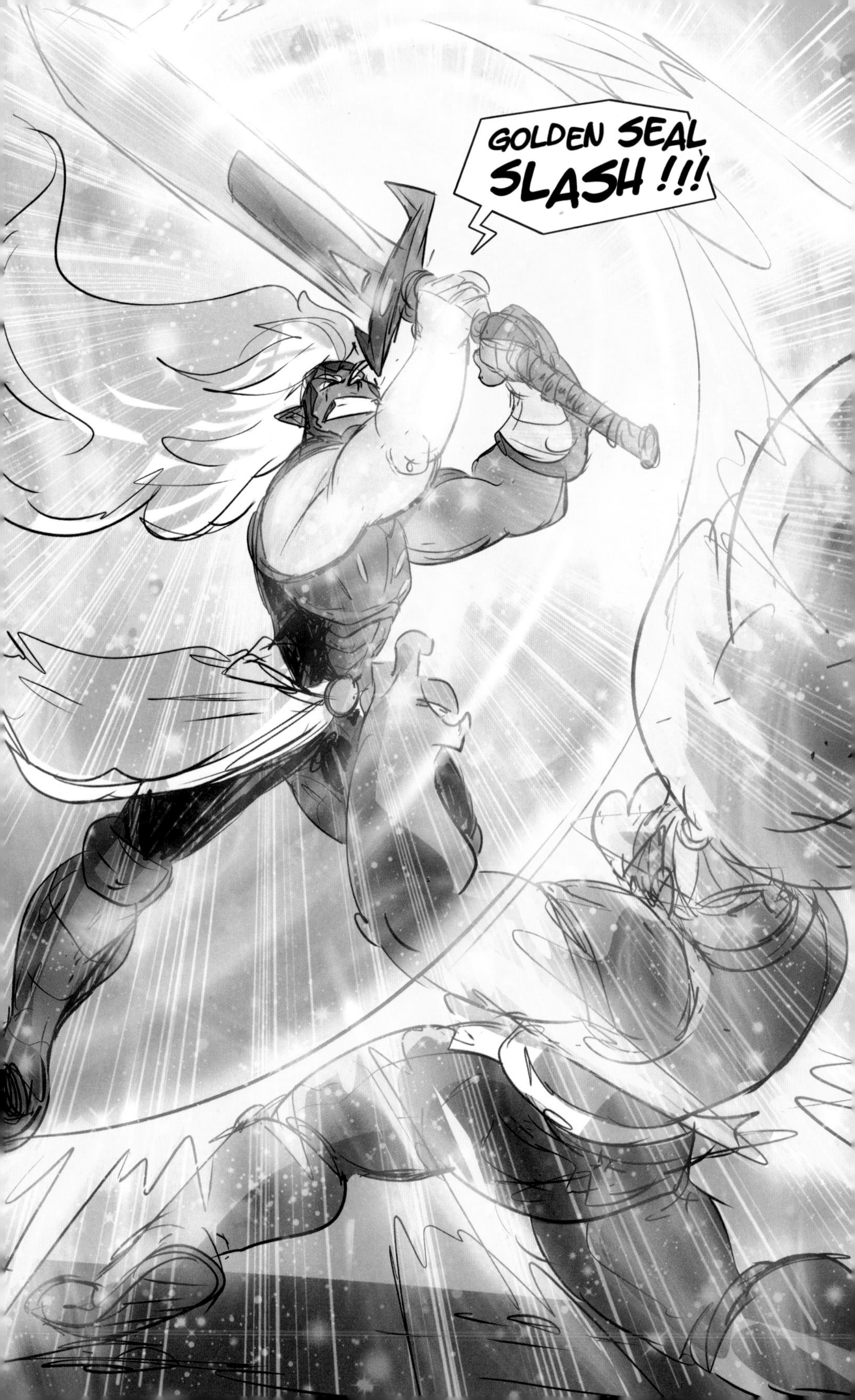
GOLDEN SEAL SLASH !!!

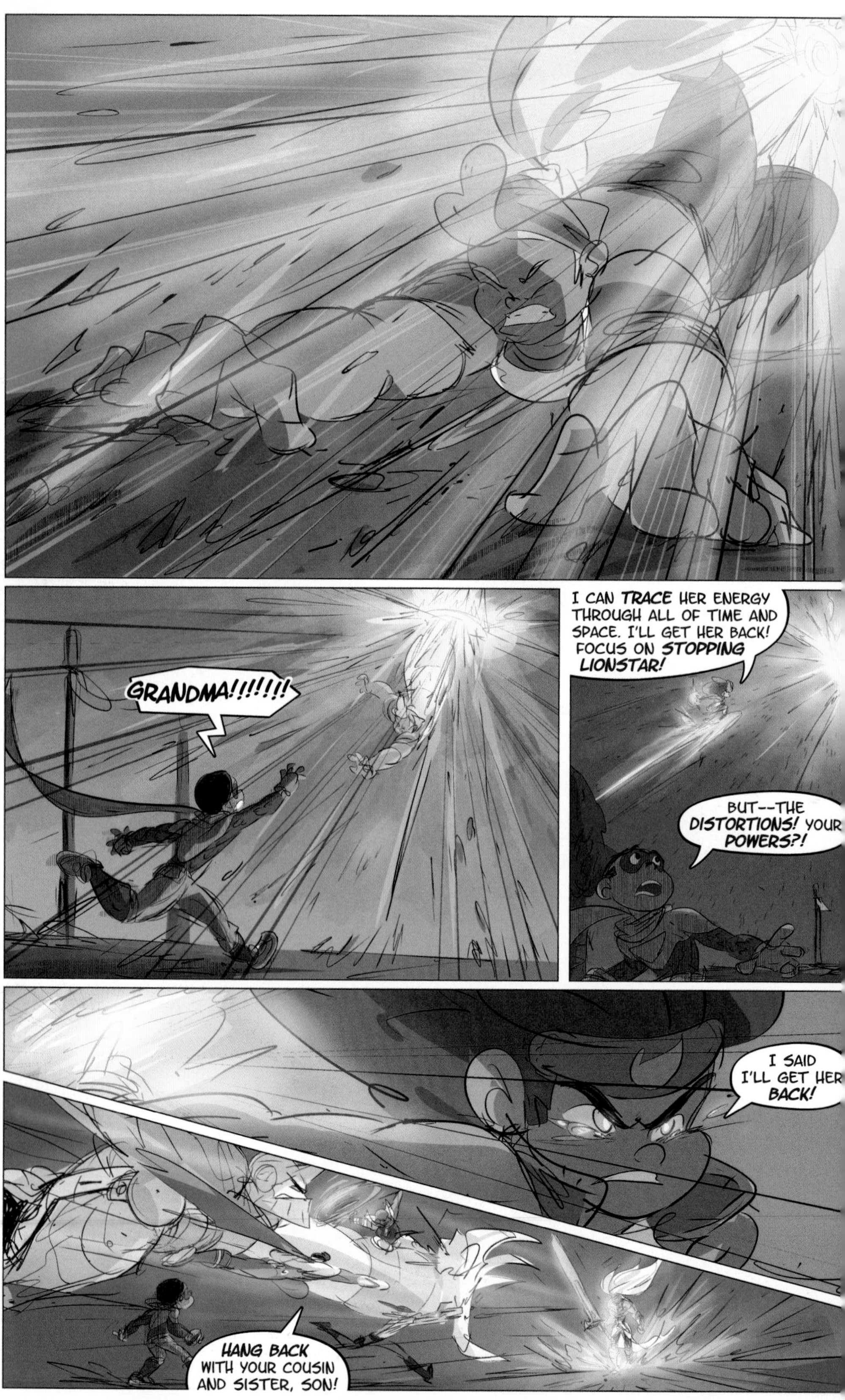

GRANDMA!!!!!!!
I CAN TRACE HER ENERGY THROUGH ALL OF TIME AND SPACE. I'LL GET HER BACK! FOCUS ON STOPPING LIONSTAR!
BUT--THE DISTORTIONS! YOUR POWERS?!
I SAID I'LL GET HER BACK!
HANG BACK WITH YOUR COUSIN AND SISTER, SON!

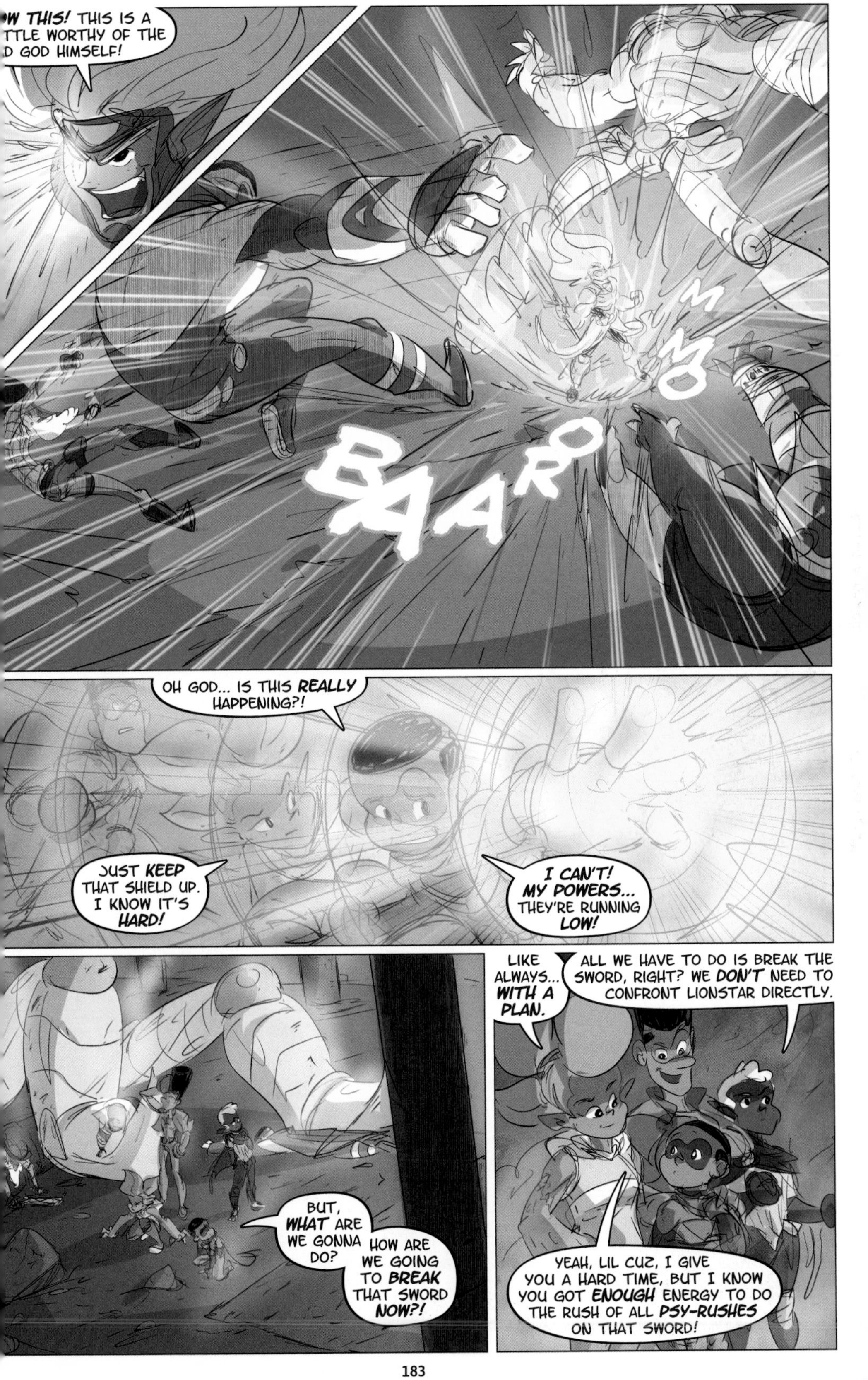
W THIS! THIS IS A
TTLE WORTHY OF THE
D GOD HIMSELF!
BAAROOMM
OH GOD... IS THIS REALLY HAPPENING?!
JUST KEEP THAT SHIELD UP. I KNOW IT'S HARD!
I CAN'T! MY POWERS... THEY'RE RUNNING LOW!
BUT, WHAT ARE WE GONNA DO?
HOW ARE WE GOING TO BREAK THAT SWORD NOW?!
LIKE ALWAYS... WITH A PLAN.
ALL WE HAVE TO DO IS BREAK THE SWORD, RIGHT? WE DON'T NEED TO CONFRONT LIONSTAR DIRECTLY.
YEAH, LIL CUZ, I GIVE YOU A HARD TIME, BUT I KNOW YOU GOT ENOUGH ENERGY TO DO THE RUSH OF ALL PSY-RUSHES ON THAT SWORD!

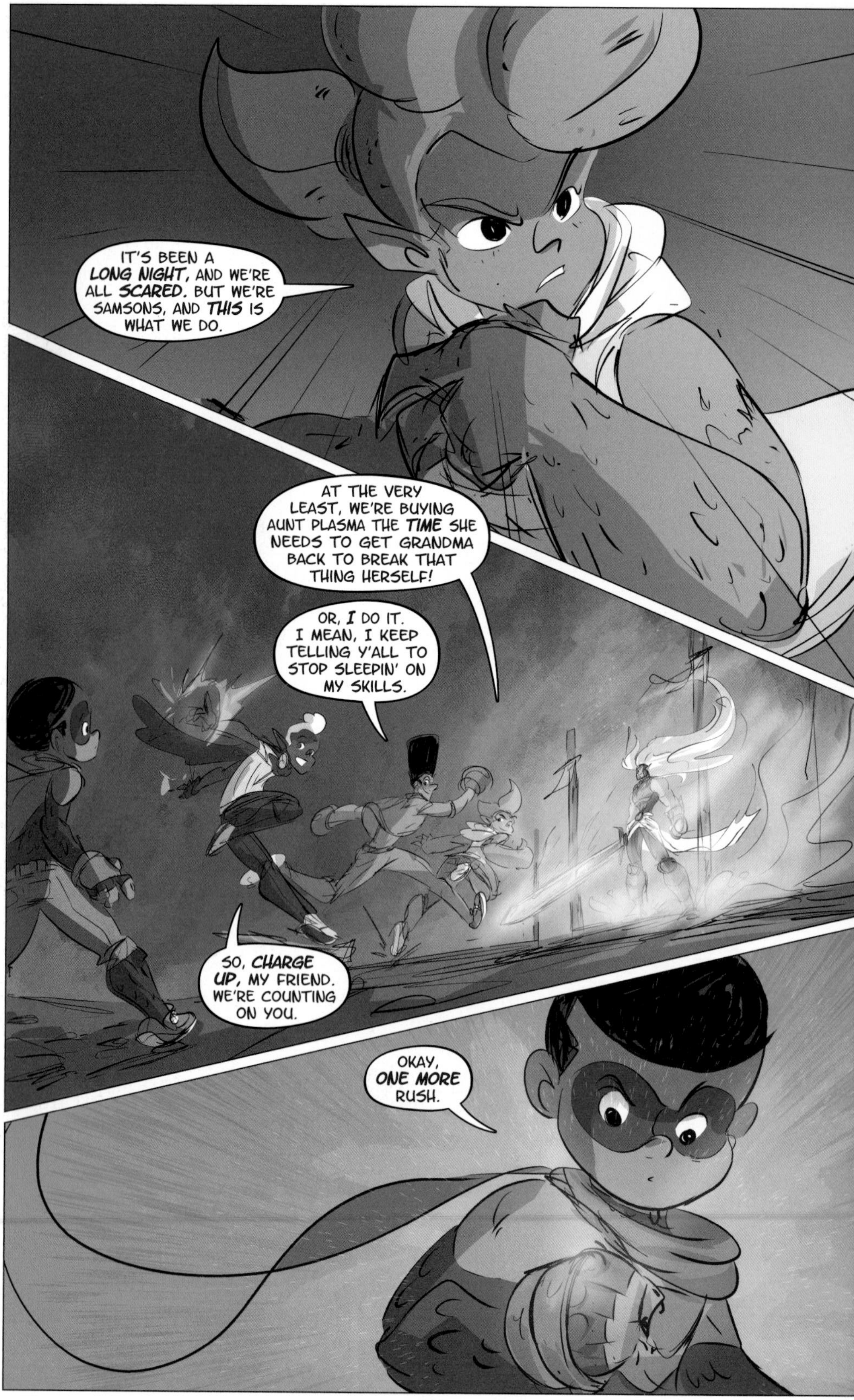
IT'S BEEN A LONG NIGHT, AND WE'RE ALL SCARED. BUT WE'RE SAMSONS, AND THIS IS WHAT WE DO.
AT THE VERY LEAST, WE'RE BUYING AUNT PLASMA THE TIME SHE NEEDS TO GET GRANDMA BACK TO BREAK THAT THING HERSELF!
OR, I DO IT. I MEAN, I KEEP TELLING Y'ALL TO STOP SLEEPIN' ON MY SKILLS.
SO, CHARGE UP, MY FRIEND. WE'RE COUNTING ON YOU.
OKAY, ONE MORE RUSH.

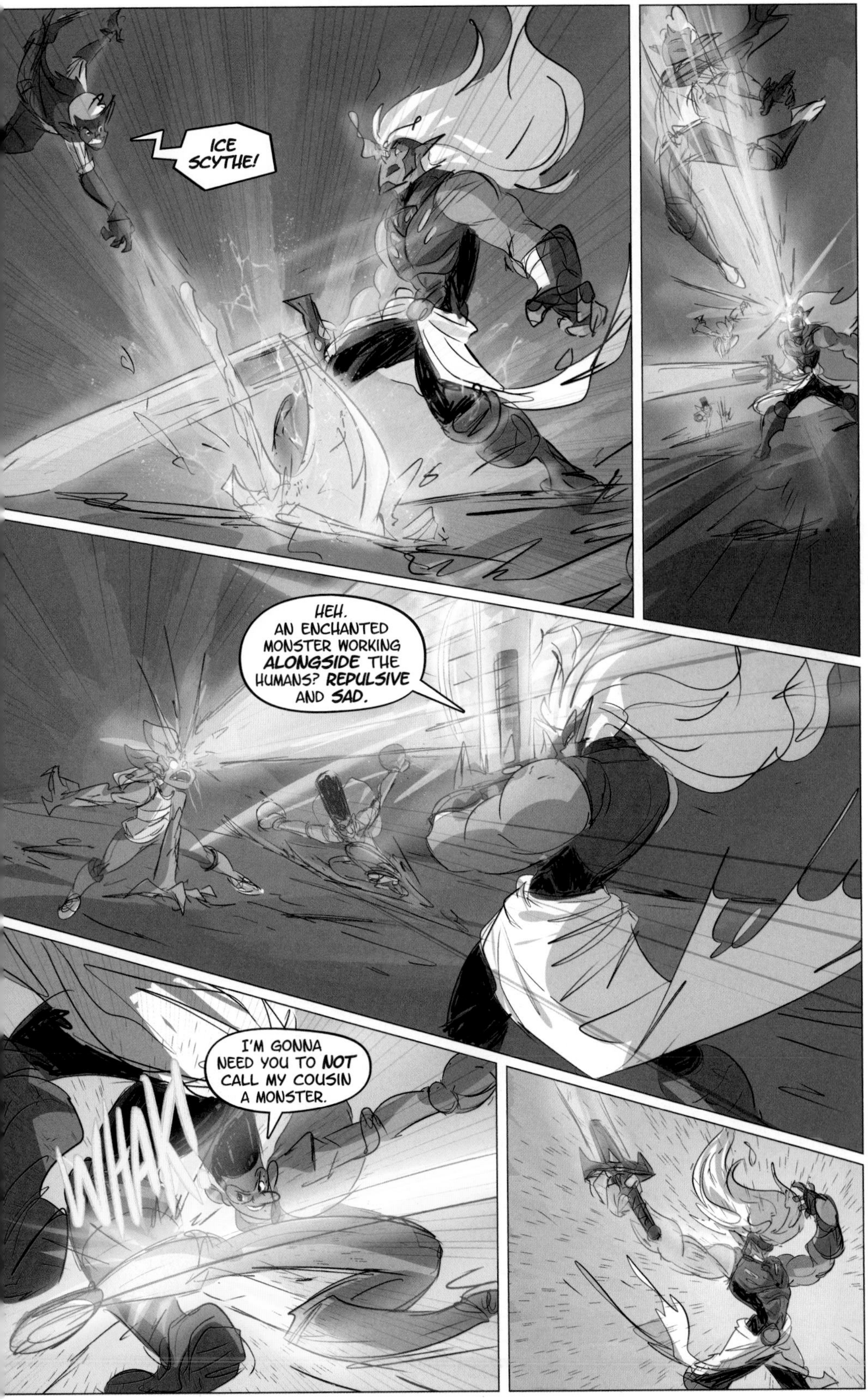
ICE SCYTHE!
HEH. AN ENCHANTED MONSTER WORKING **ALONGSIDE** THE HUMANS? **REPULSIVE** AND **SAD.**
I'M GONNA NEED YOU TO **NOT** CALL MY COUSIN A MONSTER.
WHAK

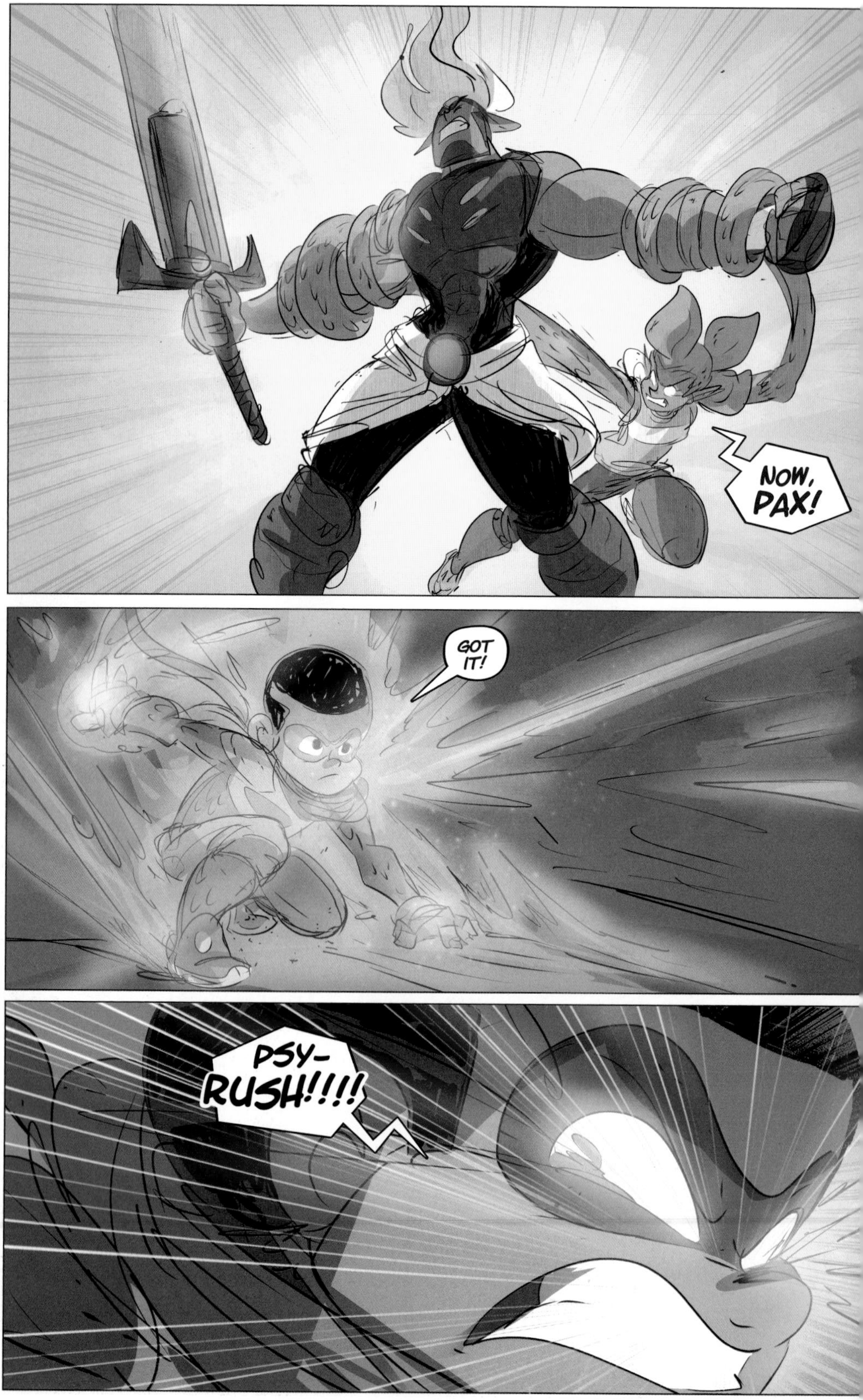
NOW, PAX!
GOT IT!
PSY-RUSH!!!!

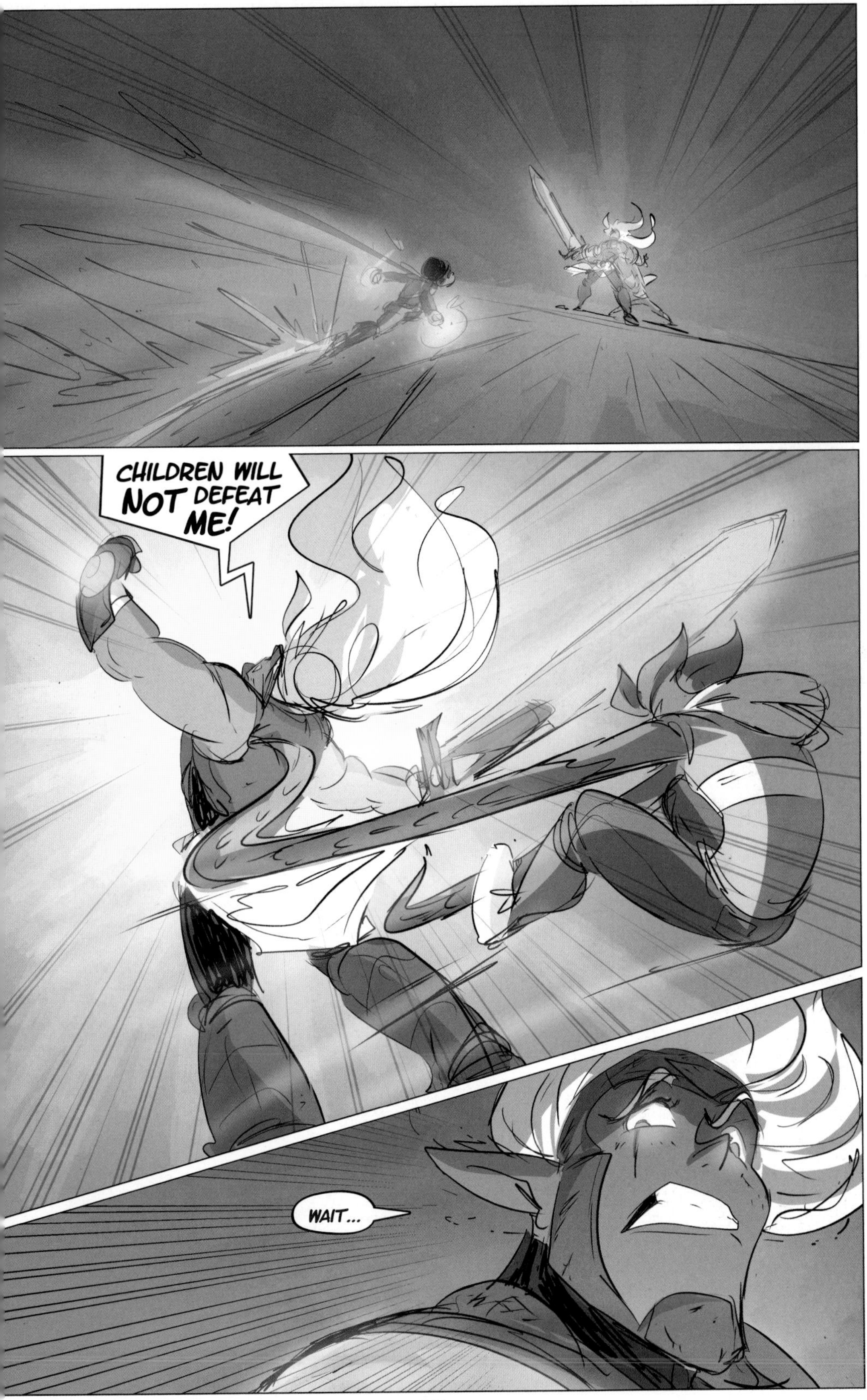
CHILDREN WILL NOT DEFEAT ME!
WAIT...

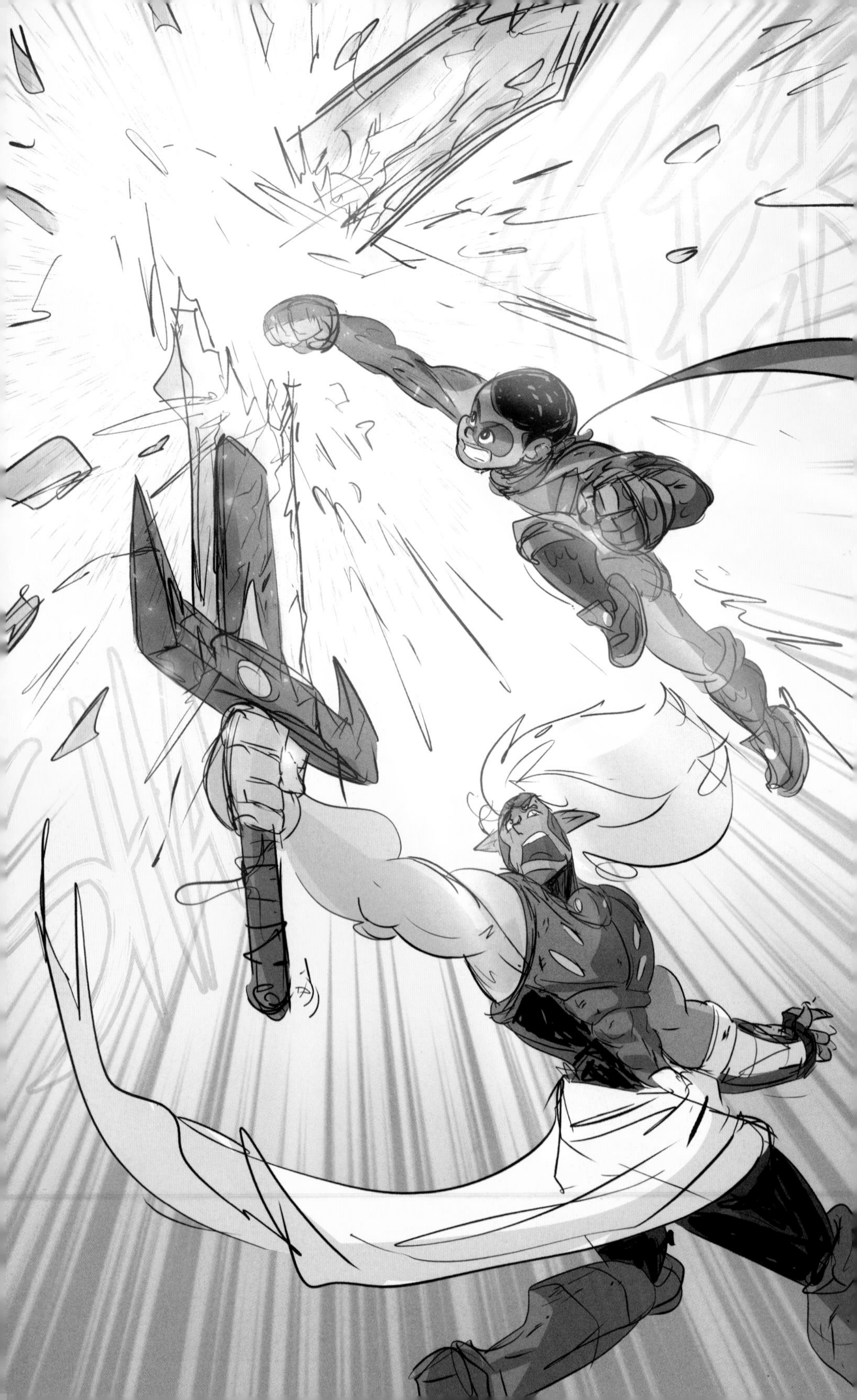

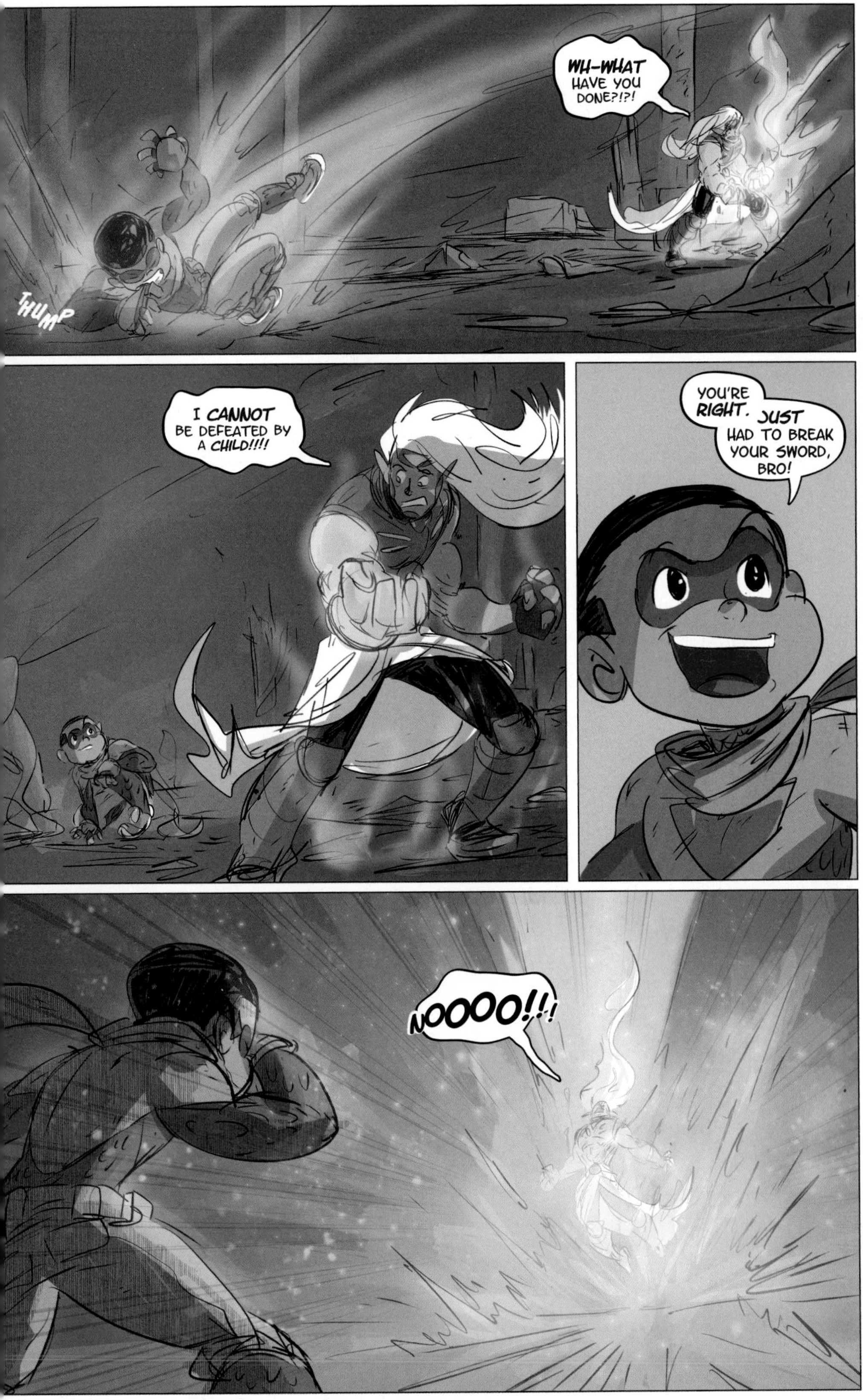
THUMP
WH-WHAT HAVE YOU DONE?!?!
I CANNOT BE DEFEATED BY A CHILD!!!!
YOU'RE RIGHT. JUST HAD TO BREAK YOUR SWORD, BRO!
NOOOO!!!

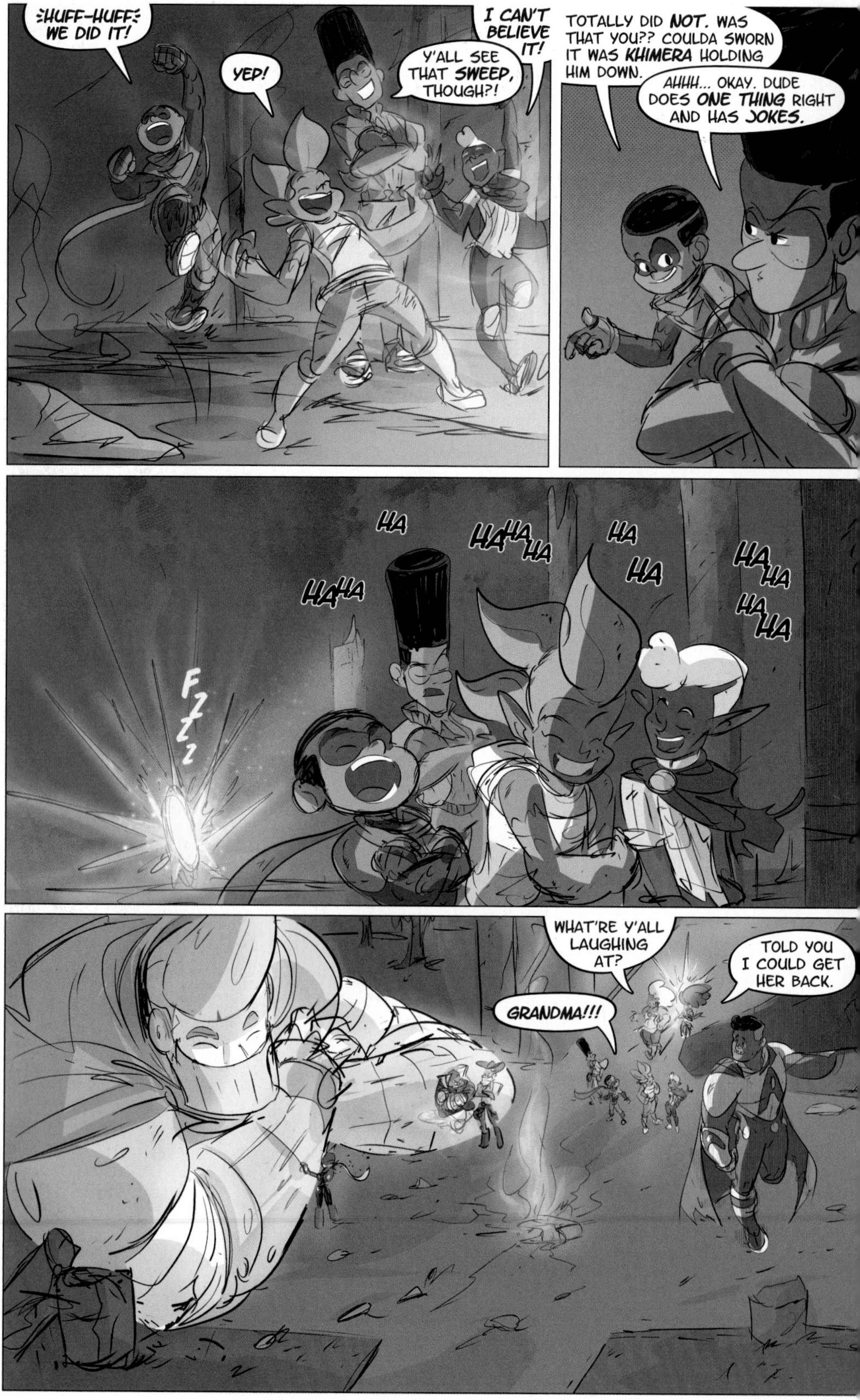
HUFF-HUFF
WE DID IT!
YEP!
Y'ALL SEE THAT SWEEP, THOUGH?!
I CAN'T BELIEVE IT!
TOTALLY DID NOT. WAS THAT YOU?? COULDA SWORN IT WAS KHIMERA HOLDING HIM DOWN.
AHHH... OKAY. DUDE DOES ONE THING RIGHT AND HAS JOKES.
HA
HAHAHA
HAHA
HA
HA
HAHA
HAHA
FZZZ
WHAT'RE Y'ALL LAUGHING AT?
GRANDMA!!!
TOLD YOU I COULD GET HER BACK.

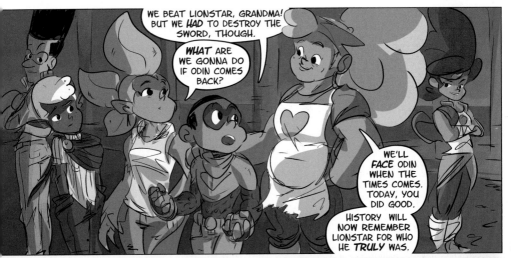

WE BEAT LIONSTAR, GRANDMA! BUT WE *HAD* TO DESTROY THE SWORD, THOUGH.

WHAT ARE WE GONNA DO IF ODIN COMES BACK?

WE'LL *FACE* ODIN WHEN THE TIMES COMES. TODAY, YOU DID GOOD.

HISTORY WILL NOW REMEMBER LIONSTAR FOR WHO HE *TRULY* WAS.

MAN, WE *REALLY* BEAT HIM. CAN YOU BELIEVE IT?!

OF COURSE I CAN. Y'ALL ARE SAMSONS, AIN'TCHA?!

AZUL, THAT MEANS *YOU*, TOO.

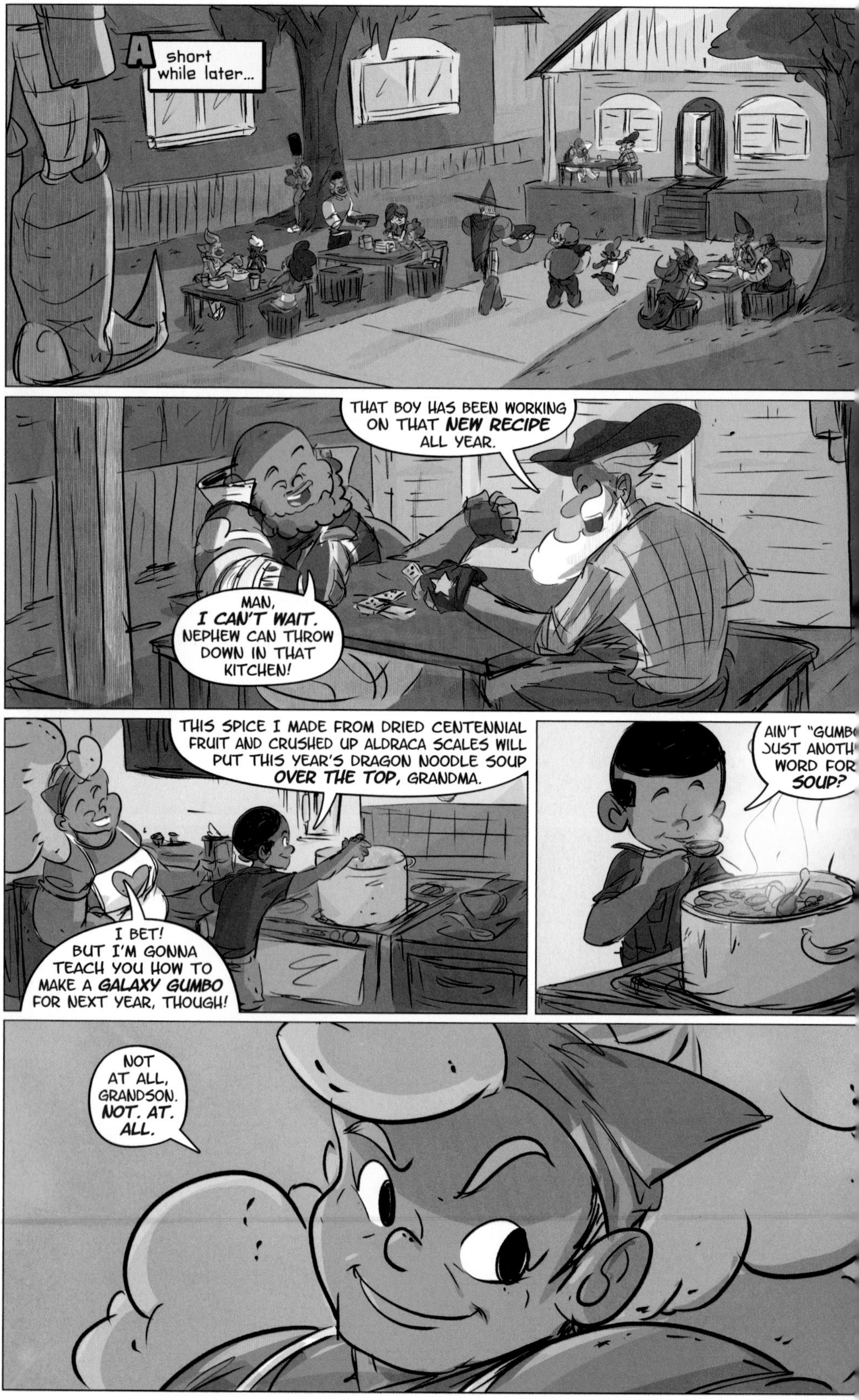
A short while later...
THAT BOY HAS BEEN WORKING ON THAT NEW RECIPE ALL YEAR.
MAN, I CAN'T WAIT. NEPHEW CAN THROW DOWN IN THAT KITCHEN!
THIS SPICE I MADE FROM DRIED CENTENNIAL FRUIT AND CRUSHED UP ALDRACA SCALES WILL PUT THIS YEAR'S DRAGON NOODLE SOUP OVER THE TOP, GRANDMA.
I BET! BUT I'M GONNA TEACH YOU HOW TO MAKE A GALAXY GUMBO FOR NEXT YEAR, THOUGH!
AIN'T "GUMB
JUST ANOTH
WORD FOR
SOUP?
NOT AT ALL, GRANDSON. NOT. AT. ALL.

BONUS MATERIAL

PAX SAMSON

Hey, new *Pax Samson* fans and readers! A ton of planning went into creating this story. Here's some of the early designs and concepts. These are two of the first drawings of Pax, including little notes made to update his design.

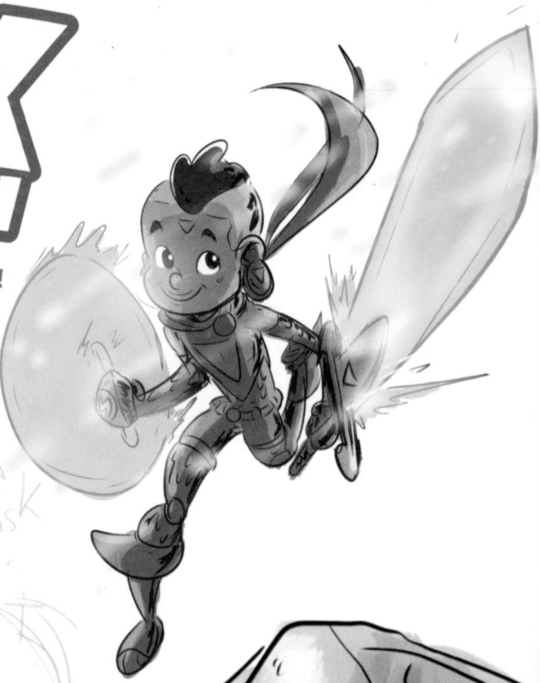

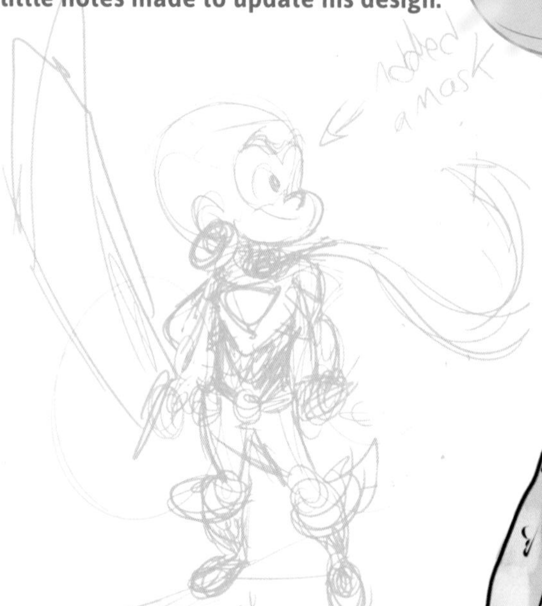
added a mask
Lost the shorts

DAD SAMSON, A.K.A. ALPHA-MAN, became a superhero around the same age as Pax is now. He was jokingly called Alpha-Boy, which he updated when he grew up.

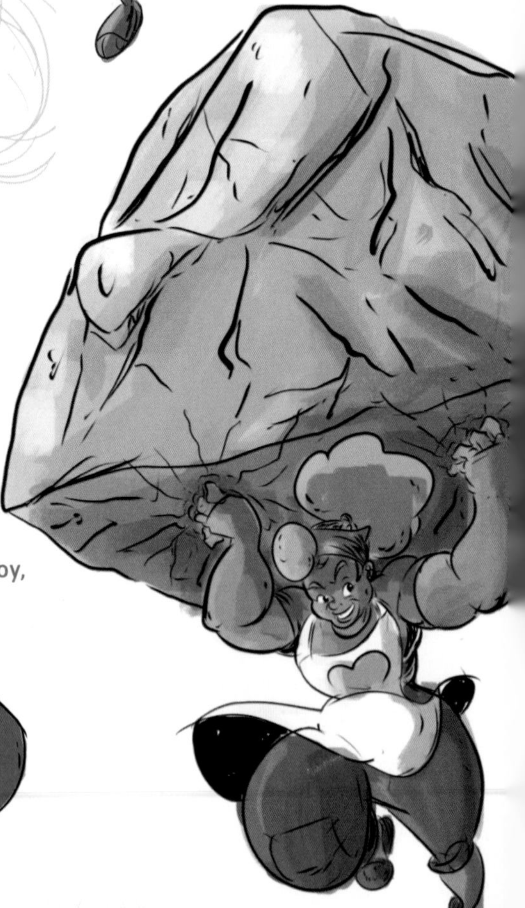

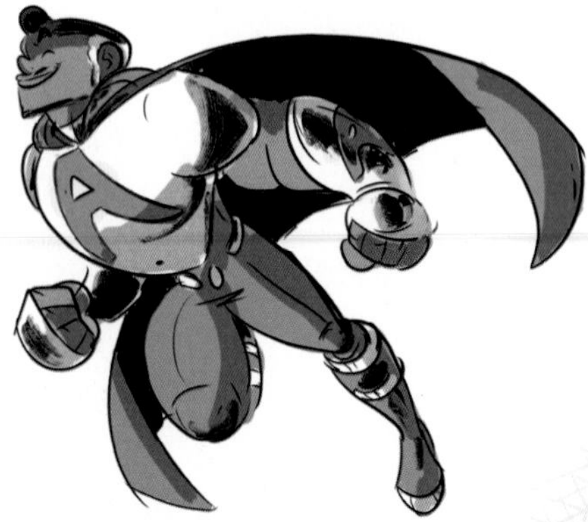

PINNACLE'S
ego demanded we give him a full page to flex.

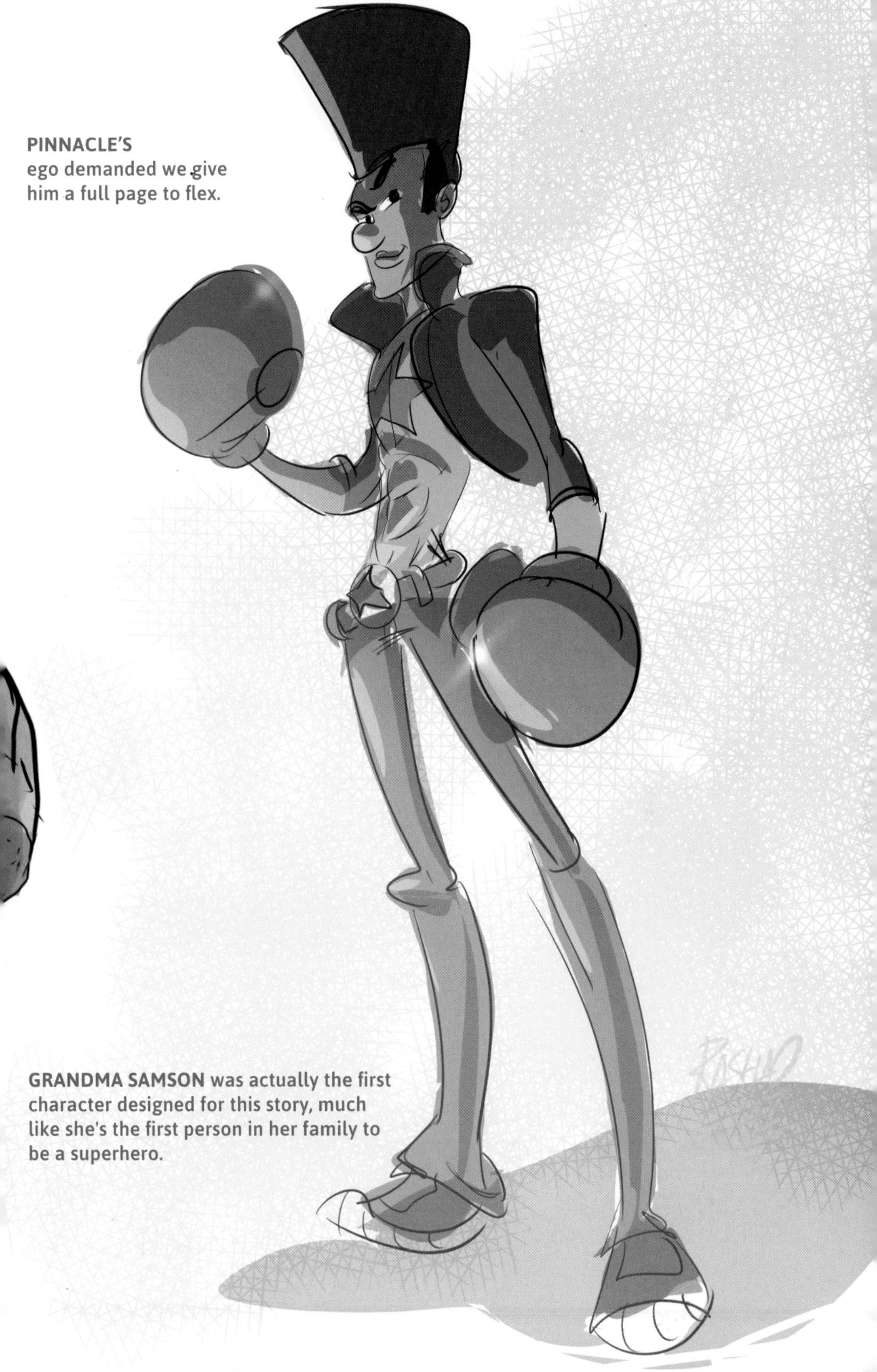

GRANDMA SAMSON was actually the first character designed for this story, much like she's the first person in her family to be a superhero.

Here's a peek into Rashad's creative process! All the art—from sketches, to black and white lines, to color—was done digitally.

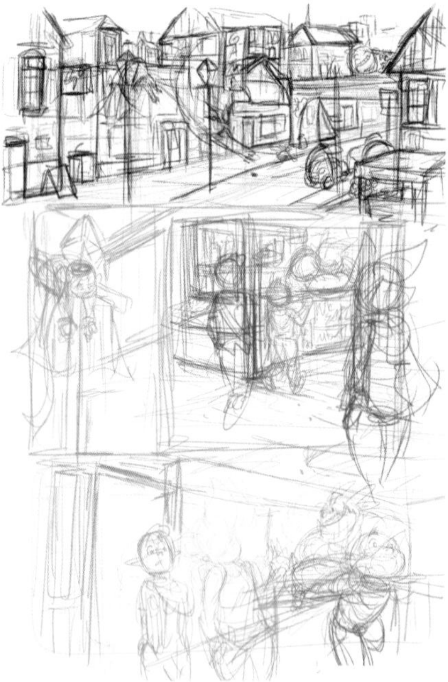

This is page 41 of this book.

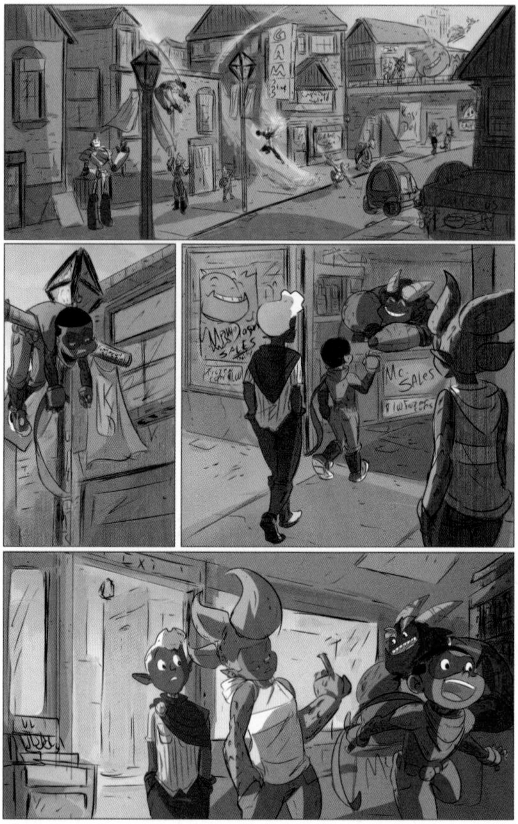

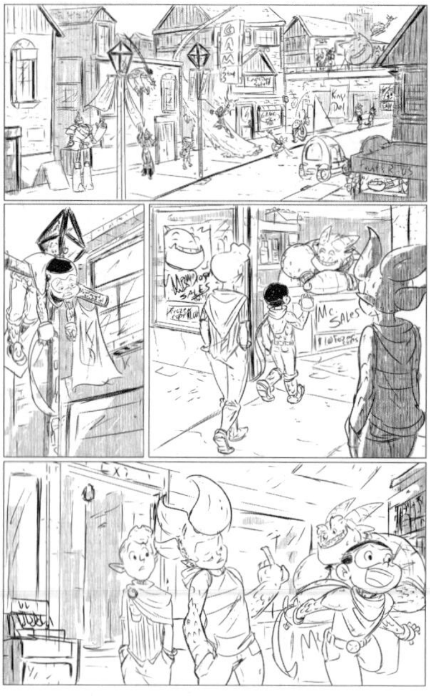

RASHAD is a very messy artist and has ruined many pieces of paper with his constant erasing and redrawing of scenes. He finds that working digitally helps keep his art a bit cleaner, but admits he still doesn't like coloring inside the lines.

Here's some of the ideas and sketches
Rashad and Jason came up with for Pax's
school, St. Savant's Academy.

RASHAD drew a bunch of random
students and teachers to populate
the school grounds.

JASON, a great artist as well, sketched out the general look of the academy
itself, as seen in the drawing below.

Rashad Doucet is from New Orleans by way of Eunice. He is a Ville Platte, Louisiana, native who's been drawing comics since his grandma gave him a pencil and some paper to keep quiet during church. He's known for his work with Oni Press on comics like *Invader Zim*, *Rick and Morty*, and *Alabaster Shadows*. He's also worked with DC Comics, Stela, and most recently was a part of the Eisner-winning *Elements: Fire Anthology*. Rashad is currently a professor of sequential art at the Savannah College of Art and Design in Savannah, Georgia, where he can often be found listening to '80s power ballads and watching way too much anime.

Special thanks to my late Grandma for always inspiring me to dream big and draw superheroes. To my grandfather and parents that showed me that focused, well thought-out hard work is the foundation of all dreams. To my uncles who always know how to make life fun. To my cousins whose teasing often lead to good times and fond memories. To my extended, found family and friends from Eunice, Ville Platte, Lake Charles, New Orleans, New York, and Savannah: thanks for always having my back in this crazy quest to make comics. And to my wife whose support has definitely been to infinity and beyond. I love you all.
—Rashad Doucet

A New Orleans, Louisiana, native, Jason Reeves is a publisher, art director, and award-winning illustrator operating out of Los Angeles, California. His most recent works include being creator, publisher, and illustrator of the *OneNation* and *Kid Carvers* series by 133art Publishing. Past projects include being a featured illustrator in *Black Comix Returns* by Magnetic Press/Lion Forge, a hardcover collection of art and essays show-casing the best African American artists in today's vibrant comic book culture; and writer and illustrator on Arch Enemy/ USAToday.com's *F-00 Fighters* webcomic. In addition to comics, he has done illustration for Esquire Magazine, the USA Network, Wizards of the Coast, Heavy Metal, and HASBRO.

Thank you to Braine, Brandon, and Jonathan. I take y'all with me wherever I go. To John and Lee, you are my creative fathers, my foundation. And to Kemi and Jason, you bring your whirlwinds into a life that would be static without it. I love you.
—Jason Reeves